Where

"The Sec

By
Helen F. Wand

"The Second Wave of Pioneers"
After years of delay, the railroad from St. Paul to the
northwest finally opened on September 8, 1883 allowing
accessibility for throngs of people to emigrate to Portland.

By the time the first train arrived, the initial wave of
pioneers, had come by sea or overland by wagon growing
the little town on the banks of the Willamette River to a
population of 17,600. Seventeen years later, in 1900, the
second wave of pioneers continued to arrive by rail and had
increased that number to over 90,000.

Broughton Bluff, seen above, is located at the confluence of the Columbia and Sandy
Rivers. The early 20th century author, Ben Hur Lampman, (August 12, 1886-March 2,
1954) stated in his book, "The Coming of the Pond Fishes," that this 450 foot bluff was
where the eagles nest.

It was on top of this hill that Alex and Julianna, along with their friends, Franz and
Katherine settled on adjoining homesteads, with Lampert and Marok Roads still marking
the approximate location.

www.helenwandbooks.com

ISBN: 978-0-9889063-2-7

Library of Congress Control Number: 2013939143

Second Edition, 2014.
Printed in the United States of America by:

Snohomish Publishing Company Inc.
Snohomish, WA

Printed on Recycle Paper

Soy Based Ink

Acknowledgements

I would like to thank the talented people at Snohomish Publishing Company in Snohomish, Washington. Without their expertise this manuscript would still be in a spiral bound notebook. I also want to thank the following people who helped guide the story through its final edits: Sharon Nesbit, Pat Lichen, Pat Wand and Christy McClure. Your enduring patience brought this endeavor to fruition.

I have spent many hours pouring over local data, in order to bring a sense of how life was lived in the late 1800's. These books in particular, were valuable references: "It Could Have Been Carpdale, a History of Troutdale," by Sharon Nesbit, "Living East of the Sandy River Volumes I & II," by Clarence Mershon, and "Crown Point Country Schools 1874-1974," by Dorothy Klock. A special thanks goes to Bea Graff, who provided me with laboriously typed and mimeographed volumes of Crown Point Country pioneer oral histories. I am deeply appreciative to these author/historians and beg forgiveness if I have changed a date here and there to aid in the flow of the story.

And a hearty thanks to the Chrysalis writers group at Clackamas Community College. Their continued support, great critiques and enthusiasm helped me develop my writing skills and gave me most of my beta readers: Alice Lynn, Barbara Froman, Elizabeth Miles, Rose Lefebvre, and Linda Appel. Other beta readers, whose efforts and time I greatly appreciated, were Bobbie Wand, Mary Bryson and Terri Johnsen.

Finally, great appreciation goes to my mother and father who instilled in me a love of storytelling, to Carolyn Eslick for her help in getting this printed and to Donna Anderson, for her encouragement, support and inspiration.

Many thanks to all!
Helen

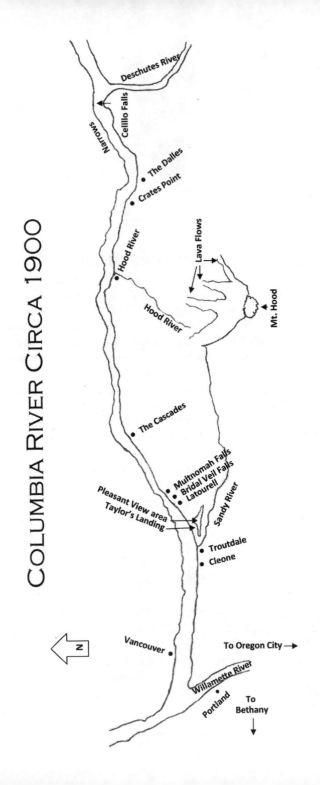

Columbia River Circa 1900

Chapter 1

July 1881

Mein Gott, he's handsome! Julianna's admiring glance fell once again on the young man talking with her father. Well dressed, with a neatly trimmed mustache, he wasn't quite as tall as Papa, but he looked lithe and strong. His eyes brushed hers with an irresistible twinkle, and the corners of his mouth curled into a charming smile.

Julianna's heart raced, and she felt her face burning. Helpless to stop her blushes, she hastily looked away, but not before the ever attentive Hans, standing beside her, caught her slight gasp.

"What's wrong, *fraulein*?" he asked, his arm encircling her shoulders, protective and familiar.

Julianna shook her head, but didn't answer. She liked Hans, the quiet, dark-haired boy next door, but he did hover, which she found annoying. Worse, her father expected them to wed.

Reluctantly, she'd agreed to his invitation to today's Summer Festival. She didn't want to encourage his ardor, but she loved the excitement of the people and the gaiety of the festival. Besides, she wanted to see the play tonight, and Papa thought it not proper to go unescorted to an evening event.

As they listened to the lilt of the accordion band, she noticed the young people surrounding them on the riverbank. The sun shone in a mottled yellow maze through the trees, providing shade for what promised to be a sizzling summer afternoon.

Her father and his cronies were chatting nearby. Who was the stranger with the enchanting smile? She admired the way he seemed so at ease with the older men.

"Let's dance," Hans said, interrupting her thoughts.

She nodded, and soon they were whirling around the wooden pavilion, weaving among the other couples. Julianna, proud of her dancing skills, took pure joy in stepping in time to the music. When she dared to glance again at her father, she caught the stranger staring at her and quickly looked away. Tossing her head, she let herself be caught up in the beat, lost in the moment.

When the song ended, Hans steered her toward a booth where they were serving punch, beer and chilled lemonade. They sat on a bench in the shade and watched the next dance set. Julianna loved seeing the antics of people and in Baden there were a lot of them to watch this time of year.

Visitors came to the little village, nestled in Germany's Black Forest, for its healing hot springs and pure fresh air. People said the crystal clear atmosphere got its purity from Mt. Merkur, which stood as the sentinel for the village. Julianna smiled as she reflected on that supposition. It was a nice idea, but she had her doubts.

She scanned the milling crowd for the handsome young stranger, and wondered if her father was trying to rent the creekside cabin to him. That would be like Papa to talk business during a holiday.

Her father dealt in property, and although they weren't wealthy, Julianna had never wanted for anything, except maybe a part in tonight's play. She frowned when she remembered how upset Papa was when she told the family she was going to try out. She had quickly decided against it, knowing that once Papa took a stand, he was rarely swayed. Mama always said Julianna and her father were too much alike.

This summer's play was a delightful light comedy that had the audience laughing throughout the evening. On their way home, Hans said he liked it and Julianna agreed.

"We have a date for next summer's play then?" he asked as he lingered at her front gate.

"We'll see." She smiled. It was the only commitment she could make.

The next morning at breakfast, Papa told Mama that two brothers from Lichtenstein had rented the cabin.

"Did they say why they are in town?" Mama was curious when it came to newcomers.

"Their uncle, Joseph Lampert, got them on with the crew remodeling the casino." He poured himself another cup of coffee. "Alex is a finishing carpenter and his brother Leonhard is learning the trade."

"Did you get the rent money?" Mama asked. Her head for figures made her the bookkeeper of the family business. Long ago, Papa had relinquished the job because he said, "it made them partners as well as mates." Julianna knew that Hans would never accept terms like that in his marriage; she would have to obey him and that was something she couldn't do.

"No rent money yet," he said, reaching for the cream. "Alex, the one with the mustache, will bring it by today or tomorrow."

Mama shook her head, but said nothing.

At the sound of the young man's name, Julianna flushed and turned to hide her face, but not before her younger brother spied her embarrassment.

"Julianna has a boyfriend," he announced.

"For heaven's sake, Johann, I haven't even met the man." She frowned at him.

"Leave your sister alone," Papa said. "She's going to marry Hans."

***

A week later, Alex stood in the door of the rental cabin, gazing at the tree covered mountain across the creek. He shook his head as the vision of his landlord's daughter crowded into his mind again. Since the festival, her face haunted him, wrapping itself between his thoughts and interfering with whatever chore he attempted to do. To make matters worse, when he'd taken half the rent money to Mr. Gross, her father, she'd answered the door, startling them both.

"Aah, I er, I have some money for, for…," he had stammered, embarrassed that he was unable to find words, and feeling even more awkward as she stared at him.

"Just a moment," she said and retreated into the house. He heard her call, "Papa, a young man is here to see you."

"I'll be right there, Julianna." Alex heard a muffled reply.

Julianna! What a beautiful name! Her voice sounded as fresh as a breeze through the trees on a warm summer evening. He couldn't remember much of the conversation with her father, but at least he knew her name. He'd seen her twice since then. The first time being when he'd delivered the rest of the rent money to the Gross household. Leonhard had offered to go, but Alex would have none of that.

"It's easier for me to take it," he told his brother. "I know the way."

The second time he saw her was in the village. A long black skirt swirled around her ankles and she wore a blue shirtwaist with a white shawl thrown carelessly over her shoulders. She was bending over, absorbed in conversation with two young girls and pointing to something in a shop window. When she straightened, she spied him and greeted him with a smile. It had warmed his heart like the glowing fires of his childhood home.

"Good day, *fraulein*!" He snatched his cap from his head and grinned.

"It is a beautiful day, isn't it?" she said. Her rosy cheeks showed her beauty in a way that no rouge could match. Her hair, neatly tied back, released one small light brown wisp that formed a ringlet on her forehead. She brushed it away with the back of her hand.

He nodded and felt his knees wobble. His mind seemed unable to continue the conversation or even form words, so he simply waved to her, turned and walked nonchalantly into the blacksmith shop. When the smithy asked what he needed, Alex shook his head. "I have no idea."

***

The casino work crew was already two weeks into the job. The remodel was moving rapidly. Too fast, Alex thought as he sanded the molding around the big double doors. He'd only talked to Julianna once. What if they got the job done and had to leave before he had another chance?

On top of that, he found it humiliating to be unable to say anything intelligent to her when he did see her. Gone were the days when his best friend Franz Frommelt called him a ladies' man because he'd flirted with the prettiest girl in school.

The following day when the workers took lunch, the subject of eligible young women came up. Alex casually asked about Julianna.

"Sorry, Julianna's engaged to a fellow who lives next door to her family," Otto, a crew member, said as he wolfed down the last bite of an apple.

"Engaged?" Alex blinked, feeling as though he'd been kicked in the stomach by the family cow.

"*Yah,* his name is Hans. He's apprenticing in the bakery down the street." Otto's voice was too casual to suit Alex. "I went to school with them." His voice droned on, "Hans told me he has her father's permission."

Alex caught his breath, gulped, and then excused himself. Away from the others, he leaned against the brick wall of the massive casino. He tried to compose himself, shaking the fog from his head.

Was zur hoelle! I don't even know the girl. What am I thinking? Fury slowly built, forming a thin armor around him. Somehow it brought a measure of comfort. He had no intention of falling in love anyway and certainly not with someone from a foreign country.

There were a couple of girls back home in Triesen that would be interested in marrying him. He always thought Leisl was pretty, but she wasn't interested in books and had no desire to travel. Well, never mind, he thought, I'm going to America anyway and get some of that free land. A wife would only get in the way.

He shook his head and reached in his pocket to feel his coin purse. It was getting fat. Good, I'll need lots of money and hard work will keep me from thinking about her.

On the last day of the job, the crew boss announced another assignment. The Café and Beer house up the block and the next street over had been damaged in a kitchen fire a few nights before and they wanted to hire his crew for restoration work.

"Guess we'll stay here a while longer," Leonhard said as they cleaned up the last of the *spaetzel* at supper that evening. "At least the food's good."

"*Yah*, and the money, too," Alex said with more enthusiasm then he felt.

"You wanna go to Mass with me tomorrow?" Leonhard asked.

"Mass? Why do you want to go to church now? We haven't gone to a service since we've been here."

"I want to make *Mutter* happy," Leonhard said, trying unsuccessfully to hide his mirth.

"What the…?" Alex gave him a stunned look.

Leonhard burst out laughing. "Haven't you noticed all the pretty girls walking home after church on Sunday morning?" he said after he'd managed to compose himself. "I'm going to Mass and see if I can meet someone." After a pause he continued. "Besides, *Mutter* always said the best *maudchens* attend church. I'm going to see if she's right."

"Wake me in the morning and I'll decide," Alex said as he strode out the door to watch the sun go down over the mountain.

Despite missing more Sundays of church than he could remember, Alex found himself in a back pew beside his brother the next morning. Guilt played into his decision and, of course, there was always a chance he might see Julianna. He wasn't sure if she was Catholic but most of the town seemed to be.

The church was smaller than their home parish, but beautifully decorated with stained glass windows and ornate statues. It wasn't until she got up for communion that he spotted her. She was with her family, and Hans was nowhere in sight.

As she came down the aisle, she saw him. Her quick look of surprise was followed by a hint of a smile. He smiled back, got up, wiped his palms on his pants legs and approached the altar. He could feel her eyes on the back of his neck. Why would she watch him if she were in love with someone else?

After Mass everyone crowded outside near the front door to catch up on the week's news. When Julianna came out into the sunshine, Alex looked for a ring on her finger, but he didn't see one. Could Otto be mistaken?

***

The brothers attended Sunday Mass from then on, but Alex never found a chance to talk to Julianna on those mornings. He decided, if she answered the door the next time he delivered the rent money; he'd strike up a conversation.

Leonhard met Anna the second Sunday they attended church and by the third Sunday, he had been invited to her parents' home for dinner. She was kind enough to extend the invitation to Alex, but he declined, bringing a laughing comment from his brother about how he'd changed since he left home. Alex shrugged and turned away.

Each time the crew finished a job that summer, another one came along. So they stayed in Baden, their bankrolls growing. The church had many parties and dances, and Leonhard and Anna attended all of them.

"Come with us tonight," Leonhard pleaded one Saturday evening, "Lots of nice girls will be there. You won't want for a partner. You never missed a dance at home, Alex."

"I think I'd better stay here. I'll just spend money if I go," Alex said, resisting.

"Suit yourself," his brother replied, "but that pretty Julianna was there last time. It'd be a great chance to dance with her." He paused and added, "I did."

Alex frowned and doubted his brother was telling the truth.

After Leonhard left, Alex sat on the front step, trying to read the town newspaper.

He could hear the faint sounds of the music. Suddenly, he was back home and Liesl was in his arms, dancing to the strains of a polka, laughing at some casual comment. She'd always found his jokes amusing.

Homesickness swept over him, washing him in melancholy. Maybe he should just leave Baden. There didn't seem to be much here for him.

Leonhard and Anna were together most of the time and he hated to intrude. If Julianna was engaged, what was left for him in Germany?

Then again maybe he should attend the party and see what dances were like in a foreign country. It'd been a long time since he'd held a pretty girl in his arms. He sat for what seemed like a long time pondering and tapping his foot to the beat of the music. Then he yawned and stretched, got up and made his way to bed where he lay unable to get Julianna's smile out of his mind.

Chapter 2

August 1881

"Papa, I have only spoken to him to say hello. What could possibly be wrong with that?" Julianna and her father sat on the steps of their front porch. She gazed down the tree-lined street and thought of the dark haired, handsome young man who'd brought the rent over yesterday.

"I don't care, *Leibchen*. He's a stranger, from a different country with different beliefs, and I don't want you to encourage him." Her father's voice was firm and decisive.

"What did Johann tell you, Papa?"

"He told me he saw you talking with Alexander on the street not long ago."

"That's true, Papa, I ran into him when I took the children on a walk. I didn't plan it." She'd often found her father much too strict and fervently hoped he would mellow as time passed.

"He seems to be a nice enough young man, but we've chosen Hans for you and that's that. We know him and his family. They're good people and Hans will make you a fine husband." He arose abruptly, and before he turned to go into the house, he added, "We know nothing of this young man."

"He does pay his rent," she called to his back.

Julianna sat for a long while after her father left. She watched the day turn to twilight and then, just before dark, the lamplighter lit the street lamps. There was no reason to be upset. Papa was right, she barely knew Alex.

But there was something about the curves in his face when he smiled and the way his eyes lit up when he looked at her. True, she didn't know him, but she wanted to, more than she'd wanted anything for a very long time.

One summer afternoon, a few of her old school mates were visiting in the backyard of her friend, Anna. As Julianna poured herself another cup of tea, someone asked Anna about Leonhard.

"Well, yes, he does come to dinner most Sundays," Anna answered and seemed taken aback by the question.

"You're lucky," Josephine said, taking a sip of her tea. "My family would never let me entertain a stranger, let alone a workman from any foreign country."

"Mama told me to ask his brother, too. They both look like they could use a good home-cooked meal, but Leonhard said his brother wouldn't come and he said he'd been acting strangely since he'd come to Baden. He said he knew something was wrong with him when he turned down a chance at some good cooking."

Anna appeared indignant as she continued. "I don't know what's wrong with entertaining him. He is a perfect gentleman. My parents think he is very nice. Besides, they are impressed that he works so hard and goes to church."

Julianna sat in silence and sipped her tea, wondering about Alex. It was strange that he turned down a dinner invitation. Maybe he didn't know that Anna's mother was one of the best cooks in town. She was sure that her brother would never refuse food.

The conversation turned to the dance that was scheduled to be held in the church hall the next Saturday evening. "Are you going with Leonhard?" Mary asked, turning to Anna.

"Yes, if he asks me," she replied resolutely.

"Let's all go," Bertha chimed in. "We don't have to have escorts. Those of us that don't have a date can go together. There are plenty of young men who show up."

"I'd like to go. I think it would be fun not to have an escort," Julianna agreed.

She wondered how Papa would feel about it, but was surprised at how little she cared.

***

Alex walked into the brightly-lit church hall and blinked away the darkness. It had taken some time, but he'd decided to finally accept one of Leonhard's invitations to a dance. He leaned against the back wall, tapping his foot to the familiar polka. The memories of how much he loved good music flooded back.

He scanned the crowd. *Where's Julianna?* He'd half expected her to be on the dance floor in Hans's arms. Eventually, he spotted her at the other end of the room, serving drinks behind the refreshment counter.

Gathering his courage, he slowly made his way around the dancers to the line waiting to be served. Finally, only one person stood between him and Julianna. Her mouth, half smiling as she spoke, intrigued him. Her eyes glistened in the lamplight and her cheeks flushed pink. Using the back of her hand, she absent mindedly, as if by habit, moved a loose curl away from her eyes as she handed the gentleman his drink and took his money.

Then he was there, in front of her. She had turned her back to him and was adjusting the clip that held her shoulder-length brown hair in place. Looking back over her shoulder, she started to say, "May I help ...", her voice trailed off as she recognized him.

Their eyes met for a moment.

"You finally came to a party," she said looking at him in disbelief.

Once again he was tongue-tied. He'd never had trouble talking to a girl, and yet he could only nod his head.

"Come on, *Kumpel*." A rough voice from behind, startled him to life. "Order something or get out of the way!"

"When will you be done here?" Alex asked, ignoring the intruder.

"Someone will take over in a few minutes," she said, with that now familiar smile crinkling her face.

"I'll help until they arrive," he replied moving around the bar to join her.

"Okay fellow, what can I get you?" he asked the rough voiced man. Alex now remembered seeing him around town.

He said he wanted a beer, so Alex pulled one from the tap and handed it to him. After that, Alex and Julianna worked in silence. Occasionally, he caught a hint of her perfume and once his arm touched hers when he picked up a full stein.

After what seemed like an extraordinary long time, her friends, Mary and Bertha, came to join them.

"Before we dance, I think we should have a cool drink and let you rest a bit," Alex said, feeling somewhat more confident.

She threw him a grateful look and accepted the glass he handed her. After they found a table he took a long drink, and leaned back.

"Where's Hans tonight?" he asked, suddenly bold.

"I don't know," Julianna shrugged, appearing unconcerned. "He may show up later."

"I thought you two were engaged. Everyone tells me he's asked your father's permission."

"Maybe he asked my father, but he hasn't asked me," she said. Her smile vanished.

"Really? You'd never know that from the talk around town."

"He and Papa may have decided this. Apparently I have nothing to say about it." Julianna scowled. Alex sat for a moment, stunned, both surprised at her sudden flash of anger and happy she wasn't engaged. She didn't want to marry Hans.

"Then you don't mind dancing with me?" He managed to spill out the words.

"No, I don't mind." Her face lit up. "I thought you'd never ask. It's taken you over a month to even show up at a dance."

His heart racing, he stood and led her onto the dance floor. With an arm around her slim waist, he drew her as close as he dared and deftly whirled her to the familiar Strauss waltz that filled the pavilion.

They danced every set the rest of the night. Anna and Leonhard were waiting for them by the door at the end of the evening, but Alex shook his head when Leonhard asked if the four of them could all walk together.

"No, I've got her for just a few more minutes, and I'm not sharing her." He smiled at Julianna and led her down the steps.

For a while they walked in silence. The warm night held a hint of fall peeking through the summer veil.

They chatted about the dance, his work and her friends, inconsequential things, and then, before he could stop, he blurted, "I'm saving my money to go to America." The words came out, surprising him as much as Julianna.

"You want to go to America?" She stopped and stared at him, her mouth open. "Why in the world would you want to go there?"

"Lichtenstein, where I'm from, is a country that's only ninety square miles and mostly mountains at that. All the good farm land is taken and someday I hope to live off the land."

"But you're a carpenter, and from what I hear a good one." She sounded a bit in shock.

He smiled at the compliment. "Have you been talking about me behind my back?"

"Maybe," she said in a teasing voice.

"Well, I'm flattered." Stopping, he turned and took both of her hands in his.

"Have you ever thought of going to America?"

"It never crossed my mind," Julianna said, a bewildered look on her face.

They walked again in silence. "What are you going to tell Hans?" Alex finally asked.

"I won't have to tell him anything. Didn't you see how everyone looked at us? You're such a good dancer, people couldn't help but notice. Remember this is a small village. He'll know by morning." Her voice took on the stillness of the night.

"I didn't notice anything unusual." He squeezed her hand. "What else is there to look at when you have the town's prettiest girl in your arms? Besides, if I were engaged to a girl like you, I'd never want her to go to a dance without me."

"Hans and I will never be anything but friends. We grew up together. He's a nice man, but I'm not in love with him."

"I can't tell you how happy that makes me," Alex said, turning toward her and suddenly he found her in his arms, and he was kissing her, at first hesitating, and then lost in the embrace.

***

Julianna attended Mass with her family the next morning. Alex sat in his usual seat in the back row. She smiled and nodded, careful not to be obvious. Afterward she walked home ahead of her family, in a dream world with a rainbow around her shoulders, her toes never quite touching the path. This good-looking young man had waltzed into her life, and suddenly everything was turned upside down. America? She had barely heard of it.

And that kiss! Her lips still burned. She remembered his mustache brushing faintly against her cheek. The moment started out softly as an early summer rain and ending in a torrent of hail, the kind that shuts the rest of the world out, and thirty years later when people get together they'd reminisce about the fierce storm.

When she arrived at the front gate of her home, her heart stopped. Waiting for her was Hans, red-faced, a belligerent look in his eye.

14

"What are you doing here?" she mumbled, wishing there was some place to hide.

"You know very well why I'm here. You, my dear, are the talk of the town." He spat the words out.

"I can dance with whomever I choose. You weren't there." She felt herself flush with embarrassment, which made her angrier.

"You know I have to work Saturday and Sunday evenings. That's what apprentices do; they work nasty hours and do scut work." Hans' face turned shades of purple. "I'm going after that no-good scoundrel. How dare he come to town and chase after our women!"

"Our women! Our women! Who do you think you are? I'm not your property and never will be. You and Papa hatched up that scheme for us to marry. Don't I have something to say about it?" Julianna's anger clipped her words. "You leave Alex alone! He is a perfect gentleman."

"Perfect gentleman, my foot." His eyes narrowed into thin black gashes. "Otto saw him kiss you in the park last night."

"I don't care what Otto thought he saw. You leave Alex alone. You fellows need to mind your own business," she said, trying to push her way around him to the gate and the front steps.

"You are my business. For God's sake, Julianna, I'm in love with you. I've been in love with you ever since I can remember. I want to marry you."

Julianna blinked and stepped back. She had wanted to tell him for a long time that she didn't share his feelings, but had not realized it would be so difficult. It was one thing to know it in her heart and another to validate it with words.

"I'm so sorry, Hans," she said after what seemed like an eternity. "I've tried not to lead you to believe my feelings for you were anything but those of a dear friend. I...I guess I've not been very successful."

"Are you saying you don't want to marry me? Is that what you're saying? I'm gonna kill the bastard. How dare he come into our town and take you from me."

"He didn't take me from you. I've never been in love with you, Hans," Julianna said, surprised at the sadness she felt. Over the years she'd been so busy discouraging him that she never realized what a good friend he was. "I am truly sorry."

"That no-good foreigner," he snarled and shook his head as if not comprehending her words. He turned on his heel and strode purposefully toward town.

***

Alex looked up from the cabinet door he was shimming. He was glad to have a chance to work on Sunday afternoon and make some extra money.

15

Besides it might keep his mind off Julianna. He'd thought of nothing else since last night.

When he'd seen her in church this morning, it took all his strength not to go to her, but it would never do to make her father angry now.

He thought about Leonhard and how understanding he'd been this morning. They'd sat on the cabin steps after Mass, eating breakfast and enjoying a few minutes of calm before Alex went to Mr. Steinman's house to fix some kitchen cabinetry.

"What's the big attraction for America, Alex?" Leonhard had started off the conversation.

Alex finished his last bite of bread and pulled up a piece of grass from beside the steps. He pondered the question and then replied, "I think it would be an adventure, such an impossible journey. I'd like to see if I could do it."

They sat in silence for awhile before he added, "Remember when we used to go out to Grandpa Lampert's farm when we were kids?"

"Those were fun times, huh?" Leonhard said staring out over the creek. "Grandma could really cook," he added.

Alex pulled up another piece of grass. He felt the sleek smoothness on his lips and tasted the sweetness as he bit down. "I wanted that farm when Grandpa was done with it. I begged Papa for it. I am the eldest son. It should've gone to me."

"Yah, you'd thought so. That's always been the rule, except...," Leonhard's voice trailed off, leaving them both to ponder.

"Except for Cousin Emil," Alex mumbled. He hesitated as he felt his composure falter. He didn't want his brother to know how strongly he felt. Emil inherited the farm because his father was oldest of that generation, and he didn't even want to farm.

"So that's why the two of you got into that fistfight?" Leonhard sounded surprised.

"Yah, not too bright, huh? He's older than me and outweighed me by at least 10 kilos," Alex spat out a piece of the stem into the weeds.

"You really took a beating. I remember that."

"I thought *Mutter* was gonna give me some more when I got home," Alex said

"Did you ever tell her what it was about?" Leonhard asked.

Alex shook his head. "She didn't need to know." He sent what was left of the shaft of grass sailing through the air.

The sound of footsteps on the path startled Alex, interrupting his thoughts and bringing him back to the present time. Looking up from the cabinet door, he spied a red- faced young man heading straight toward him. Han's hair was tousled and his eyes were full of rage. He outweighed Alex, but not by much.

16

Alex rose and went to meet the bristling young man. Before he could say anything, Hans landed a fist on Alex's chin and sent him tumbling backward.

"Listen, fellow, I don't want any trouble. Let's talk about this like gentlemen." Alex tried to wave him off as he climbed back to an upright position.

"Gentlemen don't steal other gentlemen's women," Hans spat the words into the air. Alex could see the man's fury escalating.

"Hey, the lady doesn't have a ring, and she told me she wasn't engaged. I believe her."

Heat crawled up Alex's back and neck and he knew there was no way to avoid a fight. Before he could devise a plan, Hans rushed in, catching him square in the gut. The blow folded him over and drove him to his knees.

Alex gasped for air and then rage came forth in a wall of fire. He slowly regained his feet and, forgetting strategy, blind anger replaced it.

As Hans approached him for the defining blow, Alex leaped forward, landing a hard blow to the mid-section, followed by a solid punch to the chin, a maneuver he'd devised since his humiliating fight with Cousin Emil.

Startled, Hans stumbled backward, yet somehow retained his balance. Alex followed, pushing him hard with both hands onto the grass where he landed firmly.

"Lucky for you, it's not muddy out here," Alex said, wishing fervently that it was.

Hans was on his hands and knees trying to get up, but Julianna's voice stopped him, "No, Hans! No more!"

She came up behind them, out of breath, her voice angry.

"Go home, Julianna. This isn't your business," Hans demanded roughly.

"Yes it is. It is my business. You leave him alone. Yes, Alex did kiss me and you know what? I wanted him to. Now go home, before anyone gets hurt."

"But...but...," Hans sputtered.

"You heard the lady. Leave!" Alex commanded, thankful for Julianna.

Hans regained his feet, dusted off his pants, and headed down the street without another word or backward glance.

Alex didn't know how, but suddenly Julianna was in his arms and he was hungrily searching for her mouth.

"You wanted me to kiss you?" he asked between kisses.

"Silly boy...of course. Can't you tell?"

Chapter 3

September 1881

"Papa's furious. Hans told him about us." Julianna sat on a park bench looking down at her hands in her lap, her voice flat.

"What did he say?" Alex spoke softly. He couldn't lose her now. He'd just found her. He'd seen her three times since the dance, and each time he became more convinced that she was the only girl for him.

"He says that I am not to see you ever again," she replied, still not looking at him.

"How do you feel about that?" He said after a moment, almost afraid to ask.

"I want to see you," she said, her voice resolute. "You must know I do."

They sat in silence for a few minutes. He looked out over the park to the spot where he'd first kissed her. It was mid- September now and the grass had lost its lush, green sheen to become a withered yellow-brown dryness that matched his parched throat. Soon his work here would be done, and he'd have no excuse to stay.

"Would it help if I talked to him?"

Julianna shook her head. "I doubt it. I've never seen him so angry."

"*Guter Gott*, it's not like you're a child. At twenty-one years old, you're an adult. You should be able to choose who you want to be with." Alex spewed his words, letting them tumble over one another, like a brook over boulders.

"I know, but my father is old-fashioned. If he'd had his way, I'd already be married and have children."

"Leonhard and I discussed this. He thinks I should ask your father for permission to see you." He paused and then continued. "I agree with him."

It seemed to him his words made her shrink, as if pulling away from a possibility too frightening to acknowledge.

"Julianna, I'll have to leave in a few weeks. I want to be in your father's good graces. The only way I can do that is face him, man-to-man." He reached for her hand. "This is your last chance to stop me. I'm going to see him tonight."

"What will you say to him?"

"I haven't decided yet," he shrugged. "I'll think of something."

"I don't want you to get hurt. Papa has a terrible temper."

"I can run fast, don't worry." He grinned at her.

She held tightly to his arm. "Promise me you will, if you feel things are getting out of control."

He drew her gently to him and assured her that he would.

***

That evening Alex found himself on the Gross' front porch. He pulled himself to his full five feet, ten inches and knocked firmly. He waited, rapped again, and heard footsteps in the hall.

Julianna's mother opened the door. "Alex, the rent isn't due until next week." Her voice held a hint of surprise.

"I know, but I need to speak to your husband," he said, determined to carry out his plan.

"He's in his study," she said. "You must know, Alex, he isn't pleased with you." She shook her head and continued, "Although for the life of me, I can't understand why. You're responsible and pay your rent on time."

"Thank you, ma'am!"

"I'll see if he's free." She turned and left him standing on the porch with sweat beading on his forehead. Grabbing the handkerchief out of his back pocket, he hastily wiped it away.

A few moments later, Mr. Gross filled the doorway. "What are you doing here?" Before Alex could speak, he continued. "The only time you're welcome here is when the rent is due. If you're smart, you'll send your brother with the money next month."

"Sir, I need to speak to you about an urgent matter." Well, it was urgent to him.

"And what is that?"

Alex hesitated, seeing that he wouldn't get any help from the older man. Wiping his moist palms on his trousers, he proceeded. "I've come to ask your permission to call on your daughter. She is a lovely young woman and I... I like her very much."

"I don't want to see or hear of you coming around her again," the older man spoke in a soft, firm voice. "Stay away from her!"

"I'm sorry you feel that way." Alex felt his fury rising and struggled to compose himself. He heard his own father telling him to think before he spoke. His father had always been diplomatic, so he took a deep breath and continued. "Sir, I just want to escort Julianna to the dance next Saturday and to Mass on Sunday. My intentions are honorable."

"Get off my porch now!" Mr. Gross bellowed, all restraint gone.

"Papa, *um Gottes willen*! He's a nice young man and he has done nothing wrong," Mrs. Gross intervened from the living room door where she had been standing. "All he wants is to see Julianna. If she wants to see him, then we shouldn't stand in the way."

She walked to her husband's side. Alex could see the rage in his eyes and momentarily feared for the woman's safety, but she continued. "Your daughter has told you many times that she doesn't want to marry Hans. Do you want her to be an old maid?"

"Better that than have her leave Baden and never return."

"All Alex wants to do is take her to a dance. I haven't heard anything about leaving Baden." She put her hand on his sleeve. "Don't you know

19

our daughter is as stubborn as you? She'll do what she wants." She patted his arm. "I, for one, would like to see her happy. If she wants to go, Papa, let her."

Alex wiped his palms on his pants again and said nothing. Something was being played out here that he had no control over.

Gross's eyes flared at his wife's words. After a moment, he sighed and slowly nodded his head, "All right Mama, have it your way, but if she leaves us it'll not be my fault."

To Alex he said, "Young man, take her to the dance, if you wish. Just know that she is loved and no harm had better come to her."

"Thank you very much, sir. And thank you, Ma'am, for believing in me. I'll watch over her." Alex reached to shake the older man's hand, but the gesture was ignored.

"Oh, Papa, thank you!" Julianna came around the corner where she had been hiding. "I promise we'll be home at a reasonable time. Thank you, Mama, thank you!"

She slipped her arms around her father's waist and squeezed him.

Over the next six weeks, Alex and Julianna spent many evenings together with her father seeming more comfortable around the couple as time went by. He still grumbled, but occasionally he sat with them and joined the conversation.

With the changing of the season, the temperature dropped noticeably and there were fewer prospects for jobs. One day after work, the boss called a meeting to tell the crew that the following Friday would be their last day. A couple of local fellows would stay for odd jobs over the winter, but the bulk of the work would resume the following spring.

That evening, Alex went to Julianna's house and told her that he and Leonhard would have to leave for Liechtenstein the following week.

"I have to go. We promised *Mutter* that we'd help Papa redo the kitchen floor and make her a new table. She'd like us to be done by Christmas, but I doubt whether we can do it that fast. When we're done, I'll send for you," Alex said choosing his words carefully.

"America is still your dream?" The question was more of a statement.

"Yes, it is." He hesitated, knowing how important Julianna's family was to her. He understood the sacrifice he was asking from her. "I hope it's become yours, too."

"I just want to be where you are," she said. "If you go, then I will, too."

"I don't know if we'll ever see our families again," he hesitated. "Do you think you can do that?"

"It'll be the hardest thing I've ever done," she said quietly, "But I'll come when you send for me and we can go to America, if that is your wish."

Chapter 4

Late February 1882

Julianna bowed her head, concentrating on the bread dough she kneaded. It was hard to ignore her mother's questions, knowing that Alex's letter stuck out of her apron pocket.

"And how is Alex these days, *meine liebe*?"

A tear dropped into the dough before Julianna could stop it and another rolled down her cheek. She caught it with the back of her hand, leaving a smudge of flour on her cheek. A lock of hair dropped onto her forehead and she flung it back with a flip of her head.

Alex had been away for over four months: she'd counted every day. He'd faithfully written and now the letter with money for a train ticket had come, asking her to meet him in Triesen on March tenth.

When she received the letter her heart leaped at the thought of being with him again. She'd missed him more then she ever thought she would. Then last evening and now this morning it occurred to her that she might be leaving forever. What if she never saw the beautiful mountains and rivers of Baden again? And what about Mama and Papa? And Johann, Greta, and Josey? She pounded the bread harder.

"His letters sound as though he is fine." Her voice was sharper then she wanted it to be. Her hands flew as the bread rolled back and forth, mixing, folding, and flouring. Another tear forced its way down and dropped off her chin. Thank God, Mama isn't looking at me, she thought. She squeezed her eyes shut, willing the tears to stop, but they persisted. She wiped her hands on her apron and turned to go outside.

"Where are you going, *Leibste*?"

Her mother had a way of sensing problems. She wondered if that talent came with childbirth?

"Just out for a breath of fresh air," she replied, closing the door.

She stepped off the porch and walked around the yard, shivering as the north wind bit into her bare arms. Buds had broken on the snow apple tree and her mother's daffodils, up a few inches, were getting ready to bloom. How she loved them! "A promise of spring," her grandmother called them. They had awakened this morning to a skiff of ice, but it had melted quickly.

Mt. Merkur, swollen with a cloak of snow, wrapped large, outstretched arms around her, seeming in some odd way to sense her dilemma. I am acting like a lovestruck school-girl. Most people my age had long since left their parents home. Her thoughts jumbled, she couldn't make sense of anything at the moment.

On the other hand, most of her married friends had moved down the street from their parents' or to a village close by, not across the ocean to another country, especially one with a different language.

The icy wind drove her back into the kitchen. Mama was putting the pans of bread on the warming rack above the stove to rise. She turned when she heard Julianna close the door.

"Come *tochter,* tell me about the letter from Alex. You've been quiet since it came," her mother said. Taking Julianna by the arm, she sat her at the kitchen table and pulled a chair up beside her.

Julianna shook her head. "I promised Alex that I would come when he sent for me. He wants me to go to America with him to get some land."

"And he has sent for you?"

"Yes."

"Then why are you not happy?"

"I am, *liebe* Mama, I am." Julianna's eyes filled with tears again.

She welcomed her mother's arms around her and when the sobs came, they came with a deep, heartfelt cry of grief. She took pride in her strength, but this was beyond her control.

"What if I never see you again?" Julianna held her mother tight.

Her body heaved with sobs, punctuated by silent moments as Mama gently rocked her oldest child. Finally she said, "*Liebste*, you're a woman now. It's difficult for me to admit it, but you are."

She paused for a moment, and gently stroking Julianna's hair, she asked, "Do you love this man, this Alex?"

"Yes," her reply was muffled and barely audible.

"Then follow your heart. Go with him. Life's a journey. You never know where it'll take you."

"But what will Papa say? Remember he didn't even want me to talk to a foreigner?" Julianna said, looking at her mother. Was that a tear running down her cheek?

"I'll talk to him, *leibe.* I'll talk to him. You get yourself ready for your trip. We'll be fine. Maybe we can come and visit you someday. I'd like to see America."

The following days were filled with sorting, packing, and good-bye parties. She had not spoken to Hans since that fateful day. She wondered if she should seek him out, but decided it would be best to leave him alone. She knew there was nothing she could do to change it.

At the train station on the day of her departure, Julianna was surrounded by her friends and family, receiving their hugs and shedding tears. She knew she may never see any of them again.

At the last minute, Papa came to see her off. She hadn't been sure that he would, but there he was. He gathered her in his arms just as she was about to board and, with misty eyes, wished her a safe journey.

"My prayers go with you, *liebe!*" he whispered in her ear.

She held him tightly. "Oh, thank you, Papa. I'll love you always." She turned and tearfully climbed onto the train, knowing that his love was not the same as his forgiveness.

Chapter 5

March 1882

Her first views, just before dark, as the train traveled through first Switzerland, then Lichtenstein were of the highest, most rugged mountains, she'd ever seen. She thought they were magnificent. It was dawn when she arrived at the station in Triesen. The air was crisp and light and smelled like Mama's fresh laundry.

"Pretty high, aren't they?" Alex's voice startled her. She had looked for him from the window, and was not able to find him. She'd felt a moment of panic then, but now she flung it away and turned to look into his laughing dark eyes.

"Am I glad to see you!" He caught her in his arms, picked her up, and swung her around. "I almost forgot what you looked like."

Her doubts faded. Throwing back her head, she laughed with a delight she hadn't felt for many years.

She couldn't wait to write and tell her family. Later that evening when she was alone in a quiet room at the Lampert household, she took out her pen and paper and by candle-light, wrote her first letter home to her family in Baden.

March 10, 1882

Dearest Family,

I arrived in Triesen early this morning. Alex, Leonhard, and their sister, Verena, were at the station to meet me. Alex looks wonderful. Leonhard was his own funny self and Verena is a lovely young girl. If I were staying here, I know we would become fast friends.

We had to go by horse and wagon to the family farm a few miles out of town. I was surprised at the rugged country, but their farm is located in a small valley where the ground is flat. The mountains in this part of Liechtenstein are higher and more magnificent than the ones at home. The air is crystal clear and in places there was a marvelous view of the Rhine River Valley from the train. When I asked Alex why he wanted to leave this beautiful country, he shrugged and said there wasn't enough land here for everyone in his family. He has promised himself that he will have a farm of his own some day. I only hope we can find one in America.

Alex's people are wonderful. They welcomed me into their home and treat me as one of their own. I'm sorry I only have a week or so with them. His mother and Verena are the only two who seem to be upset that he is leaving. They are disappointed that he doesn't want to get married here in their parish church. Alex says we don't have the time to give me the kind of wedding I deserve, if we marry here. I'm not sure what he means by that because I don't want a fancy affair, but he says he wants to wait until we get to America. His best friend, Franz and his wife, Katherine, are in America and he wants them to stand up for us. If I had my way, I would like for Leonhard and Verena to be in our wedding.

His father and brothers are encouraging him to leave. "A man is measured by the amount of land he has acquired in his lifetime," is what his father told me. "I'm proud of Alex for wanting to go out and explore, especially now that he has a pretty sweetheart to share his adventures. A man should not be alone."

Alex has three other brothers besides Leonhard; Joseph, Johannes, and Arnold. Needless to say, it is a busy and noisy household. They are all handsome and as kind as Alex.

Alex has the train tickets to LeHavre, France. That's the port where we board the ship. It will leave on March 22, but Alex has to report in the day before. He has signed on as a joiner and will be working all the time we are at sea. I'm so proud of him; he does such beautiful finishing carpentry. You should see the oak vanity he built for Verena. He'll get free passage because of his job, but he'll have to pay for mine.

I miss you all, but am so very happy. When I saw Alex this morning, I knew I had made the right decision. I'll write to you when I am at sea, but doubt I can mail it until we make port.

Please remember that I love you.

Julianna

They left the following Monday on a train bound for the port in France.

***

"I've never seen so much water," Julianna said with amazement.

"You'd better get used to it." The man in a dark blue uniform smiled as they approached the ship. "You'll see a lot more." He smiled and winked. She blushed and was glad that Alex was busy with the trunk and hadn't seen him.

After they got on board Alex helped her find the single women's quarters. Once she was settled, she explored while he went to check his quarters and talk to the purser about his job. Much to her surprise, the ship was larger then she'd guessed and it made her less frightened about the voyage. Nothing with this expanse could sink.

She admired the highly polished wooden railing, but noticed a few rust spots here and there showing on the white metal along the starboard outside wall. A redheaded deck hand was painting them at the front of the ship. She remembered Alex calling the bow *des schiffes.*

She found a place out of the way, but close to the gang plank where she could watch the crew load everything from luggage and food supplies to large crates marked in many strange languages. People were starting to board even though it was a day early. Maybe they were workers, too.

The ship left the next morning and stopped before dark in London. After two days in port, they headed for the high seas.

"I think I'll pass on breakfast this morning," she told Alex when he stopped in her room to give her something to eat. "I feel *mulmig.*"

"I don't feel so *gut* myself. Maybe if we eat we'll feel better." He offered her some bread.

She shook her head and decided if she lay on her stomach it might help. It didn't.

Julianna saw very little of Alex after the journey started. He worked twelve hour shifts that often turned into fifteen hours. She was glad because she hated for him to see her when she was so ill. She startled herself when she looked in the mirror and saw her pale cheeks and the deep dark circles under her eyes.

After three days at sea, she began to feel well enough to eat small amounts of food. When the weather was fair, she spent much of her time, sitting on the deck in the fresh air, wrapped in a blanket. She had packed several books for the trip and found that reading helped the hours pass.

***

It took the ship almost a month to travel from the LaHavre port to America. They docked at the Battery in New York City beside two other large oceangoing vessels. Alex's excitement to be on solid ground was second only to having Julianna as his fiancée. She was sitting on a bench, her trunk beside her, when he finally disembarked. The captain required the crew to wait until all the passengers were safely on shore, which worked well for him since he needed to collect his pay before he left.

Too bad I hate the ocean. I could make a good living working on these ships, he thought as he stuffed the bills into his money belt. As he walked briskly down the plank carrying a satchel and his tool box, he smiled at her. Julianna looked a bit overwhelmed. He couldn't blame her; New York was a large bustling city, a boom town as someone had described it.

He beckoned to a surrey that had "passengers" written on the side and asked, "Can you get us to a *gasthous*?" The cabbie shook his head and indicated that he didn't speak German.

"Hotel?" Alex said speaking slowly. He'd been practicing his English on board ship. One of the carpenters was an American who had taught him many words.

The driver nodded and jumped down to help load the trunk, while Julianna climbed into the back seat. Soon they were on their way up Broad Street.

"We want to be near to *da* train station," Alex said, in broken English as he climbed in beside Julianna.

"I know a good place close to the trains," the driver replied.

They passed Wall Street, its sidewalks filled with activity. The energy took on a physical presence, one that clung to him and took its release with every breath. Alex held tightly to Julianna's hand, trying to shield her from the heady force of avarice.

"Look at that church. It's so tall," Julianna exclaimed, interrupting his thoughts as she pointed down the street. Again the driver shook his head.

Alex repeated the comment in English, and the driver explained, "That's Trinity Church. The top of the steeple is the tallest point in New York City." Then as if anticipating the next question, he said, "It's Episcopalian."

Alex translated, with some difficulty. He wasn't sure about the last word, so he didn't try it.

The route took them through a wealthy part of town, where mansions on large lots had beautiful manicured gardens. A few children played here and there. He saw a woman in a white dress and black apron, hanging wash on a line by the side of a large white house with dark green shutters.

They came to an area of markets and shops. Again the bustle of busy people, but the feeling was different here. Less greed? Maybe. He couldn't be sure, but he felt more comfortable. Small shops lined both sides of the street. People were laughing and talking, their baskets filled with goods and groceries. As he and Julianna traveled, they heard many languages. One place was strictly German with a northern accent, but he still could understand what they were saying and it felt good. A glance at Julianna told him she too was enjoying it. He squeezed her hand and a smile lit up her face.

"Everything is so big," she said, her eyes wide with excitement.

Several times he caught his breath as he spotted some interesting item: a newspaper boy singing out a headline or the woman and the fish vendor haggling over the price of the catch. Life in this city was something he had never imagined. He knew he'd always remember it. Part of him felt a longing to stop and join this German neighborhood. But the pull for land was too great. He needed a farm of his own.

When they stopped in front of a large hotel, the driver announced, "Grand Central Station is just down two blocks. The hotel has a surrey that will take your trunk when you want to leave. It's walking distance for you young folks. That will save you another cab fare." He smiled his good-bye.

They checked into adjoining rooms. Then wanting to stretch their legs, they went for a stroll around the large block. This area had a more commercial feel, probably because of the railroad station, Alex thought as they walked with her arm in his. He suddenly felt very proud with this beautiful woman beside him. Straightening his back, he held his head high. Something inside whispered words he'd heard as a child, "pride goeth before the fall." But he shook off the thoughts, grinned at Julianna and reminded himself to enjoy the moment.

The next day, flush with cash from his job on the ship, they rented a carriage and went for a long ride in Central Park. They debated about attending a play in the evening.

"I'd like to go, Alex, but I'm sure it would be all in English and I still am struggling with the language." Julianna's voice held uncertainty.

Alex laughed. "You speak the new language pretty good for only practicing four weeks." He hoped he sounded encouraging.

"But I have a hard time understanding what people are saying. Do you suppose they will speak slowly?"

"I doubt it. Maybe you're right. Instead of the theatre, let's buy a couple of books for our trip to Illinois. We can do that tomorrow."

"That sounds wonderful, Alex. I've read everything I brought at least twice." It was Julianna's turn to laugh. He kissed her and wished with all his heart that they had gotten married in Treisen.

On the third day, they boarded the train to Freeport, Illinois. "Will we tour Chicago on the way?" Julianna asked. "I had such fun seeing New York."

"I did too, but it looks like there's only a short time there. All we can do is stretch our legs a bit." Alex put his arm over her shoulders.

"That's fine," she nodded. "I'm anxious to get where we are going so we can hang up our clothes and stay awhile."

A day and a half later they stepped off the train onto the streets of Freeport. Alex put his arms around her as they touched the ground and said, "This is where we'll get married, just as soon as we can find a priest."

She smiled and kissed him. She suspected it would take most of the summer to plan the kind of wedding that Alex wanted her to have.

Chapter 6

August 1882

August 16, 1882 started out as a miserably hot day as often happens during the summer in northwestern Illinois, but by midmorning large cumulus clouds rolled in. Although the air clung to the moisture, the temperature dropped a little, much to Julianna's relief. Ever since they'd scheduled the wedding for August, she'd dreaded a ceremony in the muggy oppressive heat so foreign to her.

The Wedding Mass was set to take place at eleven o'clock in the morning, in the tiny St. Joseph Catholic Church on West Washington Street, close to where Franz and Katherine lived in their small cottage.

Julianna smiled as her thoughts traveled back to May when she and Alex arrived in Freeport. They had stayed with the Frommelts until Alex found a job a mile out of town on a large farm. He had told her on the trip over that he wanted a rest from "building things".

"I think it would be good for me to study agriculture methods in America. Maybe I'll pick up some good tips," he'd said one evening when they were sitting on a coil of ropes, gazing out over the open water. "I hope I am able to make a living off our land. Then the only building I'll be doing is for us." She remembered he'd taken her hand during the conversation. The simple gesture touched her soul and brought a prayer for their success.

Because the farm was out of town, Alex stayed in a bunkhouse during the week, only coming back to visit on weekends. Katherine invited Julianna to stay with her and Franz until the wedding.

"Are you nervous?" Katherine asked, interrupting Julianna's thoughts and bringing her back to the present: the church hall where Julianna had just put on her wedding dress. Katherine was finishing the final touches on Julianna's veil.

"No, not really. I was worried about the weather. Everyone wilts in this summer heat." Julianna was busy at the mirror, making sure each strand of her rich brown hair was in place. "I'm more excited than nervous. I can't wait to see Alex in his new suit. I do wish he had wanted a simpler affair, but you know my Alex." She shook her head and added with a giggle, "It has been fun though."

She had liked Katherine from the first time she met her. In the last couple of months, they had become fast friends. She smiled into the mirror as she spoke, happy that Katherine had consented to be her matron of honor.

Katherine caught the smile and nodded as she pulled the needle through the lace for the last time. "There now, that job is done." She smiled back at her friend. "Let's try it on." She slipped it over Julianna's head.

"I don't know what I would've done without you these last weeks," Julianna said as she adjusted the veil to just the right place.

"Well, I feel the same. It's nice to have company when Franz is away working." She paused and continued, "I wish I'd had someone helping me at my wedding. Franz's Aunt Gretchen helped as much as she could, but with so many children, it was hard for her to find the time."

The clock chimed once, startling Julianna. "We've got thirty minutes to wait. Maybe I shouldn't have gotten ready quite so soon," she lamented.

"Not so fast," Katherine said with a laugh. "You may be dressed, but I still have to get ready, and I'm going to need your help getting at the top two buttons in back."

"I can help you," Aunt Gretchen said entering the small room in the back of the church that was reserved for the bridal party. She had two of her young children in tow, little Eileen dressed in a new pink gingham frock and three-year-old Emil in knee britches.

"Julianna, your dress is beautiful!" Eileen squealed.

Julianna smiled at the five-year-old, and felt her cheeks glow warm. Glancing in the mirror, she viewed a flushed, hazel-eyed woman in a long white satin dress gazing back.

"The dress is lovely, isn't it," Julianna agreed. She hadn't wanted to spend the money on such a magnificent gown, but Alex had pressed the issue.

"This is your day," he said and insisted she and Katherine take the money and buy the fabric.

They had hunted all over Freeport, but finally found something she felt they could afford.

Katherine was clever with fabric and a needle. She had drawn several patterns before they settled on one for each of them. All in all, to Julianna, it was a massive undertaking. Again, she thanked God for Katherine and her talents.

A month before the wedding, Alex and Julianna had found a small white house, with the front porch covered by a twisting grapevine. Franz said it would yield large purple fruit. The cottage was located close to the road leading out to the farm and within easy walking distance to the Frommelts'. The landlord offered them the first month's rent free if they'd fix up the place, so on weekends they had cleaned, made repairs and planned. It was mostly furnished, but they bought odds and ends that suited them which helped to make it theirs.

Julianna splurged and bought a beautiful mirror to hang on the wall in the bathroom. Even if they didn't have an indoor toilet, they at least had the mirror and the tub. It didn't matter to her because she was almost out of her teen years before her father had installed an indoor water closet at home. It was a sign of a successful man when he brought his toilet inside, Papa had told her.

"Here is your nosegay, Julianna." Aunt Gretchen's voice once again brought Julianna back to church and the reality of her wedding to Alex. She handed Julianna a beautiful assortment of zinnias and asters with three tall white gladioli.

"Lucky my next door neighbor, Mrs. White, has a large garden," Aunt Gretchen said.

"Oh, isn't it beautiful?" Julianna said as she buried her nose in the flowers. The smell brought her a sudden memory of her own mother's garden.

With that, a momentary sadness gripped her as she realized that no one in her family would be able to see her beautiful dress. I'll just have to write them a long letter and tell them all about it, she thought, not wanting to let anything dim the joy of the day.

"I'm going to take Emil to the men-folk now so they can give him the ring. Come now, child." Aunt Gretchen led the little boy out the door. "I waited until the last minute because I was terrified he'd get dirty before the ceremony even begins," she called over her shoulder.

The girls laughed and settled down, going over the details, impatient to hear the music. Julianna felt herself getting more nervous. How could she be so excited and yet anxious at the same time?

"I know how you feel," Katherine said as if sensing Julianna's sudden uneasiness. "It's perfectly natural. I felt the same way."

"Oh thank you, Katherine," Julianna said, relieved at her friend's understanding. After a pause she added, "I wonder how Alex is feeling right now?"

"Don't worry, dear, Franz is holding him up," Katherine chuckled. "You should've seen Franz on our wedding day. Uncle Henry told me he thought Franz would faint before the ceremony even began."

The first muted chords of the organ sounded and she hastily checked Eileen, noting her basket was full of flower petals, probably from the wild roses which grew on the fence in their backyard.

"Well, it sounds as though this might be the start," Julianna said with another glance in the mirror.

"Yes, it does," Katherine agreed. "Eileen, do you remember what you are supposed to do?"

"Yes, ma'am!" Excitement danced in the child's eyes. "Is Emil going to walk with me?"

Katherine went to the door, letting the once stifled tones of music flow through the room. "He's out here, dear, with your mama," she said. "Go now, stand beside him."

Julianna gave Katherine a quick hug, smoothed her skirt and adjusted her veil one last time. Then she started out the door and up the aisle, her eyes searching for and finding Alex in his brand new black suit and tie, looking proud, excited and a bit frightened.

Chapter 7

September 1882

It was only mid-afternoon in early September, but clouds had been drifting in and there was a black angry sky in the northwest. Unseasonably warm, the day turned muggy and uncomfortable. Alex and the rest of the crew worked faster to get the last of the hay into the barn before the rain hit. Sweat poured from their faces in rivulets across the grime.

"Whew, that cloud sure looks threatening." Mr. Schmidt, who owned the farm, glanced nervously once again toward the approaching darkness. "Alex, the boys and I'll get this last load in the barn. You better head for home. I think a tornado might be brewing."

Alex stuck his pitch fork in the hay high up on the wagon, turned and walked down the path through the open gate and onto the main road. There was not a breath of air, no breeze at all. He realized the only sound he could hear was his own footsteps.

He had an eerie, uneasy sense of some impending doom. The silence grew ever more ominous. The sweat beaded on his brow and rolled into his eyes. His handkerchief did no good. Earlier he had tied it around his head, under his hat, until it was so wet and grimy that he put it back in his pocket. Hayseeds stuck to the perspiration on his back. He unbuttoned his shirt, took it off and shook it. Then he put it back on because he didn't want to carry it. Ignoring his aching muscles, he picked up his pace.

He knew Julianna would be worried if the storm came and he wasn't home. They'd been married only a few weeks and he didn't want to cause her concern. Neither of them had experience with the kind of wind storms that people talked about around here. What they had heard didn't sound good.

For the first time since he left Triesen, he wondered if he'd made the right decision. The flat land here in Illinois made it easier to farm, but he could think of nothing else he liked about it. He shook his head when he remembered how the clay soil built up on his shoes when it rained so he could hardly lift his feet. The heat was so oppressive and relentless, that some nights they couldn't sleep.

True, the long warm summers were great for the growing season. He couldn't believe that Mr. Schmitz had three cuttings of hay this summer; but he missed the clear air and the green, raw smell of the freshly turned soil of his mountain homeland.

All summer, people had told him about tornadoes: what they were and what they did. Was the approaching cloud getting blacker? Maybe he was imagining it? No, it was closer and darker! He saw a lightning bolt close-by and terror took over. He broke into a trot. Then forgetting how tired he was, headed home in a dead run. A rumble of thunder broke the silence.

The storm kept pace and began to close in. Suddenly the roar, like the loudest train he'd ever heard, filled his ears. Instinctively he looked over his shoulder before he realized he was far from the railroad tracks. *Mein Gott*, it's the wind! He glanced around, looking for the black tunnel and there it was in the neighboring field, not a quarter mile away, whirling and circling; bearing down on him. He was directly in its path.

A few paces ahead, he spotted a dry creek bed. He ran as fast as he could, breathing large gulps of hot air. A slight cool breeze broke the stillness and the oppressive heat. A warning wind perhaps?

He leaped into the ditch and pressed himself as close to the edge as he could get, just as the deafening roar took over his thoughts. Even with his hands over his ears, he couldn't keep the sound from filling his body.

The wind tugged at his clothes until he felt like they might be shredded off his body. Something ripped his arm, making him try to pull even tighter into himself. Time stood still. How long did the roar last? He couldn't tell. It seemed a lifetime and yet it was suddenly over as quickly as it had come.

Stunned, he lay still, not able to get up or wanting to. He wasn't sure that he could. Cautiously he raised his head and peeked over the side of the creek bed. The black cloud was racing away and had turned a wimpy gray color. A few drops of rain washed at the dirt, cooling the earth. Unconsciously, he touched his arm. When he drew his hand away, he was surprised to see it covered in blood.

The sight of his own blood brought a wave of nausea. His sleeve was gone and he saw a long laceration running down his upper arm. Blood dripped off his elbow. It didn't hurt, which he thought strange.

He ripped off what was left of his shirt and fashioned a bandage, wrapping it as tightly as he could around the wound. Taking the two ends of the wrap, he placed a twig through them and turned it until he was sure the pressure would staunch the flow. He resisted the urge to vomit, as pain scalded his arm, shoulder to fingers.

Slowly he rose to his feet. Blinking back the dizziness, he stumbled out of the hole. At home he would've picked up a walking stick, but here there was nothing sturdy close-by. He made his way slowly up the road, struggling to stay upright. Eventually he came upon a stand of willow trees, limbs scattered as if Thor himself had walked through. He struggled to break off a six foot piece of a sturdy branch.

Wrapping his good arm around it, he leaned on the stick and made his way slowly toward home and Julianna. Amazed that he wasn't hurt any worse, he thanked God he wasn't dead. He wondered if soldiers who fought in wars felt like this.

His arm burned with the intensity of the pain. He tried to walk without leaning on his stick, but he was weak and unsteady. He wasn't sure if it was the trauma of the tornado or the blood loss. He decided it was both and was glad he was nearing home.

Julianna must've heard the front gate open, because she was on the path, running to him. He was in her arms before he reached the porch. "Oh you poor, poor darling! What happened to your arm? Look at your clothes!" Julianna cried out when she saw the bloody shirt wrapped around his arm.

"I was in the tornado. I had to lie in a ditch. I thought it was going to kill me."

"*Mein Gott*! I saw the thunder clouds! Come sit here on the step. Let me look at it," Julianna said as she helped him down. She slowly pulled off the bandage, examined the damage and quickly wrapped it back up. "You need a doctor to sew this up," she said, taking charge. "I'll run next door and ask if they can take you to Doc Krohn's."

Emil quickly hitched up the buggy. Shortly after Julianna had gotten a clean towel to rewrap Alex's arm, he was there, anxious to help. His children, ever curious, ran across the yard to see the wounded man. The kindly neighbor helped Alex into the wagon and soon they were at their destination.

"It was smart you got him to me," Doc said as he finished the last stitch. "This man's arm is badly mangled."

"Will I get back the use of it?" Alex asked, almost afraid to hear the answer.

"Well, I've cleaned it good and it's sewn up, so barring any complications, I think you will. It'll take some time though. Don't get anxious and try to do too much. I don't want you pulling out those stitches."

Chapter 8

November 1882

The snow swirled and blew, frozen bits pinging as they hit the window. Julianna stood watching it from the warmth of the living room.

"At least it snows here, even if it's not home," she said half to herself. She tried to hide her homesickness, but there was little about living on these low rolling hills that she found appealing.

"This is some storm, isn't it?" Alex sat on the stool by the fireplace sharpening his axe. He'd spent the morning replenishing the supply in the wood box.

After a time he continued, "We rarely had these kinds of storms in Liechtenstein. Mostly we'd just wake up to another meter or so of snow. Look out there. Some places are blown bare and other places are drifted high. We won't be able to see out of the window before long."

She nodded, grateful to have him feeling better. He had spent two weeks with his arm in a sling and when it was healed, he had to exercise it to get full mobility. He still worked it daily, but insisted that it was as good as new. Thank goodness it was his left arm rather than the right one.

"As soon as this storm is over, I'll start building that rocking chair for Mrs. Schmitz. I don't want to dip into our savings," he said. Grateful for his building trade, he'd been promised several carpentry jobs around town and out at the farm during the winter, but the wound held him up and their ready cash supply was dwindling.

The snowstorm lasted for another week. The temperatures remained well below freezing. Julianna worried about Alex walking out to the farm in such cold weather, so he stayed in town and caught up on the odd jobs he'd found before his bout with the now infamous tornado.

They spent Thanksgiving with the Frommelts at Aunt Grace's. The conversation was filled with weather related topics starting with Alex's windstorm adventure. The men visited in the parlor, their stomachs growling, while trying to ignore the aroma of roast turkey and gravy,.

"That's quite an introduction to our fair land," Uncle Henry said with humor in his voice. "It's pretty hard to outrun a tornado." Uncle Henry was a large man with an ample belly. He was known for his gaiety and laughter. Franz smirked and Alex flushed.

"He did his best," Julianna said, sticking her head out of the kitchen door. She was not one to let anyone embarrass her husband.

"I'm glad it was Alex and not me." Franz joined the conversation. "I saw that funnel cloud cross old man Pogeman's field. It was bigger than what the paper said and it was traveling faster than a train. Alex has always outrun me. I think I wouldn't have gotten away as easily as he did."

Alex nodded. "A fellow can run pretty fast when he's motivated by sheer panic. Frankly, I'm grateful to be alive."

Aunt Grace called the men and children to dinner. As they sat down, Katherine suggested they add a prayer of thanksgiving that Alex had escaped the tornado and lived to tell about it.

Uncle Henry made the sign of the cross and said the blessing before the meal, followed by a moment of quiet joy.

"I heard that there's still a lot of donation land claims in the west," Franz said, as plates were being served. "I was down at the hardware and a couple of men were talking about a relative who had written them to come out to Oregon. One of them said that his cousin lived on a homestead somewhere near a town called Salem."

"Isn't that the Willamette Valley?" Alex asked, remembering something he'd read somewhere.

"That's what I understand," Uncle Henry replied, after taking a swallow of wine.

"Does the west have mountains?" Julianna passed a bowl of mashed potatoes, thinking of her beloved Mt. Merkur.

"The men said it's mountainous country, with fertile valleys."

The conversation lagged as the hungry group filled their plates and mothers tended to the children's needs.

"I've known several people who have migrated out there, but the problem is you have to go by horse and wagon at least part of the way," Uncle Henry broke the silence. "They still don't have train service to Portland. I've heard you can go to Omaha and take the train to California, but there's no railroad from California to Oregon either. You have to take a sailing ship from San Francisco."

Julianna's stomach turned queasy at the thought of getting on another ship, but she couldn't help feeling excitement at the thought of country that may look like home. She hadn't realized or let herself think about how badly she disliked this flat land country, especially after that terrible wind storm. Maybe they wouldn't have to stay here after all. Her eyes met Katherine's and she knew instantly that Katherine shared her feelings.

But there was a possible problem that she hadn't discussed with anyone. She was pretty sure she was going to have a baby. She'd been nauseated for several weeks starting in mid-September which was her first clue. Being in a family way, either traveling across the prairie in a wagon or sailing by ship, did not sound appealing. Well, we haven't gone yet, so I won't worry about it, she thought.

***

The month between Thanksgiving and Christmas saw another serious snowstorm, which stranded everyone for several days. Julianna was glad they didn't have livestock to care for. It was all they could do to survive themselves.

35

Alex went to the feed store and brought home several sacks of coal. Wood was scarce and they needed something to burn, even though she hated using it. It turned the walls sooty and gray and it smelled bad. But the week before Christmas, as if on cue, the temperature rose and the weather grew balmy. They went out to restock their groceries and Julianna bought Alex two new shirts and a pair of woolen socks. She had darned his other pair until there was no stocking left in one of the heels, only her careful sewing.

She wondered when to tell Alex about the baby and decided she would make it a Christmas present to him. She purchased some soft white cotton fabric to make a christening dress.

For the next few days, while Alex was working, she rushed to sew the tiny gown. She was almost caught one day when he came home early, but he was cold and hungry and didn't seem to notice her haste to push the project under their bed.

Two days before Christmas Eve, Alex brought home a pine tree no more than three feet tall, which she balanced in the corner on a small table. They strung strands of popcorn, made tiny wreaths of evergreen limbs that Franz brought from his back yard and decorated their first Christmas tree.

"What's all this?" Alex asked as he came in the door the following evening and spied the presents under the tree.

"No fair peeking. We have to wait until tomorrow evening or Friday morning to open these." Julianna could barely contain her excitement.

Alex laughed and kissed her eyelids. "Now *Leibe*, what makes you think I would cheat and open them early?"

"Because I know you. I'll be watching you every minute." They both laughed and sat down to dinner.

On Christmas Eve, before Midnight Mass, they couldn't wait any longer. Alex brought out a large package from the woodshed and sat it in the middle of the floor. It was wrapped in newspaper and tied with a red bow.

"Ok, you go first," he said.

Julianna carefully untied the ribbon and unwrapped her present. It was a chest, beautifully varnished, with her name painted in red letters on the lid. The workmanship had been done with his loving hands. Tears welled up as she turned the latch and opened it to find a much smaller identical jewelry box, with her name in tiny letters.

"Alex, this is beautiful!"

"Open it," he said, his eyes shining.

She opened the lid and there on the velvet lining was a jade cloisonné brooch on a gold chain. She took it out and held it to the light.

"Where did you get this? Did you make it?"

"No dear, I bought it in New York. I wanted to give it to you for the wedding, but I decided to let you enjoy your ring and give this to you on our first Christmas together."

"Here, help me put it on." Julianna held it to her throat.

36

Alex got up, attached the clasp for her and gently kissed her neck. "I got it because I knew it would go with your eyes."

"You are the most romantic fellow I've ever met."

"I hope so!" Alex grinned at her. "Now can I open mine?"

She handed him the package wrapped in white tissue paper and watched as he unwrapped the tiny dress. He looked at it in disbelief.

"What the...?" After a moment his face lit up. "Does this mean...?"

"Yes dear," Julianna nodded and put her arms around his shoulders. "Merry Christmas! You're going to be a Papa."

"You're sure?" Alex looked a bit dazed.

"Absolutely positive."

"Do you know when?"

"As near as I can figure, sometime in June."

Alex was quiet, which Julianna momentarily took as disappointment. But then he smiled, as only he could and said, "Well, that settles it. We can't go to Oregon until there's train service. I won't have my family riding all those miles in a wagon."

Chapter 9

April 1883

According to the old timers in Freeport, the winter was worse then usual, but spring came early and by the first of April, farmers and their help were busy getting the fields ready for planting.

Julianna felt like she was growing bigger by the minute and was more than a little uncomfortable. Her earlier sickness had passed, but her movements were cumbersome and unwieldy. Alex worked long hours, which gave her time to rest between her household chores.

There were questions she wished she could ask her mother. She missed her terribly and regretted not being able to share this time with her family. She wondered when she would see them again.

One pleasant afternoon, she opened the door to Katherine and Aunt Grace. She hadn't seen them for awhile because Katherine hadn't been to church the past two weeks. Franz had told them she was down with the grippe.

"You look well," Julianna said as she took their coats and sat them down.

"Oh I'm much better now. I didn't want to visit you while I was ill. You don't need that ugly disease when you're so close to your time."

Aunt Grace nodded in agreement. "I was ill when I delivered Eileen and believe you me, I didn't think I would live. The doctor told Henry he was surprised that I did. You can't be too careful when you are going to have a baby." She clucked her tongue.

Julianna stifled a laugh. She dearly loved Aunt Grace. She was a funny little lady, short with an elfish round face and a serious countenance. Many times she reminded Julianna of her mama's dear friend in Baden, Mrs. Woehlers. She would lovingly advise her mother about childbearing and rearing, even though her mother was a practicing midwife, with Julianna often assisting.

Cookies, coffee, and cheerful chatting helped Julianna forget her homesickness, and the afternoon passed quickly. She was surprised at how much better she felt. I'm going to spend more time with them, she decided. It's not good to be by myself.

She made an effort after that to spend at least one afternoon a week with Katherine. Sometimes they chatted quietly while working on a sewing project. Sometimes they would seek out another friend or go by Aunt Grace's. Julianna noticed that she wasn't quite as homesick after these visits.

Alex was all for it. He never complained when he came home to a cold supper, which amazed Julianna. She knew Papa would never have stood for that. One day she asked him about it.

"Why am I not angry when we have a cold supper?" he repeated, a surprised look on his face.

"*Leibe*, I'm glad you have friends to visit. I'm gone all day and I worry when I know you're alone." He grinned at her, "Besides, you're in better spirits after a day with Katherine. You two are good for each other."

"You really don't mind then?" Her father wouldn't believe this.

"Six days a week I have a warm meal. I can live with that. At least you don't make me fix my own." Alex reached for her hand. "I have the best wife in the world. No need to worry about it."

April crawled slowly into May and much to Julianna's dismay, she got even bigger and more awkward. She calculated she was still at least a month from delivery. Her quandary was who to have in attendance at the birth. Aunt Grace's friend Cecilia helped with births; maybe she would ask her.

She knew birthing was woman's work. She had no business asking Alex about it, but she wanted his opinion. He was her best friend. It puzzled her why none of the women she knew would discuss things of this nature with their husbands. She pondered the dilemma for several days and one night when Alex looked particularly relaxed, she decided to bring up the subject.

"Alex, I have something I need to ask you."

"What is it dear?" he said as he sat absent mindedly gazing into the fire.

Julianna hesitated. Was she doing the right thing? She took a deep breath and said, "I know this isn't a man's issue, but I need to know your thoughts on who should help deliver the baby."

Alex started, staring at her with that now familiar surprised look and said, "Who said it wasn't a man's issue?"

"All of my friends. In fact, Papa always scoffed at Mama when she'd bring up things about babies. I remember him laughing at her when she'd ask a 'woman's' question."

"This is my baby, too!" Alex came to where she was sitting with a diaper half hemmed in her lap. He put his arm around her and squeezed her shoulder.

"Don't you know I'm as excited about this child as you are? At this point maybe I'm more excited because I don't have to bear it." He paused a moment and continued, "You bet I want to be involved."

"Really?" It was her turn to be amazed. She knew Alex was excited, he told her every day and in every way, but to actually want to share everything!

Alex sat on the footstool in front of her and looked at her for a long moment. She met his gaze and wondered what he was thinking.

"*Leibe,* who do you want to help you?"

"I have been thinking about it. Katherine said she wanted to be with me."

"Does she have any experience birthing a child?"

"No, but she tells me I am her dearest friend and she wants to be here."

"I think that is a good thing." He hesitated and added, "But I still want someone here who knows more about it."

Julianna nodded, "Cecilia is a practicing midwife. I'm thinking about asking her."

"Then do it. Don't wait. We need to have a plan well in place." Alex relaxed and with a smile said, "I'm glad Katherine will be here, because then I can ask Franz to come and stay with me."

***

The days turned into weeks and Julianna's time grew closer with everything ready and in place. She tried hard not to let the coming days frighten her, but she knew about childbirth and what could go wrong. Everyone told her that Cecilia was very good, so in the end she felt she'd made the right choice. She had then made a conscious decision not to worry. She could after all assist if need be.

They were sitting at the table just finishing dinner when Alex leaned back in his chair with a sigh of contentment. "Have you thought of any names for our new baby?" he asked.

"I thought if it was a boy, I would let you name him," Julianna replied with a smile.

"I'll have to give that some thought." He was quiet for some time, and then added, "I think I'd like to name him Ferdinand after my grandfather."

She nodded and said, "That's a fine German name. I like it, too."

"What do you want to name it if it's a girl?"

"I'm still thinking about it," she said. "I'm not sure yet."

Alex nodded and took her hand. "It's fine, *leibe,* you have some time left to decide."

When June finally arrived, Julianna found herself excited. Now maybe things would start to happen. But time continued to drag.

"Dearest, you look much too pale and uncomfortable to come over here. From now on, I'll come to your house until the baby arrives," Katherine told her one afternoon while they were busy sewing a baby quilt.

"Mama always said it's good to walk when your time is near," Julianna said, wincing as the baby kicked a low rib.

"Well, then I'll come to you here and we'll walk together. I just don't want you walking alone."

Julianna nodded, "All right, then we'll walk together."

So every afternoon, she and Katherine walked up the street to the park, visited in the sunshine, and walked back. The month passed slowly.

***

The last week in June came and went and still nothing. Alex didn't want to leave Julianna, even to go to work. She looked so uncomfortable, but he couldn't help her. Excitement about the baby had turned to worry and doubt. Maybe this wasn't as great as everyone said? He hated seeing his wife so miserable. He insisted that she not cook, he could eat cold meat and bread, just as long as she was all right. That's all he cared about.

On the last Friday of the month a thunderstorm raced through, leaving the road a muddy bog. When quitting time came, Alex wanted to hurry home, but the mud kept building up on his boots, slowing his pace. He scraped his soles again and again, cursing the soil, the prairie, the rain and everything else he could think of in this Illinois country.

When he finally arrived, he stamped his boots hard on the path, went into the house and found Julianna leaning over the cold stove, one arm tightly wrapped around her waist.

"I, I think I'm in labor!" was all she could say, between gasps. "You'd better go get Katherine and Cecilia."

He helped her to the bed and made sure she was safe before he turned and ran to Katherine's, staying on the grass and gravel to avoid being slowed by the sticky mud. Franz was home, so Alex sent him to get Cecilia, while he and Katherine hurried back to Julianna.

They got her as comfortable as possible and then Katherine sent him outside to wait for the others. He sat on the steps, leaning forward, his head in his hands, not having the slightest clue what to do. Franz joined him as soon as he and Cecilia arrived.

"You look worse than you did at your wedding, fellow," Franz said with sympathy in his voice.

"*Yah,* I feel worse, too!" Alex's voice cracked.

Later, Katherine came out with two cups of coffee. "Here, Cecilia thought you might need this. She says it's going to be a long night, so I made a big pot."

"Thanks, Katherine," Alex said, his hands shaking as he took the cup. Some of the hot liquid spilled into the saucer and on to his thumb. "Ouch!" He wiped it off and stuck it in his mouth.

Time dragged on. It seemed like an eternity, but sometime in the early morning hours, a baby girl with a very loud voice was born.

She was in her mother's arms when Alex first laid eyes on her, and he was sure he'd never seen anything quite as beautiful.

"What should we call her?" he asked, one of her tiny hands wrapped around his finger.

"I love the name Theresa," Julianna said. "It's the name of my favorite saint."

"Then Theresa it is," Alex said, gazing in wonder at his baby girl.

41

Chapter 10

Late September, 1883

It was Franz who brought the news. The railroad was through to Oregon. They'd pounded in the last spike somewhere in Montana. When he heard about it, Alex's first instinct was to pack his family and leave immediately, but Julianna and Katherine intervened.

"It's going to be winter soon," Julianna said, wiping milk from Theresa's chin. "I'm not sure it is a good idea to go out there now, especially with a new baby. Let's wait until spring. That'll give us time to plan for the trip."

"You're right! We don't know about the winters. It's like a foreign country." Alex had learned to value her opinion.

"We have a place to stay when we get there. We can go to the Foeller's."

"Cecilia's brother, Matt, lives in Portland," Franz chimed in.

"But we don't know him, Franz," Julianna said, untying the baby's bib.

"I met him once when he was here on business, and we know Cecilia."

In the end, they decided that Katherine and Julianna would ask Cecilia to write to her brother and his wife, Sophie, on their behalf. Alex and Franz would begin planning for emigration the following spring. One thing was sure, they all wanted to go whether they had a place to stay or not. Free or at least good inexpensive land was on their minds and they all yearned for the mountain country.

***

Time passed quickly in the winter of 1883-84. The storms were shorter, warmer, and less intense than the year before. The old trunk that had brought their belongings to America had belonged to Alex's family. It was now worn out, so he spent several evenings building one for them and another for the Frommelts.

Julianna carefully planned what they would take and what they would give to Aunt Grace and other church members. She packed the baby things in her Christmas chest and contemplated how life became so much more complicated when a baby was involved.

"What should I do about these beautiful plates?" Julianna asked. She and Katherine were working in the Lampert living room.

"Aren't you going to take them?" Katherine folded a blanket and carefully laid it in the trunk.

"Alex and I decided that we would only take things we need to survive. I'm quite sure this is something he would think frivolous." She picked up the pink dish with flowers and admired it. Several families in the parish had given the couple a plate from their own collection of china, most from the old country, as wedding gifts. They were some of Julianna's favorite things.

"Why don't you just wrap them in Theresa's clothes and put them in the chest? You can discuss it later with Alex," Katherine suggested. "Perhaps after we've arrived in Portland," she added, smiling.

Julianna nodded and began to wrap them carefully in the small sheets and blankets.

They were trying to earn as much money as possible for the trip, so Julianna was gone for long periods of time, helping deliver babies. She shared her earnings with Katherine who watched Theresa.

Theresa grew and changed, a contented child who adored her father. Much to Julianna's dismay, Alex began to call her Tracy. One night after they settled down in bed, she brought up the subject of names to Alex.

"I thought you liked the name Theresa," she said, pulling the covers up to her chin.

"I do, *Leibe*. Why do you ask?" Alex rolled over to face her. He sounded puzzled.

"You keep calling her Tracy. Why do you do that?"

He put his arm around her and matter-of-factly said, "Because it's easier to say."

After a long silence, Julianna nodded in the darkness and said, "That makes sense."

***

Spring came in early March and brought with it a renewed exuberance for the trip and all its adventures. Julianna and Katherine frantically attended to the last minute packing issues, while Alex and Franz tried to cram in a few more days of work, not knowing what they'd find out west.

Most information they read or heard was that Portland was a wide open town, bursting at its seams with construction. Floods of people were flocking to the fledgling city.

The highlight of the season was a letter they received from Sophie Foeller, postmarked February 22, 1884. Katherine and Franz brought it over one evening, and the two couples carefully studied it.

It read in part, "We are so eager to have you folks come to Portland. Cecilia speaks very highly of you. Matt does remember Franz. As you probably know, we own a small grocery store near the western outskirts of Portland up on 16th and Johnson, near the forest. We live upstairs, above the store. We have a small apartment over the carriage house that you folks could rent for as long as need be.

Matt tells me he thinks he knows of some land near the community of Bethany in the Tualatin Valley that might be available. He hears things when he is working in the store. He says he'll inquire about it for you. Just let us know what evening you'll arrive on the train and we'll have someone there to meet you."

"Sounds promising doesn't it?" Alex said, looking at Julianna.

"Yes, it does," Franz agreed. "Especially about the part that says he remembers me. She didn't follow the sentence with anything *abfaollig*, so I must've made a good impression." Tracy was on his lap and he chuckled as he patted her head.

***

By the first of April, everything was packed and tickets purchased. Shortly after midnight on Friday April 11, the excited young people were prepared to board the train in Dubuque. Aunt Grace and Uncle Henry drove them to the station from Freeport and stayed to see them off.

"Don't you young fellows take any chances out there. I hear it can be pretty wild," Uncle Henry said as he shook their hands all around. After a moment he leaned over to the men and said quietly, "If I had my way, we'd be going with you."

"Now Henry, you know you don't mean that." Aunt Grace had overheard the comment. "You swore you'd never step foot out of Freeport once we landed here. Don't you remember?"

Henry laughed, shook his head and winked at Katherine and Julianna.

After their last good-byes and a wave from the train window, the engine bellowed smoke, blew its whistle and was on its way to St. Paul.

Chapter 11

April 1884

Alex pulled out his silver Elgin pocket watch. It was 8:00. Hmm, right on time! The morning sun shone on St. Paul, in Minnesota Territory, as the Pacific Express roared and hissed and left the city behind. We're on our way. He breathed a sigh of contentment and smiled at his drowsy wife and sleeping daughter.

The conductor, in his starched white linen shirt and vest, appeared on the scene and asked for tickets. Alex pulled them out of his vest pocket and handed them over, careful not to disturb the baby in Julianna's arms.

They rode all day, seeing nothing but flat land and stopping only once in Fargo, a small town bustling with enthusiasm for the new railroad and the prosperity it had brought them in such a short time.

"We're going to get something to eat." Franz announced as soon as the train came to a full stop. "We'll bring it back. You girls don't need to come with us."

"Do you have time?" Katherine asked.

"Long enough to grab a bite," Alex said. "At least that's what the conductor told me."

"Then hurry," Julianna urged. "I don't want to end up in Portland without you two."

New passengers boarded the train and others left, while workmen unloaded freight and loaded sacks of grain onto boxcars.

The men brought back large slices of homemade bread, slabs of meat and cheese, and a large bag of dried apple slices, plus coffee all around and milk for Julianna.

Soon the train continued its trek through the prairie. Darkness quietly slipped over them, dancing to the tune of the clack of the rails. Alex woke when the train stopped. It was past midnight when he looked out the window and saw a sign that said Bismarck, Dakota Territory.

Everyone was asleep when the train stopped so he stayed aboard, although he was too excited to nod off. He was sure he was going to see mountains before long. He shifted his position, stretched his legs, and glanced at his wife. She didn't seem to have any trouble sleeping in her seat; maybe she was right not wanting to get a berth.

Since they had agreed before the trip to avoid the expense of the dining car whenever possible, they ate some of the bread and cheese for breakfast. Daylight revealed the passing terrain, which was flat, with rocks and prairie grass. The scenery didn't change for several hours and many passengers remarked about the breadth of the landscape.

When the train stopped it was late afternoon and they were in the Montana Territory. The depot sign read "Glendive."

Tracy fussed and Julianna said, "Let's get off and stretch our legs. We all need to move around."

"I don't care if we get left, we can catch the next train," Katherine agreed. "Besides, I need something to take this grit out of my mouth."

"These aisles are narrow, aren't they?" Alex said with a chuckle and asked, "Who knew America was this big?"

"I'm ready for something to eat," Franz said pulling his coat from off the back of the seat.

They walked a block to a café for a quick dinner and took a leisurely walk "to limber up". It was dark before the train left Glendive on the trip west. Tracy slept quietly in her mother's lap as they rolled away from the station.

Their next stop was Billings just as the sun began to peek over the horizon. Alex's heart leapt. There in the distance was a mountain range. Our first mountains and aren't they beautiful!

The conductor laughed when Alex asked about them and said, "You're in good company, young fellow. Those are the Beartooth Mountains and they're a favorite of Fredrick Billings, too. He is president of the Northern Pacific Rail Road Company and he built this town."

No one was particularly hungry at this early hour, but the conductor said they wouldn't arrive in Butte until past midday so Franz and Alex went in search of coffee and something light to eat.

"Would you look at that sky?" Alex said, admiring what seemed like a huge upside down dark bowl against the pink, orange sunrise. To the west he could see nothing but high snow-covered mountains. A hint of mist covered their base so they appeared to float on the clouds above the horizon.

"*Yah*, it's about the biggest sky I've ever seen," Franz agreed. "It's cold, too."

Alex nodded. He was glad he had thought to put on his hat.

Before long they were headed for Butte. The tracks followed the Yellowstone River, bringing the mountains closer with each mile. When they arrived at the bustling mining town, they were high in the Rockies, in a rugged landscape that brought memories of his home in Liechtenstein. It was late in the day, and the air was light and clear. Alex and Julianna's eyes met, for the first time it felt like home.

The conductor said they were on the continental divide and warned the train would be staying here for at least a couple of hours. As they disembarked they saw several armored wagons lined up by the train, each pulled by four large, tired appearing draft horses. Burly workmen in shirtsleeves were unloading sacks and putting them onto a boxcar.

"What do you suppose is in those sacks?" Julianna asked.

"I don't know, but they look like they're heavy." Katherine shook her head.

"They're from the silver mine up yonder," A gentleman from the train had overheard the conversation and chimed in.

"You mean there's silver in those sacks?" Franz said. "No wonder they weigh a lot."

"Yes, the train often has trouble getting up some of the hills after they load it. They may have to use two engines. It depends on how much silver there is," the man continued. "That's why it sometimes takes longer here than other stops."

They went to eat and when they returned the wagons were gone, the boxcar door was shut, and it looked like nothing had changed. The single engine blasted three whistles as a sign they would be leaving in ten minutes. They hastily boarded, found their seats, and settled in for the next leg of the trip.

Alex noticed a well-dressed stranger sitting in the seat across the aisle, toward the back of the car. A rifle leaned up against the window beside him. Something about the slick haired gentleman sent shivers through him and he glanced at Julianna. She was busy trying to clean the coal dust out of the baby's eyes and seemed not to notice, but Franz gave him a curious look. The two of them got up, walked out the rear door, and stood on the platform as the train pulled away from the station.

"I wonder what that's all about," Alex said, motioning inside the car. They weren't used to seeing guns in the open and it concerned him. He'd heard about arms on trains in the old country, but only during times of war.

"I don't know, but I don't like it." Franz shook his head. They gazed out the back and watched the town of Butte disappear.

"I wonder if it has to do with that load of silver." Alex glanced at the boxcar with a degree of trepidation. "We have our families to think about."

"One of us'll stay awake at all times," Franz said after a pause. "I'll take the first watch, you get some sleep. When I can't keep my eyes open anymore, I'll wake you."

Alex nodded and followed Franz back through the door. He gazed at the other passengers. No one else looked worried or even seemed to notice. "Let's not tell the women what we think about it," he whispered. Franz nodded.

It was dark when the train stopped at Helena. No one stirred when two people left and a family with several small children boarded. Then it was off again into the black night, the rhythm of the wheels soothing the sleeping passengers.

It was Alex's turn to take the watch and Franz immediately fell asleep.

Alex sat beside his sleeping wife and child and committed himself to stay awake. He yawned and noticed a fine grit in his mouth. His tongue moved over his teeth and he tried to spit it out. Dirty smoke coming out of the engine, he thought as he coughed and moistened his lips.

With dawn came the Blackfoot River, the Bitterroot Valley, and soon the small town of Missoula. When the train stopped, the stranger got off ahead of them. Alex watched him disappear into the depot.

"This is a pretty place," Julianna said, taking Alex's hand as he helped her down the steps, the baby balanced in her other arm.

"I guess you just don't know where you'll find beauty," Katherine agreed, gazing at the high snow-covered hills surrounding the small town. "And after all that flat land."

The two men nodded in agreement and steered them to a small eatery for breakfast.

When the train left Missoula, another stranger wearing a side arm joined the first, but sat closer to the front of the car. Neither talked to anyone or to each other, but sat alert, their eyes seeming to look everywhere. Alex started when he saw them. Worried, he glanced to see if Julianna noticed it. She seemed fine, so he relaxed and leaned back, but couldn't help wondering about those guns.

The tracks wandered through steep wooded hills and high mountain valleys. They stopped at a small outpost called Lake Pend Oreille in the wilds of Idaho Territory, before heading out to Spokane Falls in the northwestern-most Territory. Alex had read about Washington, named for the first president of the United States, and even wondered if they should settle near the city of New Tacoma. But the more he read and heard about the Oregon country with its rich Willamette Valley, the more he felt it calling to him.

**

Julianna stirred, moved her legs and stretched. Sleeping in a chair and entertaining a small child for these many miles was taking its toll. Oh, to lay my head on a pillow. She had discouraged the men when they wanted to pay for a berth because she wanted to save money, but now she wasn't so sure she had done the right thing. Her dress was gritty with coal dust from the engine and there was nowhere to change.

Julianna was grateful that Tracy was such a good baby. I'd hate to take this trip with a fussy child. She moved again to try to find a comfortable spot and smiled at Alex, who had fallen sound asleep. That was so unlike him, to sleep in the middle of the day. Franz was strangely silent.

She sighed and looked out the window, astonished at the skill of the Indians fishing with long spears in the small stream that ran along the tracks. She looked at Katherine, who had just opened her eyes and pointed silently, careful not to awaken Alex.

The train had begun a slow steady climb up the mountains shortly after leaving Lake Pend Oreille and now, looking out the window, she noticed the train was pulling up an exceptionally steep hill. As it continued to lose speed, she began to wonder if it could make it to the top, when it suddenly lurched to a stop, the cars banging into each other with loud crashes and jolting bumps. She could see the engine spewing steam as it had partially rounded a curve, smoke from the brakes curling up its side.

"Oh *holle!*" Alex said, suddenly awake and leaning over her trying to see out of the window. "What the *teufel* is going on out there?"

Katherine startled awake and turned to look. "What happened?" she said to no one in particular.

The two strangers jumped up; one disappearing out the front door, the other out the back of the car. Julianna could see the one in front had a gun in his hand. The other passengers were stirring and a baby cried. Several children could be heard questioning their parents, but as near as Julianna could tell, no one appeared to be hurt. The climb had slowed the train enough that the sudden stop had not done serious damage to the passengers.

She could see several men running up the hill toward the engine. Alex put his arm around her and watched. She could feel his heart racing.

She saw Franz and Alex exchange glances. *What's going on?* She caught her breath. Tracy whimpered and Julianna bent to comfort her.

The passengers talked among themselves, and shortly the conductor and the stranger came through from the car in front of them.

"Ladies and gentleman," the conductor began. "There is a good-sized log across the tracks up ahead. A windstorm must've blown it over, because it is still attached to the roots."

Alex and Franz glanced at each other again. Alex nodded and looked relieved.

"We have a cross-cut saw and several axes, but it'll take two or three hours to clear the tracks. If there are any men who would like to lend a hand, we would appreciate it," he continued. "In the meantime you are free to move around if you wish, but please remain close by. We don't want anyone lost, and when the tracks are open we need get on the move immediately."

"I don't know about you, but I could use the exercise," Franz said to Alex.

"Yes," Katherine said. "Please go and help so we can get to Spokane Falls. This ride is exhausting."

Julianna nodded, happy for the chance to move about and stretch her back.

Alex looked reluctant, but squeezed her hand and followed Franz out the train and down the steps. A short time later, Julianna, Tracy and Katherine left their seats and climbed the hill toward the engine to watch. The crew spent the morning sawing through the giant log; the sound of axes rang in the air as the men hacked limbs.

The two strangers stood on their side of the train, down by the car containing the silver. They were joined by a third man with a long rifle balanced in the crook of his arm. Julianna noticed on the other side of the train, two men with holsters and guns and one bearded man with a large double-barreled shotgun stood guard in front of the car door.

"Do you see that?" Julianna asked Katherine. "Those men have guns, too."

"Yes," Katherine nodded, "And it scares me. I hope the men hurry."

"Do you suppose someone might try to rob the train while it's stopped?" Julianna squinted in the distance, fearing the thieves might ride in at any moment. She'd read about things like that happening in the west.

The crew worked hard, but time crept by and each moment made Julianna more nervous. Was that someone coming over the hill? She looked again. No, thank God it was only an old snag. She brushed the dust from her skirt and picked up Tracy in case they had to flee.

Shortly after noon the men rolled the pieces of the log to the side of the tracks and hauled away the last of the brush. Julianna didn't relax until everyone was on board. The train slowly began its way up the hill, unable to gain speed until it reached the crest. Sighs of relief were heard from several of the passengers.

Alex's suit pants were scuffed and stained and his white shirt was splattered with mud and wet with sweat. "Well so much for this suit," he remarked as he sat down.

"I think you're a hero," Julianna said, patting his arm. "Most of those stains will come out."

"You're a lot cleaner than Franz," Katherine said with a laugh, shaking her head at her husband.

"Yah, I worked harder." Franz laughed heartily at his own joke. "At least they let us wash up in the caboose. That was generous of them."

The rest of the ride into Spokane Falls was uneventful and both men got a good nap believing the danger was passed. They pulled into the station shortly before dark. The conductor came through and told the passengers they wouldn't stay here long because they were behind schedule and needed to make up time. "Otherwise the Portland-bound train at Wallula Junction will have to wait and engineers hate to have that happen," he said. His once white linen suit was now gray with coal dust.

"They've just opened the new railroad bridge at Ainsworth," he continued. "We won't have to be ferried across the Snake River. That'll save a lot of time." The conductor looked pleased and Julianna could feel an air of excitement in the car. "In the meantime, please take a short walk and stretch. The falls are beautiful. Just be back in twenty minutes," he said. Everyone disembarked to see the sight.

"They look treacherous." Julianna exclaimed as they admired the falls in the setting sun. They watched, opened mouthed at the Indian fishermen, with large spears in their hands, standing out on planks over the river. One had a long-handled net, and was dipping for fish. Spray washed up over his hands and face, as he hauled a large salmon onto the platform.

After the short walk, they arrived back at the train and went directly to the dining car, hoping to beat the crowd. They got the last seats and were grateful for a warm meal of stew, with large chunks of beef and warm bread. It seemed like a long time since they'd had breakfast in Missoula. The train pulled out just as they were finishing a piece of prune kuchen topped with thick whipped cream.

"That tasted like home," Franz remarked as he scraped the bottom of the dish.

"What a reward," Alex agreed. "*Menschenskind*! I'd cut up another tree if we'd get this dessert when we're finished."

Julianna and Katherine looked at each other and laughed. "We'll remember that the next time we have something we want you to do for us," Katherine said, patting Tracy's tiny cheek as she picked her up and put her over her shoulder. "My goodness, *leibe,* you're getting heavy," she added.

Tracy giggled as Alex took her from Katherine and laid her on the seat on a blanket between him and Julianna.

They settled back in their seats for a rest before the next stop, hoping that Tracy would sleep until then.

***

Light in the eastern sky was just breaking when the train came to the edge of the small settlement of Ainsworth, showing bleak, dry terrain, sand and sagebrush in the rocky soil around the town. Julianna shuddered and hoped Portland would be greener.

The houses in the small village had a few young shade trees planted along the streets. A large sawmill stood on the banks of the broad mouth of the Snake, with piles of railroad ties stacked neatly around the periphery.

"They look like giant matchsticks," Katherine said, giggling.

Julianna loved Katherine for her fun-loving ways. At the moment Julianna, with dirt in her mouth and dust in her eyes would've been miserable if it weren't for Katherine's laughter and good humor.

The train blew its whistle, stopped at the small depot to load and unload cargo and passengers in what the conductor said was record time. Within the hour, the train started across the Snake on the brand-new bridge.

When they arrived at Wallula Junction, a train was waiting on a sidetrack.

"That must be ours," Alex said as their engine came to a hissing stop.

The conductor came through just then and announced that the Oregon Railway and Navigation Company train was there to pick up Portland passengers.

"Anyone going on to New Tacoma please do not disembark as we will be leaving as soon as possible to make up time," he said. He looked exhausted.

"I thought we made up all the time we lost," Julianna said. "I was hoping to rinse out some diapers. I'm running low."

"Not quite," Alex said, "we were delayed almost four hours back there." As if an afterthought he continued, "I'll bet by the time they get to New Tacoma they'll be just about on time, though."

"I'll bet you're right," Franz agreed, as they gathered up their belongings and shoved them in their traveling bags.

Julianna and Katherine hurried off the train and into the restroom to wash a few diapers, bath the baby and change her clothes. They took a moment to wash their hands and splash some water on their faces.

Refreshed, soon they were aboard the Oregon Railroad and Navigation Company train bound for Portland.

Chapter 12

April 1884
The Columbia River

Tracy cried and woke Julianna shortly after boarding. After she was fed, the moving train rocked her back to sleep, leaving Julianna to gaze out the window at the arid countryside. How desolate, she thought. It's so rocky and barren, how could anyone farm here.

She dozed off for a few minutes but her aching legs kept her from sound sleep. She was sorry she hadn't insisted on a berth. For three nights they had slept sitting up, and her back felt as if it would never straighten out. She didn't dare move for fear of waking Tracy.

She glanced out the window again and could see the wide Columbia River rushing beside the tracks. The water's energy soothed her and she felt herself relax. She remembered how she loved to sit by the stream at home on warm summer days and listen to its hurried journey.

Before long the conductor walked through the car and announced something she couldn't understand. His voice awakened the rest of the group. This language is so difficult, she thought.

"We're arriving at the Umatilla Landing Station," Alex said to her questioning look. She nodded, and watched as the train came to a stop. She was amazed at the number of people milling around on the platform at such an early hour and wondered where they were all going.

Alex, Julianna, and Tracy disembarked, following the other passengers to a café in the only hotel in town. Julianna shivered in the crisp breeze, snugged her shawl around her shoulders and adjusted Tracy's bonnet. When they stepped into the diner, Franz and Katherine were already seated, and Katherine beckoned to them.

"Isn't the river beautiful?" Katherine pointed toward the Columbia as they sat down. "But look at the desert country it flows through."

"I was thinking the same thing," Julianna agreed. "Do you think the land is even inhabitable?"

"As long as you're farming near the water and the fields aren't hard rock, I guess you could live here," Franz said. "I don't think I want to though," he added.

"Nope, I'm holding out for the mountains. The Cascade Range is between here and Portland. We should see some changes in scenery soon," Alex said. He'd devoured railroad advertisement pamphlets, especially about the country they were about to make their home. He often surprised Julianna with his ability to read English. He'd studied many evenings by the light of the fireplace. One of his prized possessions was a tattered translation book, which he used to struggle over words in the Freeport Bulletin, while ignoring the local German newspaper.

After breakfast they walked along the river's shore, water lapping at their feet. They watched a steamboat, the name *D.S. Baker* painted on its bow, pull away from the dock, its deck full of waving passengers. They'd heard it was bound for the Snake River en route to Lewiston and the nearby gold fields.

The train whistle blew and they scurried to their seats where they watched other people board. The train headed due west, the clack of the wheels lulling the passengers into an early morning nap. Julianna caught a glance of what she thought was a snow-capped peak to the southwest, but she wasn't sure.

It didn't seem like much time passed before the conductor announced that the train would be coming to Tumalow Station at Celilo Falls.

"The village of the Waimpums is located here and is the most important native trading area in the Northwest," he explained, and then quickly moved down the aisle and out the door to the next car.

Alex translated, and they searched for the falls as the train moved in harmonious time with the river. They crossed a high bridge over a broad stream. Someone sitting behind them called it the Deschutes River.

The train rounded a bluff that shot out almost to the water and a large canyon that seemed to stretch forever came into view. Ahead as far as they could see, the basalt floor looked as if a huge hand in some ancient time had poured black syrup into the stream. The sticky liquid ooze had then run down the gorge, searched its way through the rocky maze, and solidified. The water cut deep channels and, as they approached the great falls, mist filled the air over the plunging water, dancing from place to place in some chaotic, ancient ritual marking its own time.

As they neared the falls, they saw not one, but many areas where water poured over the edge of the rocky ledges in a haphazard horseshoe shape. The main river was a high cataract plunging at least forty feet in some places to the surface below, broken into two parts by a giant wall of rock. Farther out a cascade of water raced through smaller falls, and with a burst of a great finale, shot water down a chute with such force that a rainbow of spray reached above the highest edge.

Julianna watched in disbelief as an occasional salmon struggled to jump the lower barriers on its homeward journey. Scaffolding dotted the top of the rocks, with some hanging part way down the walls in an attempt to get closer to the water. The platforms were framed with lumber and held in place with enormous cables. Men with large nets stood on many of them. She wondered how they managed not to slip and fall into the roiling vortex below.

The area between the tracks and the water was filled with people tending to the catch. They worked among the wooden houses and rickety outbuildings worn from years and wind. Fish on drying racks stretched in every direction, some in open sheds and some partially enclosed. Women tended them while children played nearby and many of them stopped to watch the train pass. Julianna waved to them and several waved back.

On the other side of the train, sand dunes whipped into a frenzy in an effort to match the tumbling water, a fine dry dust blowing from them as they slowly move their bulk.

"That sand blows onto the tracks and stops the trains," Alex said, looking at a pamphlet he'd picked up at the last stop. "This paper calls them the walking hills."

The train pulled into Tumalow and when it stopped, the passengers rushed down the steps to see the sight. The roar of the falls greeted them. Julianna had never heard water with a voice like mesmerizing thunder.

A blustering west wind buffeted them. Julianna held tight to Alex's arm, her other hand holding her bonnet. He stood bareheaded, holding Tracy.

"This is *verwunderlich!*" Alex exclaimed his eyes wide with amazement.

The train stayed only long enough to pick up two people and let the Indian families disembark; the people Julianna had seen board at the Umatilla stop. The whistle blew and everyone climbed back on board.

***

As the train traveled west, it followed the lava bed. The passengers watched the river rush through rough basalt barricades, with more Indian fishing villages and platforms suspended off the cliffs dotting the river's edge.

Soon they came to a long narrow place in the river, where it looked like the hot syrup had been sliced with a monstrous knife just as it was hardening. The water was forced to "turn on its side" before it was allowed to run through the restricting gash.

The deep, almost-straight chasm continued for at least three miles, with the water bubbling, elbowing and churning as it battled its way to the end of the sluice. The banks gave testimony to the whirlpools of high water when it rose to peak levels, showing huge circles and swales the rush had carved into the rock over the millennia.

Julianna saw many people living on the banks of this constricted waterway; two large villages on this side and five smaller ones across the river nestled under the high hills that fell onto the black lava rock.

"That channel looks to be only about twenty-five meters wide," Alex said.

"*Yah*, that's a lot of water to be forced into such a small space," Franz agreed. "It must be *sehr tief.*"

"It must be deep," Julianna agreed. She had forgotten about her sore back.

Even Tracy stared out of the window and sometimes pointed to something, jabbering in German.

The train pulled into the bustling town of The Dalles in mid-afternoon. A sternwheeler named *Wild West* was loading at the main river dock, a short distance from the railroad station. In smaller letters it declared itself to be owned by the Oregon Steam Navigation Company.

As usual, crowds gathered, ready to meet arriving passengers. Workers hastened to empty and fill boxcars. The energy of the settlers in these remote villages continued to astonish Julianna. The four of them with Tracy, seized the opportunity to get a bite to eat and take a short walk.

"What do you suppose those broken down *bauen* were used for?" Franz said, while striding down the path in the lead. He was pointing to a clump of dilapidated and partially burned buildings nestled up the hill away from the river.

"I don't know," Alex shook his head. "It doesn't look like they have been used for quite awhile."

"There's an American flag flying over one of them," Julianna said, wondering how anything in this new territory could look so old.

"I'll bet it's the old fort," Alex said. "I read there was one here."

"It looks as though its not been used for a long time," Katherine chimed in as she rushed to catch up to the fast-walking group. "Well, maybe not quite deserted if they're still flying the flag," she added.

They walked along the worn path over the lava rocks to get a closer look, but the train whistle blew, cutting their exploration short. As they hurried back to their seats, they watched the *Wild West* pull out into the rushing water, turn into the river, and let the current speed it downstream.

Soon the train was on its way, headed north a couple of miles, then around Crate's Point, they were once again they traveling west with the afternoon sun in their eyes. Miraculously, the sage covered hills of the steppe began to turn from yellow with splashes of chartreuse where winter springs popped out of the ground, to the darker, richer greens and browns of oak and pine and finally, a few miles downstream, to the conifers of a temperate rain forest.

The bluffs on either side of the river dwarfed the train and the steamboat headed downstream was just a dot in the shimmering water. Across the Columbia, high-water marks left white tell-tale signs of seasonal change on the rocky cliffs.

The train stopped at a stream dumping spring run-off into the Columbia, with a depot sign reading Hood River. Two people boarded, but no freight was picked up or delivered so they were not delayed.

The Columbia widened, but was still a narrow ribbon between the high gorge peaks. On the north side a high, perfectly conical, mountain came into view. Julianna caught her breath at the sight.

"I never expected anything quite this wonderful!" she exclaimed.

"It reminds me of our Rhine River." Franz said and added, "But I think this is more beautiful."

As the tracks wound their way westward, the bluffs on the south side became taller, almost straight up from the tracks. The northern mountains had a more gradual ascent; a few of them appeared to be hacked by a gigantic axe that sliced and split and left a hulking exposed cliff face on the hillsides.

They could see up ahead where the river narrowed again and began to churn. Huge rocks dotted the channel. White water danced around them, sending spray into the air. At the upper end of these rapids, where the water was still, there were boat landings on either side. Moored nearest them, the steamboat *R.R Thompson* appearing fully loaded, bobbed on the quiet pool. Across the river another steamboat was pulling out into the main channel, heading upstream.

They followed the rapids downriver and, much to Julianna's surprise, she saw a small camp with men working on top of the rocky bank.

"I wonder what they are doing out there."

Alex shook his head. "I don't know."

"They're starting to build locks that will by-pass the cascades." A man in front of them, with a German accent, turned to comment. "It's impossible to get steamboats up the rapids, so they have to unload all the passengers and cargo and haul everything on railroad cars to the upper landing."

"A locks?" Julianna asked.

"A canal," Alex explained.

Julianna nodded and watched until the camp was out of sight.

They stopped at the small settlement of Eagle Creek. A sawmill held a prominent place by the tracks with a few homes and other buildings dotting the area. Ahead she could see the train tracks, laid on huge pilings driven into the river bed. The tracks hugged the edge of the river and looked like they might not hold the weight of the engine. She shuddered.

The train waited just long enough to hook a flatcar loaded with lumber onto the line of cars behind them and then they were off again for more spectacular sights. Julianna held her breath, but the train stayed on the tracks and rounded the next bend without mishap.

From then on they began to see magnificent waterfalls. The one that Alex called Multnomah Falls was by far the highest. But no more beautiful than the others, Julianna thought. Unlike her companions, she couldn't pick out a favorite.

The mountains on either side of the river looked like they had been covered with vast timber stands at one time, but now there were places where it had been cut almost to the point of baldness. I wonder where all the lumber went, Julianna thought.

They passed by another waterfall close to the tracks with a small mill next to the creek near the falls. The mill, built on high stilts, was powered by a large waterwheel that turned nimbly by the rushing stream. Two houses were tucked into the hill. A young boy with a fishing pole in his hand and a dog by his side sat on a rock where the mouth emptied into the Columbia. He waved at them; Julianna and Katherine waved back.

Minutes later the train roared by a depot with a sign reading Latourell Falls nailed to its wall. That was one of the few places they didn't stop. She asked Alex about it. He and Franz went to get some air and see if they could get an answer from someone.

"The conductor said the signal wasn't out so we didn't stop," Alex explained when they came back.

"What signal?" Julianna asked.

"There's a manual signal that the station master displays if they want the train to stop and pick up passengers or cargo."

"What if someone wants off?" Katherine was the practical one.

"I guess the conductor knows by the ticket," Alex shrugged his shoulders.

They passed an interesting rock formation on the river side and on the other side of the train was a high bluff with sheer cliffs dropping into a large lake. There were several landings along the way, where a few fishing boats and various other craft were moored.

The train suddenly lurched and braked, and with smoke flying and cars banging, it slid to a stop. A young blond man scampered up the train steps and waited as the conductor made his way to him.

"I'd like to purchase a ticket to Portland," he said, pulling off his cap and handing him a coin.

The conductor said nothing, but gave him a punched ticket and left out the same door that he had entered.

The man sat in the seat across from Alex and introduced himself.

"I'm George Hurlburt. We live about five miles south of here."

Alex reached over and shook his hand. "I'm Alex Lampert and this is my wife, Julianna, and my daughter, Tracy," he said in his best English. "These are our friends, Franz and Katherine Frommelt." After a moment he continued, "Do people often stop the train like this?"

"Oh yes, we do it all the time. It's how I get to work in Portland. I work for my brother, we're surveyors," George answered with a charming smile. Soon they were chatting like old friends.

They passed the last high bluff on the west end of the gorge. Julianna's eyes followed it up to its highest point and saw a bare steep spot near the top. When they crossed the Sandy River, she noticed a magnificent eagle swoop down and carry off a salmon, still squirming in its claws.

"There's an eagle's nest up on top of that hill," George said, pointing toward the top.

Julianna squinted, searching as high as she could, but didn't see anything that looked like a likely spot for a nest, while they crossed a river, that George called the Sandy. This is a lovely place, she thought, even if I can't find an eagle's nest.

The Columbia River, a still wide mirage with hidden currents was now making its way, uninhibited, toward the ocean. The train stopped in Troutdale where a man got off, and then passed a depot at Cleone, the last scheduled stop before the end of the line.

"What time is it?" Julianna asked Alex. Tracy was getting restless.

He pulled out his pocket watch and said, "Its 6:05 and we are due in Albina at 7:00."

Chapter 13

Late April, 1884

At forty-five minutes after six o'clock, four days after leaving St. Paul, the ORNC train pulled into the Portland terminus at Albina depot.

Julianna let out a sigh as exhaustion consumed her. After they bid George good-bye, she saw Franz staring out of the window and wondered if he was searching the crowd in the covered waiting area for a familiar face.

"Do you see Matt?" Julianna asked as she slipped a pink jacket on Tracy.

"Not yet," Katherine said, stooping beside Franz to peer out of the window. "He's here somewhere."

"I'll go look for him," Franz said. "Wait for me here." He climbed off the train and disappeared into the crowd.

"There must be a hundred people out here," Katherine said, folding blankets and tucking them into a small bag. "I guess I shouldn't be surprised. They haven't had train service very long."

A few minutes later, as they stepped off into the crowded throng, Julianna spotted Franz coming toward them accompanied by a tall, sandy haired young man with a friendly grin.

"Alex Lampert, I am glad to make your acquaintance. I'm Matt Foeller," he said giving a hardy handshake. He turned and said, "This must be Julianna and Tracy."

Julianna nodded and smiled at him. Franz and Katherine were right, he does seem like a nice fellow. His easy manner put her mind at ease.

As he turned to Katherine he said, "I'm glad to see you again. You are looking well after your trip."

"Thank you," Katherine replied. Her eyes met Julianna's and betrayed her self-conscious embarrassment. She stood with one arm resting across her belly as if trying to hide her pregnancy.

"Lucky we found each other," he continued, not noticing the women's discomfort. "This place is a madhouse when a train comes in."

After visiting a few more minutes, Matt took charge.

"Katherine, you and Julianna go with Franz to the wagon," he said. He was the youngest of the group, but experience in this bold new city gave his face and manner a maturity beyond his years. "I'll take Alex with me to get your bags."

They slowly made their way to the wagon, excusing themselves as they ducked and pushed through the masses. Franz helped the women on to the wagon seat and handed Tracy to Julianna.

Alex and Matt soon returned with the baggage stacked neatly on a dolly. The men loaded it and scrambled aboard, Franz in front, while Alex sat in the back with his family and Katherine.

"I'm glad that didn't take long," said Matt. He climbed over the wheel of the buggy and grabbed the reins. "We've got to make the Stark Street Ferry by ten o'clock. It's the last run of the day." He slapped the horses and added, "Sophie has rooms waiting for you folks." He laughed. "Sophie is a proper hostess and would be mortified if I didn't deliver you in a timely fashion."

Dusk dropped into darkness as the horses made their way through the muddy streets of Albina, and then over the trail to East Portland, while the young people chatted.

"We're lucky it isn't raining. I was worried, but it quit this morning. I don't know how I would've kept you dry," Matt said, carefully guiding the horse around a broken limb lying across the road. "Though I guess I could've borrowed the neighbor's surrey."

"Does it rain a lot here?" Alex asked.

"*Yah!* It rains a lot in the spring . . . and the fall, but we often have droughts in the summer."

"How are the winters?" Julianna asked shivering as she remembered last year's harsh midwestern snowstorms.

"The winters can get cold and it rains a lot. I guess I should say the winters aren't very nice."

"I've never met a nice one yet!" Alex said with a grin.

"So Matt, what have you heard about the homestead you've staked out for us in Bethany?" Franz asked.

"You better get out there right away. There're rumors that people are stealing land claims in the area. It's prime farmland, some of it doesn't need much clearing, thanks to the Indians who burnt it off to harvest berries." Matt squinted into the darkness; the lantern on the wagon was too dim to light the road.

"We'd better go tomorrow!" Alex said turning to look at Julianna who nodded.

"That's not a bad idea," Matt continued. "Just the other day a man from out that way came into the store and told me that a neighbor of his was murdered in his own barn. His wife and young son found him. People are saying it was claim jumpers."

"My *Gott*!" Julianna grabbed Alex's arm. She remembered the men with the guns on the train. What kind of country is this?

"Sounds like there's no time to waste," Franz said with an edge to his voice.

"What about the women? We don't want them out there until it's safe," Alex questioned.

"Oh don't worry," Matt said. "Sophie says she would like Julianna and Katherine to stay with us as long as need be."

"You men go. Katherine and I'll be fine," Julianna said, pulling Tracy tighter to her breast. She shivered and wondered if it was the chill of the night.

They caught the ferry in East Portland to take them across the Willamette River. Theirs was the last wagon to board and the crew pulled a chain across the back. The flag on the steerage house whipped in the easterly breeze as the flat boat pulled into the darkness.

A short time later, they landed in Portland on Front Street and made their way uptown to the Foellers store on 16th and Johnson Street. They arrived a few minutes before midnight.

Sophie welcomed the weary travelers with warmth, hugs, and the smell of coffee and fresh baked rolls. She was short, shorter even than Katherine, and wore her dark hair pulled back, showing off her fair skin and soft hazel eyes. When she smiled, her whole face lit up, comforting the exhausted group after the grueling trip. Julianna liked her instantly and knew they would be friends.

Sophie showed them their quarters above the stable. The apartment was warm and clean, but small. Curtains partitioned off the two small bedrooms, but it had a large kitchen, with a table and four chairs. A small steam heater hissed from the corner next to the window. She helped Julianna fashion a bed for her sleeping child, out of a large dresser drawer, complete with a goose down pillow.

After the men unloaded the luggage and helped Matt put up the horses, they joined the tired women for the late night snack.

***

The next day the two men left, headed out toward the approximate location of their claims. They walked briskly south on Sixteenth Street admiring a beautiful home and estate on Seventeenth. Sophie had told them it belonged to Richard Knapp who owned an implement company downtown. It took up almost the whole block.

"That guy must have a lot of money," Franz said, straining to see through a fence and across a garden.

"Hey, that'll be us before long." Alex walked with a spring in his step. He knew they would be successful. "We're a couple of talented guys. We'll have houses like that some day."

"I'm sure we could build one that pretty, but I just hope we can find the land to put it on." Franz shrugged his shoulders.

They glanced back, waved to the three faces pressed against the second story window and quickened their pace as they turned west onto Burnside Road.

"The girls will be fine!" Franz said after what seemed like a long silence. "Katherine told me that Sophie plans to take them around town and introduce them to the local folks. Apparently there is a large German community here, complete with a church congregation that speaks our language." He stopped and leaned against a large tree by the side of the road. "You'll never guess the name of the church," he said with a grin.

"Don't tell me it's another St. Joseph's," Alex said, shaking his head.

"*Yah*! Another one!" They laughed. The humor helped Alex feel less apprehensive about leaving them alone.

"The girls will feel right at home," Franz continued. "Katherine isn't due until the first of August, so she'll be fine," Franz spoke with an assurance that bolstered Alex even more.

"Julianna hasn't been left by herself much. I'm glad she and Katherine get along well."

They walked along the muddy cordwood track. Eight foot lengths of peeled logs laid side by side made up Burnside Road.

"I guess they have so much timber here, they use it for everything," Alex said with laugh.

"Matt told me this road's vital for the farmers in the Tualatin Valley, but it was so muddy during the rainy season that the only sensible thing to do was use the timber. The problem with it is that the logs get slick when it rains and horses have been known to slip and break a leg. A fellow can't stand a loss like that," Franz related.

They had walked only a short distance when a freight wagon stopped. The driver leaned down. "Where ya' fellows headed?" he asked, then he spewed a stream of tobacco on the road beside them.

"Over by the Bethany area," Franz answered.

"I'm on my way to Helvetia. I'll go by the road to Bethany, so's I can drop ya' off, if ya'd like."

"That would be friendly of you," Alex answered, trying to speak English without an accent, but not having much luck.

"Patrick's my name. Patrick O'Reilly," he said as they climbed aboard.

"I'm Alex Lampert and my friend here is Franz Frommelt."

"What are you fellows wanting out in Bethany, anyhow?" Patrick asked as he swatted the horses with the reins.

"We have claims staked in the area, near a small creek. We've heard rumors that there's been trouble out that way."

"Be gorie! They have been having a lot of trouble with claim jumpin'," Patrick frowned. "Someone kill't a farmer out there while he was in his barn doin' his chores."

"That's what we heard."

Patrick nodded his head. "I own 20 acres between Helvetia and Bethany. No one has bothered me, but I proved up my claim ten year or so ago. I reckon' it's mine now. Mine and my litt'l wife's. I got this freight job to tide us over during the off season."

"Tell us about the poor widow woman whose husband was murdered," Alex asked. "Is she still on the place?"

"As far as I know, she is. She's got two children. Sons they are, but still young. I hear the three of 'em are gonna try to run the farm by themselves. Their land is right near where you say yours is. You may run into her."

"Seems like she'd be too scared to stay there," Franz interjected.

"Oh no, not her. She's a tough lady. Don't sneak up on her. She owns a shotgun and isn't afraid to use it," he warned.

Shortly after noon, they came to an intersection with a sign that pointed to Bethany. "The store's about a mile down this road. That's all that's there," Patrick said stroking his beard. "You boys planning on staying out here tonight?" He pulled the wagon to a halt and the young men jumped down.

"*Yah!*" Alex said, slipping on his pack board. "We got some provisions and whatever else we'll need we'll get at the store."

"Well, good luck to you fellows. Be careful," the older man cautioned as he bent down to shake their hands.

It didn't take long for them to arrive at the mercantile. It was a large store with a tall false front and a wooden sidewalk. On one side was a stable and a feed store. A large sign on the front window proudly stated it was a U.S. Post Office.

"Howdy! What can I do for you?" A middle-aged man with a handlebar mustache and sideburns greeted the pair. He wore an apron that had not been white for a long time.

"We need provisions and directions."

"I think I can help you. Where you headed?"

"We have claims staked on a small creek about two miles northwest of the store."

The storekeeper's expression changed, "That's a bad area out there. People aren't friendly. There's been a murder and land's been stolen. Are you sure you even have a claim?"

Alex shrugged. "No. We've got to check." A pang of fear nudged his heart, but he tried to appear calm.

"Well, when you go out in that area, be aware. You'll come across the Widow Small's place about a mile from here on the same crick. Her husband got kilt awhile back and she's spooked. She's likely to shoot first and then ask if you're friendly."

The pair nodded, bought some jerky and bread and headed out.

"Franz, I think we need to heed his advice and be careful. I've got an uneasy feeling about this," Alex said as they walked down the steps and onto the wet, worn path.

"*Yah!* Me, too!"

After they had walked a short distance, they came to a stand of willows and birch intersected by a small stream. They left the trail following the water and soon came upon what they thought might be the widow's farm. It was rundown, but livable. Cautious, they stayed on the other side of the creek.

Alex crouched behind the bushes and said, "We don't need to borrow trouble."

Franz nodded, bending low as they moved on.

64

"The man at the store said our claims probably aren't far up this creek. I'll be glad to have land near water," Alex said stepping over a large fallen willow branch.

They walked into a clearing. "The southeast corner marker of our claim should be around somewhere close. Matt said it's a six foot long lead pipe with a white stripe painted on it." It took them awhile to find it and when they did it was by a big leaf maple sapling.

They struck out diagonally across the property, pacing it off step by step. As they crested a small rise, they saw a shack in the distance.

"Hey, that house is on our land!" Franz said, "What the....?"

Alex put his hand on Franz's arm. "Listen, friend, you'd better let me talk. Your temper has landed us in many a problem over the years. Let me find out what's going on."

Franz mumbled, but stayed back saying, "I remember the time you got your nose broke after I picked a fight with the two biggest fellows in school."

Alex nodded, remembering the pain.

As they drew closer, a grizzled, disheveled man appeared out of nowhere. "Who ya' be and whadaya want?" he growled.

"We're Alex Lampert and Franz Frommelt. We've claims here. They're marked on the southeast corner with a piece of lead pipe back there. You've built your cabin on the wrong place."

"You're the ones on the wrong place, young fella, and if ya don't get off my land right now I'm gonna call my son. He's in the house, and he has a rifle."

Franz stepped forward. Alex put his arm out to stop him and asked, "Do you have papers to prove it?"

"I do, but I don't need to prove anything to you."

Alex took a deep breath and pulled from his pocket, the papers Matt had given them. "These papers show this claim in our names, it's on record at Oregon City. Unless your papers are dated before ours, we're going for the sheriff, because you're on our land." Alex could feel anger flush his face. He stood his ground, terrified that maybe there was a man with a gun behind the door of the shack.

He heard Franz move behind him and knew his friend well enough to know that if the man didn't produce papers, he wouldn't be able to stop what could result with someone's blood being shed, most likely theirs. He held his breath and after what seemed like an eternity, the unsavory fellow threw up his hands, turned and walked into the house.

He emerged a moment later, wrinkled papers in hand, with the date April 22, 1882 smudged, but readable.

Alex and Franz looked at each other. Were they forged? It was impossible to tell. Alex had a sinking feeling that they couldn't win this fight. The unkempt fellow had notarized papers in the name of S.J. Nelson.

Dejected, they turned and walked away, with their papers dated June 23, 1883.

The disappointed men traveled in silence and, by the time they reached the store, a soft rain had begun to fall.

"Let's rent a room from the storekeeper. He seems like a nice enough fellow," Franz suggested.

Alex agreed.

***

The next morning Franz proposed they look around. "Maybe there is some land for sale or still left to claim."

"We've got nothing to lose. Might as well," Alex said. It was all he could do not to be angry or disappointed. He'd come all the way from Lichtenstein for this kind of land, and they were a year too late. They decided to take a chance and visit the widow woman, figuring they had escaped being shot at yesterday, so maybe their luck would hold out.

When they arrived at her house, they knocked on the door. When she appeared, she was short and round and had a blond braid wrapped around her head.

"Is this place by any chance, for sale?" Franz asked.

"No, I'm staying. My children want this farm and I'll see that they have it," she insisted. Her pretty face was lined with the kind of strength brought on by anger and despair, and her eyes flashed with determination.

"Aren't you afraid?" Franz asked.

"Of course," she snapped. "But what does that have to do with anything?"

"Do you know of any land around here that might be for sale?" Alex persisted; hoping against hope there might be a farm in this beautiful, apparently fertile area.

She shook her head and closed the door.

"She's a strong woman," Alex said, turning away and heading toward the trail. "I'll bet she makes it."

Franz laughed. "I'm sure of it."

They spent the next couple of days searching, but it became apparent to them that there was no good land left in the area. Most of the marginal land was occupied as well.

"I wonder if old man Nelson really filed on that claim a year ago," Alex said as they sat eating a plate of beans at a small eatery they'd found on the main road.

"I've been wondering that, too." Franz's expression of anger belied his calm demeanor.

"How could Matt have gotten papers if there were already papers filed?"

"Maybe we should go to Oregon City and find out."

"Tomorrow, we'll ask how to get there."

The next morning, loaded with provisions, they started out. It was about a twenty-five mile walk, but they got a couple of rides. It started raining mid-morning. One of the rides was in a covered buggy, which gave them several miles of shelter. Still, by the time they arrived, their clothes were soaked and Alex was never so glad to see civilization.

Oregon City was a good-sized town, with several hotels and eateries. Two grist mills, a paper mill and several sawmills dotted the banks of the Willamette near the falls, which extended across the river in a horseshoe shape, barring any upriver traffic without portage. Near the Oregon City Woolen Mill they noticed a large dilapidated building with many windows and two brick chimneys. A sign over the door read HOTEL, but Alex shook his head when Franz pointed to it.

"I'm cold and tired and hungry, but not bad enough to stay there," he said. "There's got to be better places and we still have a bit of money left."

They found a nicer place to stay at the Cliff House. They paid two-bits for a hot bath, laying their clothes over the steam heater to dry. After getting themselves presentable they went to the hotel and ate their fill before retiring for the night.

"That food was almost as good as Katherine's," Franz said on the way back to their room. "I didn't realize how hungry I was."

"It's the first real meal we've had since breakfast at the Foellers and that was three days ago. No wonder we were hungry."

"Let's get some sleep. We need to be at the courthouse early," Franz said, flopping down on the bed nearest him.

***

In the claims office the following morning, they presented their papers and told the clerk about S.J. Nelson. He searched the file cabinets and then disappeared into the back room. After what seemed like a long time he returned with copies of both sets of papers. Alex's set of papers were dated June 23, 1883. Nelson's were dated first.

"How did this happen?" Alex asked, crestfallen.

"I'm not quite sure," the clerk said shaking his head. "I suspect Nelson's were misfiled." He looked perplexed. "I had a hard time finding them myself. It's too bad, but they are dated prior to your set. This is an unfortunate accident. I am sorry," he replied.

"Is there anything we can do?" Alex asked, stepping in front of Franz, worried that his friend's temper might get the best of him.

"No. If Nelson has a building on the property, and he has made the improvements, the land is in his possession for now."

"Very well, thank you," Alex said and put a warning hand on Franz's arm. "There's nothing we can do. Don't make it worse."

Franz's face was scarlet, but he said nothing.

They caught the ferry across the Willamette to Linn City and spent the last of their money on train fare to Portland.

67

Chapter 14

Early May 1884

The loss of the land stung like a sharp slap. Another season and he was no closer to owning his own farm. Maybe they should've stayed in Illinois. At least he was able to put his hands in the soil there.

And Alex hated telling the women. He knew Julianna would be disappointed and he couldn't bear to make her unhappy. She was already homesick and that broke his heart. He knew she tried not to let him know, but once in a while he caught the sadness in her eyes. Now this!

"We lost our claim," Franz blurted out the minute they walked into the room, before the women had a chance to welcome them.

Alex startled, looked at Julianna, almost afraid to see her face, but much to his surprise he saw a look of relief.

"Some fellow and his son were living on the claim. We went to Oregon City to see how it could be that he owned the land, and they said he did." The words tumbled from Franz before Alex could stop him.

"I had bad feelings about moving out there," Julianna said, shaking her head.

"There'll be other land," Katherine said, nodding to Julianna. "We're just glad you're home and in one piece. Neither of us relaxed the whole three days you men were gone."

"Sophie said we can have the apartment as long as we need it. We can work in town while we look for land." Julianna brushed a lock of hair out of Tracy's eyes. "I can use my mid-wife skills. We met a woman from St. Joseph's who will soon have her baby. Her husband will come and get me when she needs me. There's some work already."

Julianna had a way of bringing him back to reality, but Alex was too upset over the loss to comment. Her hand touched his arm and he covered it with his.

That night Alex tossed and couldn't sleep. Up early, he slipped out into the quiet of the morning, and walked briskly downtown, letting the crisp air invigorate him. The city was stretching and yawning awake. He inhaled deeply and allowed Portland's energy to soak into his soul.

Pulling his collar up, he tucked his hands in his pockets. His fingers curled around his rosary, and before he knew it he was silently in prayer. He heard his mother's voice reminding him, "Son, hard times only mean pray harder."

He passed St. Joseph's church, then many homes and buildings, some under construction. He stood and admired the post office and federal courthouse on Sixth and Morrison and wondered about the master who could create such a magnificent building.

Walking down the next block, he noticed a small, partially completed building. A man came out of the main door and nodded to Alex as he approached.

"*Guten Tag*," Alex said tipping his cap. "Is this your place?"

"Yes it is."

"When does your crew start work?" Alex thought it strange that no one was on the job site.

"I expected two men here twenty-minutes ago."

"I'm a carpenter and I'm here," Alex said, suddenly coming alive.

"Are you a good one?"

"Yes, I am. I worked my way over to America as a joiner on the ship," he said, straightening his shoulders with pride.

"Well then, I'd say you have experience." The man paused and looked at the front of the structure. He took off his cap and rubbed his forehead. After a moment he continued, "I'll take a chance and hire you at a dollar and two bits a day."

Alex shook his hand. "You don't by chance have any work for my friend? He's a brick mason."

"I'll put him to work helping you until I get supplies for him." The man looked pleased.

"I'll be right back," Alex said. He turned and sprinted back to the apartment shook Franz awake and together they hurried back to the site.

"Well, they said Portland was a bustling place," Franz said.

"Matt did say that the banks are lending money for new businesses," Alex said, surveying a partition that needed finishing touches. "He told me there's a lot of jockeying for number one position, with Vancouver, East Portland and some of the other outlying neighborhoods all fighting to be the largest city." At least there were jobs in town, even if they didn't have a homestead.

***

Hopes revived, the two young families settled into the cozy flat. They paid the Foellers $10.00 a month rent and the men did minor repairs in the store and carriage house. Time passed, and the money jars filled quickly. Alex wanted to open a bank account, but Julianna thought better of it.

"You know what happened to Papa's friends when they put their money in banks in Baden," she warned. "You just go down and have them put the smaller bills into larger ones that are easier to store."

Alex shook his head, but followed her request. It was true; people had lost a lot of money when a bank in Baden was forced to close its doors.

Katherine grew larger with her baby as time passed. Alex could see that taking care of Tracy when Julianna was out on a birthing call was becoming more difficult for her. He admired the fact that she never complained and marveled at the strength of the women in his life. He'd known Katherine since she was a spindly little girl in school and he remembered what a crush Franz had on her even then.

***

One day in early August, as they came home from work, they were greeted at the door by Julianna.

"Here, take Tracy and go fetch Sophie!" She pushed the child into Alex's arms. " Hurry, Katherine is having her baby. *Eile! Eile!*"

"What can I do?" Franz asked, his face taut with fright.

"Not much," Alex said, holding the squirming Tracy with one arm. "C'mon let's go!"

"But I...I..." Franz stammered.

"Friend, *kommen sie jetzt!* Julianna has the situation under control." Alex put his hand on Franz's arm to guide him down the stairs, afraid he would stumble. "There's nothing we can do here," he said. He'd never seen Franz like this, muttering and frightened; this tall man, with the big hands and the confident gaze reduced to trembling. God, I hope I didn't act like this when Tracy was born.

"Katherine will be fine. You know how skilled Julianna is," Alex said as they hurried on to the sidewalk.

"I...I...I don't know. I should do something."

"What do you want to do?" Alex asked, turning to look at his quivering friend.

"I don't know. What do men do when this happens?"

Franz hands shook so badly that Alex had to reach around him to knock on the door when they arrived at Sophie's.

"I prayed a lot," Alex said.

"What if I lose her?"

"You're not going to lose her."

"Are you sure? What makes you so sure?"

"Listen, Franz, Katherine is a strong, young woman." Alex was beginning to get concerned and somewhat annoyed.

Sophie answered the door and Franz practically leaped at her. "You've got to go now, Katherine needs you. Julianna wants you to help her." His words flung out, stumbling over each other like dry leaves in the fall winds.

"Now, now Franz," Sophie soothed. "You boys come on into the house. There's bread and cheese on the table. Help yourselves. Matt will be closing the store soon. He'll come and join you."

After Sophie left, Franz paced. "I don't feel hungry."

"Franz, you worked all day. C'mon, ya' gotta eat something," Alex said a little impatiently. "You don't want to insult them," he added.

"I doubt that would happen."

"Well by golly, I'm gonna eat," Alex said, heading for the kitchen.

"*Yah! Yah!* I'm coming." Franz followed him.

70

Franz picked at his food. The quiet, it seemed to Alex was unnerving. Franz got up, paced the floor, went out onto the sidewalk, came in and repeated the process again.

Alex gave Tracy a cup of milk out of the icebox. She didn't like it cold and fussed, but ate the cheese. He held her and watched Franz. Tracy fell asleep on his shoulder so he put her on the couch and surrounded her with pillows. Rubbing his arm where she'd rested, he wondered what time it was.

Matt came up the stairs, passed Franz, and burst in the door. "He's not doing very well, is he?" he asked, thumbing back toward the frazzled young man on the porch.

Alex shook his head. "I hope Katherine has this baby soon. He may not survive."

Matt laughed as they headed out the door and sat on the porch, where they could keep an eye on Franz and hear Tracy if she woke up.

Darkness came and the hours dragged on. A quiet westerly breeze cooled the air. No sounds came from next door. Matt lit a cigar and offered them one, but they refused. Franz got up and paced the sidewalk once again.

"How about a glass of wine?" Matt asked. "It might help your nerves."

They nodded. Matt went into the house, came out with a bottle and three glasses. He poured each a glass of the hearty Italian red wine that they had come to enjoy, thanks to the Italian neighbors down the street. Time seemed to stand still, and Alex wondered if the baby would ever arrive. He pulled out his watch and saw it was 10:30. Is that all? It seems like midnight.

Shortly after 1:00 AM, Mary Katherine joined her family. Franz raced to his wife's side as soon as Sophie came home and announced it. He couldn't be coaxed away for the rest of the day.

When eleven month old Tracy was presented with the newborn, she immediately took possession of her and became her most ardent advocate.

"Baby!" she exclaimed. "Baby eat?" "Play!" Toddling around the tiny apartment, Tracy was never far from the infant's side. She shared her toys and blankets with the newcomer. One day she tried to feed Mary some potatoes from breakfast, but Katherine swooped in to rescue the infant.

***

Franz made the acquaintance of Harvey Schwartz at Sunday Mass. He was a brick layer, too, and when Franz's job ran out, Harvey got him a job building piers for the new Morrison Street bridge project.

When Alex's job finished a couple of weeks later, Benjamin Stark was beginning construction of a three story building on Front Street, so Alex, along with five other carpenters, hired on.

"But Alex, three stories up is too high. What if you lose your footing?" Julianna protested when he told her about his new job. "Please don't fall."

Alex shook his head. "I'm not going to fall. Remember, I had to climb high up on that ship when we were coming over here," he said. Seeing her fear he added, "I'll be careful, I promise."

Overwhelmed with activity, Portland seemed to keep everyone busy. It was hard for Alex and Franz to get Sundays off to go to Mass. The docks always had ships loading and unloading, and everywhere it seemed there were mercantile stores, hotels, and offices under construction.

***

The women got along well, even in the cramped quarters of the tiny flat. On the days that Julianna wasn't delivering babies, they sewed, mended, and knitted at Sophie's. Their supply of clothes began to build. They hadn't acquired many new things in the last year, so there was much work to be done.

As Julianna grew to know Sophie, she became fonder of her practicality and inner strength. She liked the way Sophie interacted with her tiny son, Victor, and decided to handle her children the same way; with a gentle but firm hand.

"I'm sewing you a new shirt," Julianna whispered to Alex one night while they were lying in bed. "It's a blue work shirt."

Alex rolled over and put his arm around her.

"Thank you. I sure need a couple more."

"I know, and the three of us are having such fun sewing together. We get along well. I'm going to hate to leave here."

They lay quietly, enjoying the silence that came with the darkness.

"How much money do we have in the savings jar now?" Alex asked after a few moments.

"I don't know. I haven't had a chance to count it lately," She held him close and suddenly money was the last thing on her mind.

***

"I met a man today. His name is Eldon Taylor," Franz announced one evening as he walked in the door from work. "He lives about twenty-two miles out east in the Gorge. We passed his place on the train; it's called Taylor's Landing. He's got 360 acres out there, some of it up some steep bluffs. He needs a skilled mason to build culverts. He offered me forty dollars a month and a free place to live." His face flushed with excitement.

"That's wonderful news," Julianna responded, joining his enthusiasm.

"A free place to live," Katherine said with astonishment.

"Yes, dear, you and me. He has a cabin up the hill a ways from the train stop. We can live in it rent free as long as I work for him."

"When does he want you to start?" Katherine asked.

"As soon as we can get there, but that's not even the best news." Franz put his arms around his wife. "There's prime land close to his property and it's available for homesteading."

"Oh! I can't wait till Alex gets home!" Julianna couldn't believe her ears.

After supper in the quiet of the evening, the four of them sat at the table and planned the next few months.

"I'll go tomorrow and check out the situation," Franz said holding Katherine's hand. "If it looks as good as it sounds, I'll be back on the weekend and Katherine and I can pack up." He smiled at his wife who held their sleeping child cradled in her other arm.

It hit Julianna: Katherine would be leaving. She would miss her terribly. Who would watch Tracy when she was called to work? With great effort, she shook off her adverse thoughts. This is wonderful news and a great opportunity, she reassured herself.

"How did this fellow find you?" she heard Alex ask Franz.

"I was working down on the East Portland waterfront and he just walked up and started to talk to me. Said he'd been watching me work and liked my craftsmanship." Franz spoke with an air of confidence, bordering on conceit.

Julianna smiled at his lack of humility. So like Franz, she thought, but he is a fine man and wonderful friend.

The discussion lasted far into the evening and they decided that if Katherine and Franz liked living out in the Gorge country, Alex would go out in late fall to look over the available land. If there were creeks or springs nearby and it had good soil, the couples would file papers right away. Alex and Julianna could move out there next spring.

Chapter 15

July, 1884

Immediately after Franz and Katherine left amid hugs and good-byes, Julianna missed them. Tracy fussed and asked to play with Mary. When Alex went to work, Julianna was alone with her thoughts and, try as she might, she couldn't shake her forlorn mood.

She kept herself busy, and often visited Sophie whom she had grown to love, but the loneliness was unrelenting. Her family was never far from her mind. I do miss Mutter, she thought. I haven't heard from her for such a long time.

"Come Tracy; let's go to the post office. Maybe there's a letter waiting for us."

"Letter…letter," Tracy mimicked.

"Yes, *Grossmutter* might have sent us some mail," Julianna said as she patted Tracy's hair and slid on her sunbonnet. The thought brightened her day.

It was a short pleasant walk, with the sun playing in and out of the clouds and the promise of a hot afternoon. Tracy toddled happily along.

Julianna welcomed the short letter from Baden waiting for her. Mama just isn't much of a writer, she thought, but I'm happy for any bit of news. She found a bench outside in the shade and sat down, eager to hear the news from her family.

June 30, 1884

> *My dearest daughter,*
> *I pray this letter finds you well and happy. My thoughts are always with you, but today especially as it is my darling granddaughter Theresa's first birthday. I close my eyes, yet I cannot picture her. From your description, she must be a beautiful child. I pray that I get to meet her one day.*
> *I hope you are safely on your land and have a good crop in. We are all well here. Your Papa is working too hard, but that is his life and I would not take it away from him.*
> *Johann wants to go to Hamburg and join the Merchant Marines. Of course we do not want him to go, but it is his choice. He is almost 17, so he is a man. Papa is broken hearted as he wants Johann to join him in his business.*
> *The girls are well. Greta is enjoying her music studies. She would like to attend the music conservatory. I doubt that Papa will let her. Josie is doing well with her studies, but she isn't a student*

and does not like school. I think she will marry young. They miss you and speak of you often.

Hans married Josephine in May. They seem happy.

We are looking forward to a prosperous summer. The city fathers are predicting that many people will come to the resort for a holiday. That makes your Papa happy.

We miss you and hope that you can come for a visit someday. I close this letter with love and prayers.

Mama

A tear slid down Julianna's cheek before she could stop it. A tiny hand reached up and caught it. "Mama, Mama!" Tracy cried.

"It's alright, dear one. Mama is fine, just a little sad today."

"Sad?"

"Yes, *liebe*! Mama misses *Grossmutter*."

Tracy put her arms around her mother's neck and buried her head on her shoulder. They sat there for a long time, Julianna's mind sliding back to Tracy's birthday. It had been a Sunday morning and Alex went to get the baby out of her bed.

Julianna had watched Tracy smile at him, arms outstretched. "Papa! Up Papa!"

"Today you are one year old," he said as he picked her up and held her close. "Just look at our beautiful little girl," he said bringing her back into their bed. "She smiles all the time. How can we be so lucky? That Schwartz child is the fussiest baby in church. We rarely get a peep out of Tracy."

"You're so funny, Alex. You forget the times she cries." Julianna had laughed and kissed her husband's cheek as he crawled in beside her.

The blast of the noon whistle startled Julianna and brought her back to the present. "Come dear, let's go home and write a letter," she said rising from the bench and taking Tracy's hand.

She spent the day blinking back the tears that bubbled close to the surface. I thought I was over being homesick. I guess the best that can happen is that I learn to live with it and take comfort in the memories. Sighing, she finished the letter to her mother.

"It sure seems quiet around here, doesn't it?" Alex said, later that evening. He understood her moods and seemed to sense her loneliness, and she loved him for it.

Julianna nodded and bravely attempted a smile.

***

Over the next few weeks, Alex and Julianna spent time getting to know one another again. It had been months since they had moments to themselves, and Julianna cherished them. These times brought her light and life, and her melancholy lessened.

Sunday mornings found them at early Mass, followed by dinner, then afternoons with the Foellers, the Boecks, or some other parish family. The German community helped and comforted each other, so far from home, and soon they felt they were part of an extended family.

July turned to August, and the days weren't quite so warm. In the evenings, when Alex wasn't too tired, they took Tracy for strolls around town and down by the waterfront where steamboats and ocean going vessels moored.

"Look at all those sacks," Julianna exclaimed one evening as they watched a particularity large vessel unload. "What is that stamped on them?"

"It's wheat," Alex said. "I guess part of that sagebrush country our train traveled through is trying to raise grains now. I heard just the other day that they were perfecting a method of dry land farming up there." Alex had a far-away look in his eye.

Just for a second, Julianna thought she saw a hint of an idea that maybe he wanted to go back up to The Dalles and live. She was about to protest, when he shook his head and the mountain man in him said, "A fellow would have to be plain crazy to want to live in that godforsaken place."

The flurry of activity that most interested Alex and Julianna, and as the rest of the Portland population, was the continued work on the Morrison Street Bridge. There had been a lot of politics around building a span across the Willamette for fear of navigational obstruction, so work had shut down several times. The project had finally resumed earlier in the year and now the crew worked until dark every night to meet the scheduled opening in '87. The bridge builders long work days suited the Portlanders just fine, giving them many hours of free evening entertainment.

"Look how far they've gotten!" Julianna exclaimed one evening. They were standing at their favorite viewing spot, slightly up the hill from the waterfront.

"They are moving right along, aren't they," Alex agreed.

"I heard this morning that the Pacific Bridge Company put out a call for more workers a few days ago," the tall German gentleman standing next to Alex said overhearing their conversation.

"Is that right?" Alex said.

"They brought in two extra crews, one from Oregon City and one from Vancouver. I guess they're still hiring."

"Do they need carpenters?"

"Yes, and they pay pretty well," the man nodded and moved up for a closer view.

"I don't want you to work on that thing," Julianna said taking his arm. "I don't care if you would make more money." She paused and put her hand in his, "Look at how they climb around up there."

"Honey, I have all the work I need with Mr. Stark, and he pays me well. I'm a happy man." Alex laughed and put his arm around her.

One evening, Alex came home excited. "Let's hurry and eat!" he exclaimed. "They tell me there is a Chinese ship down at the end of Oak Street. Let's go see it!"

They gobbled their supper, left the dishes on the table, and headed toward the waterfront. On the way, they passed the edge of Chinatown on Second Street. Two elderly Chinese gentlemen, sitting on a bench visiting quietly in the shade, eyed the trio as they passed. Alex hailed them and smiled. They smiled back, looking somewhat surprised.

"Many local people view the Chinese as outsiders and don't like them," Alex said, in a quiet, thoughtful tone.

"But why?" Julianna asked, puzzled. "They look quite pleasant."

"I have found them to be on the few occasions I've had dealings with them. We do have a hard time talking to each other though. My English isn't that good yet and neither is theirs," Alex smiled as he spoke.

"Look! There's the ship!" Julianna pointed at the small brig in front of them, bobbing at its tethers. "There are people disembarking!"

Fascinated, they watched as stragglers in twos and threes disembarked, chattering in their strange language. They wore dark-colored, loose flowing pants with lighter colored cotton blouses and sandals. Many wore broad-brimmed hats, and all of them had long braids down their backs.

"I wonder if they are as frightened as we were when we left the ship in New York," Julianna said softly. "They're new in a foreign land, too."

"I wonder where they will end up," Alex said, echoing his wife's thoughts.

Julianna nodded thinking, for that matter, I wonder where we'll end up.

***

In late September, Alex came home with a letter from Katherine.

Come any time, the sooner the better, she wrote. *There are at least 250 acres available up on top of the mountain between Taylor's place and the Sandy River. Franz has been up there exploring and he is sure this is what we want. Some of it has burned recently which will help with clearing. The soil appears fertile and Franz has found two good-sized springs.*

"You must go soon." Julianna's eyes flashed with excitement.

"I'll make arrangements with Mr. Stark and leave the end of the week." He paused. "It does sound promising, doesn't it?"

Friday morning found Alex on the eastbound train wearing his clean work pants and a blue cotton shirt. "It's fine to wear my work clothes," he'd told Julianna earlier. "They're clean and mended. Once I get there, I'm going to be hiking around in the forest. Besides my new boots make me look like a wealthy man."

After purchasing his 25 cent ticket, he bought a local newspaper printed in German, with articles of interest to the local German community. It had been a long time since he'd had the luxury of sitting and reading, especially a paper in his native tongue. He spent the whole trip absorbing the news from front to back. He still struggled with the English papers, so this was a treat. *Franz and Katherine will enjoy this, too. It'll make a nice little gift for them.*

When the train pulled into Taylor's Landing, Alex stepped off and stood admiring the broad, flowing expanse of the Columbia River. He'd heard it was almost a mile wide here, unlike the wild, narrow savageness of this same river between Celilo and The Dalles. He shaded his eyes and gazed across its girth. Looking upstream, eastward where a large rock stood guardian, he caught his breath. *It does remind me of the Rhine.*

"What can I do for you, stranger?"

Startled, he turned to put a face to the voice. He saw a tanned, gray-haired, grizzled man a little taller than himself.

Sticking out his hand, he introduced himself in his best English, adding, "I'm looking for Franz and Katherine Frommelt."

"Yes, they're expecting you. I'm Eldon Taylor." His friendly manner put Alex at ease. "Franz is building a rock conduit on the road near the south end of my place. A winter spring washed it out last season. The school up there is nearly finished and we have to get the road open." He spoke with the earnestness of a man who'd endured hardships, but had not let them steal his dreams. "That Franz is a fine mason, one of the best I've seen."

"That he is," Alex agreed, happy that his friend's talents were appreciated. "That he is."

"His missus is home, up the trail in a little cabin," Taylor said pointing to a path meandering westward up the wooded hill, beneath a treeless bluff. "It's only a quarter of a mile or so. In the winter when the leaves are gone ya' can see it from here."

"*Danke,* sir!" Alex waved as he headed up the trail. Thick foliage, ferns, and underbrush lined the path through some of the biggest trees he had seen for a long time. The sweet smell of the lush woods reminded him of the forests of his youth. *I'll bet its ten degrees cooler in here when the weather's hot.*

"Hello, hello, Katherine!" he called as he got closer.

"Alex! Oh Alex, it's so good to see you." Katherine ran down the trail, catching his hands in hers. "Here, let me look at you. I've missed you and Julianna."

"All my girls talk about is seeing you again," Alex said. "You are looking well. How is the little tot doing?"

"She's sleeping now. She's such a sweet darling."

"So Franz has done some exploring?" They chatted on the way to the cabin, and sat on the steps within earshot of the baby.

"Yes, he has. I can't wait for him to come home and tell you of the places he's found." She pointed to the top of a steep bluff as she spoke.

Franz found them, still on the steps, as he walked up the path for supper; the two school mates engrossed in conversation about land, building homes, and farming.

Chapter 16

September 1884

Alex wasn't sure when he realized that the search for a farm might be ending. The perception began to fill the void left by the lost claim in Bethany. He'd felt it when he stepped off the train yesterday, but thinking back, it might have been even earlier. Perhaps the day the train stopped at Taylor's Landing to take on Portland-bound passengers last spring. That was when he first caught sight of the tall, heavily timbered bluff.

Franz's voice startled him back to the present. "We'll follow this blaze, for about a mile. Then it butts into the Wire Trail." He pointed to a shallow cut just above eye level on a tall Douglas fir. The two men were hiking up the bluff, which was a steep brutal climb, with switchbacks that were not cleared in places.

"Wire Trail?"

"*Yah*! It's where they strung the telegraph wire from The Dalles to Portland about fifteen years ago. Taylor says the Indians used the trail when they traveled from the fishing grounds at Celilo to their gathering place near the falls on the Willamette at Oregon City. He says the low lands down on the Sandy River delta are too marshy much of the year to travel so they had to come up over this hill."

When they reached the top, the two friends picked up their pace, slowing only for fallen logs and places where buck brush, sword fern and lush growths of salal blocked their progress.

"If we come this way often, we'll have to clear out a better path," Alex said, fighting his way through a patch of prickly Oregon Grape.

Franz nodded. "As long as we stay at Taylor's cabin, I think this is our best route." He stopped to scan the area and continued, "If we homestead up here, I think we can find a shorter way to the train."

The early morning dew covered the low vegetation and drenched the men's pant legs. They welcomed an open area, where the sun shone with the promise of a warm clear day where they stopped to rest and admire the beauty surrounding them. A wide patch of underbrush and alder trees ran up the hill to a second bench almost due west of them. Burned remnants of huge stumps, much larger at the base then he and Franz together could reach around, stood here and there. What few trees remained standing reminded Alex of flags, the way their limbs were all pointing west.

"Taylor said there was a bad fire here three years ago in October. The east winds blew it clear to the point overlooking the Sandy River," Franz said. "Blew it fast, too! He said no one could've outrun that blaze, even on horseback."

Alex rubbed his chin thoughtfully as he remembered a fire he'd witnessed back in Illinois last year. It had started over a millinery shop in downtown Freeport. Everyone available rushed to help the firemen, but it burned three buildings before they had it contained.

Taking to the trail again, they arrived at the fork of the Wire Trail, their pants legs mostly dry. This path was well worn and wide enough for a team and wagon, making the walk easier and they made better time. Along the right side, a wire high above their heads, strung on large blue insulators was nailed on trees. Here and there the trail intersected the fire's path, showing wide open areas where dark red fireweed bloomed profusely. Stands of wild huckleberry bushes were beginning to grow; some even had ripe magenta berries. The men jammed handfuls of the sweet fruit in their mouths, their chins staining red with the juice, and laughed at each other.

After another three quarters of a mile, Franz said, "My stake is right up this way. See, I made a blaze so we could find it again."

Sure enough, a mile north of the Wire Trail, they came upon a large wooden stake, pounded in the ground, with the initial 'F' scratched on it. "I paced off 40 acres here and staked it at each corner." Franz pointed and added, "I suggest we share the eastern boundary. There's about 160 acres that stretches lengthwise around the upper edge of the bluff and an old falling down cabin in the woods, so there was a claim here once. Taylor says the place has been deserted for years." Looking off in distance he said, "If you want it, we'll be neighbors."

"Want it, *mein Gott,* Franz just look at this beautiful soil!" Alex stooped and ran the soft, rich dirt through his fingers. Breathing in the musty fertile smell of virgin loam, he put his head back and looked up. He saw a stand of tall green firs that climbed almost forever into the blue cloudless sky. A hint of a breeze fluttered across his cheek and he laughed as he hadn't laughed for years. "A hundred and sixty acres of this! We are lucky lads, my friend." he shouted!

"Come; let's pace out your acreage. I have extra stakes over here in a cache." Franz walked over to a rock pile and pulled out an armful. "Hey, first let me show you the home site I've chosen," he said, leaving the small pointed poles in a pile.

They walked down to a large flat area nestled between two rises. Although it was heavily wooded, Alex saw that it would be a perfect home site. Plenty of room for a barn and outbuildings too.

As they explored, Franz pointed to a low area and said, "Over there's a spring. It's the driest part of the season right now and it's still marshy so I think I can get enough water out of it. If not, I'll build a cistern. God knows it rains enough in this country."

Alex chuckled.

They walked back, grabbed a handful of stakes and headed east over a small hill to explore what Alex had already decided would be his and Julianna's farm. Less then a half a mile away, just over the property line, through some dense forest, they came upon another level spot, tucked under a tall rise to the east.

"This looks like an ideal place to build a home," Alex said. "I'll bet there's water not far from here."

They spent time looking over the area and eventually found a nice spring coming out of the hill just north of the building site.

"Look, you can see the Columbia through the trees," Alex said. "This is perfect! I can't wait for Julianna to see it! This is where we'll build, Franz. Right here!" Alex began to pace off the outline of the house, first around a moss covered log, then over a fallen large alder branch. "There's so much more underbrush here than at home," he added, stomping down a tall sword fern.

They wandered around the perimeter, discussing plans. They decided which trees needed to come down, and even where the barn should be built. Franz, never far from his appetite, suggested they sit on the fallen log and eat the sandwiches Katherine had made for them.

"Look at the tiny fir trees growing out of this rotten wood. At home, Papa called these mother logs," Alex said as he sat down.

Franz nodded, too busy eating to reply. Alex followed suit. He couldn't remember when bread and cheese had tasted this good. By now the noon sun was hot and he welcomed a drink of cool refreshing water from his canteen.

"We've got a lot to see yet. We'd better get going," Alex said, eager to explore his land.

Franz groaned.

"*Yah! Yah!* We'll go, Alex We'll go," Franz said with a laugh. He reached over and patted his friend's shoulder. "We'll go up to the top, the peak of this mountain," he said pointing to a heavily forested hill to the southwest.

With no more blazes to follow, Alex pulled out his compass and took a reading. "It's hard to get lost as long as we know the river is north, but the timber looks thick up there and neither of us wants to be late for supper," he said shading his eyes.

Slinging their knapsacks over their shoulders they climbed up through the timber until they came to a clearing made earlier by the fire. The higher they climbed the easier it was to see the beautiful forested mountains across the Columbia River.

Further up the hill they came upon an immense pile of rocks, huge boulders strewn over several hundred yards. As they scurried over the obstacle they discovered a large hole in the middle of the debris.

"What do ya' make of this?" Franz asked.

"I don't know." Alex took off his cap, stuffed it in his pocket, and thoughtfully rubbed his forehead. "Most of these mountains around here are volcanoes. I wonder if it's a crater." He pondered, "I guess that's a question to ask at the Land office."

Looking around they realized they had reached the summit. Alex picked up a heavy rock and with slow deliberate strokes drove in the southern boundary stake of his claim in the dirt beside the pile of boulders.

"Looks like we could just reach down and get a cup of water," Alex said as he stood up and admired the river below them. They were high enough to look east and see the river come out of the narrow gorge and flatten like a blue-green ribbon that sparkled and danced its way to the Pacific. The southern edge of this vast and powerful river, seemed to pass just below their feet, instead of the hundreds of yards below the bluff where they stood.

Alex couldn't believe the splendor. It was more, much more then he'd ever hoped for; truly a sight to delight his poet's heart. Maybe this is where we should build our house. The thought drifted through his mind. No, I'll bet the wind is brutal up here, he cautioned himself, noticing a slight wind blowing through the flag trees so prevalent at the top of this hill.

Thirsty, he raised his canteen to his lips, threw his head back, and looked toward the southeast. It was then he saw the beautiful snowcapped peak brighter and bigger then he'd ever seen it. Mt. Hood, the sentinel, stood watch over the entire domain. He'd seen the mountain from Portland and gotten a glimpse of it from the train, but never had he seen anything like the way it looked from the top of his hill. Not even his beloved mountains of Liechtenstein were this beautiful. The breeze stirred his hair as he stood transfixed. I'm home, he thought, I'm truly home.

Chapter 17

October 1884

"Let's pack," Alex said as he walked in the door. In a swoop, he picked Julianna up and swung her around.

"Are we moving now?" Julianna asked, wide-eyed and startled.

"Not now, next spring, but I want you to see the land now and taste the red huckleberries, if there are any left, and smell the soil." His face glowed. "This is just what we wanted, better even then Bethany."

Tracy tugged on her father's pant leg, "Go, go!"

"Yes, dear, we're going to see Mary." Alex picked up Tracy, swung her around and they laughed together.

Later Alex and Julianna sat on the bed, holding hands, and watched Tracy at play. He told Julianna all the things he and Franz had found and seen. He told her how Franz liked his job with Mr. Taylor, and that Katherine missed her and Tracy.

"We'll go tomorrow and walk the place. Katherine said to bring an extra blanket and she'll make us a bed on the floor," he said and smiled at her. "Then we'll take the train to Oregon City and file papers."

The rest of the evening they prepared for the journey until finally exhausted, they crawled into bed.

"I have something to tell you, dear," Julianna said as she snuggled up beside him.

"What's that?" Alex asked, thinking how nice it was to be in bed with his wife.

"I am quite sure we'll be having a baby in the spring, possibly May."

Alex turned and held her tight. "I'm glad we've found a place to raise our children. It looks like we may have a few."

***

Julianna and Katherine talked and laughed and enjoyed visiting as if they hadn't seen each other for years. "Thank goodness we'll be together so I can help you," Katherine happily exclaimed when Julianna told her of the pending new arrival.

Katherine cared for the children, letting Julianna and the men explore the top of the hill and the home sites. They found three apple trees and a pear tree, evidently planted by the earlier homesteaders. They ate their fill of the juicy fruit and gathered as much as they could carry to take to Katherine.

On top of the hill, Julianna caught her breath at the view; the river appeared close to her feet with the pristine snowcapped mountain behind her just as Alex had described. A bit desolate perhaps, she thought, but I'm sure it will be fine. Better than fine really, it will be our little piece of heaven. Oh, how I wish Mama and Papa could see it! They would be so happy.

"Look Alex, there's a mountain beside Mt. Hood. See there, with all those trees and that funny knob on its top."

"Taylor says that's called Larch Mountain. He says there's gold in the timber up there, but no one knows how to log in rugged terrain," Franz replied squinting in the sun.

"I'll bet it won't take long for someone to figure it out," Alex said ruefully.

Back at the cabin that evening, Julianna was stiff and sore, but elated that their friends were going to be close. Very few settlers lived in the area, and she was sure wild animals roamed the woods, but having Franz and Katherine nearby cheered her.

And oh my, the soil is so fine and rich. Even as a city girl, she could appreciate the men's exuberance when they had showed her the loamy loose mixture sliding out of their hands and back onto the forest floor. She loved its pungent earthy smell.

The following morning Alex and Julianna left Taylor's Landing. When they reached Portland, they had to wait for the next train to Oregon City. Tracy, although sometimes a bit restless, felt at home on the train and fell asleep shortly after boarding.

Oregon City, a bustling, busy town was not unlike the familiar towns in the midwest. The dynamic energy surprised Julianna. She noted the contrast to the relatively uninhabited, wild area where they planned to homestead.

"It's too late to go to the courthouse today," Alex said as they stepped off the train. "We'll check in at the place where Franz and I stayed."

The next morning they filed the papers on their land and were back on the train before noon.

***

Franz and Katherine arrived back in Portland the second week in November. "It's so nasty and rainy out there we aren't able to get any work done and besides, Katherine couldn't stand that musty old cabin any longer," Franz announced as they walked into the apartment.

Julianna didn't think she'd ever been as glad to see anyone as she was to see the Frommelts. She had wondered if Katherine would have to stay the winter in those crude surroundings. The two women got right to work making baby clothes for the new arrival, while the two little girls played with their dollies.

Franz joined Alex in helping Mr. Stark with a new project. Although it rained, it was not cold by midwest standards so they worked every day. The weather continued mild into December, but the city had an air of anxiety, like a coming unknown change.

"I don't understand. It's too nice outside for December," Josie Boeck said one Sunday morning as she and Julianna were walking together after Mass. Talk at St. Joseph's inevitably turned to weather this time of year.

"I know. Matt remarked the other day about how much colder it was last year at this time," Julianna said, as she straightened Tracy's bonnet and pulled it down over her ears.

"I don't trust it at all," responded old man Ruehr, another parishioner walking beside them. "I've been here more than ten years now, and I've seen it turn on you overnight. Portland weather can be vicious."

His words were prophetic. The following Saturday afternoon, December thirteenth, the temperature fell rapidly and two inches of snow blanketed the city, turning the sidewalks into icy playgrounds for children. By eight o'clock Monday evening, the east wind blew in the strongest, most memorable windstorm on Portland record. The city had twelve inches of snowfall and a record number of broken water pumps and frozen troughs. Everyone but the livery stables and the saloon keepers were paralyzed. There was so much ice on the Willamette River that the ferries quit operating after dark for fear of damaging their hulls.

Although the storm kept Alex from working, Julianna was secretly grateful that it forced Alex to take some days off. She worried that he wasn't getting enough rest.

He and Franz went out on Wednesday for supplies for themselves and Foellers. When they returned Alex shook the snow from his coat and said, "You should see the walkways out there."

"*Yah*! They're piled high in most places. We had to walk on the street. They're jammed with snow," Franz said. He stomped his boots on the porch and hurried through the door.

"*Kommen Sie!   Eile*! You two look frozen," Julianna said, relief softening her face, as she took the bags from Franz. "We've hot coffee ready for you."

"We ran into Mac McCoy. He's been working for a livery, helping chip ice out of troughs. He said there's plenty of work. We can meet him tomorrow morning. He'll help us get a job," Franz' enthusiasm didn't seem dampened by the freezing temperatures.

Katherine seemed fine with the idea, but Julianna wasn't excited about it. Alex looked pale of late and some of his exuberant energy seemed lacking. She shook off her anxiety.

"On one condition," she cautioned him. "You promise to dress warmly and rest often."

Except for an occasional Sunday, those first few days were the only days the men took off work during that cold winter season. The money in Julianna's savings jar grew as the days passed. She delivered two parish babies and a neighbor's baby, splitting the money with Katherine, grateful that Tracy had such good care while she was away.

86

"You are a blessing to me," Julianna said, one evening after a neighbor's long and difficult labor. She had left at ten o'clock the evening before. At three o'clock the next afternoon the baby finally arrived. After a seventeen hour day, Katherine had hot cider and a bowl of warm oatmeal waiting for her, though she was almost too tired to eat.

"You go to bed now, Julianna. I'll take care of Alex and Tracy."

Julianna handed Katherine a dollar, her half of the money and wearily did as she was bid.

***

When February arrived, the snow was gone, and there were even a few balmy days that promised spring, but March brought howling winds and more rain.

Alex began to get restless, anxious to catch the eastbound train to their farm. He found himself wondering what the place looked like after the bad winter. We've saved up enough money to start on the houses anyway.

"I want to get out to the land by the first of April. Franz and I'll go out and take a look around. That way we can plan on how best to attack our building project." Alex and Julianna sat enjoying some quiet time after the children had gone to bed. Franz and Katherine were out for the evening at a church gathering.

"What did Franz say?" Julianna asked as she sat by the fire, her knitting needles busy.

"We talked about it today. He agreed with me. He wants Katherine to stay here with you until the weather gets better." Alex sounded more confident then he felt. He hated to leave Julianna and Tracy. He missed them terribly.

"That's a good idea. We can keep each other company while you men are gone." Julianna set her needles in her lap, and looked at him. "I hate it when we're apart, you know."

He nodded silently.

"It's wild country out there."

"I'll be all right."

"You don't even have a gun."

"I know," Alex agreed adding. "I can run fast." He stifled a chuckle, knowing that Julianna was dead serious.

She shot him a "don't-you-dare-laugh" look.

"Katherine told me about a man out there last summer who was chased by a bear," Julianna continued. "The only reason he escaped is that he played dead after the 'blessed' thing had him down. He could've been eaten, you know." Her back straightened with indignation.

"I heard that. I promise I'll be careful. I just hate to spend the money on a rifle when we need every penny for our house." Alex paused, and then added, "If I can find a cheap one, I'll buy it."

This time Julianna nodded.

"Franz and I decided that we'd build one house this summer and all of us can move into it," Alex said, trying to get Julianna into a less serious mood. "Then we'll start on the second house. Hopefully, by fall we'll all be living out there."

"Oh, that would be wonderful." Julianna smiled that smile he couldn't resist.

Chapter 18

Late April, 1885

By the end of April, Franz and Alex had dug the basement and were starting on the foundation around the perimeter of Franz's house. Franz could store produce toward the back of the basement where it wouldn't freeze. The front area could serve as a woodshed. In bad weather, everything they needed would be right outside the kitchen door and down the cellar steps.

"I think if we dynamite the rock pile, we can use the pieces for the foundation," Franz said as they rested one afternoon under one of the tall firs. The rain shower had finally stopped, and the sun, hot for so early in the year, peeked out from behind huge billowing clouds.

"That's one problem solved," Alex said after walking down and looking at the heap of boulders. "Now we need to get some blasting powder. We'll need to order the lumber soon, too."

"As far as I'm concerned, it doesn't need to be fancy. Rough cut boards will do just fine and be less expensive." Franz scratched his head thoughtfully. "I heard last summer that there was a saw mill up at Latourell Falls. I wonder if it's still operating."

"We've done about all we can without supplies. Let's go back to Taylor's cabin tonight. He can tell us all about sawmills," Alex said, as he stood and stretched the kinks out of his back and shoulders. "I'm about sick of camping up here in the rain."

They finished digging out the spring, leaving it open to catch the late rains, and spent the next hour packing what they wanted to take back. They stashed the tools in a hideaway down by the bluff. A small cave with an entrance too small for a man to squeeze through served their purpose well, and would keep everything dry. A few well placed rocks hid the entrance from anyone who might chance by.

They arrived back at Taylor's cabin close to dark. "I'm going to let him know we're here and make sure it's all right to stay. We'll talk to him in the morning about the mill." Franz said as they stepped into the clearing. "Besides, our lantern's out of fuel. Maybe, he'll have some we can buy."

They spent a comfortable night indoors, listening to the rain on a roof that didn't leak, unlike the fir boughs they had slept under for the past few weeks. The next morning they inquired about the lumber.

"There's a fellow named Dr. McKenny up at Latourell," Taylor said leaning lazily against a stump in his front yard. "It's only about five miles east of here," he jammed his thumb up river. "He's runnin' the company that's building a flume to bring timber down from Brower." He pointed toward the western bluff of Pepper Mountain, with Larch Mountain standing behind it.

A steamboat whistle blew for the landing. "Whoops, I gotta get ready. The boys on the *Joseph Kellog* will need help with that wood pile," Taylor jumped up and started down toward the dock.

"What about Dr. McKenney," Franz hollered to him.

"He's a good guy. Why don't ya' go up and see him?" Taylor stopped and yelled back. "Catch the east-bound train. It's due in a couple of hours, they'll let you off right at Latourell."

"We'll walk. I'll bet we can beat it," Alex said in a loud voice, as they started out at a fast clip. "I don't want to wait. I want to get to Portland tonight. We've got to find lumber before we leave."

The town of Latourell was tucked back in the curve of the bluff where a high tumbling falls plummeted into a wide creek, which meandered through part of the town, eventually losing itself in the Columbia. The dock close to the creek welcomed steamboats regularly. The town sported several saloons, a mercantile store and many residences. A salmon cannery, the depot and another large building were tucked in close to the railroad tracks.

"There's more people here then I thought there'd be," Franz said as they briskly walked through town.

"*Yah*, I'm surprised about that." Alex shifted the weight of his pack board and nodded. "When we passed through here on the train, I didn't realize it was so populated."

Alex asked a couple of boys skipping stones at the creek to point out Dr. McKinney's mill. Then, unable to resist, he picked up a smooth round rock and sailed it bumping across the water. He got admiring glances from the boys as he and Franz headed toward a sign that read Brower-Thompson Office.

"May I help you fellows?" A tall slender gentleman with a mustache asked when they knocked on the door. In spite of a chilly wind blowing outside, he sat in his shirt sleeves and vest. His coat hung from a peg on the wall.

"We were told you might sell us some lumber," Franz said, stamping the mud off his feet, and ducking quickly inside.

"We'll have some the middle of June, if all goes well."

"Do you deliver?" Alex asked. He wasn't sure how they'd get it to the farms if they didn't.

"Where do you want it delivered?"

"We're homesteading, up on the bluff, south of Taylor's Landing and east of the Sandy River."

"Oh yes, I know the place. I heard about the fire up there a few years ago." The man paused, leaned back and lit a small cigar. "You fellows like one of these?" he asked, offering them the box of stogies.

They shook their heads.

"If the road's passable, I can have a fellow bring it to you." Sticking his thumb in his suspenders, he raised his head, blew cigar smoke to the low ceiling, and watched it waft over the room. "Won't charge you much."

Alex's eyes began to water. I'm glad I don't smoke those things, he thought. Franz shot him a glance telling him he felt the same way.

"We're about a mile or so off the Wire Trail. We can get started widening the road into our places this spring. By June it should be dry and we'll make sure you'll be able to get a team and wagon through to the place," Alex said, coughed a bit and longed for some fresh air. "How about we come back the first of June? We'll firm up the order and give you a check."

"By then I should have a price for you." McKenney clenched the cigar between his teeth as if he were afraid it would explode in a whirl of smoke. "We're just getting back into the woods now, so I don't know what lumber will bring this year." He stood up and stretched out his hand, "Nice to meet you fellows."

They bade him good day and started for the railroad station. As they made their way through the town, an elderly gray-haired lady, hanging clothes on the line, waved to them.

They waved back.

"Where you two headed?" she said in a thick accent that Alex didn't recognize.

Before they could answer a short, gray-haired gentleman, appeared from around back of the house. He shook their hands. "I'm Frenchy Latourell," he said, "and this is my wife, Gracie." He slid his arm around her waist and continued, "You strangers in town?" He had friendly, laughing eyes and Alex liked him immediately.

"Yes, we're homesteading out where the Sandy River runs into the Columbia."

"Oh, out on the bluff where eagles nest." The old man's face lit up. "We have a nest here, too." He pointed up to the steep cliff behind the town. "Up on the way to the Mountain School, in that tall snag, there's a nest. See, the one right by the trail."

Alex squinted in the sunlight. "*Yah*, I see it." Alex said, noting the dead tree with what looked like a tuft of hair sticking out of its top. He added, "That's one steep switchback. Do the children climb that everyday?"

"*Oui*, and so does the teacher." Frenchy paused and scratched his thinning hair. "They have it easier than the Taylor children though."

"Why's that?" Franz asked.

"When they were growing up they had to go to school in Washougal. They rowed their father's boat across the Columbia River. They could only go in summer and fall, when the water was low."

Alex shook his head. Tracy's going to school, but she's not going to row across the river to do it.

"Where are you boys headed?" Gracie joined the conversation.

"Back to Portland to get our families," Alex said.

"Portland's a big city now," she told them. "When Joe and I first married, it was a swamp with a few buildings and a lot of stumps." She

91

laughed and said, "That's been over thirty-five years now." She paused, Alex thought a bit wistfully, before she added, "It certainly doesn't seem like that long ago."

"I'm sure it doesn't, ma'am," Alex said, trying to imagine a swamp where that dynamic young city now stood.

"I'm curious about that building in the meadow over there," Franz said, gesturing toward an open park- like space.

"That's our dance pavilion," Grace said. "We have dances several times during the summer. Joe and our children play music for them. Everyone comes from miles around."

"*Oui,* you'd better plan on bringing your family to the Fourth of July celebration," Frenchy added.

"That sounds like fun," Alex said. "We'll have to do that."

They caught the afternoon train and arrived at Albina at seven o'clock. By the time they made their way across the river to the apartment, it was late.

"I hope we don't scare the girls," Alex said as they walked up the front stairs.

"They'll be so glad to see us; they'll forgive us," Franz chuckled.

"I don't know about that, but I'll be glad to see them." Alex said. He quietly pushed open the door and was greeted by two sleepy women.

"We had a feeling maybe you'd be home tonight, so we decided to stay up and wait a bit longer." Excitement danced in Julianna's eyes replacing the weariness he'd first seen.

A single lamp burned on the kitchen table beside the women's unfinished needlework. Alex thought his wife's face in the pale light was even more beautiful then when he'd left.

Chapter 19

May 1885

Julianna knew Alex was anxious to get back to the land and part of her was grateful he hadn't mentioned it. Soon her second child would be here. She was large, bigger than she had been with Tracy, and it was difficult for her to get around. It made her cross and she hated that about herself.

She had counted the days and knew the baby's arrival could be any day. When she finally told Tracy about the new family member, she was immediately sorry she'd said anything.

"Baby soon," Tracy had chattered. "My baby."

"Yes, your baby, sweetheart," she murmured for the thirtieth time.

Another week passed and still nothing. Alex and Franz had construction jobs and were gone most of the day, but Alex was home in the evening and having him there made the pregnancy bearable. It had been those long days in April that she'd despised, when he had been gone and it had rained incessantly.

"I want us to stay in Taylor's cabin when you and Franz go to the farm," she said one evening when everyone was sitting around the table.

"Me, too," Katherine stated. "We're not going to be left behind this summer. The weather'll be better by June and the baby should be here."

"That suits me just fine," Alex said. "I'm not the least bit interested in going out there and spending the summer without you girls either."

Another week passed. Julianna began to wonder if the baby would ever come. She'd given up hope that Tracy would stop asking. Sophie came each afternoon and took Tracy and Mary to play with Victor, a favor that helped Julianna cope with mood swings and labor pains that dead-ended.

Then on May 24th, a bright sunny Sunday morning, during Mass, Julianna had several sharp pains and knew the time was near. She nudged Alex and whispered to him to get Matt's carriage and take her home. Sophie and Katherine rose when Alex signaled them.

Less than six hours later, the baby arrived.

"It's a girl," Sophie said holding the crying infant up for all to see, "and a beautiful one at that."

"Tracy has a little sister," Julianna murmured, grateful for it to finally be over. "She'll be excited."

Sophie laid the tiny infant in Julianna's arms. What a beautiful child! Perfect hands and toes and such dark curly hair. In fact, Julianna thought, she looks exactly like Alex.

They'd already decided to name a little girl Emma, after Alex's favorite aunt.

On the first of June the men made a trip to the homesteads and returned with news that the lumber shipment would be delayed. The woods had been closed three weeks longer than previous years due to extended snowfall.

"*Yah*, we're supposed to check back with McKenney the first of July," Alex said as he sat down at the table, his mouth watering at the supper aroma. "Just in time for the 4th of July celebration up there."

"Fourth of July celebration?" Kathleen asked.

"Every year the whole town turns out for a big party. Everyone's invited." Franz said shoveling in large spoonfuls of the warm meaty stew. "They play baseball and dance."

"That sounds like so much fun," Julianna said, quietly from the corner where she was feeding Emma. "We haven't done anything like that since we left Baden." Her thoughts flashed back to home and the fair where she first laid eyes on Alex, remembering how handsome he was. How her knees had gone weak when she saw him.

"Well, that settles it. We'll combine a little business with our holiday." Alex grinned. "In the meantime, we'll go out as soon as possible to get Franz's house foundation finished. We've got a shipment of dynamite headed out to Taylor's in the morning."

"*Yah*, we got some rocks to blow up," Franz said, in his usual off handed manner.

"O, Lord," Julianna said, shaking her head. "Will you two be careful, for heaven's sake?"

Alex walked over to give her a long, loving hug. "Of course we will," he assured her.

By the second week of June, the two families had snuggled into Taylor's cabin with the rental agreement of fifteen dollars a month. Julianna was feeling better every day and was sure that there would be babies to deliver, which would help with the expenses.

Even though they had quite a bit of money saved, Julianna was not one to feel comfortable, just because they had a little savings. They needed building materials and provisions for winter, and she didn't want the men to have to leave in bad weather and go to Portland to get a job.

"Will this rain ever stop?" Julianna asked as she took off her soaked coat and shook the water into the open fire.

Watching it sizzle and fade, Katherine slowly shook her head. "I'm beginning to wonder."

"Mama, Mama!" Tracy ran to greet her exhausted mother.

"*Leibkind!*" Picking her up, Julianna turned again to her friend. "Mr. Cole gave me a ride to Taylor's, thank God. I can't imagine walking the whole five miles in this downpour."

"Julianna, you look tired. Let me give you some of this soup. Tracy can sit on your lap while you eat. She's been asking for you all day."

Julianna smiled and kissed her toddler on the forehead. "How is baby Emma, darling?"

"Baby sleep."

"Good, that means she had enough to eat. I wasn't sure if I left enough milk for her. She can be a little piggy sometimes."

Tracy giggled and laid her head on her mother's shoulder.

"So how did it go?" Katherine asked. "You've been gone a long time."

"Fine really, it was just a long labor. The missus had a baby boy about eleven this morning. I'd have been back sooner, but her husband didn't want me to leave her right away."

Katherine's soup warmed her. "Where are the men folk?" Julianna asked, while savoring every spoonful.

"They're in Taylor's barn working on some of his equipment. He was eager to put them to work and I wasn't sorry to see them go. The rain is driving them crazy. All they could do was pace the floor. This little cabin doesn't hold two restless men and three babies." Sighing, Katherine added, "I know Alex would not have been so uneasy if you had been here. He just doesn't do well when you are gone."

"I know. If we all didn't need the money so badly, I would never leave."

"It'll be better when we get moved into our house on the hill. Even an improvement in the weather will allow us to spend some of the time outside," Katherine said ladling Julianna another helping.

The door opened suddenly and the men came in, stamping their feet and pulling off wet clothes. "Ah, Julianna, I'm glad you're home," Alex said kissing his wife and then taking Tracy from her. "We've been fixing Taylor's wagon. It had a broken axle." Wiping his face with a dry handkerchief he continued, "It's a two man job."

"I'd like a little glass of wine," Franz said as he reached in the cupboard for the bottle. "I'm cold clear to the bone."

"*Yah*, that sounds good," Alex agreed.

Julianne shook her head, "None for me, thanks." She met her husband's dark hazel eyes and he smiled at her.

"If this rain ever stops," Alex said, taking a sip, "we're ready to go up to the farm and put the finishing touches on the place in time for the lumber."

"Old timers around here say it won't quit until after the 4th of July," Franz laughed.

"Well, we only have a week to go," Katherine said, looking at her calendar. Julianna smiled at her friend. It was like Katherine to know the exact date. She was the organizer, the anchor of the group. Julianna valued her more every day. They were family now, all of them.

She missed her folks back in Baden, but it was no longer unbearable, more like the dull scraping of a windblown broken limb, than the sharp pierce of a jagged sword. She hoped her *Mutter* and Papa could come and meet their grandbabies one day.

"Taylor said he'll take us up to Latourell on the 4th in his wagon."

"That's nice of him. I'm looking forward to it." Katherine's face glowed.

"It's time we get to know more of our neighbors," Julianna said, excitement rising. "Alex says the people in Latourell are very friendly."

***

The rain finally stopped on July 2nd. Water dripped from the trees in little pools on the path to Taylor's Landing. The sky remained overcast into the afternoon, but no more rain. Julianna, grateful for the chance to get Tracy outside to play, didn't mind her wet feet. They walked down to the landing where Alex and Franz were helping Taylor unload a steamboat full of supplies from Portland.

"Julianna, this is Tom Evans." Alex introduced her to a stocky, dark haired gentleman standing next to a team and wagon loaded with cord-wood. He smiled at her through a full beard, tipped his hat, and extended his hand. "Nice to meet you, Ma'am!"

Julianna smiled back, "*Gutten tag*!" Followed by, "Hello, very nice to meet you also." She and Alex practiced often talking to each other in English. She still had trouble understanding many words, but she felt a bit more confident now.

"Tom has been clearing his land, so he sells a few wagon loads of wood every month to the steamboats," Franz chimed in.

"They use a lot of wood. About four cords an hour when they're churnin' up the river," Tom said. "Keeps me in pocket money." His eyes twinkled as he reached down and patted Tracy on her pink and blue bonnet. Tracy beamed back. "We're planting a prune orchard up on our place. It's southeast of Gage, past the Hurlbert district," he continued.

Julianna had no idea where he was talking about. She'd only been to the family homestead once and to the Cole place, up in the mountains to deliver a baby. But Alex and Franz seemed to understand, so she just smiled and nodded.

"Julianna helps deliver babies," Franz said. "If you know anyone in need of her services, let them know."

"I surely will." Tom smiled and turned back to his chores.

Tracy and Julianna wandered up to the Taylor house. She thought of poor Mr. Taylor. He'd lost his wife back in '67 and raised two sons and a daughter by himself. Julianna shook her head thinking of the hardship he had to endure without his spouse. I can't imagine how terrible that would be, she thought with a shiver.

"What happened to Mrs. Taylor?" Julianna brought the Taylors up again that evening at supper. The thought of people losing their mates here in the frontier was a horror to her.

"I hear she died in childbirth along with the baby." Franz said reaching for another slice of bread.

"How terrible," she said. "I can't imagine losing my husband." Julianna shuddered at the thought.

"Neither can I imagine losing Franz out here," Katherine agreed.

"Do you know, Taylor gave the county an acre of ground in the high lands for a school?" Alex said changing the subject.

"Really, when?"

"I guess he did it last year, but it's taken them this long to get it processed and ready to build. They plan on having school in it this fall. They've hired a teacher and everything. There's a couple of schools in the country, but not an official District 39. The community is pretty excited." Alex paused and held his plate out for a second helping. "I guess the loss of land doesn't hurt Taylor much. He has 639 acres left." The men laughed.

"I think it's wonderful of him," Katherine said.

Chapter 20

July 4, 1885

The Fourth of July dawned sunny, promising a warm day. The wind came from the east, drying everything in its path. Julianna chose her prettiest blue church dress, a gingham with puffed sleeves. Might as well get some wear out of this, she thought, It'll be awhile before we go to church again.

She watched Alex button his clean white shirt. "You look so handsome," she said, kissing his newly shaven cheek. "I like you without whiskers."

"No whiskers," he said rubbing his face. "Don't you want me to look like a mountain man?"

"No, I like you to look like you did when I met you, with just a bit of a rakish mustache."

The families walked down the path to Taylor's.

"I wish you'd waited for us to help you hook up the horses," Alex said to the old man.

"No, no today is my treat," Taylor said. "You young fellers help me all the time."

It's true, Julianna thought, Alex and Franz helped Taylor as much as he helped them.

The hot east wind dried the road enough to harden the mud, but not enough to be dusty, which made the trip pleasant. Julianna noticed Taylor smiling as he listened to them chatter.

The horses strained as they plodded up the steep winding trail. There was a spring almost at the top of the hill where they stopped to water the horses and everyone got out and stretched their legs. Then one more short pull to the top where they hit the Wire Trail and turned east.

"In the summer, the east wind is hot and dry. By tomorrow it will be in the 90s, mark my words and that's fire season," Taylor chatted as they drove. "I encourage you young folks to cut timber down around your houses as a fire break and keep the dry grass down. Get a goat if nothing else to keep foliage under control."

It was close to noon when they arrived at the city park in Latourell. Tables, already collecting huge platters of food, were set up under the shade trees. People were arriving from all directions. Musicians were busy setting up their chairs and stands in the pavilion

Julianna couldn't believe her eyes. Here in the middle of the wilderness were people eager to dance and celebrate their independence.

"There must be a hundred people here," Alex said.

"You bet. Everyone comes to this. It's the biggest event of the year. It's in the summer so people can get to it." Taylor stopped the team so the group could disembark. He smiled and nodded to an older balding gentleman and his gray-haired companion. "That's Fred Hicklin and his wife Sarah."

"Must be where Hicklin Bottoms on the Sandy River got its name," Alex said.

"Yup, they're the ones. Been there before I came to this country and I came in '66," Taylor said as he climbed back up in the driver's seat.

He took the horses to the trough and gave them a long drink. Then he handed the reins and a coin to a teen-age boy, who led them to the edge of town, unharnessed them and turned them out in the Latourell pasture to graze.

Out on the outskirts of town, near the railroad tracks, a group of men were throwing a ball. Alex and Franz headed towards them. Julianna watched them go, excited they had something to take their mind off the homesteads.

"Last year the mill workers won, so the settlers are ready to even the score," said a sweet looking, young pregnant woman. "Oh, I'm sorry I should have introduced myself." She spoke German and Julianna thought her Swiss accent was delightful, "I'm Anna Luscher. That's my husband Fred, over there. The one with the brown vest throwing the ball," she pointed to a handsome bearded fellow on the baseball field. "He loves to play baseball. He's hoping to get the game going soon because he has to quit before five o'clock to go home and milk. We have a dairy down the road."

"I suspect that Alex and Franz will want to get in on that game," Julianna said, introducing herself and Katherine. She instantly liked the young woman and it was fun to make a new friend who could speak her language.

As soon as everyone finished the noon meal, the game began. Many of the women gathered in the shade of two large alders near third base, chattering together, one eye on the game and one eye on their young children playing nearby. Two of the Latourell teen-age girls were organizing games for the older children.

"Those Latourell girls are wonderful with children," Anna commented as the women wandered over to watch the children's games when Tracy and Mary began to get restless. "Alice, the older one, is being courted by Newell Courter. He's the handsome young man who is pitching for the mill workers."

"My, he is good-looking, but no more so then she," Katherine said as she admired the young lady with dark hair and petite features. "From what I see of the Latourell family, they're a handsome lot."

Anna sat down on one of the wooden benches. "I think I'll sit for awhile, I'm getting a little tired."

"I'm not surprised," Katherine said. "Did you know Julianna is a mid-wife?"

"Oh! Julianna, that's wonderful. I have been worried. Fred wants me to go to Portland to have the baby, but I don't want to go without him, and he can't leave the dairy. Can I hire you to come help me?"

"Of course. Just send Fred when the time is near. I'll come right away."

All through the warm afternoon, the women visited, met new friends and wondered who would win the ballgame. The suspense mounted. By the 7th inning the score was tied 11 runs to 11 runs. It would've been 14 for the mill workers, but Tom Evans caught a long-line drive in left field, an unheard of feat with no glove, and left two men on base to end the inning.

"Well, I guess we'll be tending to Tom's hands tomorrow. The last game he played he hurt his shoulder," Tom's wife said with a laugh. "I tried to tell him he was too old for this kind of foolishness." Hannah was a pretty woman, with striking brown eyes. Julianna could tell she was half teasing.

"How long do they play?" Julianna wondered.

"They usually play nine innings, but if they are tied they play longer."

"Two years ago, the game went 15 innings," said Hannah. "The mill-workers won that game, too."

"Oh my, it's getting late," Anna said, with a sigh of relief. "Fred has to leave soon."

"Who'll play in his place?" Katherine wanted to know. She was watching Franz guarding the sand-filled flour sack representing third base.

Not much later the dilemma was solved when Fred hit a long fly ball over the fence into the pasture. He scored easily, bringing in Alex who had been walked earlier. The score was 13 to 11 and there it remained. Thus for the first time in history the farmers won the annual baseball game. Julianna was sure it was because Alex and Franz played for the farmers team.

The jubilation lasted into the evening. Fred came back to celebrate with a little homebrew after he finished the chores, but Anna claimed exhaustion and stayed home.

After they put the children to sleep in the back of the wagon, Alex and Julianna danced into the night. She felt like a young girl in Alex's arms under the moon. The music was different than she was used to, but she loved it. Joe's fiddle rang out tune after tune, from slow waltzes to refrains that someone called Cajun.

The dawn was just peeking through the darkness when Taylor dropped a slightly tipsy, very happy Fred near his house. Then the tired, but light-hearted group headed back to Taylor's Landing, the babies fast asleep in the wagon.

Chapter 21

July 1885

At Latourell on the 4th of July, Alex verified their lumber order one last time with Dr. McKenney.

"We can expect our shipment on the 11th?" Alex inquired, wishing he felt more confident.

"Yah, yah, we'll have it for you. Probably around noon." McKenney assured him.

Over the next few days, he and Franz worked feverishly getting the foundation in place, and putting the finishing touches on the project. Alex hoped they weren't rushing around for nothing.

"What if we don't get the lumber day after tomorrow like he promised?" Franz asked, his face mirroring Alex's concern. They'd prepared everything, even widening the trail for the horses and delivery wagon.

"He'll do it." Alex hoped his voice sounded confident.

"But what if he doesn't?"

Alex continued to work, his face twisted with determination. "We've got to get started framing this house. If we don't, we can't get it done by winter." Perspiration beaded on his forehead. "We can't ask the girls to stay in that tiny cabin with the babies during bad weather," he said, stopping a moment to wipe the sweat from his eyes. It might not worry some men to see their wives unhappy, but it bothered him and he knew Franz didn't like it either.

"I got a feeling about that delivery." Franz sounded skeptical.

"So have I," Alex admitted. "But let's not invite trouble."

The day of the delivery, the men were up on the homestead just after daylight. They found a good place to pile the lumber, close enough to be handy but out of the way. They made plans and watched the sun climb.

Alex talked himself into believing they would have their supplies today, but noon came and went with no sign of the lumber. They busied themselves making fire wood, all the while peering down the trail. Shortly before dark, dejected, they headed down the hill to Taylor's cabin.

*****

"They promised!" Julianna was furious. "How dare they not show up and not send word? You go to Latourell tomorrow."

"I will. Franz is going up to the home place to make sure there wasn't a mix up and it gets delivered tomorrow. I'll catch the earliest train and find out what's going on."

Katherine, looking like she was going to cry, turned to the stove.

"I don't know when I've been so angry. We gave them almost all of our money, too," Julianna said. Then she was silent for a moment, trying to gain composure and put her arm around her friend to comfort her. "The men'll find out what's going on. I'm sure they'll straighten it out," Julianna said, knowing she wasn't convincing.

***

The next day was hot even for July. Julianna waited impatiently for word from Alex. The children whined, seeming to feel the frustration hanging in the air. Tracy, usually an independent explorer, clung to her mother's skirts, and Emma and Mary fussed and cried.

"We need to get some fresh fruit and vegetables to put up. We'll never have enough to eat next winter if we don't." Katherine said as she busied herself in the kitchen.

"It's too bad we didn't get out here early enough to put in a garden," Julianna was grateful to her friend for trying to get their minds on something besides the homestead and the heat.

Katherine brushed a curl out of her eye and Julianna noticed her hand was shaking.

"Ella Smith told me we could get produce from them. I had a nice visit with her on the Fourth. She said they have several acres of prune trees and two acres of produce." Katherine paused to give Mary a drink of water.

"Where do they live?"

"Down in the Gage area, south of here," Katherine said. "Fred makes produce deliveries up at Brower for the logging families. She said we could have him deliver to us, too."

"Maybe we could buy from Tom Evans, too. His farm is in Hurlburt," Julianna added as she finished feeding Emma and put her back into her cradle.

"The problem is, I don't know how much money we have left to pay them." Katherine sounded worried as she wiped Mary's chin with her apron.

"Let's see what we have." Julianna pulled the money jar down from the shelf and poured the contents onto the table. After carefully counting it out she announced, "It looks like we have $74.06. If we don't need any more building supplies, this might be enough."

Katherine nodded. "But I'd rather have more of a cushion."

"If we'd just hear from Alex. I know I'm not being patient about this, but I can't stand this waiting," Julianna said, her voice heavy with frustration.

"I know, dear Julianna, but Alex will tend to it." This time it was Katherine's turn to console. "There is just a little mix-up. You wait and see. When he comes back, it will all be fixed." But her face was sallow and pale, belying her comforting voice.

Alex returned later in the afternoon, his face furrowed in a deep scowl.

"McKenney says it'll be at least two more weeks before he can get our lumber together. He's got two other large local orders as well as ours."

102

Alex lifted the ladle and took a long drink from the pail on the front stoop. "The good news is they have plenty of logs but because the woods have dried out, now they're afraid of fire. When it gets too dry, they have to shut down the whole operation."

"It seems the mill is either shut down because of snow or because of sunshine," Julianna said, and immediately wished that she hadn't.

Alex shrugged and walked back down the path, Tracy running after him.

When Franz got home later that day, they discussed their options.

"We're down to $74.06 in our jar," Katherine informed them.

"Taylor told me the City of Portland is stringing electrical wire all over downtown." Franz sounded enthusiastic. "He said he heard they are paying 50 cents an hour. I'll go to town and try to get on. Alex can go up to the homestead and start clearing a bigger area around the foundation for fire protection, like Taylor told us."

"That's a good idea," Katherine said a little wistfully. "I just hate to have you leave, but we have to have food to get us through the winter."

"You girls give me a list of supplies you'll need and I'll get them while I'm in town," Franz said.

"I'll be at Matt's, unless they have the flat rented. Otherwise I'll go to St. Joseph's and put out a plea for a room with someone in the parish."

"I'm afraid it's the only option we have," Alex said.

Franz left next morning carrying a small satchel. He ran down the trail as he heard a train whistle coming from the east. Alex waved good-bye and headed up to work at the homestead. The warm wind promised another hot July day.

Four days later, Alex retrieved a letter from Franz when he went to the Landing. It said he got on with the electric company and was staying at Matt's. They didn't want to charge him rent, but he planned to give them two dollars a week.

August came, but the lumber didn't. Alex went back to Latourell to find out what was holding it up. His patience worn thin, he was determined to either get his order or his money. He'd heard there was a sawmill in Cleone and had about made up his mind to take his business there. If they had to move back to Portland for the winter, so be it, he thought clenching his fist. It was almost too late this year to get it done anyway.

"Hello there, Alex." McKenney greeted him with a smile and a handshake.

"Where's my lumber?" Alex demanded without even a hello.

"See that wagon over there?" Mckenney pointed to a long freight wagon stacked high with boards. "That's yours. We'll finish your order by tomorrow night. It'll go out day after tomorrow."

"I upgraded your lumber because of the delay. I feel bad that we've taken so long. I hope that will help make up for it," McKenney said, as if reading Alex's thoughts.

"It certainly helps. I know the Frommelts will be happy with it. Our biggest concern now is to get the house habitable by winter."

"Franz says you're a good carpenter. If anyone can do it, you can."

"We'll see," Alex said. "In the meantime I'll look for your hired man day after tomorrow up at the Frommelt place."

Back at the cabin that evening, Alex added a note to Franz on the bottom of Katherine's letter saying he had seen the load and it would be delivered August 5th. The next day he walked to Taylor's to mail it.

When the lumber came, McKenney sent two men as a courtesy to help Alex unload and stack the boards. As soon as they had gone, he began nailing the sill on the top of the foundation. He fashioned a sawbuck out of scrap lumber and some sturdy limbs. But even so one man with a handsaw couldn't get a lot done in a day.

He'd only gotten half the sills in place by dark and realized he'd have to work from sunrise to sunset to finish the house before winter.

He arrived home well after dark, ate a quick supper, fell into bed and was asleep before Julianna, busy with Emma, could get away to kiss him good night.

Friday afternoon Franz arrived back at the cabin, amid boxes and sacks of supplies. Jubilant, he kissed his wife and daughter and gave Julianna a big hug.

"There's a little over sixty dollars in there," he said handing Katherine a wad of bills. "That ought to help out with winter supplies. I got everything on your list and even some candy treats."

When Alex got home, Franz had a surprise for him, too. "Matt and Joe Boeck are coming out on the train next week to help get our house up. They say they can stay for at least two weeks. Sophie's going to run the store. I told them all we could pay them was two dollars a week and food. They didn't care. It sounded like fun to them."

For the first time in many weeks, Alex believed they had a chance to get the house done before cold weather set in.

Chapter 22

Fall 1885
Hurlburt, Oregon, U.S.A.

Nov.10, 1885

Dearest Mutter,
We've finally arrived. We moved into Katherine and Franz's home on October 8. The men borrowed Taylor's team and wagon. They took Katherine's stove, the windows for the house and some of our household necessities, and hauled them up the hill. It was a heavy load, but his horses are young and the road was dry. They came back to the cabin and loaded the rest of our things and we rode back up with them. Tracy was thrilled with the horses and the ride. Truthfully, I would've rather walked, but the men would not hear of it.

"You girls have to move into our home in style," Franz told us. The men are so proud of the house.

One of the windows arrived broken. Katherine and I were unhappy because it was the kitchen window, the one that looks out over the trail coming into the place. The opening is boarded up and we work in a dark kitchen, much like when we lived in Taylor's cabin. The men promised us a new window as soon as spring arrives.

The week following the move, Franz and Alex went to the Evan's farm near the Hurlburt district south of here. They bought two bushels of cabbages, three hundred pounds of potatoes and two bushels of carrots. I'm sure this won't be enough for winter, but he promised to deliver more if we need it.

He had a poor onion crop so we were unable to get any but he did sell us three large bags of unshelled dry beans. They also brought us a special treat, freshly dried Italian prunes and two bushels of apples and pears. We dried the apples and pears as soon as we got our stove working. The men love Katherine's apple kuchen. We have enough fruit for winter now because we have a small orchard someone planted on our place.

Everything seems to be storing well in the cellar. The only thing we're having trouble with is flour. It gets wormy so fast. Franz brought us a five gallon tin container with a tight lid the other day. We are going to try that and see if it keeps better. Flour is expensive and the men have to carry those heavy sacks all the way up that steep trail.

We bought onions and some more potatoes and carrots from Fred Smith, who lives not far from Mr. Evans. He also sold us a butchered hog last month. Most of it is ham and bacon. We have it stored in the cellar in a large crock. They advised us to cover all the meat with layers of melted lard which then hardened. They said the meat would keep best that way. So far it is doing well and is very tasty. I am growing fond of baked beans and bacon.

I helped deliver Anna Lusher's baby girl in August. They have a dairy in a town along the river just east of us called Latourell. In payment, they gave us five pounds of cheese and a sack of English walnuts.

Katherine's baby is due in February. She says she's glad that her best friend is a trained mid-wife as we are miles from the nearest doctor.

Alex brought a goat home last week for milk. We have no place to keep it out of the weather, so he made a log lean-to for her. We are lucky, she'll eat anything. The children gather weeds to feed her along with table scraps. If it gets very cold, we'll have to bring her in the cellar. We girls are not at all happy about that but Alex says it's the only way for now.

People up here tell us the winters can be very severe, usually snow and ice with a vicious wind coming down the Columbia River. I am mildly concerned because we are so isolated. No one lives between us and Taylor's Landing which is about three miles northeast by Alex's trail. Our nearest neighbor to the west is the Hicklin place on the east side of the Sandy River across from the Troutdale depot. The Smith and the Evans's farms are about three miles south which means the four of us here have to depend on each other. I am so grateful for Katherine and Franz's friendship and they say the same about us. Alex and Franz work well together. They remind me of brothers, rather then friends.

The children play nicely. God is truly good to us. Emma is such a darling baby, so happy and plump. Tracy is very protective of both her and Mary, the Frommelt's daughter. They will miss playing with each other when we move to our own place next season.

Our land is just over the hill from here, maybe a quarter of a mile at the most, so we'll see them often after we move. As soon as we get our house built, I hope you can come for a long visit.

Being out here so far away from civilization, I miss going to Mass. Alex promised me we could take the train into Portland in the spring and visit the Foellers and the Boecks. Then we can go to church at St. Joseph's.

Franz said the monastery at Mt. Angel sends priests out riding the circuit. He thinks we can ask Father Kempf at St. Joseph's to see if we can get on the route. They come to different families houses

*and say Mass several times a year. That would be wonderful, but
it's so far out here and I don't know if there are any other Catholic
families around.*

*I must finish this letter tonight. Franz and Alex are going to
Taylor's tomorrow. They can mail it from there. Taylor needs a
retaining wall built. We had a hard three day rainstorm last week
and it washed down part of the hill behind his house. They are
going to help him shore it up at least temporarily. I will try to get
you another letter soon, but it depends on the weather. I understand
the winter rains keep everyone close to home because the roads get
muddy and people are unable to travel. It's raining again today and
I'm already growing tired of it.*

*Please know that we are safe and warm and well. Merry
Christmas and Auf Wiedersein meine dear Mutter.*

Julianna

***

"There, that's done," said Alex.

"Julianna would've never forgiven you if you hadn't caught that train to
post her letter." Franz gathered up his tools as they talked. "I hope the rain
holds off until we get this job done. I looked at the slide yesterday. The
ground's unstable. If it rains again we could lose more of that hill."

"I wish Taylor hadn't let those fellas log that upper piece, but I got the
idea he needed the money," Alex said.

The men climbed the hill behind the train station. A small raw piece of
the bluff stood out with a pile of brush and trees underneath.

"We'll cut these alders and lay them crossway to shore up below the
slide. That should hold it until it dries out and we can get enough rock to do
a more permanent job," Franz said softly as if thinking out loud.

"I'll go up and get some of those trees that didn't make it all the way
down. They'll make good poles."

"Just be careful. I don't trust this. The ground is still way too unstable."

Alex made his way up the steep muddy bank. He worked with his axe,
swinging it in wide accurate strokes, limbing the trees. Some of them were
so submerged he had to pry them out.

"I'm not going to waste a lot of time digging these," he hollered down to
Franz.

Franz nodded as he pounded poles in the ground to hold the stacked
beams.

The skies stayed cloudy into the afternoon. Keeping one eye on the sky,
Alex noticed approaching dark clouds over to the west.

"Look at that black cloud," he yelled down to Franz.

"I've been watching it."

"I've got two more poles to cut up here. How are you coming down
there?"

"I'll definitely need at least those two. I'll come up and give you a hand as soon as I get this one," Franz shouted back.

Alex noticed Franz's wall was about four feet high. We shouldn't need to go much higher, he thought. If four or five feet won't hold it, nothing we can do on this short notice will. Deftly, he cut limbs from another alder. It was about ten inches in diameter at the base and about eight feet long. This one and the one over there should do it, he thought.

The dark angry cloud came closer. Franz came up and started working rapidly on the second tree. A splatter of rain hit Alex in the face.

They worked faster, but in less than ten minutes the storm hit them full force. Taylor left the steamship he was helping load and ran up to help the men. Alex tried to roll the pole down the hill, but the mud was too sticky, so he picked it up and carried it down. They put it in place between the posts Franz had ready for them and ran up the hill for the last pole.

"Here, let me help with that." Alex headed to the upper end of the tree and cut out the top. "This is a good one." He said, referring to the hefty fourteen footer, "but it's darned heavy."

As soon as they finished the limbing, the three of them hoisted the log and started down. Suddenly Alex felt the ground start to give out under his feet.

"Drop it and get to the edge!" He heard Taylor yell.

"*Schnell! Schnell!*" Franz hollered.

Alex dropped the pole and ran for the edge of the slide, but the ground was moving, picking up speed. He heard Franz yell at him, just as he grabbed for an upright overhanging tree limb. He caught a piece of it, but it slipped through his fingers. He felt himself being pulled under and threw his arms up to protect his face. His boots were covered and then his knees. Struggling to stay upright, he shut his eyes to keep the mud from blinding him and held his breath.

A sudden stop jolted his eyes open. Franz's wall had stopped him. He'd lost his hat and his axe and he was buried almost up to his waist. The rain pelted his bare head. Frantically he searched for Franz and Taylor. He saw Franz waving to him from the edge of the slide.

"Where's Taylor?" Alex yelled.

"He's safe. Thank God!" Franz pointed to the other side. "Are you all right?"

He saw Taylor and waved back to him. "Yes, but I'm stuck." He looked down at the sticky ooze and tried to dig his way out with his bare hands, but with every bit he threw away, more seeped in, pulling him further down into the murky grime.

The men carefully made their way down the bluff, afraid of setting off another round of slides or getting stuck themselves.

"Let's get him outta here before more trouble comes." Franz grabbed his shovel and started to dig.

"I think I lost my tools," Alex said, still trying to help dig himself out. "Damn, I need those, too."

It took ten minutes to free him and Alex was shivering and wet. The mud stuck to his clothes and filled his boots.

"We gotta get him over to the spring and get this mud off," Taylor said, his voice urgent. "Then we'll take him in the house."

Alex jumped into the water, surprised at first that it didn't seem cold. But by the time he got outm he was shivering. When they got to the house, he was cold to his very marrow.

"Oh my God! What happened to you?" Lydia, Taylor's daughter, grabbed a blanket and handed it to Alex. "Get those wet things off this instant. And you," she said to Franz. "Get over by the fire. I'll get you men some dry things. You can't go home like this. It's too far to walk up the hill tonight."

"I'll have to go as soon as I warm up a bit. The women will worry if I don't get word to them. Alex can stay here. He can come home when the rain stops," Franz stood shaking in his drenched shirt.

"I'm going with you. Julianna will be worried if I don't come home."

"All right, but I wish you wouldn't."

"No, just let me rest a minute and get some dry things. I'll be fine. I'm afraid I lost my hat, though."

"Robert has one you can borrow," Lydia said, handing them dry pants and grabbing her brother's hat off the rack by the front door.

Alex, warmed slightly, put on the clean dry pants and boots. They started up the trail with the rain pummeling them. They were soaked before they got to the top of the bluff. Darkness was closing in.

"It'll be dark in a half hour in this weather." Alex said, his teeth chattering.

They walked as fast as they could, but the mud was deep and they sank in with every step. By the time they got to the second rise, it was dark enough to light the lantern Taylor had lent them. It took another three quarters of an hour to get home.

The door flew open as they reached the steps. "Thank God you're home!" Katherine said. "Julianna said there had been an accident, she was sure of it."

"There was, wasn't there?" Julianna gasped. "I knew it, Alex, what happened?"

As Katherine ran for blankets, Julianna ladled hot beans into bowls. While the food cooled, she poured them each a glass of wine. The men, wrapped in blankets, sat in front of the stove and told their story.

Tired to the bone, Alex fell into bed. The next morning, every muscle in his body hurt and he was still cold. So cold, he thought, he'd never warm up.

"You're burning with fever!" Julianna exclaimed, feeling his forehead. "My God! Alex, get back in bed."

He remembered falling back into bed, Tracy curling up beside him, but it was many days before anything made much sense to him. There were blurred images of Julianna and Katherine, but mostly he slept. He had periods of intense sweating, when he couldn't stand the covers and his bed clothes were wringing wet. Then there was the wracking cough. He coughed until he thought his insides were coming up and his ribs hurt. He hacked until blood came, and still he coughed and sweated.

By the second week in December, he felt better, but he couldn't believe the weakness. Up from bed, just an hour or two and he was ready to lie back down.

"I'm no good for anything," he growled at Julianna one morning. He was beginning to feel well enough to be restless.

"You're going to take care of yourself. There isn't anything you have to do. Franz can milk the goat. You split so much wood for us, we're fine. You just get your strength back so you can build our house in the spring."

And so Alex spent the next few months regaining his strength and waiting out the winter storms.

Pleasant View District, Oregon

Circa 1893

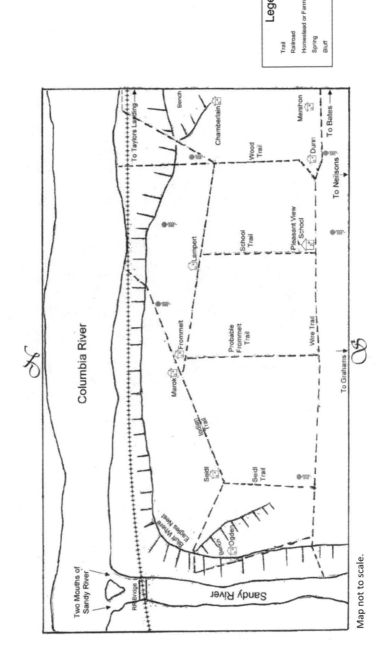

Map not to scale.

Julianna Gross Lampert

Circa 1882

Alexander Lampert

Circa 1882

Left to Right: **Julianna** holding baby **Ferd**,
Bertha (Bertie), **Theresa (Tracy)**, and **Emma**
Circa 1889

Standing, left to right: **Ferd, Theresa (Tracy), Josie, Arnold**
Sitting, left to right: **Emma, Alex Jr., Julius (Jack)**
and **Bertha (Bertie)**
Circa 1895

Chapter 23

Spring 1886

One Saturday evening in early April, after the children were settled in, Julianna quietly announced that Katherine was very near her time. "I think she'll have this child before the week's out."

"I'm not going into Portland then. I've got plenty to do around here," Franz said, with a look of concern.

"I wouldn't go if I were you," Alex agreed. "I'll go in, make a bit of money, and buy supplies."

Alex and Franz sat by the fireplace and discussed the situation. "I'm going to try getting to the railroad tracks by following the Wire Trail west, instead of going down to Taylor's. I've been studying it and I think it may be a faster way to catch the train," Alex said.

"I'm sure that's true. I'll walk down with you." Franz nodded.

The next morning after breakfast, the two men left. About a mile down the trail on their way to the Sandy River bluff, they spotted a path leading north into the woods.

"I'll bet that's where those people live that we heard about last time we were at Taylor's. Let's go meet them," Franz said. He turned and walked down the heavily wooded path.

"I hope they do live here, it's close and it would make me feel better about leaving our families out here by themselves." Alex hated leaving his family and working so far away. "I'm anxious to get my house up so I can start farming."

The small trail led up a slight incline for less then a quarter of a mile, coming to a stand of beautiful Western Red Cedars. They pushed past the forest's edge, and came to a clearing where they saw a small log cabin, with a stove pipe on one end of the roof and a single window beside the front door.

A large dog turned the corner of the house and barked his surprise at the men's arrival. A pile of shingles stood neatly by a well-worn splitting stump. A large cedar log lay at the edge of the clearing, with axes, saws, awls and an assortment of tools in a nearby three-sided tool shed.

The cabin door opened and a muscular middle-aged man greeted them. Behind him, a women in a faded green gingham dress peered over his shoulder. He called the dog and smiled a warm welcome.

"Hello," Franz answered. He introduced himself and Alex. "We have homesteads about a mile east of here," Franz continued in his best English as they shook hands.

"Welcome! I'm Harold Ogden and this here's my wife, Alice. We've never had company up here," he said. "We've lived here for over a year. Come in, come in!"

"We can't stay today. Alex is on his way to Portland to work and my wife about to have a child."

With that news, Mrs. Ogden's face brightened. She looked to be old, but Alex knew life in the frontier aged people. "A new baby! It's been so long," There was a faraway look in her eye.

"How long have you folks lived up on the hill?" Ogden asked.

"We built Franz's house last summer and we'll build ours this year." Alex said

"That's good! It'll be nice to have close neighbors," Ogden said, putting on his hat. "My sons and I made shingles, down by the Sandy River near Camp Harlow before we moved to this place," he continued in a friendly manner. "After our oldest sons left, the wife and I found this stand of cedar trees, so we filed our claim and moved our business up here. When I get a good load and the trail dries off, I'll have someone come up with a horse and wagon and haul them down to the railroad."

"You don't by chance know of a shortcut down to the Hicklin Place, do you?" Alex asked.

"You bet, young fellow. Just go back out to the main trail and head north to the bluff. There's a good trail there. A bit steep, but it's the only way down there at the moment."

"I knew there was an easier way to catch the train, than to go all the way back to Taylor's." Alex said with a grin.

After visiting a few more minutes, the men made their way back, and walked along the bluff. Sure enough Ogden's trail was well maintained and went straight north, dropping steeply into the Sandy River canyon, close to the ferry landing and just down river from the railroad bridge.

In less than an hour, Alex climbed aboard the west bound train and settled into the seat.

The week could not pass quickly enough for Alex, and he was relieved when Saturday finally came. He hiked up the hill home about mid-afternoon, and found tired adults and very excited children.

"Baby brother!" Mary babbled.

"Where's my brother?" Tracy demanded to know. "I want one, too!"

"Tracy wants brother!" Mary danced around her playmate.

"There, there, *Leibskind*. We will see what we can do for you." Alex laughed as he stepped in the door and suddenly found himself encircled in his wife's arms. "How's Katherine?"

"She's tired, but just fine and so is baby Albert," Julianna said holding Alex close.

"Tis a fine boy and my wife is beautiful," Franz said, joy written on his face.

Within a week, Katherine was almost back to normal, but they chose to have Franz stay home anyway. He needed to finish splitting the firewood for the families for the following season, and with a house to build and a garden to make, it seemed the prudent thing to do.

Alex and Franz went over to the Lampert homestead the following weekend and began laying out the foundation in earnest.

"We'll get this done now so when the weather turns nice we can get started framing the house," Alex said, digging into the fresh soft soil. He was anxious to get as much done on the foundation as possible before leaving Monday morning.

"I'm going to bring some baby chicks home next weekend. I can get them for a cent apiece from one of Boeck's neighbors. I don't know how many I can bring on the train, but I'll bring as many as I can. Everyone is hungry for fresh eggs."

"That would be good. I'm going to go to Cleone and try to get another goat and some garden seed," Franz said, as he threw a fresh shovel full of dirt away from the perimeter of the house.

"*Yah*! Get every kind of seed they have. We're gonna have a great garden this year. This new soil is rich. Things'll grow well."

They finished digging the perimeter that weekend. Franz would begin building the rock foundation during the week.

The following Saturday, Alex brought home a large box with twenty Rhode Island Red chicks, much to the children's delight. The box sat by the fireplace with a dish of water and two plates for their tiny feed pellets. "We'll only leave these here for a week or so, until they get big enough to be outside," he assured the wives.

"They better not smell." Katherine said.

"If they do, out they go," Julianna echoed with a firm voice.

"Yah! But remember, you wanted fresh eggs. These are the critters that'll give 'em to ya." Alex teased.

Alex went to join Franz in the garden, which was a clear spot that had burned years before. What brush was left Franz had cleared during the past few weeks and had about a quarter of it spaded up.

"I hope we have a horse by next season. This hand shoveling's too slow," Franz said, turning over a scoop of the loam.

"*Yah*, a horse is pretty high on my list, but I doubt if I can get one this year. This house is going to take all my money."

"I suppose so, but it would be nice."

They worked until dark and with the rest of the quarter acre spaded; they left it ready for the women to plant the next day.

***

"When you're feeling better, we'll take the children and visit the Ogden's," Julianna said, dropping another potato in the row.

It was a sunny spring day and Albert and Emma were asleep in their cribs on the porch. Tracy and Mary played nearby. Their instructions were two fold; "Do not wake the babies and if they do awaken you must come and tell us immediately."

117

"I'm feeling better every day," Katherine said. "Alex said the Ogden's don't live too far away, maybe a half mile at most. It would be a pleasant walk for us."

"We've been cooped up far too long. The walls are beginning to scream at me." Julianna loved the outdoors. She closed her eyes for a moment and put her face toward the sun, letting the rays warm and relax her. "We should be able to put up enough food to last clear through next winter. This is a huge garden, much better than I'd have hoped for."

The women were ready for spring and happy they'd survived their first winter on the hill. And what a winter it had been: almost as bad as the winter before when the railroad had paid men $1.50 a day to shovel the trains out of the drifts in the gorge.

The winter of '86 held the two families snowbound for several weeks. By the time of the thaw, they were close to being out of food. The men went out and shot a couple of gray digger squirrels and several rabbits, which immediately went into the stew. As soon as the trails were passable the men hiked to Hurlburt and bought vegetables from Tom.

"It's a good thing we're such good friends or we'd never had made it in those close quarters," Julianna said as she carefully moved down the potato rows, covering them both ways with dirt.

"Yes it is." Katherine sighed and said, "I'll miss you and the girls when you move. I'm glad you won't be far over the rise."

"Me too," Julianna said. "At least we can visit often." She stood up and took a deep breath, inhaling the moist fresh smell of the overturned soil. Putting her hand on her abdomen, she said, "I just felt the baby move."

"That's a good sign," Katherine said, stepping across the rows of beans that she had just put in the ground. "At least you know it's all right."

"Yes, it's the first time I've felt it."

"When are you due?"

"Early September, I think."

"Oh my, just in time for your move," Katherine said, her face masking the concern in her voice.

"We'll just have to wait. We'll be busy canning and harvesting our garden at that time anyway." Julianna felt no angst. She'd been through enough to know that these kinds of things had a way of working themselves out.

***

Once the foundation was in place, their supplies came in a huge wagon drawn by the prettiest team of white Percherons that Julianna had seen in a long time. The work on the Lampert house began in earnest.

By the end of June, the framing was complete. The men spent the next several days nailing up one- inch by eight-inch side boards: one man sawing to size and the other nailing them in place. Julianna brought the children over several days and helped to hold the boards up while Alex nailed them.

"It's nice to have you here," Alex leaning over to pound the first nail, grinned at his wife. "Besides you make my work easier."

She bent over and kissed his ear before he could straighten up.

Tracy was old enough now to watch Emma and Julianna was comfortable as long as she could hear them playing. After the noon meal, she put them down for a nap under a nearby fir tree. Usually they were tired enough so they went to sleep easily. At about four o'clock or so she would take the children and go back to Katherine's to help with supper.

Julianna treasured these days. Having Alex close by, working together, was the dream she'd always cherished. She hoped against hope they had enough supplies to finish the house this summer.

"We'll be out of nails next week and we're almost out of money again. I guess I'll have to go back to Portland and see if I can find work," Alex said one evening as they were getting ready for bed. "I hate to leave you, but if I get a good job, I should be able to make enough money in a month to finish the house." He paused, unbuttoning his shirt. "Well, not finished exactly, but it will be good enough and sound enough to move into."

"Please try to be back by the first of September. I know this baby won't wait until the end of the month." Julianna pressed her hand against the bulk of her pregnancy.

"I will," he promised.

***

Alex spent the next five weeks away, with only two short visits to bring back supplies. He arrived home the last week of August to stay. On his way back up the trail he ordered the roofing for their house from the Ogdens. They delivered it four days later. He and Franz finished putting on the shingles on the eighth of September. Baby Bertha Lampert arrived the next morning.

Katherine helped with the birth, but Julianna had to talk her through the process, at least until the last few pains of the ordeal. Alex and Franz watched the four children, with Franz even changing Albert's diaper. Katherine laughed when she heard that and said it was a first for him.

Later Julianna had nothing but praise for her friend, telling her she performed admirably considering the circumstances.

"It's a good thing birthing comes easy for you because, frankly, I was scared to death," Katherine said.

Bertha was a beautiful, roly-poly baby with the gentle disposition of her father and grandmother who lived somewhere in Liechtenstein.

Two days later, Julianna arose from the birthing bed, sat in the shade, and peeled apples to dry for pie-making in the winter. Bertha slept next to her.

Alex dug a cellar under their house and the next weekend Franz helped him haul several loads of potatoes and carrots up to the new homestead. When that was finished he made a table and benches out of a slab of wood that he and Franz had sliced with the cross-cut saw.

By the end of October, the house was livable, so with the help of the Frommelts, they carried bedding and clothes over the hill. Julianna was thrilled with her cozy little cottage. The evening before the move, Alex had stayed up at the new house with the lantern until after midnight.

"It's late. What have you been doing?" Julianna asked when he accidentally woke her as he crawled into bed.

"You'll see tomorrow," he replied as he put his arms around her. "In the morning."

The next day when she walked into the living room of their brand new home with Bertha in her arms, the first thing she saw was a beautiful vine maple rocking chair with limbs that twisted and bent in a whimsical way, on top of sturdy rockers.

Chapter 24

Fall 1886

"Taylor gave me two of these yesterday." Franz laid a huge salmon on the drain board. "He says he's got all the salmon he can eat so he had to start giving it away."

"Then I'll cook some of it for Thanksgiving dinner," Julianna said. "Alex can smoke the rest of it."

"And here's a couple of ducks he gave me, too." Franz pulled the cleaned, plucked birds out of a sack. "Katherine thought we could have these."

"We'll have both," said Julianna. "After all, Thanksgiving is a feast and we have much to be thankful for."

"Don't we though." Franz chuckled and added, "Katherine said we'd bring a pie." He paused, sampling another of Julianna's fresh cookies. "She said to tell you to plan on coming over to our house for Christmas if the weather isn't too bad."

"We'll certainly do that and tell her thank you."

Franz nodded and turned to leave. "We'll be here about noon tomorrow," he said over his shoulder.

Thanksgiving 1886 was cold and rainy, but no snow. The two families who had lived together the last three years, gathered again around the table. Julianna thought nothing could smell as good as that duck, all roasted and browned, except maybe the smell of Katherine's apple pie in the oven.

"In the name of the Father, the Son and the Holy Ghost." Alex made the Sign of the Cross, said the blessing, taking care to give thanks, and then reached for the platter of duck that he had just carved.

"I met a new neighbor named Elijah Chamberlain last month. He bought a place just east of yours, Alex, down on the bench above the river," Franz said. "He was down at Taylor's looking for work on the seining grounds at Rooster Rock. He told me he has a family and knows his wife would like some company."

"That's wonderful news," Julianna said, filled with excitement. "I hope she's as nice as Alice Ogden."

"Maybe you and I could walk down that way tomorrow if the weather doesn't turn. We could get acquainted and see where they live. Then we can take the families down when the weather gets better," Alex said to Franz.

"That would be such fun," Katherine agreed and as an after thought asked, "What is seining?"

"We saw them doing it up at Latourell during the spring salmon run in April when we were getting our lumber," Alex explained. "It is a process where they fish off the beaches using big nets. They use row boats to pull them out into the river. When they get ready to haul them in full of salmon, they have to use horses or mules to pull them back on the beach because they're so heavy."

"What do they do with the fish after they catch them?"

"Remember, we saw that cannery at Rooster Rock when we came by on the train?" Alex said. "The salmon are processed there."

"I think I was trying to get Tracy to sleep about that time. You had to wake us both up when the train stopped at Taylor's."

"They're processed right away and the canned salmon is shipped out by rail."

"If the salmon tastes as good canned as it does fresh, there must be a huge market for it," Katherine said, reaching for another filet.

The day ended far too soon. Before dusk the Frommelts reluctantly left for home with their tired children.

"Do we have enough money so that you don't have to go to Portland for work until spring?" Julianna asked after the children were fed and put to bed. These were the times she most enjoyed. She had Alex all to herself in the quiet of their home. The fire in the little wood stove crackled with warmth.

"I think so. I'd like to spend the winter making more furniture. I certainly won't be leaving in the next couple of months."

"Good, I love having you home."

"We have enough food to tide us over. If we run short, I can always go down to Taylor's and pick up some more salmon."

The next day, Franz and Alex walked to Taylor's and asked directions to the Chamberlain cabin. They followed the trail up the hill to the first bench and turned east onto a tiny side path. Soon they came to a house set in a grove of firs. Two small children were playing outside, bundled up against the chilly wind.

A tall slim man came from around back and greeted them with an outstretched hand.

"Hello strangers. My name is Lige Chamberlain and these are my children, Bert and Nettie." Then he recognized Franz, "Frommelt, I believe."

"Yes, Franz. This is my friend Alex Lampert. We live up on the hill, not too far from here." He motioned in the direction of their homes. "Our wives sent us down here today to meet the neighbors."

"Come in, come in. I'll introduce you to the missus." Lige opened the cabin door and waved them inside. "Sarah, here are some folks that came down to meet you."

Wiping her hands on a dish towel, a young woman with a warm smile came to greet them. "So nice to meet you both," she said after they repeated their names to her. "I certainly hope you have families. It gets lonesome here, and I do miss the womenfolks."

As they sat sipping a warm cup of coffee, they chatted about the country and the river. "I fell in love with this area the first time Lige brought me out here," Sarah said. "We moved to Latourell first. We didn't know where else to go. The Latourells told us about a piece of ground with a cabin on it for rent down at Hurlburt so we stayed there until we found this place. This is God's country, that's what I tell Lige."

"Katherine and Julianna say that, too," Franz said as he finished his last swallow and put his cup down. "We'll bring the families down as soon as the weather gets warmer."

"I'm eager to visit with them. Maybe Lige and I can get to your houses sometime this winter. As soon as the fish stop running and he has some time, we'll try to visit. When he's down on the seining grounds, I don't see him much."

"We'd like that. I know the children would be delighted to have new playmates," Alex said as he went out the door amid good-byes.

"They are nice people. I am a little worried because our wives speak so little English," Franz remarked on the way home.

"You know our girls, they'll make themselves understood somehow," Alex laughed and shook his head. "I'm not going to worry about it. If worse comes to worst, Tracy and Mary can interpret and they would love it."

The two oldest children of the families both spoke passable English. Tracy, almost five, could talk to Alex in English, and to her mother in German, without pausing to take a breath.

Chapter 25

Summer 1887

Alex stayed home most of that summer, clearing another acre and tending the small potato field and kitchen garden. The spring had started off cool, but by mid-July the weather was warm and the potatoes grew lush, a few in bloom here and there.

"I think the children and I will visit Katherine today," Julianna announced one morning.

"Why not? It's a beautiful day and I know you've been missing her." Alex leaned against the back doorjamb, sipping a cup of coffee before heading out to work. The cool air smelled of fir boughs and moist luxuriant grasses. Julianna drank in the aroma, enjoying it as much as Alex seemed to savor his coffee. "I'm going to cut down a couple of these alders close to the house anyway. I'd just as soon not have the children nearby."

After breakfast Julianna and the children started out down the path towards Katherine's. The first third of the way had been burned out and was brushy, with few trees. The path, now well worn, wove around the small hill, into a wooded ravine, and then wound its way up another forested hill and finally down to the Frommelts' back yard.

Julianna carried Bertha and a small packsack. Tracy and Emma followed behind, stopping often to smell a flower or watch a June bug scamper over a moss covered stump. Mostly, Julianna thought, they just wanted to rest their short legs. Julianna wished she had a pack board for the baby. It would be so much easier, she thought, shifting Bertha onto her left shoulder. I'm going to talk to Alex about it.

"Come children," she urged them on. "Mary and Albert are waiting to play with you."

As they walked down the trail and rounded a curve, there in the morning shade, blocking the way, was a large dog. Teeth bared: a trickle of foam etching its way down the side of its mouth and dripping off its chin. A low growl rumbled from deep inside the beast.

Julianna sucked in her breath and stopped short. Heart racing, she searched for anything that would protect them.

"Tracy, take Emma and get behind me," she commanded her voice low and firm.

"Mama, is that a bad dog?"

"It's a sick dog, maybe part wolf." Julianna trembled and clutched Bertha closer. "Hush now, don't talk."

At last she noticed a heavy limb lying near the edge of the trail, several paces closer to the beast. Do I want to get closer? She took a small step forward, but stopped as the dog, head down, took a step towards them and staggered. His growl grew more menacing.

She stepped back. The noise subsided, so she took another backward step.

"Girls, slowly move back down the trail." Her heart felt like it was going to come through her head. "Slowly now." She forced herself to remain calm. Two more steps back. "Good, that's the way," she urged.

The dog took another step. Julianna hesitated and made the bold decision to stare it down.

"Stand still, girls. Wait for Mama to tell you when to move."

She held her breath, knowing a single bite would be certain death. She'd seen a neighbor child in Baden die from the bite of a rabid bat, a horrible screaming death.

She waited for what seemed like an eternity, eye to blood-shot eye with the creature. Then ever so slowly she took another step backward, still facing the feral animal.

"Children, quietly and slowly walk to the bend in the trail. As soon as you are out of sight, turn and run as fast as you can and get Papa," she commanded quietly.

"Yes, Mama. We will," she heard Tracy murmur.

She listened to the tiny footsteps as she watched the animal. The foam from its mouth grew thicker, dripping into large frothy puddles. It shook its huge head, spewing the spittle from side to side, its eyes glazed.

Holding Bertha tightly, again she stepped backward. She heard the children's footsteps pick up speed as they raced down the trail. Thank God they're safe.

The sound of running feet seemed to awaken and enrage the beast. Showing his teeth and snarling, he lunged. Julianna turned to run, but stubbed her toe and nearly fell.

The baby shrieked further infuriating the maddened animal. Miraculously she kept her grip on the child, and regained her balance. She began to run. As if sensing the danger, Bertha stopped fussing. Rounding the bend, she saw the children had disappeared from the path. Good maybe they can get to Alex in time! She dropped her pack and ran faster, the baby bouncing against her hip.

Behind her, she could hear low gurgles and turned to see the animal spewing larger amounts of vomit. She kept on and looking back again she noticed the dog was slowing, staggering as if under a giant weight. Out of breath, panting, she slowed and leaned against a large fir tree, out of sight of the animal.

Holding her breath she listened, straining for any sound. Time ticked by, her heart thumping loudly in her ears. Bertha began to fuss again. "No, dear, no," she quietly murmured. "Not now." Julianna rocked her gently and stepped back onto a dry twig. The snap reverberated and echoed.

Quietly she waited; a low whine came from a few feet away, alerting her to the peril. She held her breath and slowly allowed herself to peer from behind the tree. The animal lay partly on the path, his large contorted head in a watery pool, facing her. Quickly she pulled back and once again waited, rocking the baby. Her heart pounding she kept her eyes up the trail, watching for Alex. Praying he would come soon.

The stillness of the forest enveloped her, interrupted only by snorting sounds emitted by the animal in short staccato vibrations. If her luck held, he might be too sick to give chase. Her breathing came easier, but she couldn't take a chance. Not with Bertha. If she were alone, that would be different; she would run for home.

Holding fast to her baby, she watched and waited. Minutes passed.

After a lifetime, Alex appeared running down the trail towards her, axe in hand.

Chapter 26

Late Spring 1888

"I guess my poor baby is stuck with the name, Berty. Emma can't say Bertha," Julianna said with a chuckle. "I shouldn't complain, I can't get Alex to call Teresa anything but Tracy. We'll just have to be a family of nicknames."

"I'm hoping we can keep Albert's name intact. I've always liked the name," Katherine said as she wiped her small son's face. Then added, "I can't keep him clean. He's happiest when he's a mud ball."

They laughed with the familiarity that comes from close sharing of time and problems. Seated on a log in front of the Lampert home, they were enjoying the spring sunshine while watching their five children frolic in the sunshine. Julianna cherished her friend and loved it when she brought Mary and Albert over the hill and down the trail to play.

"I'm glad you had a chance to visit. I miss you. We don't get to spend near enough time together these days." Julianna absently brushed Bertha's hair back from her forehead. "I guess we were spoiled when we all lived together in that little flat in Portland."

"I'm sure of it," Katherine agreed. "Remember when we had our garden together when we first moved here? That was so much fun. I wish we could still at least do that."

"I wish we could, too, but I'm already starting to show. By harvest time, I'll be so big I'm sure it will be impossible to even get myself and three *kinder* over to your place, let alone work in the garden," Julianna said. "Alex'll be home this weekend. He promised to spade up some more garden space for us here."

"Yes, Franz told me. I think he is planning on coming over to help. He misses Alex. They're so like brothers and with Alex working in Portland, they rarely see each other these days." Katherine spoke with a wistfulness that Julianna understood.

"Why don't you bring the family and come too?" Julianna said, "It'll be like old times."

"That'd be fun. I'll fry up a pullet and bring it."

"I love your fried chicken. I just can't fix mine as well as you do," Julianna said, happy at the thought of a weekend visit. Katherine and Franz were their family now.

"Not true," said Katherine. "Yours is every bit as good as mine. Mama always said her cooking just didn't taste as good to her either, but I thought it was wonderful."

Julianna paused for a moment, thinking of her own mother. I wonder how she is.

"Do you miss your *Mutter*?" she asked.

Katherine nodded, but said nothing.

"I miss mine terribly," Julianna continued, feeling a sudden stab of sadness. "I doubt I will ever see her again. When I left Baden, I was young and so in love with Alex, I'd have followed him anywhere. Now I realize my parents are an ocean away."

"I know. All I could think of was getting away from Triesenberg. There was nothing for Franz to do when his older brother inherited the farm. There was certainly not much need for brick masons. All I heard from him was, America this and America that. I couldn't wait. Now, I know I probably won't see my family again either. I am trying to get my brother, Joseph, to come over. Franz said he'd sell him the twenty acres west of the house." Katherine gathered Albert, who was beginning to fuss, onto her lap as she spoke.

"It'd be wonderful to have a family member come over. The worst thing for me is that my mother will not get to meet her grandchildren," Julianna said watching the children. "I try to describe them in my letters, but I can't seem to do them justice. Alex said that we can take the train to Portland one day and go to a photographer and get their picture made. I do so want *Mutter* and *Papa* to see their grandbabies."

"What a wonderful idea. Maybe I will go with you and have a picture made for my family. I bet that would help Joseph make up his mind." Katherine smiled at the idea. "Does Alex know about the new baby?" she asked as Albert slid off her lap, happy to be free from his mother's snuggles.

"I'll tell him this weekend. He wants a son, so he'll be happy, though, I told him it may not happen. It looks like we are well on our way to becoming a family of daughters," Julianna said with resolve.

"Mama, Mama," Mary called. "Albert is eating dirt again."

Katherine rose and picked up her small son, wiping his face with her apron. She laughed and said, "See why I wear this even when I'm not cooking?"

They chatted for a few more minutes, and then Katherine left so the younger children could have naps.

***

Alex and Franz dug a space for a large garden. When they were done spading, they smoothed the ground and Julianna helped them plant. Katherine was busy with the children and had taken over the kitchen duties.

"This is virgin soil. Everything should grow well," Alex said as he seeded the second row of corn. "But we'll have to watch for crows now."

"Yes, I'll send Tracy and Emma out with the broom to scare them away," Julianna said and she carefully covered the beet seed and patted it in.

"That broom is as big as those girls," Franz said with a laugh. "If I were a crow, I'd be afraid." They shared a chuckle at the thought.

Later in the evening, when the Frommelts had left and the children were in bed. Julianna brought Alex a glass of his homemade apple wine. "Here darling, you might need this. I have something to tell you."

Alex's brow furrowed as he accepted the glass. "This is nice, but what's on your mind? Are you all right?"

"Oh, I'm fine. I just wanted to tell you that we are about to have a new member of the family."

"A baby!" Alex looked happy

"Yes, sometime in September if my calculations are right." She bit her lip. "I'll need help with the harvest and the canning, I'm afraid," Julianna felt bad, but he didn't seem to mind.

"Have you told the girls yet?"

"No, dear, the wait is too long. When the time gets closer. Remember how time works? Four months to a small child is like a year to us," Julianna said as she took his hand. "Darling, maybe this will be the son you have always wanted."

Alex smiled back at her and said, "I'd like a son, but I wouldn't trade any of my daughters. They're my most precious possessions."

On Monday, Alex left for his job in Portland. As he walked out the door he said, "I'll stay in town for a couple of weeks. I want to get as much work as possible so I can be home with you this fall when the baby comes."

"Please do, my dear," she said as she held him, but she knew he'd be gone most of the summer. As soon as he left, loneliness crept in to envelope and consume her.

Alex came home once in June to bring supplies and more seed potatoes. They planted another four long rows, knowing this late planting was a staple that could see them through any bad weather that might happen during the winter months.

His next trip home was early July with more supplies. The money in the jar in the cupboard grew so much that Alex took half of it, put it in a tin can and buried it in the basement.

"That's our stash," he said. "Now all I have to do is remember where I buried it!" He laughed and the dimple in his cheek stood out, the one that Julianna loved.

"It is good to have you home," she said as she kissed him.

"A little over a month and I'll be here for harvest and our new little one." He held her tight.

But Alex hadn't been gone a week when Julianna began to notice things about this pregnancy that were different. For one thing, she had more swelling in her feet than before and lately she had pangs of high abdominal cramping. She ignored them in the beginning, but as time went by, they became so intense she would have to sit and rest.

The days were warm, and Julianna prayed the weather wouldn't get any hotter because she feared it would make her swelling worse. I've no ambition, she thought to herself as she watched the dirty diapers pile high. I

129

have to get them washed before Alex comes home. I don't want him to do my laundry.

"Gather the dirty clothes, Tracy, and I'll get the water ready." They had just finished breakfast and she was determined to get the job done.

Julianna and Emma went to the spring and carried back two buckets, not quite full. Emma helped her mother, holding on to one of the bails as they made their way towards the house.

Julianna placed the boiler tub on the kitchen table and built a fire in the stove, dreading the combination of the hot stove and July sunshine. She poured one bucket in the tub and placed the other one on the stove to heat. As she picked up the bucket of boiling water, a sharp pain doubled her over in agony. The water spilled, just missing her and the children, but covering the floor in a wave of boiling fury. She managed to get to the bench before dizziness swept her almost unconscious.

"Mama, Mama, are you hurt, Mama?" Tracy ran to her, throwing her arms around her neck.

Unable to talk, she held on to her five-year old until the pain subsided and she caught her breath. "Help me to bed, Tracy. I need to lie down a few minutes." The other children followed as they slowly made their way to the bedroom.

"Mama's better now, children," Julianna said. But the pain persisted, not as intense, but it was there. She felt for the baby's sake, she must stay lying down until it was gone.

Julianna knew she could count on Tracy to watch the others. At noon, Julianna instructed her to feed them each a piece of bread and cheese. Bertie fussed and lay down for a nap beside her mother. The other two children played close by.

Julianna tried to get up to help them with supper, but when she stood for any length of time the pain drove her back to bed. The children ate some more bread and cheese and came to bed at dark, all of them curled up around their mother.

Julianna lay in bed, trying to sleep. She and the children were isolated. Did she dare send Tracy to find her way to Katherine's? She was only five. It was more than a half a mile, some of it in old growth forest. There were a couple of places on the trail where she could take wrong turns and perhaps get lost. I can't let her go. I just hope with rest this goes away. But she was a midwife herself and she knew this pregnancy was in trouble. She could not only lose the baby, but she herself could be in danger. What would happen to her children if she died?

She tried to put it out of her mind and finally sleep came, but it was in bits and pieces, fitful and full of dreams, with babies crying and old women shaking their fingers at her. "Stay in bed!" they said, as they danced around her and the children. She awoke to Berty's fussing and she turned to hold her precious eighteen-month old.

In the darkness, fear gnawed deep in her heart. It would be at least a week before Alex returned and if he'd happened on a good job, he might stay in Portland even longer.

Another moment of panic seized her as she realized how much trouble they were in. This pregnancy could terminate at any time. She'd seen women go through things like this. One of them lost her baby and almost bled to death. They had to pack her in towels for hours until they got the bleeding stopped. It was months until the poor thing was back on her feet. My best chance is to stay off my feet completely, but how can I do that with three small children? Julianna whispered prayers, but a hint of daylight crept in the window before she fell asleep again.

Two more days passed. At least I think it's been two days, she thought. She heard the goat crying outside. Her bleating was getting louder, more desperate. Tracy is too young to try to milk Nanny. She couldn't even catch her. Alex! Please hurry home.

"Girls, come to Mama," she cried as she pushed herself up on one elbow.

"What Mama?" Emma pushed in to catch Julianna's hand as she reached out.

"Darlings, how much bread is left? Is there enough for supper?"

"No, Mama."

Julianna winced in pain as she bent to pat her middle daughter's cheek. "You and Tracy go to the garden and pick out some nice beets and carrots. Dig a hill of potatoes, too. Bring them in. Go, don't tarry," she commanded.

Nanny cried in rhythm, now. It seemed with every other breath Julianna took, she heard the goat. I can't let the poor beast wait any longer, besides the children need milk. She slowly pushed herself up to a sitting position. That's not too bad. I can do this, she thought, as she grabbed her dressing gown and pulled it tightly around her.

She stood up bracing herself on the bed post and with determination slowly walked toward the door. Berty played quietly on the floor with a rag dolly.

She made her way along the wall, the pain now dull, seeming to fade almost away, but she was surprised at how weak she was. At the back door, she grabbed the short rope hanging on the wall and the milk bucket, scrubbed and turned upside down on the bench. At the end of the porch, she reached over to pick up a good sized limb to use as a walking stick. She stumbled, but didn't fall.

Nanny saw her coming and bleated a greeting. Julianna threw the rope around the goat's neck and snubbed the animal's nose close to a nearby tree. Now she could lean against the tree and milk into the bucket. Nanny seemed to sense Julianna's dilemma and cooperated, unlike her usual cantankerous self.

As the bucket began to fill, Julianna's pain increased in intensity. She tried to ignore it, but soon it became too unbearable to continue. She grabbed the bucket with one hand to try to save the contents as she doubled over.

"Tracy, Tracy come quickly!" Her head spinning, she leaned against the tree almost on her knees. "Tracy! Quickly!"

The girls dropped the vegetables they were carrying and raced to their mother's side.

"Emma, take this bucket. Don't spill it!" The milk safe; she slid down the tree and onto the ground, beads of sweat on her forehead. It took all her strength not to cry out.

Tracy held on to her mother's arm, terror on her face. "Mama, Mama,' she said over and over again.

After resting for what seemed like many minutes, Julianna reached up and undid the rope that tied the goat.

"Now, dear, you must help me crawl to the house. We'll go slowly, but I need to get back to bed," she said as she started the slow process of working her way to the porch, stopping often to rest and rub her abdomen as if to dismiss the cramping that seemed to come and go in rhythmic fashion.

They reached the steps before Julianna blacked out. She regained consciousness just long enough to get into the living room where she fainted the second time. When she awoke, it was dark and she was covered with perspiration, the pain almost unbearable.

"Bring Mama a blanket" was all she could say before losing consciousness.

Sometime later, in the dim recesses of her mind, she thought she heard Tracy say, "Mama, there are some people coming down the path," but her mind drifted off, a dream maybe.

She managed somehow to get back into bed during the night. When she awoke for a moment in the dawn light, the children were huddled around her. She heard Bertie cry, a low frightened sob.

"Tracy, get some milk for the children and give them a carrot to eat." My God, am I going to die here and leave my children? What will they do? Alex! She tried to sit up and fainted. She thought she heard adult voices, but knew she was dreaming. Sometimes she thought she tasted a harsh warm substance and tried to spit it out. Once she thought she heard someone tell her to drink. She didn't have the strength to fight, so she swallowed feeling the bitterness in her throat. Then she slept.

When she awoke, she saw a lovely young native woman, in a buckskin dress with beads sewn in neat patterns around the sleeves and collar. Am I dreaming, Julianna thought. Who could this be? Where am I? Surprised she realized the sharp pains were almost gone.

"How do you feel?" the woman asked.

Julianna could only look at her, too weak to answer.

The young woman smiled and said, "Don't worry, your children are fine. They are with my father in the garden." She placed her hand on Julianna's forehead and nodded. "The tea worked well. You must drink it many times during the next days."

"My baby?" Julianna managed the question.

"Your baby is alive. It will come in its own time."

"Thank you," Julianna murmured and fell asleep.

When she awoke, the children were at her bedside. "Mama better?" Emma asked.

"Yes, dear. Where is that lovely young lady? Is she real?"

"I'm real," the woman said as she stepped into the bedroom.

"Who are you?" Julianna asked, rubbing her forehead weakly.

"They call me Ho'mow'mae. You call me Mae." She patted Julianna's arm. "It is lucky we found you. My father and I are on our way to the falls on the Willamette for a festival to meet my husband-to-be." She spoke in almost perfect English, but Julianna had trouble with the translation and struggled to understand the new language.

"We came from Celilo and walked the trail. We followed your path to see if you would sell us vegetables," Mae continued.

"How long?" Julianna attempted to rephrase Mae's English into her familiar German.

"We have been here three days," Mae said.

"Thank you." Julianna smiled weakly. "You saved my life. I was frightened for my children. I couldn't take care of them."

"They are brave girls. Father says they work hard."

Julianna nodded, thinking but they are too small to have the kind of responsibility they have had to endure. After a pause, she continued, "When is the festival?"

"Soon! We must leave."

"My neighbor, Katherine Frommelt, lives less then a mile down the path. If you could fetch her, she'll stay with me until my husband gets home."

"I'll ask my father to go. He'll bring her. In the meantime, I will stay here and help you."

"Where did you get the tea?" Julianna asked, remembering the bitter taste.

"In the forest, there are many roots and leaves that are medicinal. One is the plant you call the burning nettle. There is much around here and it is very valuable for your health," Mae said, straightening the bed. "I gathered the plants while my father fed the children. Then I made a strong tea and let it steep many hours, giving you sips often. There is much left and you will need it."

"What if I run out?" Julianna worried, remembering the terror she felt.

"You can't, I have gathered many plants. They are in a basket by the door. I will tell Katherine how to mix them before I leave."

"Julianna, I'm so sorry," Katherine exclaimed, out of breath, her hair uncombed and tears glistening on her cheeks. "I had no idea. What would I do without you? You could've died!"

"Mae and her father saved us. Thank God they found me. I tried to milk Nanny and fainted," the words came weakly.

Katherine clasp Julianna's hand in both of hers and said, "Thank God for Mae."

Julianna managed a weak smile. "She certainly was an answer to my prayers."

Mae and her father left that morning, after giving Katherine careful instructions on the art of tea brewing. Franz brought Mary and Albert over later in the day and the family moved in.

The following week, Alex came home, contrite that he'd stayed away longer then he had planned and devastated when he discovered that he'd almost lost his wife and baby.

"*Mein Gott*," he cried as he cradled Julianna in his arms, and rocked her back and forth. "Katherine, please stay until the baby is born. Julianna will need your help," he begged.

"I plan on it. But I wonder if we should get a doctor up here." Katherine sounded worried.

"I can go get Dr. Volp from Troutdale, if we need him," Alex said.

"I doubt I'll need a doctor. I'm much better and I have Mae's tea. Katherine and I can take care of things here, but I'm afraid I won't be any help for harvest,"

Julianna spent the next days resting and waiting. In the afternoons, Katherine moved her outdoors, to get "some fresh air" and to sip on her tea. The children played nearby, reluctant to let their mother out of sight.

September came bringing a few rainy days that chilled the air. The men finished the harvest at both the homesteads and busied themselves putting produce in the basements for safe keeping.

Julianna tried to walk a bit farther each day, to build up strength for the birth, but remnants of the pain continued to appear and she would have to sit. Still, with Katherine and Alex's good care, she felt she was making progress. Every day seemed to drag. There was no comfortable position and she knew her time was near. She worried the delivery might be difficult. She wasn't as brave as she let on, for she knew the possible outcome.

Then one day, her labor started in earnest. Surprising everyone after the long and complicated pregnancy, the birth was easier then anyone expected. Just four hours after her water broke, Julianna's first son, Ferdinand, named for her grandfather, was born. He was a beautiful, blond-haired child, with a tiny mouth and perfect fingers and toes.

Exhausted, Julianna slept most of the next few days, waking only to feed the baby. Katherine and her family went home, with a promise she would return to check on her often.

Alex, delighted with his new son, stayed home for the rest of the fall and the whole winter, dividing his time between clearing land, cutting and splitting firewood, and tending to his family.

Chapter 27

Late spring 1889

"What a glorious sunny day," Katherine exclaimed as they settled in their seats. The west-bound train had stopped for them at Taylor's Landing. "It seemed like a longer walk than usual this morning." She fanned herself as she settled back in the seat.

"Maybe it's because the last time we did this we didn't have seven children between us and I wasn't about to have my fifth baby," Julianna replied with a droll expression.

"That could make the difference," Katherine agreed.

"I'm certainly glad that Franz and Alex will come home with us. I don't think I could carry the baby back up that hill," Julianna sighed.

She still had days where she felt her strength leave her. Ever since last summer, when she almost died during her last pregnancy, she hadn't been strong. Katherine had come to check on her after Ferd's birth, at least once a week, until her own pregnancy became too burdensome.

By that time, Julianna was able to take her children and spend the last two weeks of March with the Frommelts helping Katherine, until she gave birth to her third baby, Aloysius. After that, Katherine was too busy with three youngsters to leave home and so the two friends hadn't seen each other for almost three months.

Just two weeks before, Mae, her new husband and her father had stopped to see how Julianna was doing. Mae had taken her up the hill behind the house into the woods and showed her which plants to use for the tea that would strengthen her. Julianna loved the taste of one of the herbs, a fern root that reminded her of the licorice candy her father used to give her when she was a child. Mae taught her how to harvest the burning nettle without getting hives.

"I don't think I could have traveled today without Mae's tea," Julianna said.

"She is a blessing and so clever."

"Yes and she promised to come again next summer. I hope I won't need her for this baby. I don't mind telling you, I'm a little afraid. I was so scared and sick last year. I can't believe I am with child again so soon. So much for breastfeeding protecting you."

"My mother told me it didn't work and she was right," Katherine agreed. "She said it was a woman's duty to have children for her husband. We're certainly doing our duty."

"*Yah,* we are. I thank God our children are well-behaved. I would never attempt such this trip to Portland if they were naughty. We'd just have to wait to have a priest come out to our homes to baptize our babies." Julianna glanced back at the children, who were looking out of the window, pointing at the farms and ranches racing by and chattering. She caught Tracy's eye and smiled, proud that her six-year old first-born was so grown-up for her age.

When the train stopped in Portland, they caught a horse-drawn streetcar from the Albina railroad terminus and crossed the Willamette River on the new Morrison Street Bridge.

"My goodness, look at Portland. It's changed in two years," Katherine said, gazing at the scene that unfolded from the height of the new bridge.

"It's no surprise Alex and Franz are busy. I wonder where they're working now."

"Franz told me he had a job shoring up a wall in a basement of one of the buildings downtown. He said it's damp and cold and he doesn't like it. Besides he'd heard about bad things happening down there."

A shiver run up Julianna's back. "I don't like the sound of that. You know where Franz is, Alex isn't far behind."

Katherine laughed, "Yes, just like two little boys."

The streetcar let them off on SW Tenth and Morrison where workmen were building a new train depot. The women gathered their children, picked up the satchels, hiked their skirts and began their walk to NW Twelfth and Couch where Sophie was waiting with open arms. Her young son peeked out from behind his mother's skirt.

"What a darling little boy, Sophie," Julianna praised as they walked in the door. "Your letter was right; he is the image of his father." She smiled and patted the toddler.

"Yes, he is," Sophie said and glowed. "And look at your sweet babies. Here lay them on the sofa. What darlings they are."

"Sophie, I swear you haven't changed a bit," Julianna laughed. "It is so very good to see you again."

"It's been ages," Katherine put down her satchel. "It seemed like more than a two mile-walk down the hill to the train. I'm sure the babies have gone through three or four diapers apiece.

"It's amazing, isn't it? I mean it's always worse at the most inopportune moments," Sophie agreed. Pausing she said, "Where are my manners? You must be exhausted. Let me show you where you folks will sleep and then we'll have a bite to eat."

After the children had eaten and were put down for a nap, the women chatted over coffee until a knock on the door interrupted the visiting. Alex and Franz stood on the stoop.

"I hear tell there are a couple of missing wives in here. Is that true?" Alex said with a grin.

"I heard they were runaways from out east of town," Franz continued.

"No," Katherine said. "If we would've run, we'd have been half way to Freeport by now."

"*Nein stipendiaten*, we aren't letting you off the hook that easy," Julianna laughed and patted her husband's wispy hair.

Alex held her close for a moment then asked, "Where are the children?"

"They're upstairs napping. I suppose you boys can wake them, but at your own peril."

***

At Mass the next day, Julianna realized how much she missed going to church and being surrounded by people speaking her mother tongue. After Mass, Ferd and Aloysius were baptized.

When the ceremony was over, the families went to the Boecks for a huge Sunday dinner. It had been months since they had enjoyed such a delicious meal. Mrs. Boeck, her usual cordial self, continued to encourage everyone to take another helping and they all ate far more than they should.

"Where are you fellows working?" Mr. Boeck asked over an ample slice of apple pie.

"I just finished a remodeling job on a warehouse on Fourth and Alder," Alex said, between mouthfuls. "Franz has been hired to do stone work on a basement under a building on Third and Couch. He says there's work for two, so I think I'll join him. I've been doing carpentry for a long time. I think it'll be interesting to do something different, and the money is good."

Mr. Beck looked perplexed. "You boys be careful down there. I've heard rumors that bad things happen in that area."

"Bad things. What bad things?" Julianna asked as she wiped Berty's face and stood her on the floor by her chair.

"Rumor has it there are a lot of opium dens and that men disappear at night around there. Some call it shanghaiing."

"Well, we're safe then because we won't be anywhere near there after dark." Franz said scraping his plate.

"I'm not sure I want our men working there," Katherine said.

"You girls worry too much. We'll be just fine. No one would dare mess with Alex and me. We're too tough!" Franz laughed and winked at Alex.

His friend nodded in agreement. "You know how big Franz's mason hammer is. No one would have the courage to attack us."

But Julianna didn't like it. She couldn't put her finger on it, but uneasiness enveloped her.

That evening she asked Alex about it again. He tried to reassure her. "Besides, dear, they're going to pay us $1.50 a day. That's a lot of money."

The next day the men went to work and the women, accompanied by Sophie, took the children down to Gifford's photography shop and had pictures taken. Julianna planned to send copies home to her and Alex's families in the old country.

Chapter 28

Summer 1889

"Now that we have the families safely home, we can get on with the basement job." Franz was looking out the train window watching the Sandy River Railroad Bridge disappear as the train sped towards Portland. The men had escorted their family's home last Friday and it seemed to Alex that Monday had arrived far too soon.

"We should make pretty good money in that tunnel," Alex said, placing his hat on the seat beside him. "We'd better because Julianna's not happy about us working down there. She tried to tell me it will be bad for my health, but I think Boeck just scared her."

"She'll forgive you when you bring her those pretty pictures of her and the children," Franz chuckled.

"I hope so. She's pretty upset."

The train arrived in downtown Portland just before 8 o'clock in the morning. They didn't get up to the Lasso Saloon until close to 8:30.

"We've been waitin' for you."

Alex looked up to see a large man with a scraggly beard and beady eyes looking at them. "You boys are the ones gonna work down in the basement?" His voice growled and his shaggy beard couldn't hide his snarl.

A shiver raced down Alex's back.

"Yes, we are. I'm Franz and this is my friend, Alex. Who might you be?" Franz asked in his best English.

"I'm Jacob and that's Earl. We just got in from Pendleton. Who's the boss here?" he growled.

"I'm surprised he isn't here yet. Mr. Marsden is the guy who hired us," Franz responded.

"That'd be me." They heard a booming voice behind them. Alex turned and looked into the coldest blue eyes he'd ever seen. They belonged to a middle-aged fellow wearing an expensive black suit, two rings on each hand, and a smile that didn't project, but plunged to the ground. He was clean-shaven, his hair slicked back in perfect place. Alex resisted an urge to take a step back and held his ground.

"You boys ready to go?" Marsden asked. They nodded.

"Follow me, then," he said as he entered the saloon. He passed the front of the bar to a door at the back of the room. They started down the stairs and into the darkest, most fetid place Alex had ever been. The damp, slick walls smelled of mold and the odor of rank critters that grow in the depths of the earth wafted up from the dank floor. Water dripped in the darkness.

Good thing this pays well, Alex thought and coughed, as he grabbed the pine torch Marsden handed him. He held back another cough and continued down the steps.

When they reached the bottom, Marsden began lighting the kerosene lamps which stood on ledges along both sides of the opening. As the room lit up, Alex saw a large open area where wine casks lined the wall.

There was a bricked in tunnel behind him. It looked to be about four and a half feet tall. I'd have to bend over to get through that. I wonder where it leads. Alex fought to shake off his doubts.

"This is where you'll start." Marsden was at the opposite end of the room. He pointed to another wider tunnel, with a higher entrance.

"I need you fellas to use rocks to line the walls and ceiling. It goes over to the next building's basement. We like to stay connected," he said with a chuckle that made the hair on the back of Alex's neck stand straight up. "We don't want the thing cavin' in on us now, do we?" he continued.

Alex shivered and glanced at Franz, who didn't seem to react.

"You fellas haul the rocks down here. There's a pile of 'em up in the alley. When you run out, one of you go to Ferguson's down on First Street and order more. They'll deliver," Marsden went on. "I noticed some water farther on down the tunnel. You may need to put in some tile." He turned away and said, "I'm leavin' now. I'll be back this evening to see how things are goin."

After he left, the men examined the opening. "We'll need at least eight-inch tiles to clear out this water," Franz said as he walked the fifteen foot length of the tunnel.

Earl grunted. Jacob growled something indistinguishable.

"Look at the wet spots on this wall. No wonder they're worried about caving in. If we don't take care of these springs, our walls won't hold either," Franz aid as he held the lantern up, examining it closer.

After they finished assessing the job, they went up to the alley and started hauling the material down the stairs.

"Alex, why don't you go to Ferguson's and order some more rock and about twenty 8 X 12 inch tiles," Franz said straightening his back. "We'll get this pile cleared out of the way, then the rest of us will start digging the ditch."

Alex nodded and left. He took a deep breath and drew in the fresh air, hoping to get the musty smell out of his lungs and nostrils. It was several blocks down to the river and he walked rapidly, relieved to be away from the oppression of the dank underground. He was back by noon. The men sat on the ledge outside in the alley and ate the sandwiches they'd brought from home.

"Julianna makes the best sandwiches. I don't know what she puts in them, but they're better than anything I can buy," Alex took another bite.

"I think it's because she's your wife," Franz said. "The reason I know is because I feel the same way about Katherine's lunches." He took a bite and continued, "I hope we can earn a living on the farm some day so we can stay home."

"I do, too. Julianna needs me now that she's expecting another baby. She rarely says anything, but I know she doesn't want me to leave, especially after the terrible time she had last summer. I told her this morning that as soon as this job is over, I'm going home to stay for the winter."

"That's a good idea." Franz shoved the last of the sandwich into his mouth. "In fact, I think I'll ask if we can work longer hours. That way we can get it done sooner."

Alex agreed, forgetting their promise to their wives about not working at night.

The next day the ditch had been dug most of the way, and they started to dig a dry well. Alex figured it should be at least ten feet deep and ten feet across. Franz explained to Earl and Jacob how they would fill it with large rock and cover the top with a six inch layer of smaller gravel.

"If it doesn't completely take care of the problem, we can tile the top out under the wall into the street. But from my experience, I doubt we'll need to do that. I think the dry well will take care of any excess water."

"That ditch under the wall would be difficult to dig," Jacob said. "I hope you're right." He was friendlier now. Maybe they have grown to trust us, Alex thought.

Marsden had come to check on the job at the end of the first day and he had agreed to up their wages to $2.00 a day if they worked 12 hour days.

"I'd like to get this done in a couple of weeks, so work as long as you want. If you get done by the end of the month there's a $10.00 bonus in it for each of you."

Alex and Franz looked at each other.

"We'll work straight through. No going home on weekends for us," Alex said.

Alex worked with Jacob digging the well and laying the tile, while Franz and Earl began building the rock wall that would shore up the tunnel and make it safe to pass through. They worked until they were exhausted and then walked the six blocks to their room at Foellers. As with most evenings, there was a tray of food waiting for them.

"Room and board for $2.00 a week. They're darn good to us," Franz said, busy cutting off a large piece of pork roast. "We've got to do something nice for them."

"We'll bring them some produce. I hear Sophie saying how much she enjoys fresh fruit and vegetables." Alex leaned back and yawned. "I'm ready for bed," he added.

"Fine by me," Franz stretched, echoing Alex's yawn.

They were up before daybreak and back in the tunnel. The dampness pulled at Alex's chest and it wasn't long before he developed a deep hoarse cough.

Franz asked him to bring in the rest of the rock from the street. Alex grabbed several deep breaths of fresh air every time he went up top, which sometimes made him cough, but helped the congestion in his chest.

He had developed an increasingly uneasy feeling down the tunnel, which had nothing to do with his cough. Once he thought he heard a man holler, and another time he was sure he heard voices far away and muffled. I suppose other people would be down here, he told himself, but he couldn't shake the foreboding.

On the way home that evening, he asked Franz if he had heard anything.

"I thought I did, but it was hard to tell. I thought I heard a man call out the other day. You heard it too?" Franz's face contorted with worry.

"Yes and I don't like it. Remember Boeck's warning?"

"I wonder if there might be something to it. For one thing, I don't like Marsden. Something about him is downright unseemly."

"I agree. Let's ask him for the money he owes us now. Let's not wait," Alex said, "It'll be safer under our mattresses. I sure as heck don't want to work this hard and not get paid after it's all done."

The next time Marsden came to inspect the job, the men asked for the week and a half's worth of pay they were owed. Marsden frowned and paused. "All right, I'll bring it by tomorrow evening, but by God, you boys had better finish this project," he said, his voice hard.

"Don't worry; we want that $10.00 bonus. We'll be done in a few days." Franz assured him.

"See you tomorrow," Marsden said as he turned on his heel and walked up the stairs.

Marsden kept his word and brought them their pay. It pleased the other men, but Alex suspected this was the only money they'd see from the job. He mentioned the matter once again even though he was happy for the cash in his pocket.

"We've come this far, we'll see it through," Franz replied in a hopeful voice.

"That's true. We've given our word, but something's not right and we better watch ourselves." Alex said. As an afterthought, he added, "I think we need to explore that tunnel. We've no idea where it goes."

"I've been giving that some thought, too," Franz said.

The next day the dry well was finished, and the tile was laid and covered. "We'll see if it holds the water," Franz said, eyeing the job. "I guess the true test will be with the fall rains."

He stepped back. "If you fellas want, you can quit for the day," he said to Earl and Jacob. "Alex and I'll finish this little area here and call it a day." He pointed to a space where several rocks needed to be cemented in. "I don't want to waste this mortar we've mixed up."

Alex and Franz worked quickly to finish and get home, enjoying the quiet and the satisfaction of nearly being done, when a loud clanging noise broke the stillness.

"What the hell was that?" Franz exclaimed.

"It sounded like someone beating on iron," Alex replied. "I think it came from that way." He pointed to the narrow tunnel by the stairs. "There it is again," he said, responding to another round of muffled staccato vibrations.

"Shall we go exploring?" Franz asked, his eyes wide.

"*Yah*," Alex said, "but not without a weapon."

"I'll take my hammer." Franz lit two pitch torches, handing one to Alex.

"I've got the crowbar. Let's go." Alex grabbed the light, turned, and headed toward the sound. They had to bend to go through the entrance, but within a few yards they could walk upright.

Alex worried about the light from the torches giving them away, but it was pitch black and they'd never find their way without them. They came upon another basement and surmised it was under the laundry next to the saloon. The tunnel turned toward the river and threaded its way parallel to Glisan Street.

They passed a room with the door ajar and saw a Chinese man with a pipe, smoke rising. The strong smell of opium overwhelmed the musty odor of the tunnel.

"Seems like a long way. Maybe we should've gone the other direction," Franz said as they entered yet another basement. Once more they heard the metallic clanging, this time it was accompanied by frantic voices.

"There they are again. We're going in the right direction," Alex said, taking a firmer grip on the crowbar.

"It's really spooky in here." Franz said as he looked into the entrance of one taking off to the right. "It's a downright maze."

"I hope we can find our way back. These torches aren't gonna last forever," Alex brushed away the cobwebs and headed toward the sounds. Stairs going up to a door on the left made him wonder where they were.

"Listen!" Alex said startled. "Do you hear that?"

"*Yah,* guys are talking. Loud! Hey did you hear that? They're calling for help."

"It came from that direction." Alex pointed to the right. "Let's go. Keep the light down low and behind us. We don't know what we'll find."

The voices grew louder. Eventually they heard shrouded conversations.

"Where the hell are we? What the hell is going on?" the voices said, now even louder.

Continuing in the direction of the voices, they came to a large room with a cave-like opening, the front closed in with steel bars. Two disheveled men gazed at them, arms resting against the cross-bars. Two other men behind them looked dazed.

"Who are you?" one asked in a gruff voice. He wore a torn shirt and had not shaved for several days.

"We heard you beating against your cell door," Alex said, surveying the situation. "We're just a couple of workers, shoring up the wall back there."

"Why are you here?" Franz asked.

"We don't know. The last thing I remember, I was in a bar in Northwest Portland and taking a nice long swig of whiskey. That seems to be what most all of the fellows here remember," the other man snorted.

"The trap door at Lasso's Saloon. The one at the end of the bar. I've been looking at that since we started working on the tunnels. These men have been shanghaied!" Alex exclaimed. Stunned he continued, "I guess Boeck wasn't all wrong." He could hardly believe it.

"Shanghaied! My God!" the man with the torn shirt groaned. "You gotta help us get out!" He pulled frantically on the bars.

"I think I can break this lock with my hammer," Franz said as he swung at it. The lock smashed, but didn't open.

He tried again and then once more. "I hope no one hears this," he said as he hit it again. The lock began to bend.

With the next blow, it opened and the door swung free. Four men walked out and two that they hadn't seen before lay unconscious on the floor.

Franz and Alex picked up one of them and the fellow with the torn shirt and his partner picked up the other. The two others grabbed the torches and followed.

"There's stairs in that last room we passed, maybe we can sneak out that way." Alex said between coughs. His chest hurt and he was gasping under the weight of the unconscious man.

"Listen!" Franz hissed. Everyone stopped.

Voices! Veiled but close! "Where the hell are they?" They heard footsteps coming from behind them.

"Hurry!" Franz stepped up the pace.

Alex held in a cough, terrified that he might give away their position.

"I wish I had a gun," one of the prisoners said.

"I got a great hammer and Alex brought a crowbar. If we need to take a stand, we can," Franz said quietly over his shoulder.

"Here's the room with the stairs. I'll run up and try the door!" Alex said. He ascended the stairs and pushed on the door, while Franz held up the now semi-conscious man.

The voices behind them grew closer. The door didn't budge. He pushed harder, pulled down on the lever and put his shoulder against it and shoved once again. It moved ever so slightly. He peeked into a room with harness hanging on the walls and barrels on the floor.

"I think it's a back room of a saddle shop. I don't see anyone. Quick, get up here," he said as he pushed the door open.

The men dragged each other up the steps and looked for places to hide. Alex gently slid the door shut, just as the light from a torch flickered on the walls of the tunnel. Sliding the bolt in place, he beckoned to Franz to help him push a barrel of harness nails on top of the door.

They could hear yells on the other side and pounding. The door shook. A gruff voice said, "You go down this way and check the Saddle Shop, I'll go the other way. Shoot to kill. Marsden is gonna have our hides."

"Quick, out here," Franz said, pointing to an outside door. "It probably goes into the alley. It's our best bet."

One of the unconscious men was beginning to revive. Thank God, I doubt whether we could carry him much further, Alex thought. One man grabbed him and together they staggered out the door into the darkness.

"When we get out into the street we'll separate," the fellow with the torn shirt yelled back over his shoulder. "We'll take Jeb here and head for the hospital. He's been knocked out too long. He needs a doctor. It's safer there anyway."

The other man said he was going to the hotel room, get his belongings and head for the train. "It'll be a long time before I set foot in this town again," he growled.

Alex thought that was a fine idea. "That was too close a call for me. I'm not going back there," he said, gaining his second wind. They doused the torches, and the darkness hid them.

They ran a couple blocks, hid in a doorway and listened. Footsteps and excited voices echoed down the street. Alex stifled a cough. No one came by, and after a few minutes, all they heard was their pounding hearts.

"Let's wait awhile longer. They may be sneaking around," Franz said.

"You never know. Men that crazy will stop at nothing."

It seemed like an eternity. Alex couldn't hold the coughing spasm back. He bent over, hands on his knees and coughed.

"If that doesn't bring them, they aren't around," Franz mused. "Let's get out of here."

Alex recovered enough to walk. They hurried to their apartment, pausing every so often to listen.

"I think we've lost them," Alex said, not quite allowing himself to be convinced.

They hurried in to the safety of the room, locking the door behind them.

"Don't light the lamp." Franz sat on the bed, still shaking.

"It feels good to be here," Alex said, gulping deep breaths.

The food on the tray was cold, but they ate it anyway.

Before leaving the next morning, they told Sophie and Matt their unbelievable tale and Matt agreed to tell his friend down at the police station, Constable Schmitz.

"As for you boys, I think you better get out of town and stay out for a long time. If they ever get wind of who you are, you'll be in a lot of danger," Matt said. "Take what money you made and go enjoy your families. You've earned it."

"You sound like you feel better today, Alex," Sophie said as she pulled the biscuits out of the oven.

"I don't think basement and tunnel work are the best jobs for me," he said. "I best stick to carpentry." His chest was still tight, but he could breathe easier.

After breakfast, they packed, stashing the pictures of their families in with their belongings and left. They took the long way down to the train station, hoping not to be seen by the wrong people.

When they arrived at the ticket window, Alex started. Is that Marsden? But with a second glance he realized he made a mistake. The son-of -a-gun owes us over ten dollars apiece, he thought ruefully.

It seemed like hours until the train pulled into the station. "Thank God! I can't wait to get out of this town," Franz said. "It'll be a long time before I feel comfortable coming back." He looked back over his shoulder at the crowd ready to board.

"Cutting cordwood for the steamships seems like a better idea all the time," Alex said with a laugh as he patted his friend's shoulder and scrambled up the steps.

Chapter 29

Late Summer / Fall 1889

"The pictures are wonderful," Julianna exclaimed, examining the photos. "Mama will be pleased to see what her grandchildren look like."

"I'll have to go to Hurlburt next week for supplies; I can mail them from there," Alex offered.

Julianna smiled, but felt a jab of fear. *He looks pale and I hate that cough,* she thought.

"I'm glad you're home for awhile, but mostly I'm glad that you're not going back to those horrible tunnels. I don't mind telling you, I had a bad feeling when you left."

"It was terrible," Alex agreed. "The strangest things happened down there." He took her hand and they walked out the door and into the sunshine. He related his adventures as they strolled around the garden and into the woods.

Julianna shivered when he told her of the men in the cell. At last they sat on a log and she caught him up on the news of the children and tried to forget his frightening tales.

"Ferd is the best baby," she said. "And Tracy takes good care of him. I swear, if something happened to me, she could take over, even if she is only six."

"Don't talk like that. You're much better this summer than last."

"*Yah*, I am having an easier time this year," she agreed.

Alex put his arm around her as they chatted.

"I suppose we should go back in and check on the children," Julianna said, looking toward the house. "Speaking of them," she continued, getting up and brushing the moss and leaves off her faded brown skirt. "Katherine and her family were up for a visit the other day and while they were here, we had a visitor; a Scottish fellow by the name of Bob Graham. I couldn't understand most of what he said, but Tracy and Mary interpreted a lot of the conversation."

"It seems he's building a home less then a mile southwest of here," Julianna said as they strolled back to the house. "He told us there's a school being built on the Wire Trail. He and his wife have one daughter ready to start school and another younger one who will be ready next year. He hoped we'd send our children."

"I'm glad to hear that. I've been worried about their education."

"I have, too. I was beginning to be afraid we'd have to board them in Portland." Julianna paused, wondering how far the children would have to walk. She continued, "Let's take a walk one day soon and find out where they're building it."

147

"I'd like to do that. I'll talk to Franz. Maybe they'll go with us," Alex said, as he took a swipe at a yellow jacket buzzing around his head.

"I'm sure they will. Katherine was as excited as I was to hear the news."

A few days later both families, armed with picnic lunches, set out in search of the new school. When their path met with the Wire Trail, they turned east and followed it along the ridge high above the Sandy River. It rambled through young fir forests seeded after the earlier burn, with patches of fireweed, buck-brush and much, to the children's delight, red huckleberries. They made a game out of who could find the most berries and before long their chins and clothes were stained a dark magenta.

"They are having such fun; I don't care how dirty they get." Julianna chuckled.

Katherine agreed, picking some of the tiny red fruit. "Mmm, these are delicious. I think they would make a good pie."

"Let's return with pails and pick some. They should make good jelly, too," Julianna said.

About twenty minutes up the path, they heard the sound of hammering and soon they saw the skeletal frame of a building. It sat on the crest of a small hill on the north side of the trail. Several large surviving Douglas fir trees, two with scorch marks, stood watch.

A short, red-headed man extended a sweaty hand in greeting as they approached. "Howdy friends, my name is John Smith. I've been commissioned by the county school superintendent to build the area a school here."

The men introduced themselves and their families and they all shook hands. Julianna nodded hello, but was unable to understand much of the conversation. Mr. Smith had kind eyes though and she liked him immediately.

"These are our children. Mary and Tracy are old enough to attend school and are excited about having one close by," Franz said.

The group conversed for a few minutes while the children explored the schoolyard. Then they shared their picnic lunches with John.

"Whose land is this?" Alex asked as he munched on a piece of Julianna's fresh bread.

"A Mr. Flechheimer from Portland traded a team of horses and a wagon for 480 acres of ground here. He named the area Banner Acres and donated an acre for the school." Sitting on the ground leaning up against the rough bark of one of the firs, John removed his cap and mopped the perspiration from his forehead and neck.

"He must be a generous fellow," Franz said.

"I don't know about that, but I know he'd like to sell pieces of the land. Maybe he figured a school would make it more appealing," John said with a rueful smile. "Besides, the county wants a school every so many miles. This is a good location, being on the main trail from The Dalles to Portland and all."

Alex and Franz nodded and translated for the women, who laughed and nodded.

"I've heard of men like that," Julianna said. "My father knew a couple of them and to tell the truth he might have had some dealings himself." She laughed remembering her father, coming home and spouting the good news of a sale. He always picked her mother up and swung her around in his exuberance. The bittersweet, memory stabbed at her heart, but she put a smile on her lips. I have no time for this. She forced away her thoughts and willed herself back to the conversation, straining to understand the English words.

"My daughter, Blanche, suggested we name the school Pleasant View because it's high on this ridge and has a view of Mt. Hood and the Sandy River Gorge," John said, taking a hungry bite out of one of Alex's Gravenstein apples.

Alex translated and Julianna's face lit up. "I think that's a lovely name," she said. "Don't you, Katherine?"

"I certainly do. It is a scenic place. Just think, the Columbia River is just on the other side of that hill." Katherine waved her hand toward the north. "I feel like we live on top of the world."

"Our wives like the name," Franz said, turning back to John.

"Well, that's settled then. Everyone I've talked to seems to agree." He paused, surveying the partially built shell. "We wanted the building ready for school next week, but it doesn't look good right now. The way I figure, I've at least three weeks' worth of work left on it."

"Franz and I will come and help you. We're good with a hammer and saw. Maybe we can help finish it sooner."

The next few days the men left early in the morning and came home at dusk. Fortunately, they found a shorter route. They walked their trail east like they were headed to Taylor's Landing. They came to the wood road that Taylor used and turned south to the Wire Trail. It cut off a good fifteen minutes and made an easier, shorter walk for the children.

School opened on Monday, September ninth, a week later than planned. Entire families came for the occasion. John Smith, who was the school clerk as well as the carpenter, greeted everyone and introduced them to the new teacher, Mary Perkins, who Julianna thought was lovely and refined. Just the kind of person I want to teach my children, she thought.

To Julianna's great joy, more people then she had imagined lived in the area and turned out for this important day. Alex interpreted some of what was said, but many of the languages spoken were Germanic so she and Katherine could understand and make themselves understood.

Bob Graham introduced his wife, Anne, to Julianna, who noticed Anne was with child, which bonded them immediately. The Grahams had two girls, Hattie and Alma. Hattie, a year older then Tracy, struck up a friendship and they were soon playing with two other girls their age. Emma entertained Alma and some of the younger children who seemed eager to seek out new friends.

Bending over to tend to Bertie, Julianna heard voices down the trail and turned to see a handsome young couple, who introduced themselves as Orilla and Sutliff Bates and their two children, Frank and Alta. Carrying her infant son, Harley, Orilla confided that her family lived in a tent just south of the Wire Trail about a mile east of the school.

"When do you think the men will finish building your house?" Julianna asked.

"I hope soon, but the tent is quite comfortable," she replied, her voice optimistic. Julianna admired her spunk and remembered when they built their own home.

Overcome with all the noise and different languages, Julianna moved to the edge of the crowd for a quiet moment. Ferd fussed and wanted down. She let him squiggle out of her arms, but held tightly to his hand. He's only one and he's not used to all this commotion. She wasn't sure she was thinking as much about the child as she was about herself. She noticed Alex, with some envy, engrossed in conversation with Sutliff and a tall gangly lad, whom she didn't recognize. Men don't have to worry about one year olds, she thought.

A young dark haired woman came down the trail from the west, leading a beautiful black horse with children on its back.

John introduced her as Anna Dunn, a widow. A shudder ran through Julianna. How can she raise four children by herself? Julianna wondered. "Mrs. Dunn is an excellent horse woman and Black Beauty is her prizewinning stallion," John continued. Franz helped the youngsters dismount and they ran off to play.

Julianna nodded hello from her quiet perch and Mrs. Dunn caught her eye and nodded back.

Another woman that Julianna liked immediately was Bella, a beautiful blue-eyed blond, and Bella's handsome husband, Carl Neilson. They came up from their farm on the Sandy River, with two their children, Frank and George, both too young for school.

"Frank will start next year," Bella said her arm around her firstborn son.

Julianna understood many of the Danish words and they became instant friends.

"I just couldn't pass up a chance to meet my neighbors, even if the children are not ready for school," Bella said. "I get so hungry for woman talk."

"I know. If it weren't for Katherine, I'd surely go mad."

"Come in now. It's time for school to begin," Miss Perkins said when it looked like most everyone had arrived. Inside the school, three rows of benches lined up, with an aisle up the middle and on each side. The teacher's desk stood in front with an American flag on a stand beside it. A large new black pot-bellied stove sat behind the rows of seats along the back wall was a long closet with pegs for the children's coats.

"Franz and I made those benches," Alex whispered to Julianna.

She smiled at him and took his hand.

"I want to welcome you all to the first day of school. We worked hard to get it ready and are proud of our accomplishments," Mr. Smith said after everyone settled in.

"We don't have a school bell yet. We hope to purchase one and get it up by next year. I'll be pricing them shortly and then we'll have a meeting to discuss the matter."

People sat with children on their laps, some on benches and many on the floor. The men stood, leaning against the walls and two small children sat on the teacher's chair, giggling, their feet sticking straight out. A parent whispered something to one little girl, quieting her down.

Julianna glanced at Alex and he nodded his approval.

Four long windows on each side of the school let in the daylight and around the room, shelves held kerosene lanterns for evening programs. Julianna admired them, remembering the dark rooms in her childhood school in Baden.

"I hope we can get a play shed built in the next year or two," Mr. Smith continued. "We'll have a barn raising when it comes time. Also, as everyone knows, the weather up here can get vicious, so the school will be closed in bad weather. We'll have school until November and then decide."

Heads nodded. A sense of excitement filled the room. There was a feeling of belonging, of the beginnings of a community. Something stirred inside of Julianna. Could it be an understanding of a broader meaning of home? She thought. Yes, I'm happy to have this for my family.

"Now we'll have the children come and take their seats; younger ones in the front, please. Children not old enough to start are welcome to join us today," the teacher said, taking charge as John moved to the back of the room motioning to his daughters, Hazel and Blanche to take their places. Women and younger children left the benches and joined the men.

Julianna noticed the tall gangly youth sitting near the back. "Who is that?" she whispered to Alex.

"That's Will Ogden. Remember I told you about his folks and brother who Franz and I met. They live not too far from Franz and Katherine's place."

"He seems awfully old to be in school."

"Well, maybe, but he said he wanted to learn his words and numbers. He has only gone through the first reader and he told me he felt that wasn't enough. I admire him. I think he'll make something of himself."

"You're right. You can never have too much knowledge," Julianna agreed, happy with her husband's enthusiasm for education.

Thirteen students started school with the recitation of the flag salute. All of the students shared readers, with the older children reciting for the rest of the morning. Some struggled with English, as families respectfully watched or stood outside visiting.

At lunch time, everyone ate their box lunches. After an impromptu sing-along, Miss Perkins dismissed school for the day amid good-byes and promises to return the following morning.

On the way home, Alex asked Mary and Tracy what they liked best about school.

"I liked Miss Perkins. She's nice," Mary said.

Tracy thought for awhile and then answered, "I liked playing with Hattie and the rest of the children. I didn't know there were so many families around here."

Franz laughed. "There are more than I thought, too."

After that Alex or Franz took turns walking the girls to school every morning and returning to the school to bring them home in the evening.

"I'm glad you men are taking charge," Julianna said one morning.

"My God, girl, you have all you can do taking care of the younger children," Alex replied, as he helped gather Tracy's jacket and lunch pail. "Don't you worry, we don't mind. We're happy we have a nice school for the girls. I can get plenty of work done while they are at school."

The weather stayed nice as September slipped into October, but Julianna became increasingly uncomfortable. They had most of the winter supply of food put up, so she felt like she could rest in the afternoon. On the morning of October 11, she woke up feeling as though her time was near.

"Go get Katherine," she said to Alex. "I'm ready to have this child."

Franz took the girls to school that morning and Katherine brought the rest of the children over to the Lamperts. Julianna labored all day and into the night. Shortly after midnight, on the 12th of October, Josephine, was born. Josie, as Tracy immediately called her, was a beautiful baby with such fine hair that Alex was sure she'd be bald. He thoughtfully didn't mention this to Julianna, but did share his worry with Katherine.

She laughed and said, "You've a short memory, Alex. You said the same thing about Bertie and look at her beautiful curls now."

Chapter 30

Winter 1889 / Spring 1890

The first week of November, the weather turned cold and wet and many children missed school. True to his word, John Smith called a community meeting on the first Saturday of the month.

"Ladies and gentlemen," he began. "For those of you who were not informed, Pleasant View School has been designated as District 48 in Multnomah County. That makes us official."

Everyone clapped and Will whistled loudly.

"I've been asked to go east and begin the process of starting a school in the District 42 area, known to many of us as Bridal Veil Falls. They are about to build a sawmill and expect a large influx of people," he continued. "Before I leave, it's important for you folks to elect a school board. Would you like to do it now with a voice vote?"

The crowd met the suggestion with great enthusiasm, and soon Alex, Franz, Sutliff Bates, Bob Graham and Carl Neilson made up the first permanent District 48 school board, replacing the temporary board hastily appointed by John the prior September. The board held a quick meeting electing Sutliff the chairman.

"Thank you, John," said Sutliff, when he accepted the gavel, "but you're still needed here. I'd like to formally ask you to continue being our school clerk. You have the knowledge we need to guide us through the everyday running of the school."

Mr. Smith nodded his acceptance and applause erupted once again.

"The weather is turning rapidly into winter," Sutliff continued. "Perhaps we should suspend school until early February."

Conversation filled the room, some heads nodding, others questioning. Orilla immediately raised her hand.

"I think that's a good idea. We don't want our children out in bad weather." She paused and looked around, "However, I move we have a community Christmas party here a week before the holiday. We can't let this wonderful building go to waste."

This time heads nodded with enthusiasm. When the meeting broke up, people began to plan for the festive occasion.

The walk home was pleasant and dry even though clouds filled the sky and overflowed into the hills. The children giggled with delight.

"I can't wait for Christmas," Tracy said as she skipped ahead with Mary.

"Christmas! Christmas!" Bertie echoed, dancing at the end of her mother's hand.

Over the next few weeks, Julianna and Katherine met frequently to sew and prepare for the holiday party. The children's excitement mirrored their own. Franz and Alex disappeared into Alex's shop for long periods of time, smoke rolling out its chimney as the weather continued its downward spiral.

"I'm mighty glad I had time last fall to finish building the shop. If we didn't have it, we'd have trouble getting these party projects done, let alone our own children's gifts," Alex stated.

"It's good you put a stove in, too. It's darned cold out here. I wouldn't be surprised to see a little snow here sometime soon," Franz replied.

"I just hope it holds off a bit longer. I'd hate to see the party canceled because of weather." Alex paused, remembering. "Well, we've walked through some tough weather in the old country. I guess we could do it again."

On the day of the party the rains stopped and a cold wind moved through the trees.

"My prayers have been answered," Julianna said as she put the finishing touches on the *apfelkuchen* and urged the older children to help the younger ones with their coats, scarves and boots.

Everyone arrived at the school by 11:00, chilled, excited and happy to see that Sutliff had arrived early and built a fire.

Several of the men brought in a small fir tree and placed it in the stand Alex had made for the occasion. Miss Parker produced colored paper, glue, and scissors. The children made decorations, hanging them on the tree in bright festivity.

Tablecloths covered the teacher's desk and the women laid out pots of beans, large pieces of fried chicken and several apple and pumpkin pies. Orilla brought delicious carrots cooked in honey. Bella brought Danish cookies she called "Spritz" and another kind with an anise flavor that Julianna found tasty. Alex gave his cookie to her after taking one bite, shook his head, and went for a second piece of pie.

After the tree had been decorated and everyone had eaten their fill, Carl brought out his fiddle and they all sang Christmas carols. Alex didn't recognize some of the tunes, but he still hummed along and thought they were beautiful. The children caught on to the words easily and soon sang with the rest.

During a break in the sing-a-long, Miss Parker handed out hard candy, much to the delight of the children. The adults huddled in groups, visiting and catching up with news, knowing it would be weeks before they would see each other again.

All too soon it was time to leave as darkness fell early in December. Even more so when it was gray and overcast. On their way home, they sang some of the new tunes and a few of the old familiar Christmas songs.

"I think we are in God's country, Julianna," Alex said as they put the children in bed that evening.

"I think you are right, dearest. We belong to a community now. I never dreamed we'ed be so lucky."

Later as they lay in bed, Julianna held him close and whispered, "As long as I have you, I'm in God's country."

He turned to her and they both smiled in the darkness.

***

February brought warmer weather and the children returned to school amid much eagerness. Emma begged her mother to let her begin her studies.

"Darling, you are not even five years old. Let's wait, at least until September," Julianna said, remembering her own enthusiasm for school. "I need you to help me here at home with the babies," she added wanting to give her young daughter a feeling of responsibility.

"I'll help you," Emma said, patting her mother's arm.

***

Winter turned slowly to spring and one warm afternoon in early May, Alex began spading more garden space, enjoying the smell of the lush undergrowth of the woods nearby.

Nanny, staked out near the edge of the clearing, grazed quietly taking advantage of the rich foliage.

I'm going to get some oxen. Alex worked faster, his thoughts spurring him on. I could raise more cash crops here. Maybe I could stay home then. I'll talk to Franz, I'll bet he would go in with me and we could buy a pair together.

Content with his thoughts, it was easier to ignore the blisters on his hands. The warm sun felt good on his back. He stopped for a moment and leaned on his shovel. I guess that's why they make handles so when you want to rest, you can lean on them. He grinned to himself and looked at the soft fluffy clouds against the blue sky.

At the edge of the forest, he noticed a beautiful tree in full cream-colored bloom. I wonder what that's called. It's magnificent. And then he noticed another one farther down, the blooms filling the branches. I'll have to ask around. I want to know its name.

A frantic noise interrupted his day dreams. His eyes searched until he saw a small, sharp-beaked bird with a white head and a black ring around her neck. She was running away from him. "I'm not going to hurt you, birdie," he called softly to her in German, but she continued the squawking. He watched her antics and moved slowly away from her, until she calmed down.

Alex shrugged his shoulders and began to spade in a different area to give her more room. It wasn't long until she began to squall again. He noticed this time she was near Nanny, who munched contentedly on her meal, ignoring the minor annoyance.

By this time, the bird had spread her tail into an exquisite white, brown and tan fan. She limped along with one of her wings appearing to be broken and hanging down. Still squawking loudly, she once again had Alex's full attention.

She lunged at the poor goat, who looked startled, and moved backward a step. The bird continued to scream and do the small, intricate dance, stepping back and forth, but not moving from the spot. Nanny, curious, moved forward, and again the bird lunged, pecking at her nose. This happened twice more.

Mesmerized, Alex continued to watch this ritual, wishing Julianna was here to see it. He'd seen that kind of courage before. He remembered his wife's bravery and determination at times since he'd met her. She would do that to protect her children. There has to be a nest somewhere close by.

It didn't take long for Nanny to tire of the game and move to the other end of her tether. The bird settled down and Alex walked over to scout the area. Sure enough, nestled in between some dead limbs was the camouflaged nest with three little gray/black speckled eggs. He almost stepped on them before he'd seen them.

He moved Nanny farther away from the nest and, for the rest of the afternoon, he was careful to avoid the area. Still amazed at the beautiful little creature, he quietly pointed out the nest to Julianna later that evening as the bird again protested loudly.

"Let's not tell the children. I don't want anything disturbing the eggs," Alex said. "The little ones can see the babies when they hatch."

"Like when I know that I am expecting another baby, I don't tell them right away," Julianna laughed and after a pause said, "Like now."

"When were you going to tell me?" Alex said, startled.

"Soon, perhaps some evening over a glass of wine," she teased, "but this seemed like an appropriate time."

He shook his head and quietly gazed over the spaded field. How is it that God gives us so many children? I pray he helps me feed them.

"I'm glad I'm staying home this summer. The farm and the children are more in need of both of us all the time."

"Maybe you could get work closer to home," Julianna said. "It was nice when you worked on the school. You were home every night."

"I'll ask around at the end-of-the-year picnic," he agreed, folding his arms under his suspenders. They turned and walked slowly back towards the house.

***

On a warm Saturday morning in late May, after the children finished the school examinations, the community gathered in front of the school house for the first end-of-the-year picnic. A dry, warm east wind blew and the sky was clear. The men set up a table under the firs in the side yard and soon it sagged with an array of wonderful food, including Katherine's now famous pies.

Miss Parker had games for the children, while the adults quietly visited. Tracy proudly led her parents to a paper pinned on the wall. The heading stated: "The following list names students who finished the first reader last year." There, part way down, was her name, Theresa Lampert.

"We're very proud of you, Tracy," Julianna said with a smile. Alex patted her head and said he expected nothing less from his daughter. Glowing with pride, he hurried off in search of Sutliff.

"Have you finished your house yet?" he asked, when he found him.

Sutliff shook his head.

"Do you need help?"

"I sure could use some, but I've no money to pay you."

Alex thought for a moment. "I could do some work for you in exchange for meat this fall." He remembered his unpleasant trip for bacon last winter. "Do you have any livestock?"

"I have some pigs. How about I give you a hog this fall, and you can help me finish the house and build a small barn."

"That would work. I'll be down on Monday to take a look."

He glanced up and saw a tree, similar to the one he saw near his garden. "Does anyone know what kind of tree that is?" he asked, pointing it out.

"Someone told me it was a Pacific Dogwood," Carl spoke up in his lilting Norwegian accent. "They're sure pretty when they're in full bloom."

"Dogwood, I'll remember that."

As they gathered around the table to dish up their lunch, he told Julianna about the Dogwood trees.

"And you'll never guess what I found out," was her reply.

"What?"

"The beautiful bird with that nest full of babies in our garden is a Killdeer."

He nodded, "The next time I go to Portland, I'm going to see if I can find a book about trees and birds."

"I think it would be a good investment."

"I won't be going to town for awhile, though, because I am going to help Sutliff finish his house and build a barn. He can't pay us cash, but will give us a hog in the fall."

Julianna smiled, happy that he would be home, but wondering if a hog, their garden, the cordwood and the potato crop would be enough to sustain them through the winter.

She expected her sixth child in late August or early September.

Chapter 31

Early Summer, 1890

The steamboat whistle wailed once and then again as it blew for the landing at Taylor's place.

"Mama, the horn sounds louder than usual this morning," Tracy exclaimed, as she helped her mother string the peas. Dew, on the foliage, kept her hands wet but not cold. The sun peeked out from behind broken clouds, warming her shoulders.

The early morning moisture brought the earthy bouquet of the nearby forest to a rich fragrance. Tracy took a deep breath, savoring the joys of the sweet aroma.

"The east wind is in the air, dear, that's why the whistle sounds so close," her mother answered, standing up and stretching her back for a moment. She returned to her task once again.

"Do you ever think we could have a ride in one of those boats some day?" Tracy found the whistles intriguing.

"It would be fun, wouldn't it?" Julianna agreed.

"I'll ask Papa as soon as he gets home," Tracy announced.

***

Alex returned from Latourell later in the day.

"I ordered Sutliff's lumber. It'll be here in ten days," he said as he stepped up on the porch where Julianna sat, looking tired as she fed Josie.

"Do you believe them?" she asked without looking up. A faint smile traced the side of her mouth.

"I have his word," he said, smiling back, "whatever that means."

"Papa, can we ride the steamboat? I heard the whistle so clearly today. I thought it was calling me." Tracy was out of breath as the last word tumbled out. The children stopped their play and ran to Alex.

Bertie chimed in, "A boat ride!" At three and a half, she was her older sister's mimic.

Alex threw back his head and laughed.

"It's funny you should ask. Some fellow at Latourell told me that he was going to The Dalles. It seems one of the steamboat captains plans on taking the Harvest Queen over Celilo Falls."

"He must be crazy!"

Alex laughed again. "I've heard that you have to be foolhardy to be a river boat captain on the Columbia." He pulled out a clean hankie and wiped his nose. "The company wants to get the boat from the upper river to the middle river without dismantling it and that's the only way to do it."

Julianna looked at him in disbelief. "That's a high falls. I suspect the boat will be dismantled one way or the other."

"The man on the train said the same thing. He said the falls aren't quite as tall this time of year because of high water. He said he didn't care how tall they were, he wanted to see it for himself."

Alex shrugged his shoulders, reached for the water dipper and drew himself a cool drink. Hot and sweaty from his walk, he dumped the remaining water over his head and grabbed the towel hanging on a nail beside the keg.

"I think a holiday would be fun. Are you feeling up to a short trip?" he asked. Julianna's past experiences with pregnancy worried him, but he thought a trip might take her mind off her condition.

"Where would you like to go?" Julianna asked innocently, her eyes teasing.

"I thought it might be fun to take the steamboat up the river and maybe see that crazy fellow." He grinned, matching her coquettish glance.

"If I have you, I'm sure I'll be well enough to do it. Especially if we can have a stateroom. Then I could rest," she said. Silent for a moment, she quietly asked, "Where will we get the money?"

Alex frowned, turned and went to the cellar. He opened the jar, containing the money and counted it.

"We have well over a hundred dollars," he stated when he returned. "We can ask Franz and the family to accompany us and share expenses." He hesitated and said, "It would make the trip even more fun to have them along and besides, we all need a holiday."

"We do need a holiday," she agreed.

"Fine, I'll check with Franz."

The children, who had been quietly listening, now squealed with joy.

"A steamboat ride!" Bertie hugged her Papa's leg. He reached down and patted her blond curls.

"Come now children, we have much to do to get ready. It sounds as if we'll be gone for several days," Julianna said rising to put the now sleeping baby in her crib.

Alex went over to the Frommelts' after the evening chores and found they were eager to get away for a few days. The group decided they had to leave the following Friday in order to see the adventurous captain.

Alex spent the rest of the week at Sutliff's getting ready for the lumber. He built a stump and stone foundation for the barn. He'd never built one before, but he liked the ones he'd seen in Freeport, which kept the barn higher off the ground. The bottom of the building rested on short log rounds, which were set on large flat stones. Sutliff liked the idea and wanted him to try it. It took them two days searching to find just the right size rocks and another day to cut and place the logs.

On Thursday, Julianna left Tracy to mind the children while the younger ones were down for a nap. She took Nanny by the rope and led her to the Graham's house.

159

"I am envious of you," Anne Graham exclaimed when Julianna shared the story of their pending journey. "I would love to go."

"I wish you could," Julianna agreed. "It'll be quite an adventure. Other than a trip to Portland, it has been four years since I've been off this hill. Not that I mind, I do love it here, but this is exciting and I find myself looking forward to it."

She hadn't felt this giddy for years, maybe not since Alex proposed. She remembered the fun she and Alex had when they traveled from New York to Illinois and how she enjoyed the vistas they'd seen on their trip west.

Thursday evening each of the children packed a small traveling bag. Emma placed her and Berty's favorite rag dolls in their bags. Julianna smiled when she inspected the totes and saw them so neatly packed. The flour sacks had to be light as each child had to carry their own.

The Frommelts arrived at daylight the next morning. The children hugged and chattered. When the older children ran ahead, they had to be called back. It took the families just over an hour to walk the now well-worn path down to the landing.

"Hello folks!" Mr. Taylor welcomed them. "I haven't seen you down here for a long time. Where are ya' bound?" he asked as he spied the travel bags.

"We're headed up river. We thought a steamboat trip would be a nice holiday."

"Wish I were goin' with you," Taylor exclaimed, "but my rheumatism's been botherin' me lately.

"Sorry to hear that, friend," Franz said.

The little group chatted and huddled in the morning mist, watching eagerly for the boat to come into view. Two men stood by a large stack of wood waiting to load it on to the deck.

After what seemed like an eternity, the children asked, "Papa, what is that? Is it the steamboat, Papa?"

"Could be," Alex said, squinting downriver.

There on the river's western horizon was a minute speck, like a flea on a log. As they watched, it grew larger and, within minutes, the outline of a tiny boat came into view, growing bigger in what seemed like seconds.

They watched as the large sternwheeler, *Lurline*, the name painted white on a black sign just under the wheelhouse, maneuvered in beside the dock. The whistle blew loudly, twice, and startled the baby awake. She fussed, but soon fell back to sleep in Alex's backpack.

The children stared, mesmerized by the huge ship and the activity on the dock. Mary and Tracy stood arm in arm and whispered, pointing to a crew member who was securing the ship to the piling of the dock with a thick line.

From the top of the gang plank a deck hand beckoned the families aboard. Holding tightly to Ferd and Berty's hands, Julianna slowly followed

160

Alex with Josie, Emma, and Tracy up the slanted wooden walkway to the ship's deck.

The walk instantly brought back memories of a different ship and an earlier time, when she and Alex were young and in love and headed for a new adventure in a foreign land. It was a fond memory and just for a moment, it transported her back to France.

***

"Come, children!" Hurry now. Don't forget your satchels," Katherine said as she scurried to gather the little ones. "They want us off the boat right away. We don't want to miss the portage train."

The *Lurline* had stopped at Latourell and had passed Bridal Veil Falls and Multnomah Falls, arriving at the Cascades at 11:00. The north side portage train was there to take them the six miles around the rapids to catch the middle river steamboat. They had picked up passengers along the way and at least fifty people waited to be shuttled to the upper landing.

Julianna and Katherine overheard the captain tell a gentleman that he doubted whether there would be accommodations in The Dalles because there were so many people going up to see the Celilo run. The women exchanged worried glances. That thought had not occurred to her. Julianna decided not to say anything to Alex, but said a prayer and hoped for the best.

The little group managed to climb on board and sit in a car far behind the engine. The river turned to turmoil here at the rapids, with white water boiling and gushing downstream at a furious rate. Huge gray and ominous boulders poked through the water daring the ships to trespass.

"And this is high water, too." Julianna overheard a man saying to the woman sitting beside him. They watched the workman across the river building the locks that would soon put the portage train out of business and serve as a waterway between the lower and middle river.

The train moved rapidly and soon they spotted the steamship, *Mountain Queen*, docked at the upper landing waiting patiently for them, a tiny ribbon of steam coiling from her smokestack. Her railing glistened with new stain encircling her freshly painted white deck. Even though she was smaller than the *Lurline*, everyone managed to find seats when they climbed aboard.

Julianna and Katherine gathered their families around them and passed out slices of bread slathered with thick apple butter. The men disappeared and returned with cups of coffee for the adults. As the *Mountain Queen* pulled away from the landing, the families sat on the deck enjoying a quiet lunch and the changing scenery.

"Do you think there'll be a room for us when we get there?" Katherine asked in a quiet voice. "Someone on the *Lurline* said there were many people coming to The Dalles for this spectacle."

"Don't you worry, we've taken care of that," Franz said as he took a sip of coffee.

"How did you do that?" Julianna chimed in.

"We telegraphed the Umatilla House and asked them to save us two rooms."

"That's wonderful. Did they say they would?"

"Well that's the problem. We didn't do it until yesterday, so we're not sure."

Everyone was quiet for a moment.

"I guess we'll just have to wait and see then," Julianna said in a quiet voice.

Alex appeared deep in thought and did not join the conversation. Julianna, impressed with his wise choice, decided not to continue the conversation.

The trip upriver took a good three hours, but the children didn't seem to mind. Julianna and Katherine put the babies down for naps in the stateroom after they were fed and they slept the rest of the way, while the women rested and enjoyed the scenery from the small window.

They pulled into The Dalles dock at 4:15 in the afternoon. The city lived up to its reputation of being the warmest city on the Columbia. People stood on deck, many in shirtsleeves, thawing out from the wet cold spring they had experienced west of the mountains.

Franz slipped up behind Katherine and put his arms around her waist, whispering something that Julianna could not make out. Katherine laughed, turned and patted his shoulder. "Go then and hurry. I for one don't want to sleep on the floor."

He turned and ran down the gangplank. "I swear, sometimes he thinks he's fifteen again," Katherine said with a nod. "He's going to the hotel to see if our rooms are ready."

Julianna nodded and picked up her satchel and the baby's bag.

Passengers disembarked at a leisurely rate. The two families followed in no particular hurry. With Franz handling the hotel problem, they could take their time and enjoy the new town.

The dark rough rock along the water's edge proved difficult to walk on and the children soon chose to stay on the path. Julianna wondered why it looked bumpy and coarse. It reminded her of burned dry pudding that had hardened. Here and there a small critter poked his head up and eyed them suspiciously.

Alex caught up with her and she took his arm. "The captain told me this is lava rock," he said pointing to the landscape.

"You did it again. You read my thoughts," Julianna laughed. "I was wondering why this rock looked so porous."

"The rattlesnakes love it. At least that's what the captain said."

"Rattlesnakes?"

"From what I understand, they're vipers that have rattles in their tails to alert you when they are about to sink their teeth in your leg," he said, as he put his arm protectively around her shoulders. "Their bite is poison."

"Oh my, I'm glad we are staying on the path."

Alex laughed and gave her his devilish grin. "Honey, I'll protect you!"

Just then Franz hurried down the trail, waving a piece of paper. "I got us a room. I could only get one, but we can make do. The hotel's beautiful. Hurry, I can't wait to show you." He grabbed Katherine's arm and hurried her, forcing the children to run to keep up.

"I guess we'd better step up our pace," Alex said as he picked up Ferd whose short legs were unable to match his Papa's strides.

The acrid odor of cigar smoke and the stale smell of whiskey greeted them as they entered the hotel and passed by the door of the lounge on their way to the desk. Alex glanced into the saloon and noted a large area with billiard and card tables. Behind the bar was a long mirror flanked by two elaborately carved women. A sign over the mirror proudly stated they were "Twin Virgins, sentries of all who came to partake."

The lobby of the Umatilla House was as grand as any hotel Alex had seen. Dark stained hardwood floors held overstuffed sofas and chairs sat comfortably around small tables. Elaborate polished brass kerosene chandeliers hung from the ceiling. A huge iron safe dominated the otherwise luxurious room.

"Why do you suppose they would have a safe in the middle of the lobby?" Katherine asked in broken English.

A well-dressed gentleman in front of them carrying a leather case turned and said, "This is not just a hotel, it's also a bank. Lots of money comes through this port, what with the grain and cattle businesses of eastern Oregon shipping their goods to Portland."

Alex glanced at Franz. Maybe we should've settled on this side of the mountains.

***

"There's a comfortable chair," Alex told Julianna. "We'll go find the room."

She nodded, amazed at the grandeur surrounding her in a country she considered far out in the wilderness. Here and there people gathered in groups and a long line inched its way toward the front desk.

"I can't believe this many people got here before us," Julianna said as she sat down in one of the overstuffed chairs and hauled Ferd up on her lap beside Josie.

"I'm grateful that Franz got here in time to get us a room. I don't know what we'd have done otherwise," Katherine said. She sat down in a chair beside Julianna and plopped Aloysius beside her. "Probably slept on one of these sofas."

She looked at Julianna with her full lap and laughed.

"I would've never guessed you could fit two more babies on your knee. Thank God, I'm not expecting until January. How in the world do you do it, friend?" she asked shaking her head in awe.

"I'm not sure myself," Julianna said ruefully. "If I ever figure out the secret, I'll share it with you." She laughed, but there was no mirth in her eyes.

Although tired from the journey, the older children, could not be contained. Tracy and Mary, with Emma, Albert and Bertie in tow, found a group with youngsters and immediately went to get acquainted.

As soon as the men returned, the families made their way to the hotel dining room. It encompassed a huge open area, divided into two parts, a sign hanging in the first one stated "two-bit section". Farther down the way a wall sporting a larger more elaborate sign, informed the clientele of elegant dining in the "four-bit section". They chose the twenty-five cent dinners.

Chapter 32

Harvest Queen

Early the next morning found them on The Dalles to Celilo portage train. The glass felt cool as Tracy pressed her nose to the window, not wanting to miss anything. The tracks at times hugged the steep cliffs or jutted out into the water. Once, as the train circled a curve, she could see the water lap against the trestle ahead of the engine.

At one point during the fourteen mile journey, an expanse of sand swept around the train like smoke from the fire of green wood, but the engine pushed through it without hesitation. Finally they rounded a curve and a large white mass of water appeared.

Seated next to her father, Tracy pointed to the wide, frothy tumbling body of water. She saw platforms on the rocks above the falls extending out over the churning water, where men stood with long poles.

"What are they doing out there?" she asked.

"*Leibe,* this is Celilo and the men are Indians. They're catching spring salmon," he said. "You were very young when we first came through here."

"I don't remember, Papa." Tracy couldn't keep her eyes off the scene as the train came to a halt on a side track below the raging falls.

"Children, there are too many people here for you to go wandering off. Everyone stay close," Julianna commanded. "I want every older child to hold on to a younger child's hand and don't lose sight of them. Stay by us at all times."

They piled off the train and climbed to a higher bank overlooking the site. Tracy heard someone in the crowd say there must be at least 500 people mingling around. An enterprising young man came through the crowd selling cups of cold water to those who had neglected to bring their own. Papa and Franz had brought canteens.

Above the falls, a large steamboat could be seen, moored at Celilo Landing east of the mouth of the Deschutes River where the Columbia turned into a placid lake.

"Is that the *Harvest Queen*, Papa?" Tracy asked. Today she found it especially annoying to have to hold on to both Berty's and Emma's hand. It would've been much easier to follow Papa if she were by herself.

"Yes, I believe it is," he said smiling down at her. As if reading her mind, he put Ferd on his shoulders, turned, picked up Bertie, and cradled her in the crook of one arm. Mama followed the group with the baby.

They walked as close to the falls as the crowd would allow. The deafening roar of the tumbling water almost drowned out their conversation, and they had to yell to be heard. The green water turned white as it seethed over the cliffs and was a stark contrast to the tall brown hills bathed in sunlight on the Washington side of the river.

The exhilarating sight almost took Tracy's breath away. "Oh look, Emma, look at the beautiful waterfalls," she exclaimed.

"Lots of water and lots of people," Emma answered with a look of wonder on her face.

"More then we've ever seen in one place," Tracy said and looked at Papa, who laughed and agreed.

Many people sat on rocks, soaking in the warmth of the day. Excitement filled the air, as if it hitched a ride on the wind blown up from the west. The *Harvest Queen*, bobbed and tethered at the dock above the falls, awaited its bold adventure.

They found a spot with a perfect view, spread blankets, and settled in to wait. A group of important looking men stood talking at the water's edge below the falls. Another sternwheeler was tied to a wharf nearby. Several fishing boats dotted the water near the larger boat, waiting in case they were called upon to pluck the captain and his first mate from the icy turbulent waters.

Papa pulled out his pocket watch. "It's pretty close to eleven," he said. "They should be getting under way soon."

After what seemed like hours, they heard the melodic sound of the *Harvest Queen*'s whistle, once, twice, and then three times, as she slowly backed away from the landing. She eased her way out into the center of the river, where the current picked up and the paddlewheel turned backward to slow her down.

Unable to sit any longer, Tracy stood and found herself holding her breath as the boat inched closer and closer to the horseshoe-shaped falls nearest the crowd. She heard a man behind them murmur over the din of the water "Captain Troup must be crazy". Several heads bobbed in agreement, but all eyes were on the steamboat, which now appeared dwarfed by the twenty foot drop.

Tracy wiped her damp hands on her best print skirt, her eyes riveted on the little boat as it crept ever so slowly toward the ledge. Suddenly the paddlewheel turned forward and the nose of the steamboat hovered on the precipice. It teetered for just a moment on the brink as if taking one last breath and then, its bow plunged over the edge.

For an instant, it looked as if the bow of the craft, with its stern wheel turning, was going to go straight into the water, as neatly as a diver heading for a pearl. Just as suddenly the boat bobbed at the foot of the fall, reminding Tracy of the empty, lidded jar she and Emma played with in Mama's wash tub.

The captain brilliantly turned the boat into the rapids and headed out of the white water, barely scraping a rock wall that jutted into its path from the left. The craft swerved again, this time to the left, barely avoiding another large rock on the starboard side. The assemblage let out a collective whooping cheer as the *Harvest Queen* straightened itself out, tooted its whistle, and under its own steam, limped downriver toward The Dalles, with only minor damage to its port side.

The crowd erupted into hoots, whistles and applause echoing so loudly they could be heard above the roar of the falls. Tracy felt herself take a deep breath as if she had just reentered her body after a wild adventure.

"Papa! Mama! Did you see that? Wasn't that ....?" Tracy stopped, surprised at the amazed look on their faces.

"Well, I guess that's that," Alex said, slapping his hand on his knee. He looked at Mama and winked.

"It certainly was worth the trip," Julianna said, nodding her head. "I doubt we'll see anything as exciting in quite awhile."

Katherine nodded in agreement.

"Not until another ship builder wants some foolhardy river boat captain to bring a steam boat from the upper river to the Portland shipyards, anyway," Franz said as he reached down to pat Mary's head. "Remember, they have to take the *Harvest Queen* over the Cascades downriver, too."

"Will we get to see that, Papa?" Tracy asked.

"I doubt it, *leibkin*, they have to repair that left side before it's seaworthy," Papa said, putting Berty down and shaking his arm to relax his muscles.

The portage train which had been waiting for the crowd took them back to The Dalles. Then they caught the early afternoon steamboat home.

167

Chapter 33

August/September 1890

I don't know how we'll feed the children we have now, let alone another one. Julianna's thoughts jumbled together. Tears trickled down her cheeks and spattered onto her lap. She sat on a moss-covered log, near enough to the house to hear any emergency, but quiet enough to collect her thoughts. Heavy with the burdens of the day, the rosary beads worked their way through her fingers, yet brought her no solace.

She glanced down and noticed her raw red hands, sore from scrubbing lye soaked diapers on the washboard, and another deluge of tears poured out, forgetting the delight of the holiday trip they'd taken earlier.

Five children and another on the way. Her sobs deepened and came with more abandon. She let them come until none were left. Then she sat in the quiet, interrupted only by small gulps of air.

Where will we get the money? I'm afraid for Alex to go back to Portland, but no one here can pay him. We can only use so many hogs. She knew pregnancy coaxed her tears nearer the surface, and today she couldn't contain them. When Alex left this morning for work at Sutliffs, he promised that he would find another job somewhere.

"Mama, where are you?" Tracy called, breaking into her distress.

"I'm here." Julianna wiped her face with her apron and stood.

"I can't find you."

"Here *liebe*. I'm here," she said as she spotted the child holding on to Ferd's hand.

"Josie's crying, Mama."

"Let's go in then," Julianna said, brushing her hands on her worn skirt. "Mama was just taking a walk. Sometimes even mamas need time for themselves."

As Julianna tended her family for the rest of the day, she was unable to shake the dark brooding melancholy. I don't know why I'm so worried. This pregnancy is easier than many of the others. She sucked in her breath and her thoughts turned to her home country. I'm lonesome for Baden. I doubt my family will ever see our children.

When Alex came home later that afternoon, he was all smiles. "Sutliff gave us all these nice cabbages. We'll make up a good batch of *sauerkraut*. It'll taste great this winter."

Julianna smiled in spite of herself, and nodded when he added, "The children and I'll shred it up tomorrow and get it into the crock."

By the time supper was over, she was feeling better. Dear Alex is my best medicine, she thought with a smile.

After the children were tucked in for the night, she joined him on the front steps to enjoy the cool of the evening.

"Did you talk to Sutliff about local jobs?" she asked.

"Yes. He didn't know of any, but he suggested I talk to Taylor. I am going down first thing in the morning. If anyone will have an idea it'll be him."

The next day, Julianna woke to find Josie fussy with teething and that kept her occupied while Alex was off to see Taylor. She had awakened with more optimism than she had felt for many days. Mr. Taylor was always good to them. She knew he'd have some suggestions.

Josie quieted and Julianna gazed out of the window at what passed for a yard. Earlier in the summer, Alex cleared a play area for the children in front of the house. He'd let the natural grasses grow up to keep it from getting muddy.

"I'll have to cut it down once in awhile, but at least we'll have cleaner children," he had laughed. Tracy was out there now, teaching the younger ones a game she played at school. "Ring around the rosy," she chanted as they laughed and fell down.

When Alex arrived home in early afternoon, his face glowed.

"Well, it seems as though the steamboats are in desperate need for more cordwood. Many of the farmers have cleared so much land, there's a shortage. The companies are paying Mr. Taylor $2.00 a cord. He'll drive the horses up the hill and haul it for us and pay us $1.50 for each cord." Alex's exhilaration filled the empty spaces in Julianna's heart.

"Alex, that's wonderful news." Julianna hesitated, "but are you feeling well enough?"

"I feel better than I have for a long time," he said, wrapping his arms around her. "This is our chance to make the money we need for winter and we sure have enough trees, especially over on the east end of the property."

"What about equipment?"

"I have that good axe, a maul, and a couple of splitting wedges. I broke my cross-cut saw, but I'm sure Taylor will loan me one. He's eager for the wood. It's a good deal for all of us."

***

The next morning, Alex began seeking downed trees, figuring that would be a good place to start. They were seasoned, so could be used almost immediately. He returned to Taylor's to borrow a saw and get an idea of how he wanted the wood cut.

"Avoid the butt end of the tree, Alex. It's too hard to split. Start your bucking at least six feet up. Then cut the log into four foot lengths and split them into several parts depending on how big the rounds are. They don't want anything shorter than four foot, though, so measure carefully."

"Sounds like something I can handle," Alex responded.

Taylor nodded. "Just stack the finished pieces up as high as you can reach. When you get a few piles, let me know."

Alex climbed back up the bluff with the saw and started in on his first log. The saw would've worked better with a man on each end, but Taylor had given him some tips on how to use it by himself. Sawing the first couple of rounds went slowly, but by the end of the afternoon, he had a medium size fir cut into twenty-one four-foot pieces. He was too tired to finish, but felt good about the progress he'd made.

The next day, using the maul and his two wedges, he started splitting each round, first into halves, then quarters. He got the tree cut and stacked by the next day and had over a cord of wood.

Well, maybe I won't be able to make a whole cord a day, but by golly I'll try, he thought as he walked the trail toward home.

In just over two weeks, he had made over ten cords, by working every day but Sunday. Mr. Taylor had already hauled off six loads and he paid when he came to pick them up. The cash in the jar in the cellar began to grow again, but Alex noticed he had more trouble breathing and with his exhaustion, he couldn't hold back his coughing.

He decided to take some time off and help Julianna get some of the produce in and put up. She was near her time and her anxiety bubbled close to the surface.

Maybe when we get more food in for winter, she'll feel better, he thought, but he knew it was more than that. The children were coming one after another. Too close, a shudder ran through him as he thought of what must be done to bring it to a halt. He quickly put it out of his mind. Nevertheless, it nagged at him for the next several days. He loved Julianna too much to see her go through these pregnancies so soon close together.

Still he tried to ignore his worries and concentrate on the winter's supply of food. "I think I'll go to Tom Evan's tomorrow and see if I can buy some of his good prunes. They should be ripe now." He announced one evening at dinner. "Our trees should bear enough by next year so we won't have to buy any."

"Papa, can I go with you?" Tracy asked looking up from her plate.

"Well, it's quite a walk. Do you think you are up to it?"

"Oh yes, Papa! I can help you. I can carry a pack-board," the seven-year-old's eyes were shining.

Alex glanced at Julianna who smiled and nodded.

"Well, I guess we'd better go out to the shop and rig you up then," he said with a grin.

After supper, Alex used a small piece of one-by-eight lumber he had salvaged. He drilled holes in the top and on the sides, and tied thongs of leather through them. This will do.

"Here Tracy, this is your own special pack-board. We'll hang it here on this nail beside mine!"

"Oh, thank you, Papa! I'm strong, you'll see."

They set out early the next morning and arrived at the Evans farm before ten o'clock. Tom sent them out to the orchard where they gathered as many prunes as they could carry, mostly off the ground because they were the ripest and the sweetest. Alex figured he could handle two bushels, more than one in his pack-board and the rest in two tote sacks. Tracy picked up slightly less than a quarter of a bushel and carefully put them in a flour sack her mother had given her.

"Ah, a nice bunch," said Tom, as the two of them laid their wares on a table in the open air porch of the Evans home.

"They're nice and ripe, just as we like them," Alex replied. "We dried some last year and wished we'd had more." He paused to take a quick juicy bite. "How much to I owe you for these?"

"Since you gathered them yourselves, I think four-bits would be fair."

Alex handed him two coins. He placed Tracy's sack on her pack-board, carefully tying it, and then did the same with his own.

"Here, let's put this on," he said slipping the leather straps over Tracy's shoulders and tying the bottom ones around her waist. Their loads secure, they said good-bye to the Evans family and headed back up the hill.

With each step, the hike became harder and hotter than the walk down. By one o'clock they reached the Wire Trail and stopped at the Dunn place to rest in the shade and get a drink of water from the pump. Anne brought out pieces of cheese and bread and they chatted.

They soon left and pushed up over the hill to the spring, stopping once again to rest in the wooded vale. The cool water rushed out of the ground, even now in the dry of the year, and raced toward the Columbia, tumbling over the bluff in its haste. The sound relaxed them both and the cool shade felt like an oasis.

Tracy didn't complain. Not even once, thought Alex, as he smiled at her.

It was four o'clock in the afternoon by the time they arrived home. Julianna took most of Tracy's prunes and stewed them for supper.

The next day, everyone but the smallest children sat around the table and sliced the prunes for drying. Alex rigged racks out of small flexible vine maple limbs. Placing the fruit on them, he arranged it on the porch roof to dry. He even put a couple of racks on the shop roof.

Later that evening, when the couple was alone, they sat in silence for a long time. Finally, Alex said, "Tom said we could come back for Gravensteins in a couple of weeks and he'll have some Jonathans in early October." He paused, "I think it wouldn't hurt, even though we'll get some fruit from our trees. We can use all we can get." He studied the knothole in the board behind the stove in the living room aware of the cool breeze from the open door.

Julianna didn't answer, but sat with her hands on her swollen belly. He put his hand on her arm and squeezed gently.

"I know, dearest," he said in a quiet voice. "I know how hard this is for you." He paused again and then continued. "We've got to take steps to stop having babies for awhile." He felt her pull away slightly and heard her catch her breath.

"I can't believe that we have to resort to sleeping in separate beds," she replied, after what seemed like an eternity. She hesitated and added, "But I don't know of anything else to do. I've thought of little else for weeks. Neither of us can keep this up. You can't stand the strain of another child any more then I can."

He nodded and tears welled in his eyes. Embarrassed, he blinked and looked away.

"I'll fix a bed upstairs under the eaves after this baby comes," he finally said and took her gently into his arms. They held each other for a long time.

Two weeks later, Arnold was born on September 16, 1890. Alex took his bedroll and climbed the stairs.

Chapter 34

Summer 1891

This was the first summer in three years that Julianna had not been pregnant and it brought a freedom to which she was unaccustomed. She accomplished more without tiring; bringing her a sense of confidence, but the price was high. She missed having Alex in her bed and she knew he hated not being there.

The older girls helped with the children. Tracy took complete charge of Arnold, rocking him, changing him and even hauling him out under the trees so he could watch the rest of the youngsters at play.

Julianna spent time in the garden, where she found solace digging in the soil. It reminded her of growing up in far away Baden, when her family tended their kitchen garden. Mutter would be proud of my efforts, she thought as she gazed across the rows of potatoes, carrots, and cabbages. She laughed, and thought of the times her mother had threatened her and her siblings when they were caught playing instead of working.

I wonder how Alex is, she thought. He'd left a week ago to find work in Portland, after planting a half acre of potatoes. Julianna had helped him plant the garden at the end of April and he'd put up over thirty cords of wood for the steamboats during the winter, but he needed a summer job.

She remembered the evening in early spring, when they sat at the table after the children were put to bed. Julianna darned socks while Alex read "Oliver Twist" aloud by the soft kerosene lamp light. He had picked up a German translated copy of the novel during one of his work trips to Portland. When he finished a chapter, he laid the book down and said, "I am ready to try my hand in Portland again this summer. I can make good money on the jobs in town. I want my family to have the advantages this country can offer them. I don't want my family to live in grinding poverty," he shivered, "like those people in the story."

"What about Marsden? You could be in danger. It's just not worth it to me." Julianna grimaced and continued. "What would I do without you?"

"I'm not going to get into any trouble. I promise." Alex laughed. "Franz went in town last week and said there appears to be a lot of work starting up in east Portland. Marsden is across the river in west Portland. I'll stay on the east side."

"Well, I suppose it would be all right, then, if you promise."

"If I can't find a good job, I'll be home in a day or two."

He must've found something, she thought. A scurrying ant caught her eye and brought her back to the present. His health seemed better this summer. He rarely coughed. Maybe he'll stay well this year.

"The Methodists are building a school in northeast Portland," Alex heard someone say. When he looked up he saw a gentleman sitting two seats ahead of him and Franz on the Portland-bound train. Franz and Alex looked at each other. Franz nodded and rose to find out more.

"The Methodists are starting a college on the east bank of the Willamette, between Albina and St. Johns. They're patterning the building after Sever Hall on the Harvard College campus in Boston," Franz said when he returned.

"Let's take a look," Alex said. He'd promised Julianna that he wouldn't go across the Willamette, but he hadn't been sure he could find something in east Portland. This might be the answer.

When the train pulled into the station, they got directions, disembarked and started off on foot. Carrying their tools, it took them almost an hour to reach the building site located high on Waud's Bluff, a cliff overlooking the Willamette River, across and downstream from the main part of west Portland.

They inquired about jobs and were directed to a tall slender man, with a neatly trimmed beard. "Henry Schmitz is the name," he spoke with a thick German accent. "What can I do for you fellows?"

They introduced themselves and the conversation immediately lapsed into German.

"*Ah, das ist gut!*" Henry said enthusiastically. "This is going to be a five story stone building, in the Romanesque style."

"I know that architecture. I worked with it in the old country," Franz said, his face lighting up.

"I can use you!" Henry said. "And you," pointing to Alex, "what kind of a carpenter are you?"

"I'm any kind you need. I have built buildings from the ground up and I worked as a joiner on the ship that I came over on from the mother country."

"Joiner, huh! Good, you can start with the structure and when we get that done, you can help with the finish work. We pay $1.25 a day for carpenters and $1.40 a day for stone masons. Finishing carpenters also get $1.40 a day. When can you start?"

"Now."

"Good! You can store your tools in yonder shed when you aren't at the job site."

They worked until seven o'clock that evening and turned their time in to the clerk in the shed.

"Do you know any place near here that takes boarders?" Franz asked the clerk.

"There's a rooming house about three blocks south on Willamette Street. It's run by a widow lady named Mary O'Donnell," the clerk said pointing the direction. "The food's mighty good."

"Let's take a stroll down there. I'm hungry."

When they knocked on the door of the newer, three-story home, it was answered by a beautiful young woman, with soft reddish hair tied back with a gold ribbon. Her white apron covered a short sleeved blue dress and a smile lit up her entire face. Alex's heart took a troublesome flop. He shook his head to clear his mind and stammered something inaudible.

"You have to excuse my friend. We've been working all day on only one sandwich and hunger has got the best of him," Franz said with a laugh. "We're looking for a room to rent. We're from out east near the new settlement of Troutdale. We have a job on the Methodist Episcopal University down the street."

"Oh, please come in. I do have a room. Would that work for you?" Her voice reminded Alex of the church music in the cathedral when he was a youngster. "The rooms are twenty-five cents a night, clean sheets once a week. You'll get two meals a day, breakfast and supper. Since you'll be sharing a room, I'll charge an extra dime a day for the meals. The total would be thirty-five cents between you fellows." She looked at them with inquisitive green eyes.

All Alex could do was nod. Franz said, "We'll take it."

"Come with me then," she said as she led them up the stairs to the first room on the right. "The bathroom is at the end of the hall." She pointed in the general direction. "I have some leftovers in the pantry. Would you like me to fix you each a plate?"

They both nodded.

"Come down to the kitchen after you clean up. It'll be ready for you."

Alex sat on the bed, tired and confused. *What is wrong with me?* He thought. *I have a wonderful family and a beautiful wife.*

The men worked long days, never getting supper before eight-thirty in the evening, so Mary kept food back for them. Alex tried his best to avoid her, but her face flashed in front of his eyes time after time during the days that followed.

They took the weekend off, rode the train home on the next Saturday evening and spent a quiet Sunday with the families.

Alex held Julianna close, nuzzled her neck, and whispered, "I missed you," before he went up to his bed in the loft. He fell asleep with his rosary in his hand, but it did not keep Mary O'Donnell out of his mind.

***

By the end of August, the outside framing of the school was done and the back and one side of the stone work was in place. Alex and a crew of carpenters started framing the rooms. It went faster than he was used to because they had hired a team of men to saw the lumber at prescribed lengths. This allowed the carpenters to do nothing but measure, fit boards and nail. This is *hilfreich*, he thought to himself, the cutting is slow. Let someone else do it until I start the finishing work.

175

The building was to house the whole school, so most of the fourth floor and the entire fifth floor were dormitory rooms and private quarters for the instructors. The first floor housed the chapel on the right side and the cafeteria on the left, with administrative offices in the middle. Classrooms filled the second and third floor.

The stone work on the front of the building, now called West Hall, was more complicated than the rest because there were two large windowed columns on each end with the main door between them.

Franz, the most experienced mason in the crew, became foreman almost immediately with a dollar raise in pay. He had no trouble blending the columns into the façade and adding the five dormers, but he had to persuade the bosses to hire several more men. "Good weather'll run out on us, if we don't get more help with this stone," he told them.

Nights were increasingly difficult for Alex. He prayed he would not bump into Mary during his short time at the boarding house. As time went on, however, the days got shorter, and his only choice was to visit the nearby tavern or spend time at the boarding house. He hated the noisy pub with its odor of stale beer. Most evenings, he and Franz joined the men who gathered in the living room of the boarding house for card games and visiting, but he often found an excuse to retire to his room earlier then the other fellows.

"What's wrong, old friend?" Franz asked one evening. "You just aren't yourself lately."

Alex started and felt himself blush. "Ah... nothing, no, nothing," he stammered. "Ah...I guess I just miss my family." He felt as if he'd spewed forth a nasty lie. Well, it's not a total lie, he thought, comforting himself. I do miss them terribly.

Franz nodded. "Me, too, but I am lucky my job is about over until next spring."

With the advent of winter, the rock work was suspended, as it was impossible to do a good finish job with stone when it was wet and muddy. "I'll be staying home the next time we go east. What are you going to do?"

"Well, Henry tells me that I'll have finishing work for most of the winter, if I want it. I'm thinking it'll be a great way to get ahead. Julianna isn't going to like it, but at least she's not expecting a child this winter."

The men went home the first week of October and disembarked at the Troutdale depot, instead of going on to Taylor's. They stopped at the new American Dressed Meat Company on the north side of the tracks and each bought a half a hog. They left it there until the following day, as their pack-boards were laden with other necessary provisions.

When he arrived at home, Alex was pleased to see how rested Julianna looked. He embraced her with a sudden yearning. The children, glad to see him, increased his joy and surrounded him with warmth. He brought a small gift and a sweet treat for each of them. Although the family had harvested much of the garden, the potatoes and carrots needed to be dug and

176

stored. After the men went back to get the hogs halves and put most of the meat in the smoke house, he and Franz started bringing in the remaining produce.

It took a week to get caught up and then Alex had to leave to get back on the job.

"I promise to be home every other weekend," he said to Julianna as he kissed her good-bye. She walked down the lane to see him off and he turned to see her waving just as he disappeared over the crest of the hill. *Not sleeping in her bed is the hardest thing I've had to do*, he thought and shook his head.

When he got back to the O'Donnell house, he purposely avoided Mary. He fell into the habit of stopping at the Pastime Tavern for a meal before going to his room. There always were a few friendly fellows in there and every once in awhile, he would share a beer with them. Mostly though, he stayed in his room, reading the paper or one of his books, keeping the German copies to take home to Julianna.

Work on West Hall continued. The Methodists called the school the University of Portland now, which brought a grand name to its campus. They were hoping to open by January, so Alex and the crew worked long hours. Sometimes Alex lit the lanterns and stayed late to finish up a project. *Am I avoiding the O'Donnell Boarding house?* He wondered.

On the weekends that he did not go home, he worked all day Saturday and walked the mile or so to Immaculate Heart Parish in Albina for Mass on Sunday. He basked in the beautiful church, so like some of the cathedrals he'd seen in Europe in his youth. The new church, built only six years before, had slender tall support columns flaring out attaching the lofty ceiling in great squares, guiding all eyes to the altar in the front. He could see the pride in which the parishioners cared for their new parish and somehow that and the Mass provided him moments of solace.

One Sunday morning after Mass, as he genuflected and turned to leave, he heard his name.

"Mr. Lampert! I had no idea you were Catholic."

Turning, he looked into Mary O'Donnell's smiling eyes.

"Ah yes, I have always been a Catholic," Alex stammered. *That was a stupid thing to say*, he thought. He felt his face burning.

"Well, what a pleasant surprise!" She didn't seem to notice his discomfort. "I see it's starting to rain again. Do you have a way to get home?"

"I usually walk."

"Then come ride with us. I always come with Nick and Laura, our neighbors across the street."

Alex followed her out through the crowd, into the street, and into the waiting buggy. It was raining hard and a cold late October wind pierced through his thin coat. He could feel his lungs tighten and worked to suppress a cough.

177

Surprised at how quickly they arrived back at the boarding house, Alex offered to put the horses up, but Nick refused.

"Would you like to join me for a light lunch?" Mary offered as they walked into the house.

"That would be nice," Alex said.

"Give me fifteen minutes to get something together."

"I'll see you then." Alex said as he went up the stairs. His feet felt like they had wings, but the effort of the climb brought a coughing spell.

Mary had bowls of hot chicken soup and thick slices of bread waiting when he appeared for lunch.

"Sit here, Alex," she said and waved toward a chair, her face flushed with the heat of the stove. She pushed one of the wet ringlets of hair on her cheek away with the back of her hand, which reminded him of Julianna and he winced.

"I hope you like the soup. It's from an Irish recipe that my grandmother used to make," she continued.

Alex took a spoonful, blew gently on it, and tasted the unfamiliar but savory blend of spices. "Very good," he said, still feeling uneasy.

"I'm glad you like it."

They ate in silence for a few minutes, and soon Alex relaxed and become more comfortable. He admired her confidence; much like Julianna's before the rigors of raising a brood of children had left her tired and worried.

When they finished, she asked, "What are your plans for the day?"

"I thought I'd go to my room and read."

"Would you like to play a few hands of Whist?

"I've never played it."

"What card games do you know?"

"Franz and I played German Solo when we were kids. It's a game where a trump is named and tricks are taken."

"Perfect. Then you'll catch on to this game easily." Mary smiled and rose from the table, dirty dishes in hand.

They spent most of the afternoon at the card table, and were joined later by a couple of other boarders.

Later in his room, Alex tried to remember the last time he had enjoyed himself as much.

Chapter 35

Fall 1891

Work on the interior of West Hall continued. Alex spent the next weekend at home, where he repaired the children's toys, brought in a new supply of firewood and enjoyed Julianna's company. He noticed her eyes appeared less distraught. For that he was grateful.

"How long do you think the job will last?" she asked in one of their infrequent alone times.

"I think I should have work for the rest of the season and into the next, if I want it," he said.

She looked perplexed, answering, "I miss you. I hate it when you are gone, especially in the winter."

Alex hung his head. "I know."

The weather remained cold and rainy, and the days darkened earlier. It seemed to Alex that the walk to and from work took more time. He arrived at the boarding house after work wet and often tired to the bone. Always, Mary had a warm supper for him and insisted that he change clothes so she could dry his wet ones by the furnace.

He found himself thinking more and more about her. Once he came upon her unexpectantly late in the evening. Her long soft red curls lay carelessly on her shoulders. His heart leaped and he felt a little faint. He turned quickly and hurried back to his room. Sleep was a long time coming. He couldn't get her image to leave.

One night, he worked later then usual. Workers left one by one as they finished their jobs. The last to leave, he locked up his tools and as he started out toward the boarding house, he was overcome by wracking pain in his chest. He could scarcely pick up one foot and put it in front of the other. Suddenly, he bent over and coughed - a deep rasping cough that signaled trouble.

Large flakes of snow mixed with rain fell as the temperature seemed to drop minute by minute. He stopped to rest in the doorway of a small neighborhood grocery store. He thought about lying down, but quickly shook away the idea, knowing he would probably freeze.

After a few moments, he started again. His pants legs were soaked, and his umbrella was blowing in the strong wind. Each step required more effort than the last, until he thought he might not make it at all. At last, he saw the lit windows of the boarding house and sucked in a sigh of relief.

Climbing the stairs and on to the porch, he was surprised when Mary appeared at the door before he knocked. "Alex, what's wrong?" Fear flickered in her eyes.

"I need to go to bed," he told her, as he clutched the door frame, "but I don't know if I can get up the stairs."

"Come this way." Mary beckoned him to a small room off the kitchen. There was a cot made up with a small nightstand beside it. "Here, take those wet clothes off. I'll get something dry for you to put on."

Mary handed him a clean set of clothes, and that was the last thing he remembered.

***

"Alex, wake up. Drink this hot broth."

He stirred and slowly opened his eyes. They caught the snow swirling against the window as he turned to see Mary holding a steaming cup in her hands.

He sat up with some difficulty and took the cup. She put another pillow behind his head and he carefully sipped the slightly spicy concoction. It made him sweat profusely.

"What is this?" he asked after a few moments.

"It's an Irish recipe for chest congestion. It never seems to fail. My mother used it when we were children," she said with a smile. "If it makes you feel better, I'll share the recipe with you."

After finishing the brew, he sank down into the sheets and almost instantly fell asleep. When he awoke the next time his breath came easier. He sat up on the side of the cot and felt stronger.

"I think I'm better," he said when Mary came in to check on him.

"You certainly look better. I think your fever broke early this morning. I checked on you and you felt cooler."

Instinctively, he took her hand. "I can't repay your kindness, Mary."

"You don't need to," she said. "Just get well."

"I will. I think that Irish broth helped. It seemed to loosen up my chest. I need that recipe."

"All I do is heat some water, add a clove of garlic, a teaspoon of hot cayenne pepper and let it steep. Then I strain the tea, add a teaspoon of honey and a small amount of the whiskey I saved after my husband passed away. I like to add a little lemon juice, but it's hard to get, so sometimes I skip that part. I'll write it down for you."

Alex nodded. "I think I can get dressed now," he said, suddenly embarrassed, as he realized he was in his pajamas and wondered how he got into them. He felt his face burn.

"I'll get your clothes. I took the liberty of laundering them," she said as if reading his thoughts.

"You're too good to me," Alex said then added, "How long have I been sick?"

"Over a week, closer to ten days," Mary said over her shoulder as she left the room.

Stunned, Alex sat down. More than a week? He hadn't gone home last weekend. He knew Julianna and the children would be worried into panic.

My God, I've got to get to the train. But when he stood, his legs buckled, and he had to lean against the wall.

He was able to dress himself, but he could not climb the stairs to his room. Mary insisted that he continue to sleep on the cot. "I can hear if you need anything," she said.

He slept around the clock. When he woke, he wracked his brain to figure out some way to get word home, but he could come up with nothing. Even if he could get a telegram out to Troutdale, there was no way to get the message up the hill to Julianna. He remembered the snow and knew Julianna couldn't get to Franz to tell him.

By the end of the week, he was finally strong enough to make it back home. He also knew somehow, he would never see Mary again if he left, and he couldn't allow himself to think about that.

Alex felt well enough to eat at the table that evening where he and Mary found themselves alone.

"Who is Julianna?" Mary suddenly asked, breaking the silence.

Alex hesitated. It wasn't that he kept his marriage and family a secret; it just hadn't come up. "Ah, Julianna is my wife," he said quietly.

Mary paled ever so slightly, and after a moment, nodded her head. "You asked for her several times," she said, "and Tracy."

"Tracy is my oldest daughter. She's eight now."

"You never talked about a family." Mary's voice sounded accusatory.

Alex stared at his plate, a feeling of overwhelming sadness pouring over him, weighing him down. His chest hurt, but not from congestion. Putting his fork down, he finally dared to look at her. Was that a tear on her cheek?

"It just never came up," he said meekly.

The quiet thickened. He didn't know what else to do or say. This had never happened before, except once when he was young and free, and able to enjoy the journey. He knew, this time, there would be no passage, no travel to great heights.

"You called for me, too. Did you know that?"

He wasn't surprised. He knew he'd loved her from the first moment he had met her. He knew he should have never stayed on the job over the winter, but somehow, he had been unable to leave.

"Mary, I, I am so sorry. You have been so kind to me and I am causing you pain. I didn't mean to do that."

Mary sat wordless: Her plate half empty, her hands in her lap.

He wanted to take her in his arms and comfort her, and for an instant he felt his arms reach out, but instead he slowly pushed his chair from the table and turned away from her. He trudged up the stairs and packed.

When he came down, she was waiting at the bottom of the stairs. "You can't go out in this, Alex. You're not well enough. It is much too cold."

Dropping his satchel, he put his hands on her shoulders and looked into her sad eyes. Somewhere inside, he realized her sadness matched his own.

"Mary, my dear, I have no choice. If I stay now, I will never be able to leave. I have responsibilities that I must tend to. I could not live with myself if I stayed. I have six children and a loving wife who needs me and I love dearly. But know this, Mary O'Donnell, I will never forget you."

"I'll never forget you either, Alex Lampert," she said softly, after a moment.

He leaned down and brushed her cheek against his.

"Please tell Roy to give my notice on the job. I'll pick up my tools within the month."

Opening the door, he stepped into the dark night.

Chapter 36

Winter 1891/92

Alex still wasn't home. It had been well over three weeks since the last time Julianna waved good-bye to him. The supply of wood was almost gone and the blowing rain continued unrelenting. She peered out the front window and down the lane and another shiver tore through her.

"When is Papa coming home?" Tracy wanted to know.

"Soon I'm sure, little one," Julianna said trying to sound optimistic.

They were almost out of flour and she had used the last eggs yesterday. She'd never felt such isolation, such overpowering fear, as if a blanket had been thrown over her head, smothering the life from her.

She heard a step on the porch and her heart leaped.

"Alex!"

She flung open the door to see Franz, his coat dripping.

"Any word of Alex yet?" he asked.

Julianna shook her head. "I can't imagine why. This is so unlike him. I hope he isn't sick, or, God forbid, that awful man found him."

"No, Marsden isn't likely to have found him, but he may have taken ill."

Julianna nodded. "I've been fearful of that," she replied, not wanting to think of such an awful thing. She noticed Franz shivering and ashamed she said, "I forgot my manners. Please come in and warm yourself."

He slipped off his coat and hung it on a hook by the stove, drips sizzling on the hearth.

"Tracy, get me a cup so I can give Franz some warm coffee. I've been keeping the pot on the stove for Alex, hoping he'll come home."

Franz was silent as she poured the thick hot liquid. "How are your supplies holding out?" he asked.

"Not good." Julianna again shook her head. She wondered if she betrayed her fear. "I'm out of eggs and low on flour and salt. Nanny's still giving milk, thank God."

"Tomorrow I'll walk over to Jacob Seidl's and ask if he'll go with me to Troutdale and help carry supplies up the hill." Franz took a sip of the coffee and shivered. "I'll need a list," he paused, "You know, that Seidl is a hardy fellow. Did you know he carried a fourteen inch, single bottom plow up the bluff trail on his back?"

"No, I didn't." Julianna laughed, grateful for the adult conversation. She'd only met Jacob once, a few months before. The Seidls had moved in just west of the Frommelt place near the edge of the bluff. They'd built their tiny cabin close by the trail to Troutdale. Jacob had come by the Lamperts once in September to introduce himself and invite Julianna over to meet his wife and their infant son, Henry. She'd been excited to have another

German speaking family in the neighborhood and Katherine had told her later that Marie Seidl was very pleasant. Best of all, they were Catholic.

"*Yah*, anyone who can carry that heavy a load, can help carry supplies up the hill for us," Franz continued. "Katherine needs groceries, too. When I'm down there I'll go to the telegraph office and see if there's any word from Alex. If we don't hear from him soon, I'll go to town and see what happened."

***

When the stationmaster told him there was no message from Alex, Franz felt a deep uneasiness. "I don't understand it,' he told Jacob, "I've known Alex all my life and he's never shirked his duties. I'm afraid something's happened to him."

"Let's wait until the train comes through today. Maybe he'll be on it." Jacob seemed as anxious as Franz.

When the train came, no one got off. Dejected the men started up the hill, later than anticipated. Franz waited until the next day to take the supplies to Julianna. Marie sent a loaf of bread, and Katherine added a bag of cookies. Franz brought in another supply of wood, and Tracy and Emma helped him bring up more potatoes and carrots from the cellar.

***

As the days passed by without a word, Julianna's fears worsened. She worked hard to hide her alarm from the children. She told herself that Alex was all right, that he just got caught up in trying to finish so he could come home before the holidays. But to keep the house running was a constant strain, and she found herself impatient with the children.

The laundry was difficult to keep up. Both Josie and Arnold were in diapers. I feel like I've been washing diapers forever, she thought as she bent over the washtub that Alex had set up for her just outside the back door. Well, I've been doing it for eight years anyway.

She was grateful though for the convenience. He'd run a pipe from the kitchen sink under the floor to the wash tub. He'd put a stopper in the end of the line that could be taken out when she wanted to fill the tub. He's such a clever fellow. She tried to smile, but tears got in the way.

"Now all you have to do is pump the sink full and pull this plug. The pipe will take the water out to the tub. When you are finished, just pull the plug out of the bottom of the tub and the water will drain," Alex had told her proudly. She remembered that she had kissed him and had promised a proper thank you at a later time. That was before we decided to have him move out of our bed, she thought grimacing.

He had set the tub on a small stove that he had fashioned out of a metal barrel, so she could build a fire and have warm water. Last summer she had used the tub to scrub the children as well, but it was too cold now. The diapers continued, however, so at least every other day found her out in the

184

shed up to her elbows in wash water. At least I don't have to take them down to the spring in this weather. She carefully hung the clean laundry on a rack to freeze dry.

Franz checked in with her two days later. Still no sign of Alex. "I promised Taylor that I'd finish the job for him by day after tomorrow. If Alex isn't home by the time I finish, I'll go to town and find him," he promised.

Julianna nodded, her eyes again filling with tears. She turned her head, but not quickly enough.

Franz touched her shoulder. "I promise, I'll bring him home," he said. "Try not to worry. I know it's hard, but I also know my friend. There's a good reason why he isn't here."

She knew he was right, but what if something terrible had happened? What if she would never know? She shuddered. Just then Josie cried and she turned to pick her up.

***

Three days later the sun appeared and with it, cold blustery east winds. When she went out to milk, Julianna could hardly hold the bucket still. She brought the little goat into the woodshed and decided to leave her there. It's too cold outside, she thought. I don't want her to quit giving milk.

She just finished the milking when she heard the children, "Papa! Papa's here!"

She almost dropped the bucket, but caught it without spilling a drop, put it on the bench, and ran to the door.

There he was, coming down the lane, a staff in his hand, and his pack on his back. He walked slower then usual. Was he staggering? When she reached him, he leaned heavily into her arms.

"I was so worried. Where have you been?" Relief welled inside of her. "Franz was going to go look for you tomorrow." She kissed his cold cheek and said, "Come, I'll help you into the house."

The children gathered around, jumped into his arms and climbed on his lap in joyful welcome. Julianna had been so overwhelmed; she hadn't realized how worried the children were.

After the children quieted, Alex sat by the fire and gradually warmed himself as he told her of his illness and how the widow at the boarding house had taken care of him. "I don't know what would've happened to me if not for her kindness," he said. "I will be forever grateful to her."

"As will I, my darling," Julianna murmured as she helped him remove his boots.

Later that afternoon, Julianna pulled on her warmest coat and hat, and taking Alex's staff, walked down the trail to tell Katherine the good news. Alex was home, recovering from a severe illness and Franz did not need to go looking for him.

It wasn't until evening, after the children had been put to bed, that they had their first chance to be alone.

"Tell me everything, please," Julianna asked.

"I learned a new card game to teach you and the Frommelts. We can play it over the holidays."

"That's wonderful, but that's not what I meant."

"I got sick on the job. One night when I was walking to the boarding house, I darn near didn't make it." He went on to tell her about the Irish tea that seemed to help and that there were days he didn't remember, and how weak he was when he awakened. "I wanted to get word to you, but I had no way to do it. I promise this is the last winter I will work away from home."

"I'm so glad," Julianna exclaimed. "It does no good for you to make all that money and not be here. You can cut cord wood and who knows, more families are moving here all the time. Maybe there'll be work closer to home. Who knows, maybe you can even start making a living on the farm."

"We can only hope that time is closer," he paused and said, "Speaking of other families, I saw a log cabin off the trail just at the top of the bluff. It looks well built."

"That is Jacob and Marie Seidl's homestead. They have a baby boy named Henry. Franz knows the family and says they are very nice and Jacob is quite hardy." She told how Jacob had helped Franz bring her supplies and how he had carried a plow up the bluff.

"Holy God, that is unheard of," Alex said astounded.

"Best of all, they are Catholic. If we keep growing we may have enough for a church up here."

"Wouldn't that be nice," Alex said and proceeded to tell her about the Immaculate Heart parish in Albina, where he had gone to church. "Someday I hope I can take you there."

They chatted, catching each other up on the news. As frightened as she had been, she had not realized how terribly lonely these last few weeks had been. He was, after all, her best friend as well as her husband.

"It's time for you to go to bed. You have to get all of your strength back. I have many things I need you to do," Julianna finally said.

When Alex started up the stairs, Julianna put her hand on his arm. "No, I need you in my bed, not up with the children. Please, whatever happens, I want to be with you."

"I hoped you'd say that. I can't tell you how hard this has been for me. I've missed you more than you will ever know," Alex said as he turned to her, slid his arm around her waist, and drew her near.

Chapter 37

Summer 1892

Julius Lampert burst into this world, in the early summer of '92, with a lusty cry, and darker hair then most of Julianna's other babies. She admired his tiny fists, flailing chaotically as he announced his arrival. This birth was the easiest one yet and, although tired, Julianna didn't feel the emotional and physical drain that she had with the older children.

"You're destined for great things, my little man," she murmured softly.

"He is a fine young fellow," Alex said as he admired his newest arrival.

"Yes, he is, and he looks like you and Emma."

"Handsome, isn't he?" Alex grinned. "Do you think you'd trust me to pick him up?" He leaned over, put his arms around them and pretended to pick them both up. "Whoops, I guess you aren't ready for me to lift you yet," he teased Julianna.

"Not yet." She managed a tired smile before saying, "Please take him in and introduce him to his brothers and sisters. They're excited to meet him."

"Papa, he's so little," Josie exclaimed as she pulled herself up to her full almost three year old height, when Alex proudly presented the newest family member.

"You were that tiny once, *Leibkin*."

"*Yah*, even littler, I think," Emma chimed in.

Only Tracy hung back. "How is Mama?" she asked. "When can I see her?"

"She's fine, dear. She wants you to meet Julius and then you can see her."

"J, Jul, no Jack, him Jack," soon to be four-year old, Ferd said with an excited stutter, "Brother Jack!"

"Papa, let me hold him?" Berty asked pulling on her father's arm.

"No, me first, I'm older," Emma said.

"Here, Berty first and then Emma." The children lined up on the bench in the kitchen and each took a turn holding their new brother. Alex couldn't help being pleased over their excitement.

He'd gradually gained his strength back over the winter and spring, thanks to the liberal use of Mary's tea and Julianna's loving care. Now he and Franz were helping each other clear most of another acre at each place. He figured that he had at least seven acres cleared and two of them plowed. The rest was used to stake out Nanny and run the chickens. He thought of the earlier conversation with Julianna.

"No, I don't want to raise chickens. It'll be up to me to take care of them and I have enough to do," she said firmly.

"No, it won't, dear. I'll be home. We can use the extra eggs to barter."

She stood glaring at him.

"It'll be a good chore for the younger children. They can gather the eggs," he continued.

"What will we do with them in the winter?"

"Well, we can eat some of them. A chicken dinner would taste good on Sundays." Alex could feel her giving in, which didn't happen often. "I'll build a nice hen house over the summer so they'll have shelter for the winter."

"All right, if you promise to teach the children how to help take care of them. It just might be a good chore for Berty and Ferd, but I need the two older girls in the house."

"I promise!" Alex assured her.

They'd gathered a flock of three dozen Leghorn hens and several roosters. Leghorns, a relatively new breed in the northwest, were imported from Italy in the 1850s. Tom Evans assured Alex they were the best layers around. "By golly, some of my hens lay over 200 eggs apiece a year," he had told him.

One morning the children came running into the house, "Papa, Papa! There's just a pile of feathers out there. Something's eating our chickens."

Sure enough, the count was down, so that evening, Alex put his new twelve gauge shot-gun under his arm and took a seat on a stump down by the chicken house. Alex quietly posted himself under the full moon.

He fought sleep for an hour or so and then nodded off.

Alex's eyes flew open at the sound of loud squawking. In the soft light, he could just make out a small form, running toward the woods, hen in its mouth. Grabbing the gun, he aimed in the general direction and blam!

Still sleepy, he wasn't braced and the recoil knocked him backward. The shotgun flew upward and caught him on the jaw. Stunned and embarrassed, he shook his head to get the cobwebs out. I'm glad it's dark out here, he thought, tenderly rubbing his face. He could feel his jaw, swelling and throbbing. But I doubt if I'm going to be able to keep this a secret.

When he recovered, he lit his lantern and walked over to the animal. There's not much left of it, he thought ruefully.

"It looks like it might have been a weasel," he told Julianna later, "but you could hardly tell. And worst of all, I killed another chicken."

"Well, at least you got rid of a pest."

"Maybe I should not clip their wings feathers quite so short next season and encourage them to roost in the trees."

"Another lesson well learned," Julianna laughed and returned to washing diapers.

Other than the weasel, the chicken experiment worked well. The children made a game out of gathering eggs. There were so many that most of the year's supply of flour and sugar was gotten by barter. Alex even traded eggs for shoes at Aaron Fox's Dry Goods store in Troutdale. The older children were delighted. The younger children, of course, wore hand-me-downs.

One evening, Franz came to the house with news. "I just got home from a job in Portland. I stayed with the Foellers and Matt, Sr. told me about a neighbor who wants to put in an indoor toilet. He needs a good finishing carpenter because he wants to re-do his bathroom while he's at it. Matt says you're the only one he would trust to recommend." He hesitated and said, "The pay is good."

"Julianna won't like it one bit," Alex said, with a frown.

"It shouldn't take but two or three weeks and it's a good chance to put away a little cash. I know the eggs have served you well, but a little extra money is always a good thing. Tell her it's safe now. Marsden's in jail."

"That's good to hear," Alex said, relieved. "Let me talk it over with Julianna. I'll let you know in the morning."

That evening Alex broached the subject, assuring her of his safety.

"I don't want you to leave again, Alex," Julianna pursed her lips, but said nothing more.

"I know and I understand, but Franz said it would only be for a couple of weeks and the way it sounds I could bring home quite a bit of cash. That would keep us until I can get more wood cut. I promise to come home every weekend and if the job lasts more than three weeks, I'll find someone else in town to finish it."

"What about the eggs?"

"Have the children gather them and store them in the cellar where it's cool. I'll take them back to Portland every Monday. I know I can sell them and I'll trade some for board and room with the Foellers."

"And the henhouse? You said you needed to make it secure against varmints and its only half done." Her eyes flashed.

"It's the hardest half though," he said, teasing her. When he saw the flash of doubt in her face, he reassured her. "I'll finish it in September," he promised. "Then I'll hire the man at Latourell to haul a few sacks of cracked wheat up here for winter feed."

***

School began before Alex finished the job. Berty started first reader, so Ferd had to gather the eggs by himself after the three oldest girls left for school.

One morning, he saw Alex coming up the lane and ran to meet him. "Papa, I can get the eggs all by myself," he proudly exclaimed to his father.

"You are growing up too fast, my son!" Alex said as he picked him up and set him on his shoulders. "You'll soon be going to school, too."

"I can't wait, Papa! I want to learn to read."

"Reading is a grand adventure. I remember when I learned to read."

That evening the girls shared their school stories. "What's your favorite thing about school?" Alex asked as they sat around the supper table.

189

"I think reading is my favorite subject," Tracy said, with a flip of her hair. She was becoming very sophisticated. Or at least she'd like to think so, Alex thought with a smile.

"I like to play with the other children," Emma said.

"And what about you, my dear little Bertie?"

"Oh, Papa, I just love the walk through the woods to school. The woods smell so good and Tracy and Emma and I skip and play games," Berty talked until she was out of breath and then started the conversation again. "And our new teacher, Mr. Farley is nice and he lets us play tag outside, and the other children are fun, except for that mean Neilson boy, he pulls Hattie's pigtails…"

Alex laughed, "Wait, wait, *Leibkin*, didn't you know little boys tease little girls? It's just as natural as the sun coming up in the morning."

"Now, Alex, don't tell them that. We don't want our little boys to tease." Julianna joined the conversation.

"No, you're right, dear. Never mind children, I didn't say that." Alex laughed and said, "Anything else you can think of, girls?"

"No, Papa." They shook their heads.

"Well, I have some good news. I only have a couple of days work left, so I should be home for good by Wednesday or Thursday and I'll be home for the rest of the winter," Alex said.

Later that evening, Julianna admitted that Alex's job had not been as bad as she had originally thought, "But I'm delighted that you'll not have to go back after next week."

Chapter 38

February 1893

Dearest Mutter and Family,

We received your Christmas package two weeks ago. The train master told Alex it had been at the station in Troutdale for over a month. The weather was so terrible that no one ventured out over Christmas. The wind has been relentless and we had several bouts of snow and very low temperatures. For over a week we had drifts up to the roof in back of the house by the woodshed and cellar. The children were disappointed that we missed their Christmas Eve pageant and party at the school. The neighbors got together the end of January, but it wasn't the same.

Everyone loved the presents you sent. You should see little Josie parade around the house in that beautiful shawl. She is the apple of her Papa's eye. Ferd is standing at my elbow and asks me to thank you for the fine shirt. The way he is growing it will fit him perfectly by the time he starts school next fall. Now he wants to go to Portland with Papa so he can show it off.

The portrait of my dear family was most appreciated. I can't believe how grown up everyone looks. I have it hanging on the wall by the stairs. I told the children to whisper "good night" to their grandmother and aunts and uncles as they climb the stairs to bed every night.

Alex is getting stronger. He spends a lot of time in the woods now that the snow is gone. He is making cordwood for the steamboats that ply the river. I do worry about him though as he often is awakened at night with heavy bouts of sweating. He assures me that he feels just fine and has no intention of getting sick. I am trying to believe what he says.

Our wonderful fruit helped get us through the winter. Along with two small apple trees already planted on the place, the first year we were here, Alex brought home two apple trees, a Gravenstein and a winesap, one Italian Prune tree and a Williams Pear Tree. (They now call it a Bartlett pear.) We got our first fruit from them last fall. Not a lot, but enough to know they will be good trees. We always get some fruit from Alex's dear friend, Tom Evans, as well.

We had enough potatoes that we were able to sell a few bushels. Sylvester Evans bought our excess. He is Tom's brother and has a store in Hurlburt, a little settlement to the south. He buys eggs from us sometimes, too.

Little Jack is such a happy baby. I see his father in his eyes and the shape of his face. I never had the opportunity to see a baby picture of Alex, but I am sure he looked like Jackie. As soon as I can get to Portland, I will get another photograph made of the children and send it to you.

We had some wonderful news over the winter. Katherine's brother, Joseph Morak, is coming over from the old country this year. Franz is going to sell him several acres of his land so he will be able to farm. Alex is excited, as he went to school with him in Liechtenstein and has not seen him for many years. Alex told me that Joseph was one of his dearest chums growing up.

Katherine had another child last summer. They named him Joseph, I suppose after her brother. That makes their seventh child, too. We are so very grateful for each other. Katherine has helped me birth all of my children except Tracy. Maria Siedl helps us now, too. She is a new neighbor to the west and has two children.

Alex is leaving in a few minutes to go to Troutdale and pick up supplies. I will have him post this. I am going to have another baby sometime in the summer. I will let you know as the time gets closer. Please give my love to everyone and know that you are always in my heart.

Julianna

Julianna sat for a moment after addressing the envelope. A tear dropped onto the paper, and she quickly wiped it away. I don't know what I will do with another child, she thought and shook her head. God forgive me.

"Come, children," she called. "Let's eat some bread and fruit, and then you can take a short nap." Julianna believed the smaller children needed a midday rest and so did she. With the older siblings in school, it was the only time she had to herself. It makes me a better mother when I have time to collect my thoughts.

Alex came home a short time later and, while he ate, she nursed the baby and brought up the pending new arrival. "I'm almost certain the baby will arrive sometime in late July or early August," she said.

"That's the best reason I know to be here this summer. I ran into Bob Graham this morning. With his logging business, he doesn't have time to finish his house or build his barn. He asked if I would take the job. For money, not hogs," he stressed the last part.

"That's wonderful news!"

"I'll take Ferd with me tomorrow and have a look around."

"I do wish I could go with you, but it's more than I want to tackle with the children," Julianna sighed. "It's all I can do to get them to the school functions. I do enjoy Anne Graham's company, though," she mused. "Do you suppose they might like to come over for an afternoon soon? Maybe you could ask them tomorrow."

"I'll do that." Alex promised.

***

In late February, the weather turned warm and beautiful. Alex took advantage of it and spent long days working on the Graham place. One morning, Julianna heard footsteps on the porch. Looking out, she was delighted to see Anne and her four-year-old son, Bobby.

"What a wonderful surprise!" Julianna exclaimed, as she opened the door.

"Yes, I've wanted to do this ever since Alex suggested it, and it's so lovely today. I thought it would be such fun to visit," Anne said.

"It's a perfect day and I needed some good company."

"I walked with the girls to school. Alex told me to just follow the path north from there and I couldn't miss you, and it worked." Anne laughed, in her quiet gentle way.

"And here you are." Julianna, elated to have adult company, beckoned to her, "come in and have some coffee. I've just finished feeding Jack, so he'll sleep for a couple of hours."

Anne and Julianne chatted over coffee and then, taking the three children with them, they strolled around the farm, careful not to get out of earshot of the sleeping baby. Julianna bragged about the fruit trees and showed off Nanny. The children were soon off playing.

Julianna basked in the warmth of the sunshine and her new-found friend. Anne, a few years younger then she, had dark, curly brown hair and a pleasant smile. Her eyes danced when she talked about her family. Julianna admired her youth and enthusiasm, and soon found herself immersed in her stories.

Too soon it was time for Anne to leave, amid promises to repeat the visit when the weather would permit. "Just tell Alex. He can be our messenger," Julianna suggested.

"I will, I promise."

And then she was gone. She left an aura of goodwill which enveloped Julianna for several days. She didn't feel as trapped or as isolated as before. There were other women in the area now who understood her need for company.

Later in the evening when everyone was settled down, she and Alex discussed the day. "I was happy to see the children when they came home from school," Julianna related, still feeling a flush of contentment.

"I was just leaving when Anne got home and she said to tell you that she had a grand time and is looking forward to seeing you again soon," Alex related, stretching his legs onto the small stool in front of his favorite chair.

"That would be nice." Julianna moved closer to the lamplight as she concentrated on the tiny dress she was mending. She added, "Anne told me of another family who moved southeast of here, by the name of Mershon. Did you know about them?"

"I just heard about them myself." Alex shifted in his chair and threw a round in the wood stove. "Their names are Alfred and Sarah and they've moved to a place across the Wire Trail from the Bates' farm. They have three sons and a daughter." He yawned and continued, "Pleasant View School is filling up."

"It seems like people are arriving fast," Julianna agreed.

"I hear it's because this land east of the Sandy River was the last to be surveyed. We were darned lucky to get here when we did. We could've been out of luck, just like we were at Bethany," Alex said. "I'm telling you, this soil is better by far than the land we lost out west of Portland. When I dug the cellar the top soil was over twelve feet deep."

"I believe it. Our vegetables are wonderful," Julianna said, with a far-away look in her eyes. "My Papa used to tell us to move our garden around, so next year I want to plow up some of the newly-cleared area for planting."

"That should work. Bob told me I could use his horse and plow in the spring to work up our ground."

"We have wonderful neighbors," Julianna exclaimed, "I'm beginning to not feel quite so isolated."

"I'm glad for that. It helps me to see you bright and happy." He took her hand and said, "You are my love, you know," and smiled at her.

"And you are mine," she smiled back.

Chapter 39

Early Summer 1893

The sun beat down on the two as they moved slowly along the onion row, working their way to the end.

On hands and knees, Julianna carefully pulled weeds and thinned the tiny plants. Her back ached and breast milk soaked through the padding that she'd fashioned, staining her blue shirtwaist.

The child in her womb kicked periodically as if to say, "Mama, stop. I'm hot."

He's hot, she thought. The heat radiated from the tilled ground, sending rivulets of perspiration through the dust on her cheeks.

Tracy crawled beside her, scratching through the plants, quiet and methodical. Finally she sat up and said, "Mama, can we rest when we come to that shade tree up the row?"

Julianna turned and noticed the dirt smooched on Tracy's tanned face. Her sun-bleached blond hair hung in wet mats around the back of her neck. "That would be a welcome relief," she said thinking they were close to finishing anyway.

"Emma, please go and fetch us all some cool water," she called to her second-born. Emma and Berty tended the smaller children, while she and Tracy worked the garden.

Overwhelmed with work, Alex was trying to finish the Graham house while helping the Mershon's build a shed. She knew he wouldn't be home until after dark.

When Julianna and Tracy reached the shade, everyone gathered around a large stump. All seven of them climbed on it and sat with their feet dangling, enjoying the refreshing water. The pungent smell of onions filled the air as several of the children snacked on the small plants. Julianna relaxed and fed the baby, glad for the excuse to rest a bit.

Soon rested, the children ran to what passed as a lawn near the west side of the house, but still in sight of their mother. Tracy joined in the children's games. The sound of their voices at play lulled Julianna and she found herself transported back to another time and the sounds of other children.

May 4, 1882 was a warm day, she remembered. The ship, oddly enough named *Canada,* had been her home for weeks, now floated serenely, tethered to the posts of the pier. She remembered her excitement and relief after the long journey. They were docked at the Battery in New York City. She smiled at her memory of how the earth felt strange after so many days at sea.

A group of children, some of them she recognized as having been on board, played with renewed energy after the confinement of the voyage.

Noisy, happy youngsters, the older ones played games while the younger boys tumbled around like wads of puppies.

She was seated near the Customs house, waiting while Alex filed his final paperwork and retrieved his pay. He'd worked nearly the whole journey repairing woodwork on board the ship and was anticipating a fat purse for his efforts.

She saw Alex in the distance, coming down the gang-plank, carrying both of their satchels. Their trunk, beside her, had been carried off earlier by a friendly deckhand. These three containers contained all of their worldly goods. A pang struck her as she remembered the family organ and collection of books she'd left behind in her parents' house. No matter, she thought. I have Alex and that is all I need.

His smile told her he was pleased.

"Now we can join Franz and Katherine in Illinois," Alex said when he reached her. "But first we are going to get rooms at a hotel and see New York City. This'll be our only chance."

"Mama, Arnold is pulling Josie's hair," Emma's voice snapped her back to the present. "Mama, help me!"

"Arnold, Arnold, come to Mama," Julianna called as she shifted the sleeping baby to her other arm and discreetly covered her breast. "Come here now and leave your sister alone." She put one arm around the child, who looked up at her and smiled his endearing innocent smile.

She patted his head and called to Josie, "Dear, come here and hold Jackie, while I finish my row."

Josie, always excited to hold babies, ran to her mother's side.

"Sit down and lean against the stump," Julianna instructed as she gently handed the baby to her small daughter. "Careful now, support his head. There, that's a good girl."

Emma came and sat down beside Josie to coach her on the finer points of caring for a tiny baby.

"Now, Arnold, you go with Berty." Julianna felt like an army sergeant, organizing and giving orders. "Tracy, let's finish these rows, so we can quit for the day."

She winced as she dropped to her knees. A sharp pang slammed through her side, leaving her breathless. She grabbed her pregnant belly, sucking in air, trying to catch her breath. Then the pain left, as quickly as it started. When she finished her row, she stood up, but the ground spun around. She grasped at an overhanging tree branch to steady herself, and after a moment, could walk without pain. Her dizziness subsided, but for the rest of the afternoon, she felt light-headed. When she pressed on one particular place on her left side, it was painful.

She and Tracy managed to get dinner on the table and feed the children, but as soon as they finished she lay down. The east wind blew hot air into the house, but she felt chilled and nauseated.

When Alex got home, he found her there. Tracy and Emma had put the younger children to bed. The baby lay beside Julianna. He took one look at her and his expression told her how worried he was.

"I'm going for Katherine, right now," he said and bolted for the door. "Do not get up."

Katherine was there in less than an hour. Alex followed her up the path, carrying Joseph in his arms.

"I had to bring the baby," she said. "I have no idea how long you'll need me."

***

"Tracy, fix some cereal for Jackie," Katherine said as she came into the kitchen from the bedroom, carrying the wailing child.

Alex followed and sat down at the table, his head bowed, hands on his thinning hair. He sat silent for a long time, oblivious to the sounds around him.

Tracy warmed the cooked cereal with a little water from the teakettle simmering on the stove while Emma finished washing the breakfast dishes. Of the smaller children, only Josie stayed inside and had a worried look on her tiny face.

"Jackie sick?" she asked, pulling on Katherine's skirt.

"No, darling. He's just a hungry boy," Katherine said, as she patted the child's blond curls. "Little babies cry like this when they want to eat. Why don't you go out and play with the rest of the children? Bertie needs you to play with her."

But Josie stayed. She climbed on the bench beside her father, as if waiting for things to be right.

Alex sighed. "What are we going to do?" he asked. "Do you think we can save the baby? What about Julianna?" His hands shook and he felt himself blinking back tears.

"She's been taking care of six young children and a baby." Katherine sat at the end of the table with Jackie in her lap, carefully spooning food into the now quiet infant's mouth. "She's still nursing and expecting her eighth child in a few weeks. On top of that she's trying to keep the garden up." Katherine turned crimson as she talked. "Alex, it's no wonder she's ill." Her mouth tightened and she remained quiet for a few moments.

Alex sat and watched her. He could see her vexation and exhaustion. "Katherine, I can't tell you how much we appreciate your wonderful friendship." He finally said. "I can see now that things are too much for her, but she never complains, so I didn't notice before."

He saw Katherine relax as he talked. He knew she adored Julianna and was as worried as he was. "What do you think is the matter? Shall I go to Troutdale and get the doctor?" he said remembering Julianna's earlier problems with childbirth.

"I don't think it would hurt. I'm not trained to see the tiny things that can go wrong while carrying a child."

"I'll go right now. I'll have him here by early afternoon. Do you need me to bring anything back for you from your house?"

"No, just tell Franz I won't be home for a couple more days," Katherine replied as she arose to take the now sleeping baby back to his mother's bed. "I'm not leaving until I know Julianna is all right."

***

Alex and the doctor arrived before two o'clock to find Julianna resting quietly. "Darling," Alex said gently awakening her, "This is Dr. Volp from Troutdale. You remember him, don't you? He speaks German."

Julianna smiled weakly and nodded to the doctor.

Alex joined Katherine on the front steps, where she held both babies and watched the other children at play. Alex took Jackie from her, and she put Joseph on her shoulder. They sat in silence for a time.

Finally Alex said, "I think I should not have brought Julianna out here to this wilderness."

"It's more difficult than any of us thought it would be." Katherine shook her head. "But don't be too hard on yourself, Alex. We all wanted to come." Katherine said sounding less accusatory.

After a time, Alex nodded in agreement. "That's true. I knew it would be harsh, but in my youth, I saw it as a lucrative adventure. In some ways, it has been. We own more land than I ever dreamed possible. Though we haven't finished proving up on it and I still haven't been able to farm full time." He scratched his head. "We've discussed selling the acreage on the north bench. That would make someone a dandy farm and give us a nice bit of cash reserve." He sighed and glanced toward the bedroom where Julianna lay ill.

"Can you sell land that you haven't proved up on?"

"No, but we should have a clear title within two or three years."

"I think that would be a good idea. I know Julianna's life would be a lot easier if you could stay home."

"I'm going to look into it. I can hardly bear to leave her anyway." He rubbed his chin, where a stubbly beard had appeared, reminding him to shave. "She never tells me if she is not feeling well," he continued. "She's a remarkable woman." He paused and said, "And so are you"

Katherine looked away and murmured her thanks. After a short silence she said, "When we were children, did you ever dream that we would be so far from the homeland?"

"I knew that I wanted to be. There wasn't enough land back home."

"Don't you miss your brothers?"

"Well, yes, but Franz is like a brother, too." Alex rose and paced the floor. "I wonder what's taking so long."

Just then Dr. Volp opened the door and called for them to come in.

198

"Julianna has pulled a muscle in her abdomen. She is not to get up for the next week, except to eat. She is not to do any outside work until the baby comes and, for heaven's sake, she must not nurse the child anymore. It takes too much out of her. She's exhausted." His tone had an edge of exasperation to it. "I want you to treat her as if she were a queen for the rest of her time."

"We'll do that." Alex felt a great flood of relief wash over him, as he reached for his wife's hand.

Chapter 40

Mid-Summer / Fall 1893

On a warm day in early August, Alexander Junior met his seven siblings. Alex reluctantly agreed to Julianna's wishes to name the newest arrival after him.

"I guess it'll be all right, if you can't think of a more flamboyant name," he said as he beamed down at the child in his arms. "He is a perfect baby, isn't he?" He announced, when he showed the new arrival to the children.

"Where's his hair, Papa?" Bertie asked, the now familiar question.

"See, here it is," Emma answered, while softly patting the baby's thin blond hair.

Alex laughed and together they examined the latest arrival's perfect fingers and toes.

Katherine, who'd returned to the Lamperts for the birth, gathered her things and left that afternoon, saying that she was anxious to get back to her family so she could help nine-year-old Mary get supper on the table. On her way out the door, she reminded Alex that her brother, Joseph, would be arriving any day.

"I'll be over to check tomorrow," Alex said as he waved a good-bye. "And thanks again for your help."

Joseph didn't arrive until the following Monday. When Katherine and Franz brought him over to visit, Alex couldn't believe his eyes. His childhood friend, here in the United States. He sounded and looked the same, except for a slight bald spot.

"It's good to see you, old friend. It's great to have you with us." Overjoyed, Alex slapped him on the back. "Julianna, this is Joseph, my school chum."

The families spent the day catching up on news and showing Joseph the farms, the river, and the view of their beloved Mt. Hood. The next morning, Alex and Franz helped Joseph step off his land. Joseph decided to build his home on a flat clear spot close to the trail leading to the Frommelt home.

He and Alex walked to Latourell to order the lumber for Joseph's house. They hoped to begin the project before the end of the month to beat the fall rains.

***

School started on August 21, much to the joy of the children.

"Mama, can I go, please?" Ferd asked once again.

"Your birthday isn't until Sept. 16th. The rules say you must be six to go to school," Julianna reminded him.

"I can learn to read and I'm strong. I can walk that far, even farther." His bright eyes shone with eagerness.

Julianna felt herself weaken. He'd wanted to go to school for so long. He beseeched her to read to him, so she had read part of her beloved German translated book, *David Copperfield* to the children. He loved the story and begged for more. She felt his age wouldn't be a handicap, but rules were rules.

She shook her head and Ferd went outside, dejected.

That evening she discussed the issue with Alex as they readied themselves for bed. "He is very bright," she said. "I'm not sure why the rules are there and I don't know how strict they are with them."

"He's spoken of nothing else for months," Alex said, as he pulled on his nightshirt. Shaking his head, he continued, "I'm not sure how many years he'll be able to stay in school. If I get another acre or so cleared, we'll be into farming full time and I'll need him to help in the fields."

"Well, he's got to learn to read and to speak English, so I'm of a mind to send him this year." Julianna slid into the comfortable bed and lay there enjoying the moment.

"I'll walk with the children the first morning and talk over the situation with the teacher. We can let her decide whether she'll admit Ferd," Alex said as he climbed in beside her.

***

On Monday, Julianna watched over the older children, making sure each of them dressed in their finest clothes. Their excitement mirrored Ferd's thrill at the possibility of getting to enroll in Pleasant View School.

The night before, Tracy and Emma had packed four tin buckets with bread and cheese and an apple. They gathered their slates and Alex presented Ferd with one of his very own, just like his sisters'.

The next morning, Franz brought the Frommelt children by and they all left together, walking up the trail, with the children's happy voices ringing through the woods. Julianna watched them leave with a smile, remembering her happy childhood school days.

When they were out of sight she turned to the chores at hand. With two children still in diapers, she spent many mornings at the washtub, and this was no different, except her good help had left with their Papa. Four-year-old Josie tried her best to assist her, but finally Julianna had to put her to work watching Arnold and Jack so they wouldn't get into mischief.

***

"I don't see any reason why Ferd can't stay in school," Miss Olla Emily, a pretty young woman with bright sparkling eyes, said to Alex after he explained Ferd's desire to learn. Almost every year, Pleasant View School had a new teacher. This one might last a few years, he thought as he spoke to her. Her family lives just a few miles away.

She turned to Ferd and asked, "You're a bright lad, aren't you?"

He nodded and grinned a gap-toothed grin, having lost one of his front teeth while roughhousing with Aloysius Frommelt the week before.

***

The rest of the summer and fall passed smoothly. With his work at the Grahams' and Mershons' finally done, Alex spent the first week of November finishing the potato and carrot harvest, piling the vegetables high in the cellar, ready to use when the cold weather set in. Alex had helped Joseph build his house and had it mostly completed before the November rains pummeled the region.

By Thanksgiving school had came to a halt. The trails, unusually muddy, didn't allow easy passage and no one knew when a massive cold storm might roll in. The board met and decided it was time to lock the school until spring, except for the annual Christmas party.

Tracy, at age ten, finished her third reader and said she felt quite grown-up. She helped her mother with her English, but Julianna's heart wasn't in it. She had many other things on her mind.

Both Emma and Berty almost finished the second reader, even though Berty was a year younger. She sat by Emma and learned from her as well as the teacher.

"There's something to be said for one room schools," Alex said when he learned of Berty's progress. "The little ones learn from the big ones." He chuckled at his brilliance.

"I did, Papa," Ferd said, waving his slate. "Look what I can write." He stuck the words under Alex's nose and Alex pushed them back in focus. There in neat print were "Cat", "Dog", and "Cow".

"Did you write those from memory?" Alex asked the small boy with the eager eyes.

"Yes, Papa, I did," he answered.

"That's a fine job, son. I'm proud of you." He patted the boy's head. "I'm proud of all of you children. Next time I go to Troutdale for supplies, I'll bring you each a special treat."

Chapter 41

1894

Julianna carried the baby over the trail to Katherine's on a warm day the first part of March, grateful that the winter had turned mild and spring came early. Her three small sons of varying ages followed her down the path, except when they found interesting flowers or funny-looking insects to detain them.

She hadn't seen Katherine for several weeks and was eager to visit with her. She'd sent word with Alex the day before, so Katherine would be expecting her, and she didn't want to be late.

She thought of the importance of each family in each others lives and remembered their days in Freeport and how fond she had grown of Katherine. It's a good thing I taught her midwifery. It's come in handy out here in the wild.

Katherine was just pulling pies out of the oven when they arrived. The two friends greeted each other enthusiastically and sent the children out to play. The older ones were now back in school for the spring session.

They spent the day catching up and their time came to an end much too soon.

"I guess I should mention before I leave that I am going to have another baby probably in September," Julianna said almost as an after thought, as she dressed Alex Jr. for the trek home.

"Oh my," Katherine said in a worried tone. "Have you told Alex yet?"

Julianna shook her head. "No, I thought I'd wait a bit longer. He hasn't felt well these last few weeks and I don't want to add to his worries." Pausing she added, "I don't know why I'm afraid to tell him. He'll just say it's one more hand for the farm." But her laughter had a hollow ring.

***

In June, the Frommelts, Lamperts and their new friends, the Siedls, welcomed Joseph's wife, Elma and their young son, Augustus. Joseph had sent for her early in the winter after the men had finished building his house.

Julianna liked the kind-faced, gentle woman who had to have a heart of steel to attempt the journey from Lichtenstein all the way to the Northwest by herself. When Julianna mentioned this, she laughed and said, "Joseph is the only man I want to spend my life with so I had no choice." Her eyes twinkled as she glanced at her husband.

The celebration took place at Franz and Katherine's, and lasted until well after supper. Because it stayed light until past nine o'clock, the families did not have to walk home in the dark.

"We're becoming a community, aren't we?" Julianna posed on the trip home.

Alex nodded and continued his silent walk. She noticed his breathing had become more labored and wondered if it was time to start him on more of the Irish tea.

The next day, she left the two babies with Tracy, and taking the other children into the woods, they gathered nettles, which she added to the Irish tea. She'd decided sometime earlier that the herbs might be good for Alex. They'd helped her when she'd had such trouble with Ferd's pregnancy. Alex made a face with the first swallow, but dutifully drank it morning and evening for ten days, and along with his work in the sunshine, he seemed to improve.

He went to bed early and tried to get as much rest as possible so he could keep up the farm. He had cleared another acre, and by the end of June, had a late crop of potatoes planted. He knew they'd do well in the "new" ground.

In September they welcomed their fifth son, Bernard, born sooner than Julianna had anticipated. He didn't weigh as much as her other children at birth, which worried both her and Katherine.

"I don't know why he's so small," Julianna exclaimed to her friend. "He just doesn't seem to be as strong as the others."

Katherine nodded, but didn't comment. Julianna noted that and believed it to be her friend's concern, not only for the new baby, but for her feelings as well. That's like Katherine, she thought. She doesn't want to scare me. But Julianna felt with good care and food, Bernard would thrive and grow strong.

By Christmas, he had gained some of the weight he needed thanks to Emma and Tracy's attention, as well as her own. It seemed as if they were on a mission, a chosen vocation to help their baby brother. The rest of the siblings gathered around him as well. It was as though Bernard didn't have a choice but to grow stronger and bigger.

An inner voice, somewhere deep inside, told Julianna he would be her last child. Perhaps the children feel it, too, she thought, and then wondered what made her feel this way.

Chapter 42

Winter 1895

A howling storm struck the fifth day of January. It blew in from the south, dumping almost a foot of snow in two days. Alex checked on the goats and the chickens twice a day and carried warm water out to melt the ice in their troughs.

After three days the winds changed and came from the east, bringing more snow flurries drifting against the house in large fluffy mounds, reminding Alex of the marshmallow confection they ate at a train depot somewhere in France. As the snow piled higher, Alex noticed the house beginning to hold more heat and the wood lasting longer in the stoves.

"The house is warmer, don't you think?" he said to Julianna as she worked in the kitchen.

Busy with supper preparation, she nodded, but said nothing.

He wandered into the living room, sat in his favorite chair close to the window and watched the snow swirl, remembering the storms of his childhood. The thick stone walls of his boyhood home insulated them much better than the lumber built ones here. Here we are on top of a knoll. Fortunately, we're sheltered somewhat by the hill behind us. I've a mind to build a stone house in the draw and tear this one down. He pondered the idea as he watched the snow blowing around the yard and heard it ping against the window.

He decided that would be his first project after he got the farm going. He needed a horse and a cow and would have to build a barn, so it would be a few years, but that's what he'd do.

The storm lasted another week and ended with freezing rain.

"Look Papa, everything's silver," Josie said, her voice filled with awe.

By the time it was over, everyone wanted to go outside, even though the earth was muddy from the melting ice and snow.

***

February came and with it, warm sunny days, which meant the children returned to school, much to Julianna's relief. Although Julianna missed her good help, Josie started school. Seeing the child's cheeks glow with excitement made the sacrifice worthwhile.

Bernard continued to make progress. Although he was still small for his age, he thrived with all the attention and continued a gradual weight gain. His brothers took Josie's place during the day and showered the baby with attention.

Alex, determined to stay home more this season and begin his farm in earnest, had cleared another acre and traded a small building project for Mr.

Graham's horse to plow and disk. He seeded a half-acre of sweet onions and several rows of tall peas as soon as the ground was ready.

By the end of April, he had an acre of the Burbank potatoes planted as well. He was excited at the prospect of finally getting his farm off to a good start. While he worked, Arnold and Jack followed his every footstep, pummeling him with questions. Little Alex did his best to keep up, falling often in the soft dirt, but picking himself up without a word. Sometimes Alex had to take them all to the spring to wash before returning to the house.

May found him taking his tools and heading for Portland to work on a project Franz found earlier. The cash in the jar in the cellar was almost gone and Alex needed money for seeds.

"Are you sure it's safe for you to go back in to town?" Julianna asked when he finally broached the subject to her.

"Franz said Matt told him that Marsden was stabbed in a bar brawl last fall. With him gone, we're safe," Alex said, his voice firm. He hoped he sounded braver then he felt.

"I hope so. We'd be in bad shape without you."

Alex took her in his arms and held her close. "You won't be without me for long." He smiled at her and said, "I'll be home in time for the school picnic. I surely don't want to miss that."

"No, the children and I would be disappointed if you weren't there." Julianna patted his cheek and said, "Hurry home then." She brushed his cheek with a kiss and added, "Please bring me home a couple of nice lemons, if you can find some."

***

Because of the long winter break, school stayed in session until June 7th, with the annual last day of school picnic scheduled for Saturday the 8th. Alex promised he'd be home to stay by then. Julianna worried, remembering the times he'd been delayed and was relieved to see him coming down the road toward home on Thursday,

"Oh, you did remember," she exclaimed as he handed her two large lemons. She smelled them, savoring the pungent, almost forgotten aroma.

"How could I forget something as important as that," he said his voice light and fun. "Now are you going to tell me why you wanted it?"

"Just you wait and see," she teased as she helped him unload his backpack.

She spent the next day in the kitchen, Bernard in his crib beside her. He rarely cried and never without good reason, reminding her of Alex and his quiet temperament. The other boys spent the day outdoors with Alex, even though rain showers came and went. The onions, in dire need of weeding, kept them occupied.

Julianna stirred and mixed and grated, enjoying the rare moments of quiet time. The house smelled of good things baking and when the day was

206

done, two lemon sponge cakes sat on the kitchen counter, one for the potluck and one to celebrate the true beginnings of the long-awaited farm life.

She fixed a large kettle of Alex's favorite sauerkraut and some of the savory leftover sausages from the hogs they'd butchered last fall. She made sure there was enough for supper and tomorrow's picnic.

She'd used the last of the sausages and decided they should buy some wiener pigs from Sutliff and raise them since Alex was planning on spending the rest of the year farming. He could pasture them with the goats and feed them table scraps.

***

By the time they reached the school on Saturday for the picnic, many people had already gathered. Julianna spotted Anne Graham as she came up the path to greet them.

"My, there's quite a crowd," Julianna said, thankful that Tracy had coached her in English enough that she could more easily visit with her neighbors.

"Yes, there is," Anne agreed, adding, "some of the older boys dropped out in early May, but they still showed up for the celebration."

They laughed at that and were soon surrounded by friends, many of whom they hadn't seen since Christmas. Julianna nodded and waved to Bella and Anne Dunn who were visiting beside the table, which was filling up with food.

The morning started out overcast and Julianna had been afraid it would storm, but the clouds moved out, and now the sun shone in brief welcome moments. John Smith had opened the school in case everyone needed to seek shelter, but it appeared the weather would cooperate.

Julianna took Bernard from his father's arms and walked over to visit with Elma and Katherine, who were cutting Katherine's pies into generous pieces.

"Julianna, you remember Sarah Mershon, don't you?" Katherine asked, smiling at the sweet looking woman unloading a large bowl of fried chicken, while balancing her ten-month-old daughter, Margaret, in her left arm.

"I certainly do. It's nice to see you," Julianna nodded. She remembered meeting her at the Christmas party. Sarah and her husband, Alfred, had moved onto a farm close to the Dunn place on the corner of the Wire Trail and the road into the Chamberlain place.

The four of them chatted as Elma spread out blankets for the babies on top of the tarps the men had placed on the ground to keep the dampness down. June was still too rainy to safely put infants directly on the grass. Her dear friend, Mae had warned Julianna of the dire consequences of that several years ago.

"Children get congested and may die," she had cautioned.

207

Sarah Chamberlain and Orilla came over to say hello and the group sat in the rays of the now warm sun. The informal program began with its well-rehearsed performers reciting poems, stories and a few songs. The three children in the first reader group, where Josie belonged, sang "Mary Had a Little Lamb". They sang their hearts out and were only slightly off key. Julianna felt herself swelling with pride watching their earnest performance.

Ferd, who was almost through his second reader, recited a poem in almost perfect English, entitled the "Wise Old Owl". Surprised at his excellent pronunciations, Julianna looked at Alex standing with Franz, Joseph, and the other men. He winked at her in his pride.

The group took a break and ate dinner. After the food, the students participated in a spelling bee. Mary, Tracy and Emma had all looked forward to it, most particularly the twenty-five cent first prize. Hattie and Alma Graham were worthy opponents as were Bert and Nettie Chamberlain, Frank and Alta Bates and Leroy Mershon.

The first words were considered easy, but Julianna, still struggling with English, could hardly pronounce them, let alone spell them. When they got to words like "Mississippi", she was completely lost, but there were still five contenders left; Mary, Tracy, Nettie, Frank and Leroy.

"Reconsideration" stumped Hattie with one too many "S's" and she dropped out. Frank got it right and remained. Mary's word, "description", proved too much and she sat down. Now it was up to Nettie, with her word, "exhaustive," which she missed because of the pesky "h."

Leroy and Tracy remained standing. Each was in the money because second prize paid a dime. Julianna held her breath as Tracy received her word, "illusion". Tracy hesitated a moment, pronounced the word and began spelling: "i-l," hesitated again, "l-u-s-s, no, no," she said shaking her head.

"I'd like to begin again please," she said politely.

Miss Emily nodded, and Tracy began again, "i-l-l-l-u-s-i-o-n, illusion," she repeated.

Julianna sucked in her breath as the teacher once again nodded and gave Leroy his word, "misapprehend."

Leroy, a tall, gangly lad of eleven, faltered a bit, recovered, pronounced the word, and began to spell, his voice confident, "m-i-s-a-p-p-r-e-n-d," and said the word again.

Miss Emily shook her head and gave the word to Tracy, who spelled it correctly without wavering. Julianna patted her daughter's head in pride, when Tracy showed her the two-bit piece.

"What are you going to do with that?" Alex asked her later.

She thought for several minutes. "I'm not sure," was her final answer, "maybe I'll buy some more lemons. I'd like to learn how to make those cakes."

Chapter 43

Summer 1895

Alex worked in his fields most of the summer, with Julianna joining him whenever she could, usually when the babies were down for their naps. Tracy, who turned 12 in June, spent her time in the kitchen, learning her mother's recipes and inventing a few of her own, while Emma and Bertie helped with the laundry. The rest of the children worked in the field, and when they grew tired and restless, Alex sent them into the nearby woods to play and cool off.

As expected the potato plants grew large, and when Alex dug a hill he was delighted to see eight small spuds growing on the roots. Mmmm, this'll bring a lot of bushels for the loggers in Brower, he thought, remembering Tom Evans telling him how the local farmers could never grow enough vegetables for the families in that Larch Mountain town.

In late June, when Alex and Julianna looked over their fields, it became apparent they could not keep ahead of the weeds with hoes. The rich ground fertilized not only the carefully planted crops, but the unwelcome lambs quarter, pig weed and sour grass as well.

"I need a cultivator to clean up these rows," Alex said to Julianna as he leaned over and pulled up some rogue grass.

Quiet for a moment, she said with a puzzled look, "What is that? I don't know what you mean."

Alex nodded, remembering she'd been raised in the city.

"That, my dear, is a piece of equipment with several small plow shafts attached to it. It's horse-drawn and works up one or two rows at a time," he explained as he drew a picture in the dry dirt.

"That would be wonderful," Julianna agreed. "But where will you get the horse?"

"I've been thinking, if we pay to have a cultivator built, we can loan it to Joseph and when he is done, he can loan us his horse," Alex answered, with pride in his voice. "That way we both can have clean fields."

Julianna laughed and threw her head back to flick her hair out of her eyes, displaying a smudge of dirt on her neck as well as the one on her cheek. Alex figured that he must truly be a farmer because he found those patches of soil on his wife tantalizing.

"I thought you'd think I was a genius," he chuckled and wondered if she felt that he was a true man of the soil. Somehow he doubted it. She'd always bragged on his carpentry.

He walked over to Joseph's house that evening after dinner to discuss the idea. The next day they hiked to Troutdale. Alex had drawn up some plans of what he'd like to have built and he gave them to Mr. Hensley, the blacksmith, who said he'd made something similar for a "fella over near

Camp Ground last year." Then he growled, "I guess they call it Gresham now."

Hensley thought it might take him a week or two and would probably cost $15 to $20. He had a couple of the small shafts already made. He called them shoes and said he figured that a two-row cultivator should have six of them.

In two weeks when they walked down to pick up their new farm implement, Hensley showed them how he'd made the shoes adjustable, so they could widen or narrow them according to the rows, "because as the plants grow the rows get wider."

"So how much is this gonna cost?" Alex asked, running his hands over the smooth wooden handles.

"Fellas, I'm gonna have to charge you $20," he said. "The price of iron is going up and I'm short of scraps." He shook his head. Alex agreed it was a fair price, and after trying to hoe the fields by hand, he was happy to pay it.

The two of them managed to propel the cultivator up the steep trail with the aid of ropes and muscle power. They left it at Joseph's with a promise that Alex would have it and the horse in a couple of days.

The new cultivator lightened all their loads. Even Franz delighted in the innovative progress, giving Alex $10 as an investment in the tool. Alex knew he'd get back the other $10 as the produce sold.

When he'd finished cultivating the field the first time, feeling the soft, warm dirt around his boots and smelling the freshly-turned moist soil, he turned and called to Julianna, who was standing on the porch waving him in to dinner.

"Look at that," he said, motioning over the potato field. "All that is done in one day. We couldn't have cleaned it up in two weeks and it never would it have looked this good."

"It's perfect." Julianna gazed at him with affection. "You're so smart."

***

As summer turned to fall, Alex and Julianna dug, cleaned and sold many bushels of potatoes, carrots and later, rutabagas and turnips. It seemed that the people of Brower had insatiable appetites, which pleased the farmers.

Tom said it was because loggers were "big fellas and needed a lot of food to fill them up". On top of that, Palmer, a new logging village, was being built high up on Larch Mountain, with a flume to the Bridal Veil sawmill. It seemed to Alex that it was a perfect time to get his farm underway.

Alex and Joseph took turns using Bess, Joseph's horse, to haul their produce, as well as Franz's once a week up to the logging communities. One week, Alex and Tom met up on the delivery route.

"Did you plant any cabbage?" Tom wanted to know.

"No, only enough for myself," Alex said shaking his head.

"Too bad. The people up here are asking for it."

"Guess we'll plant an acre or so next year."

"Spoken like a true farmer," Tom said with a grin.

On October 4, Alex turned 39 and felt better than he had for a long time. Must be the fresh farm air, he thought. Julianna teased him about his balding forehead, but he couldn't find any gray hair, so he knew he was still young. Besides, his father had a high forehead and his mother said it made him look distinguished.

By mid-November, three quarters of the field had been harvested. One evening Alex looked up from his paperwork and said to Julianna, "Do you know that we've sold over 100 bushels of potatoes alone?" He shook his head in amazement.

"Lord knows you're killing yourself doing it." Her voice rang with concern, and then softened when she said, "But it's nice to have you home."

Alex ignored the first comment, he smiled at the last. He knew he'd beaten the sickness before, and he had no doubt he could do it again.

"Let's see," he continued, "at five cents a pound, and 60 pounds in a bushel, that's over three hundred dollars just for the potatoes." Even though he'd kept careful records of his sales, it didn't cease to surprise him that they'd made such a fine profit from their efforts. They would have a good stash of money to get them through the winter.

He'd traded some of the produce for building materials for the barn. The last few loads he'd delivered, he'd brought back lumber for himself and cash for Joseph and Franz.

He and Julianna carefully dug the rest of the vegetables, except for the parsnips, which were left in the ground to get a freeze or two on them to bring up the sugar. Alex dug a large hole at the most protected edge of the field because there were too many vegetables to store in the cellar. He and Julianna carefully mounded up the unwashed root crops in the pit, covering it with rough boards and heaping soil on top.

"There now, they shouldn't freeze," Alex told Julianna. "We'll be able to sell them as long as the weather holds and the roads aren't too muddy."

***

The east wind blew most of fall season and kept the rains away. By the second week in December, the men were still making deliveries, one week to Brower and the next to Palmer, though the logging had almost halted. In the winter most of the lumbering families stayed on in the little towns, sending their children to the schools in their communities and waiting out the weather.

Just before Christmas, an exhausted Alex set out to deliver what would probably be the last load of their crops for the season. If the buried vegetables held over during the cold spells and didn't freeze, he knew he could sell the rest in February and March.

Julianna watched Alex and the rig, loaded with produce, leave out on the path towards the Wire Trail, with his load of produce. The men, as usual, loaded everything the day before the delivery so they were ready to leave at daybreak. With most of his barn built, Alex had shelter for the horse when it was his turn to drive.

I know he's weary, but I don't think I've ever seen him this content, she thought, returning his wave as he rounded the corner by the gate he'd erected last fall. She'd laughed at him when he told her, "This windy ridge needs to look like a real farm. I'm putting up a gate on the path out there at the corner." And surprisingly it added a flavor that she loved. He'd built it out of split cedar from one of Franz's winter falls. It was heavy and durable and when he closed it on his way home from a journey, she felt contentment that he was home and her life complete.

I'll fix up another batch of his tea. I'm sure he'll need it when he gets home, she thought.

Chapter 44

Late Spring 1896

In mid-April, it was dry enough for Alex to work the fields in preparation for planting. The friable soil had drained quickly from the spring rains and in spite of his ailments, the work must be done.

One morning he walked over to Joseph's, hooked Bess up to the disk, and brought her across the fields to begin the lengthy process of breaking the earth. He never tired of seeing the swathes he cut as he circled the field, one round after the other. The smell of freshly-worked ground invigorated him.

Pleased with his pace, he had the field over half done when he noticed a dark threatening cloud coming in from the west. Looks like a good size storm blowing, he thought as he slapped Bess on the rump with the reins.

"Let's go girl," he hollered. "Let's see how fast we can get this done."

But it was not to be. The wind stirred the leaves, and then set them dancing, and he caught the low-throated rumble of thunder in the distance.

The first large drops pounded Alex and the horse on the way to the barn, and by the time they arrived, both of them were drenched. The temperature, not warm that day, dropped with the storm. Alex shivered as he unhooked Bess, dried, and blanketed her. He threw her a handful of hay and hurried, wheezing, to the house.

Julianna met him at the door with a towel and dry clothes. For the rest of the day, he had a chill, and by the next morning, his cough had returned, deep and ugly.

The rains continued for the next several days, so Julianna had Ferd and little Josie take care of the horse. Joseph came over on the fourth day to fetch Bess, and when he saw how sick Alex appeared, he promised to come over and finish the field as soon as the weather permitted.

Julianna, most grateful to Joseph, nodded and told him how much she appreciated him.

He'd laughed at that and teased, "Hey, I've got to protect my investment in that horse."

For the next few days, Julianna served Alex his special tea, fixed him bowls of chicken soup and kept hot mustard compresses on his chest. At first his appetite waned, but by the end of the week, he ate a little more and his cough abated, but Julianna didn't like his ashen color.

"It appears you're feeling better," she said with a smile as she gently touched his forehead.

"That tea always does the trick," he replied. "Just keep it coming."

The beginning of the following week, with Alex still weak, Joseph finished the disking and promised that if Alex wasn't up to it, he'd come back with the plow and do that as well.

Alex slowly regained his strength and by the end of April, with Joseph's help, he finished working the fields. He found that he couldn't work as fast, but by late May had planted almost the same amount as last year, and added a half of an acre of cabbage. At the end of planting, he took to his bed for several days.

***

Julianna tried her best to hide her worry from Alex and the children, but she could see that he wasn't recovering from his last bout of sickness. Even though he would be only forty next October, he looked spent and walked slowly and bent over as though he were elderly.

At the end of June, it took him five days to cultivate the same amount that he'd done in a day the year before and afterward needed a week to rest from the exertion.

"I think Bess must be slowing up. It took her a lot longer to get the job done this year," he'd said, when Julianna mentioned it to him. He'd laughed, but his eyes, sunk deep into his sockets, didn't have the old light.

***

Alex gazed over his half-grown crop as he slumped down on a fallen log at the edge of the clearing. He'd told himself and Julianna that he'd regain his health, but he knew it was far from the truth. He shook his head and buried his face in his hands. What would she do without him?

Joseph and Franz came over the next day to help out, and Alex used the opportunity to discuss a journey to Oregon City. Whatever befell him, he had to get the homestead papers in order or Julianna might lose the land and he couldn't let that happen. He needed a witness to vouch that he'd made improvements on the farm.

Franz, set to go to Portland to work the following week, expressed frustration at not being able to go with Alex, but Joseph agreed to accompany him.

"We'll go on Monday," he said.

Alex nodded. "That's good," he said and thought, I have three days to rest up, as he struggled to hold back a cough.

"Please see a doctor while you're there," Julianna begged when he told her about his plans.

He hesitated and then nodded, "I'll do that."

***

He clutched his chest, dropped to one knee and coughed into his blood stained handkerchief.

"Alex!" Joseph cried. He reached for his friend, trying to keep him from sprawling onto the dusty road.

Alex coughed again and gasped for breath, then shook his head, waving Joseph away.

"I'm fine, I'm fine," he muttered and collapsed into spasms again.

Joseph fished a clean handkerchief out of his pocket, walked to the river, dunked it in the cold water and brought it to Alex.

The damp cloth cooled his face and relaxed him. Within a few minutes his breathing returned to its normal rhythm.

"I'm all right now," Alex said as he struggled to his feet with the help of a sturdy walking stick. "We have to get to the courthouse before five o'clock." He set his jaw and staggered off down the trail.

In the past, I would've been there by now, he lamented, willing each step and leaning heavily on the gnarled limb he'd picked up along the way.

They followed the Clackamas River, which seemed to be in a hurry to end its own journey and empty into the Willamette. If only I could muster up that kind of energy, he thought, his gaze landing on the river current. He gasped for air and put one foot in front of the other. Another step, now another one. Yes, that's it, now one more. He found a rhythm, one and two.... It helped take his mind off the stabbing pain in his chest. Gasping for air...three and four....

Joseph paused for him to catch up. Don't talk to me. Don't ruin my concentration...five and six. Sensing his dilemma, Joseph took Alex's arm and together they made the rhythm work. One foot in front of the other, step by step.

Time passed, with Alex halting his journey only when a cough surged and his choking rendered him unable to continue.

"I think we should stop for a few minutes," Joseph suggested.

Alex nodded and reluctantly slumped down on a fallen log near the trail's edge. He leaned against a small tree growing nearby and closed his eyes, his breathing heavy and labored. Joseph wiped the beaded sweat from his friend's forehead.

After a time, Alex opened one eye and saw Joseph standing by the water's edge, looking down the road, back the way they'd come.

Around the bend came a pair of perfectly matched Morgans pulling a dusty black surrey. When the horses came even with the tired men, they stopped.

"Can I give you fellows a ride?" asked the bearded driver. He had kind eyes and a portly figure. "Name's Thompson," he continued, sticking out a large work-worn hand.

"That'd be good. My friend here is ill and he wants to get to the courthouse in Oregon City before it closes," Joseph said, his face showing the relief that Alex felt.

"I'm on my way to the city myself. Let's see if we can get you there in time."

Alex rose slowly, and with Joseph's help, he climbed in the back seat and soon fell into a feverish sleep.

"We're here, Alex." The sound of Joseph's voice woke him. "This kind fellow drove us right up to the front door."

Alex stretched and tried to smile, but it was smothered by another coughing bout. When he had it under control, he managed to thank the man.

"Can we pay you?" he asked.

The driver shook his head.

"We appreciate your kindness," Joseph said, as he reached to shake Thompson's hand and help Alex to the ground.

"It's on my way. I'm glad to do it." He picked up the reins and turned to Alex.

"I hope you feel better soon, young fellow," he said and urged the horses onto the road.

Alex pulled out his watch and gave a sigh of relief. It was 4:35. "We made it," he muttered. "We did it."

"Come, let's get you registered. Maybe we can catch the evening train into Portland. We aren't going to try to walk back home."

Alex nodded, walked through the door and approached the counter where a balding man wearing round rimless glasses greeted them. Alex gave him the satchel and watched him remove the papers and read them carefully.

"You're Alex Lampert?" he asked peering over top of his spectacles.

Alex nodded.

"Who's going to verify this is true?" He pointed to Joseph. "This fellow?"

"Yes, he's my neighbor and friend. His name is Joseph Marog. He farms the place next to mine.

"How long have you known Mr. Lampert?"

"A long time, we were school mates in the old country. My sister and her husband have lived and farmed next door to him since '85. I've been his neighbor for three years myself." Joseph's face was red, but his voice was firm, belying his shyness.

"Sign here, then."

Joseph signed on the designated line and they watched as the clerk notarized it.

"I'll be right back." The clerk disappeared through a doorway leading to the back offices.

He was gone a long time. Alex dared to sneak a look at Joseph, who shrugged his shoulders.

"Try not to worry," Joseph said, but Alex wasn't convinced. He remembered what happened before.

After what seemed like hours, the clerk reappeared. "It looks like your original file has been misplaced. We're unable to find it here. Our records show that your papers have been sent back to Washington D.C. Perhaps they were misfiled when they arrived back here in Oregon City. You'll have to come back tomorrow and speak to my supervisor."

"Misplaced? Again?" The news stunned Alex and took him back to the memory of the Bethany farm. How can they lose the papers twice? How can this happen? I've done everything right.

The man nodded. "Yes, come at eight o'clock in the morning."

With Joseph close behind him, Alex picked up his papers with shaking hands and turned toward the door.

***

"Papa, Papa!"

The children's voices startled Julianna, as she slipped the last pin in Bernard's diaper. She grabbed the baby and rushed out just in time to see Alex come in through the open gate and lean against the post.

Handing the baby to Emma, she rushed to him.

Is that blood on his shirt?

"Consumption," he muttered his face pale and contorted in pain. "The doctor says I have consumption."

Julianna's legs went numb. Her head spinning, she too grabbed the post and reached out to his free arm.

"Consumption?" she echoed, processing the hideous thought. "No, it can't be. I won't let it be," she cried, shaking his arm and shouting to make him understand. "I have some tea for you. I have some tea. That'll cure you. It always does."

He nodded, leaned on her, and with the children trailing, they made their way into the kitchen where Tracy had made her father coffee, strong, "just the way he likes it."

Alex fell into the chair at the head of the table and rested his head on the back. As his breathing came easier and his coffee cooled, he chronicled the story of the trip to Oregon City.

"We have no deed. I'm sorry," his voice barely a whisper. "They mailed the papers back to Washington D.C. and then either misfiled them when they came back or maybe they were lost enroute. The clerk said sometimes that happens."

"When will we know? My God! Alex!" Julianna said, her voice panicky.

"He said he'd mail us the papers as soon as he finds them."

"It means we can't sell the east bench now."

"There's a man interested in buying it. I have his name and address here." Alex pulled out a wrinkled piece of paper and handed it to her. "He said to write him as soon as we know anything. He's willing to pay us $500 for that 20 acre parcel. As soon as the papers come, we'll sell it." The thought was small comfort.

217

"Let's get you in to the bedroom," she said, anxious to help him. "You can rest until supper." She took his arm, gently helped him up and led him away. "Tracy, call us when you have food ready. Your father is too sick to sit here and wait."

Julianna pulled off his boots and helped him lay down, cradling his head on her lap. Smiling at his thinning hair line, she didn't tease him. A dark desperate despondence spread over her as she once again focused on the blood spatters covering the front of his shirt.

"You'll feel better after a few days rest." He was tough and could out work many men, she shivered, but what if this terrible illness is stronger than him?

He closed his eyes, sleeping fitfully. When Tracy brought him a plate, he was too tired to eat. Julianna coaxed him to take a few bites while she sat on the bed and nursed the baby.

Julianna sat by his side as much as possible, mopping his face and more than once changing the sheets because of night sweats. She tried to hide her worry from the children, but they sensed bad news and huddled together, reluctant to be far from their parents. It was four days before he found the strength to get up and go outside.

Alex walked around the yard and up to the shop. Julianna didn't accompany him, as he seemed to want to be by himself and urgent household needs beckoned her.

By now, Tracy, 13, and Emma, 11, could handle most of the tasks admirably, but Julianna knew they needed her support.

Alex gradually began to get his strength back, and a few days later, Julianna left her chores and went in search of him. The day was warm and sunny and she got a whiff of autumn in the air, a gentle warm breeze brushing her cheek and whisking away.

She found Alex in his shop, leaning on the work-bench, with his carpentry tools around him.

"Are you resting?" she asked.

"Yes and no," he answered. "Resting and thinking."

She went to him and put her arms around him. They stood together for a long time.

"Mama, Papa, Tracy says to come and eat now." Four-year-old Jackie ran into the shop and danced around them. Little Alexander, who followed his big brother everywhere, imitated his every move.

Laughing, Alex brushed a kiss on Julianna's cheek, reached down and with some effort, picked up little Alex. Jack grabbed onto his legs and buried his face, "Papa, Papa," he chanted.

"Guess we had better go to the house," Alex said. "We don't have much of a choice." He laughed like the Alex of old, the sound echoing off the walls and falling on eager ears.

The next few days, as August waned and September neared, the family spent their time bringing in produce. Although weak, Alex helped shred the cabbage for kraut and peel the pears to can. Julianna saved the peelings and cooked them down for pear syrup. Alex helped her until his energy played out.

He spent his spare time in the shop. He seems to be on a mission, Julianna thought, but now that he had rallied, she busied herself with the many chores of a farm wife and didn't discuss it with him.

One afternoon, she looked up to see Alex sitting on a log out by the barn, talking to Franz. She dried her hands and headed over to join them.

"What about the hay?" she heard Franz say.

"There's enough in there to last the winter, but someone will have to help her get it in next season," Alex answered and then saw her and smiled. "Hello, *Leibe*, Franz was just offering his help."

She forced a smile, but her heart dropped and her mind raced. What did he mean? Next season? Did he think...? She put her arm around him but her heart was a lead ball and she placed her other hand over it to protect it.

***

Alex caught the edge of the bench, just as he started to fall, and managed to hold on. Blood splattered in little droplets on the fresh lumber. I've got to get this done! But the weakness won and he edged his way over to the stump that he used for a chair. Slumping down, he put his head between his knees. Sometimes it helped keep him from coughing.

After several moments he tried to get up, but his knees buckled and forced him back into his chair. He heard Ferd coming before he saw him. With great effort he forced himself to stand up so as not to frighten the boy.

"Papa, what's the matter?" he asked.

Alex shook his head. "It's nothing." Guilt washed over him. I can't lie to the boy.

"Papa, look at the blood."

"I know, son," Alex mumbled, allowing himself to sit down again.

"Oh!" The eight-year-old said, his eyes landing on the large box-shaped object on the work-bench. He asked, "Papa what are you building?"

Alex shook his head, wondering what to tell him. Soon Ferd would be the oldest male in the family and in this moment he saw his son as he never had before. The boy's hair was blonde now at the end of summer, after weeks of working in the field. He worked harder than he should for someone his age, but Alex was too sick to help. My God, how can I leave you?

After some time he said, "Ferd, you're almost a man now." Alex put his hand on the boy's shoulder and pulled him close

He paused, carefully choosing his words, and after a time said, "I'm very sick, son. I fear I won't be here much longer." He felt tears well up, and quickly blinked them back.

Ferd buried his face in his father's chest and cried long and loud. "Papa, I don't want you to go away. Please, Papa, stay with us."

Fighting the weakness, Alex held the child, feeling his soft wisps of hair brush against his scruffy beard. He hadn't shaved for several days; it just took too much precious energy.

"My darling son, I'll stay as long as I can. I don't want to leave our family." His breathing came short and gasping, "You are my loves, but I believe God has other plans for me."

Ferd sniffed and wiped his cheeks with the back of his hands seeming to understand his father's words.

"Does Mama know?" he finally asked.

"We've spoken of it," Alex said hesitating. "She cannot face it, nor can I, but my breathing is worse. I speak of this to you because I fear the end is near and you must be strong for the other children and your mother." Putting his hands on the boy's shoulders and looking into his hazel-green eyes he asked, "Can you do this, my son?"

Ferd nodded silently, sniffed and wiped his nose on his sleeve. He stood up straight, with a look of understanding about his new and important role and asked, "Papa, who will plow the field? Who will help us harvest?"

"God has blessed us with wonderful neighbors. Joseph and Mr. Graham will surely help, as will Jacob Siedl and certainly Franz will always be here for you."

Slowly and with great effort, Alex pulled himself erect.

"Let me help, Papa, let me help!" Ferd reached out and held his father's work-worn hand.

"You can help, son. You'll be helping me, by helping your mother and the other children."

Alex paused and once again gazed at the face of the sad, little boy. He reached into a drawer under his workbench and rifled around in his tools until he found the small tote sack with drawstrings he was seeking.

"I made this some time ago," he continued. "I want you to take it. Whenever you need me or miss me, or things seem too hard, you will have this."

He handed the boy a small, wooden rosary. The crucifix, made out of a piece of highly-polished cherry wood was less than an inch long. The small, pine beads, roughly finished and not perfectly symmetrical, were strung on a piece of fishing line.

Ferd's eyes shone and he moved his fingers over the soft, light wood. "Oh, thank you, Papa, thank you," he said looking up at his father,

"You're welcome." Alex smiled and putting his hand on the boy's head, he said, "I know living out here so far from everything, it's hard to get to church, but the rosary can be the next best thing. It's a powerful prayer and you'll come to appreciate it over the years."

Ferd looked at his father and ground his fists into his eyes in an obvious attempt to stop crying.

"Go now. Find your mother. See if she needs some help before supper," Alex said and watched the tearful boy turn and disappear out the door.

Sadly, Alex returned back to his workbench and ran his hand over the sturdy coffin.

"It's taking shape," Alex said to himself. It needs a tight-fitting lid though, he thought as he picked up a rough-cut one-inch slab and reached for his rip saw.

Epilogue

November 29, 1896

   Meine Liebste Familie,

   On September 9th, Franz and friends carried Alex through the gate to his final resting place on the knoll between Frommelts and our property. Katherine says it's a beautiful place, but I see no beauty in any of it. I cannot bear to go up there, let alone think of my darling out there in the rain and snow.

   I have been unable to think and writing has been out of the question, but now I must, as Christmas is soon to be here and if you don't hear from me, I know you will worry.

   The children are despondent and I am unable to console them. Thank God for Katherine and Franz. They or one of the other neighbor couples come over once a week and bring dinner. They are able to comfort the family, and for that I am grateful.

   Last week there was a Thanksgiving celebration at school, and I made myself attend with the children. I'm glad I did because the children needed me to be there, and I felt better after the walk.

   I do have something to be thankful for; I received a letter last week from the government, telling me they had found our land papers, so I am free to sell the east bench property. I will need the money as I am land poor. Alex was too ill to work much last summer.

   Baby Bernard seems to be rallying in the last few weeks, and that is another thing for which I am grateful. He's still small for his age, but his cough has lessened some and he breathes easier. The children hover over him and play with him when he is able and I think that is the best medicine for him. The doctor from Troutdale has been up a couple of times and tells me to keep him warm and dry and give him some of Alex's tea at least twice a day.

   I must will myself to make a Christmas for the children. I know

Alex would want that of me. He always loved it so and surprised us all with wonderful gifts. Franz is making toys for the younger ones.

I have two of my good dresses that I brought from home. I think I will use the fabric to make a dress for each girl. I will alter one of Alex's good shirts for Ferd. I know he will be proud to wear it.

Tracy is standing here helping me write this. She is my strength. She sends her love, as do I.

Frohe Weihnachen,

Julianna and children

Julianna reread the letter and, with a sigh, folded it. After a moment she placed it in an envelope, sealed it, and in bold hand, addressed it.

"Here, dear, take this to Katherine," she said her voice absent and distant. "Franz can post it the next time he goes to Troutdale." She handed the letter to Tracy and turned to pick up the fussing baby.

Cooing softly to him, and rocking him in her arms, Julianna walked to the front door. Shivering from the harsh wind, she watched Tracy walk up the road and through the open gate, Josie trudging behind. She managed a smile when she saw Tracy turn and take her younger sister's hand.

I enjoyed the story so much that I had to go back and reread some of the paragraphs again because of the richness of the words and your vivid descriptions. You told me that this was fiction but it's hard to believe because you made the lives of Alex and Julianna, your great grandparents, come alive through the stories of homesteading in Oregon's Columbia River Gorge over a 100 years ago.

Donald H. Mathews, Professor Emeritus,
Youngstown State University, Ohio

Where Eagles Nest has captured the true picture of what it was like to homestead in late 1800's Oregon.   Hunger, poverty, isolation intensified by a lack of communication and the dangers of the "big city" of Portland, as well as the pressure to provide for a continually growing family are artfully woven into this narrative.

I've never read a book that documented so well the ingrained need people have for community. The special need that women have for other women to share their pain and joy was addressed in a way that wasn't sentimental, but affirming.

Christine Heck , Milwaukie, Oregon

I just finished your book and I must apologize for being so very slow, but I read it like we eat a box of chocolates! I prodded and poked and reread each chapter. I used it as a reward to myself at the end of each day. I really enjoyed it and tried to imagine where all of these places were.

Gary Moore, Wasilla, Alaska

After three sittings I finished *Where Eagles Nest* twenty minutes ago. What a beautiful story, and so well written! Your research was evident in most every paragraph, and your ability to tell a good story showed in every chapter. I was impressed with the way you told the stories, almost as if you were one of the characters on site.

Tom Cowling, Author of "Letters from a Dying Town"
and "Ghost Towns on Bridal Veil Creek"